THE
GROWING
SEASON

THE
GROWING
SEASON

A NOVEL BY

DAVID HALLMAN

· · · ·

FIVE POINTS PRESS

ATHENS, GEORGIA

Published by

. · · · .

FIVE POINTS PRESS

500 North Milledge Avenue
Suite 200
Athens, Georgia 30601
706-534-9270
www.fivepointspress.com

Book and cover design by Burtch Hunter Design • www.burtchhunter.com

——————————————

Special thanks to Chris and those associated
with Five Points Press who assisted in polishing the story.

This book is dedicated to my wife, Deb.
Thanks for hanging in there with me.

——————————————

Where were you roughly twenty years ago? Did you cheer when the Berlin wall fell? Do you remember when Jeffrey Dahmer was arrested? Did you cringe when Rodney King was beaten in the streets of Los Angeles? Were you shocked when Magic Johnson announced that he had AIDS?

Much like these events might have framed our lives in some way, each event that occurs in this story creates a balance. I have set this novel, *The Growing Season*, in the state of Georgia in 1990, not a year I chose haphazardly. Historical facts of this time lend authenticity: drug smuggling by aircraft, Federal money laundering statutes, and credit transaction reports.

These facts I know because I am a retired special agent with the Federal Bureau of Investigation with thirty-five years of criminal investigative experience. Before joining the F.B.I., I was a special agent with the Georgia Bureau of Investigation.

Other interesting nuances of the time that add complexity to my story are the societal fear of AIDS, the limited access to and use of cell phones by law enforcement, the absence of airbags in automobiles, and the uniquely Southern "root doctor." The weaving of each item into the story is based on my thirty-five years of law enforcement experience and needed to be set in the time period I chose. If any detail is removed or changed, five years earlier or five years later, the dynamics of the story change and its "reality" is altered.

Twenty years ago seems like yesterday. As much as many of these aforementioned aspects influence our daily lives in new and different ways, including the ways crimes are committed and fought, it's the people we encounter over the course of time who remain as fascinating as ever.

DMH

JUNE 14, 1984

THE PILOT of the Piper Navajo turned on a heading off the Columbus, Georgia aerial beacon, proceeding toward a clandestine West Georgia strip. Scrubbing his greasy face with his hands, he tried to stimulate his senses, his head throbbing from a scented mixture of acetone and fuel permeating from the rear of the cabin. Reaching into a gym bag behind his seat, he removed a bottle of Tylenol and a jug of water, quickly swallowing three capsules and washing them down with the remaining water. He was close now. *Concentrate.*

For today's flight he would earn $150,000, a mere pittance of the profit his employers would make on the five hundred kilograms of cocaine he was carrying in the rear of the plane. Here he was, hauling millions of dollars worth of cocaine, and he had never snorted a gram much less toked on a joint of marijuana. Not that he didn't partake of any substances at all, though. His drug of choice was whiskey. This flight was one of necessity, he reasoned. He was a crop duster by trade, but hard times had forced him almost into bankruptcy. Then a friend approached him with a proposition. *One flight. No questions asked. Get yourself and your family out of debt. You've got reservations about it being legal? Look at the politicians and their pork projects, the lawyers and their frivolous class action suits, the doctors, insurance companies and patients, all screwing each other. Keep your honor and starve, or make the flight.*

The flight began the previous day at two a.m. at Tamiami, south of Miami, Florida. He and his Colombian copilot Luis, introduced to him two days before, boarded the aircraft each with a gallon of water and a quart of coffee. They flew southeast over the Bahama Islands, threaded south through the Windward Passage, entering Colombia just east of Cartagena, flying the western slope of the Occidental mountain range. At Quibdó, a city south of Medellin, they turned east, crossing the lush towering peaks that reached over two miles above sea level. Skimming the range, they settled into the valley between the Occidentals and the parallel range known as the Cordillera Central. Once they crossed the mountains they began receiving the radio transmission directing them onto the Colombian strip. Shortly after eleven a.m. local time, they spotted the paved strip next to a railway line. After making a cautious pass they landed. A Toyota Land Cruiser met them at the end of the runway and directed them to a large corrugated metal hangar on the north end of the strip.

In front of the hangar was a member of the ground crew who guided them inside. The crew chief, slashing his hand across his throat, signaled the pilot to kill his engines. As the engines slowed to an idle, the men descended upon the aircraft like a pit crew at a stock car race. The pilot and Luis exited the craft to stretch their cramped legs. Not a gun was in sight. The clean, spacious hangar was not at all what the pilot had imagined, expecting instead to land on a dusty rutted strip and be met by unkempt, gun-toting guerrillas. These men were organized and efficient.

A fair-haired man wearing a blue polo shirt and tan chinos greeted Luis as he got off the plane. "Tiburon!" he said, welcoming Luis in Spanish. The men carried on a brief dialogue that quickly reverted to business. Luis introduced the pilot to him, first names only, of course.

He addressed the pilot in accented English. "We had hoped to get seven hundred kilos aboard. But with the extra fuel necessary to get to Georgia and to cross the mountains, I would not recommend anything over five hundred. What is your opinion?"

The pilot made a quick mental calculation of the weight of the fuel and the cocaine, comparing the figures to the load capacity of the plane. The man was right. It would be pushing it, not worth the risk. "I agree. Go with five."

The leader nodded to the men behind him who began loading canvas duffel bags into the rear of the aircraft. He went to his Land Cruiser and returned, handing them two brown paper bags. "Here are some sandwiches and two Cokes—" He stopped abruptly. "Coca-Colas," he corrected himself with a smile, "for your return trip. And with my compliments."

Luis and the pilot thanked the leader for his hospitality and returned to the cockpit, crawling over the duffel bags and bladder tanks in the rear cabin. In less than ten minutes they were airborne, loaded with fuel and product.

Once they had settled in, the pilot asked, "Was that man Colombian?"

"Sure," Luis replied. "You gringos think that the only people that settled South America were Spanish. Other Europeans who didn't speak English, like the Germans, Austrians, and East Europeans, saw opportunities down here instead of the United States. That man's ancestors were from Denmark."

"Interesting. I guess traveling can broaden my horizons."

They returned, again through the Windward Passage, turning northwest toward the States, hugging the eastern Bahama chain. Approaching Florida north of Melbourne, the pilot lowered the craft to five hundred feet. Other than the landing, this was the riskiest part of the flight. If Customs were to spot them, it would be now.

Approaching Kissimmee, the pilot ascended to five thousand feet and contacted Jacksonville Center requesting a transponder code. To the controllers at the Center, it would appear that he had just left Kissimmee with the other Disney World traffic. He was assigned a code for his final leg.

The aircraft dropped suddenly from a down draft, interrupting the pilot's thoughts of his new wealth, jerking him back to the present. He was east of Columbus. He glanced over at Luis who was dozing. They were both exhausted. He turned on a course toward Manchester, Georgia.

"Jax Center. This is 492 Whiskey Pappa. Jax Center from 492

Whiskey Pappa," he said into his mike.

"Jax Center. Go ahead 492 Whiskey Pappa."

"I'm on approach to Manchester. Thank you for your assistance."

"Glad to assist, 492 Whiskey Pappa."

The pilot pushed the yoke forward, lowering the aircraft to one thousand feet, and turned off the transponder. To the Center it would appear as though he was landing. At five hundred feet, he veered north on a heading to Connally, Georgia.

"Catbird to Sourpuss. Catbird to Sourpuss, you copy?" the pilot said into his microphone. He paused briefly, then repeated himself.

"Sourpuss to Catbird. Sourpuss to Catbird, welcome home. What's your ETA, honey?" came the reply.

Nice touch, thought the pilot. It was a woman answering his call. If anyone was listening in to the transceiver, it would sound as if a pilot was close to landing and calling home to his wife. In reality, it was his ground crew standing by. The call sign "Sour" indicated everything was fine. "I'm ten away and looking forward to a steak," answered the pilot.

"I'll be waiting for you with a hot steak—rare, just the way you like it."

Ten minutes later Luis pointed out the lights lining the strip, which was pasture land converted into a runway. At least fifteen white lights lined each side of the three thousand-foot strip and bright red beacons framed the ends. A clear night sky enhanced the approach.

"Catbird, Catbird, I have you in sight. You're lookin' good," squawked the radio.

"Roger, Sourpuss," the pilot acknowledged, concentrating on his approach.

Gingerly he lowered the aircraft, playing the yoke and compensating for the lack of depth perception due to the darkness. The aircraft landed hard with a jolting bounce, then rolled roughly over the grass strip. The grass slowed the aircraft quickly without the use of the brake, leaving over five hundred feet of runway to spare. He throttled the aircraft to the end of the runway and adroitly spun it around for an emergency take-off. Luis quickly went to the rear of the aircraft, climbing over the bags and deflated fuel bladders, and opened the rear door with skilled precision.

To his left, two pair of parking lights emerged from the tree line and approached the plane. Closer, he could tell they were pickup trucks with camper shells. They pulled parallel to the plane. Dark figures caught the duffel bags that Luis threw at them, and packed them inside the trucks. In five grueling minutes the cargo was unloaded.

"Go!" shouted Luis, slamming the door. The pilot shoved the two throttle levers forward as the aircraft lurched, causing Luis to lose his balance as he climbed toward the cockpit. The aircraft responded, accelerating quickly, the landing lights flashing by like strobes on a dance floor. The aircraft reached air speed before Luis could get to his seat. Rising toward the clear sky, the pilot turned toward Peachtree-DeKalb Airport on the northwest side of Atlanta, where upon landing, the aircraft would be parked in a hanger, wiped down to obliterate finger prints, cleaned thoroughly inside and out, and abandoned.

The ground crew at the converted pasture had other duties. They quickly gathered their runway lights, tossing them into a cardboard box in the back of a truck., and in twenty minutes they were driving north on Interstate 85, heading to Atlanta. They drove within the speed limit to the south end of town, unloading their cargo at a self-service warehouse. The load would eventually find its way to New York, Philadelphia, and Washington, D.C.

During the drive back home, everyone was quiet, each one anticipating his bounty. The "Gambler," who was responsible for the pilots, the strip and the load crew, calculated his profits. After deducting payment to the pilots, the costs of modifications to the aircraft, as well as payments to the load crew and incidental expenditures, he would net $100,000 for a night's work.

Before dawn, the Gambler's crew was celebrating their mission at his home, toasting each other with cans of beer and shots of Rebel Yell. As the morning sun bathed the Georgia countryside with the warming rays of a new day and the cardinals chirped an early chorus, the group departed knowing they had succeeded in their crime. But such a stain does not disappear so easily.

CHAPTER ONE

THE SUMMER OF 1990

AT SIX in the morning I hefted the last cardboard box onto my shoulder and trudged from my apartment to the U-Haul trailer hitched onto the Jeep, spied the last existing space inside the trailer's confines, and stuffed it with the remnants of my meager belongings. I gazed toward the east, watching the first light of the morning paint the sky in its ephemeral hues of pinks, purples, and turquoise over Tybee and Wilmington Islands, the live oaks dripping with Spanish moss. The humid air was cool, with the complex aroma of salt and shellfish. The marsh in the distance stirred with the coming of a new day, the gulls circling the crab boats that were leaving the harbor to check their traps, the herons stepping gingerly in the marsh grass searching for small crustaceans.

My roommate, First Lieutenant Steve Ridley, First Battalion, 75th Regiment, United States Army Rangers, stationed in Savannah, Georgia, strolled from our apartment balancing two cups of coffee. He handed me one. "I still can't believe you're going through with this."

"Listen, I've already given Uncle Sam five years. If I reup, it'd be another four for a total of nine. Hell, I'd be nearly halfway to making retirement. That's not me, buddy. It was fun but I'm not career." I slammed the squeaky door of the trailer, locked it, and stepped into the Jeep.

"I thought at least you'd go Federal. You've got the degree and all."

"They're not hiring. At least with G.B.I. I can get a little experience, maybe work it into a Federal job. Hey... look at it this way, they can't transfer me out of Georgia."

There was an uneasy silence, the parting of men, never a comfortable situation. "I'm gonna miss you, man.... And you too, you sorry buzzard," he said to my haughty myna bird caged in the back.

"Whatever you say, sir," the bird squawked.

Then Steve got solemn on me. "We've been through a lot together: Panama and Grenada. Damn, we've had some good times."

"I know," I replied, finishing the coffee. I handed him the cup and extended my hand. "So stay in touch. I mean it."

"I will." It was a lie. Steve never wrote, much less called. It simply wasn't his way.

I cranked up the Wrangler and said a final farewell to a good friend. "You be careful. No hero shit, ya hear?"

I turned onto Abercorn heading west. I once considered taking that desolate section of interstate highway between Savannah and Macon, but as a newly appointed Special Agent with the Georgia Bureau of Investigation, I felt it would be fitting to drive the rural roads, and maybe learn the state during my travels to my new duty station, Connally, Georgia.

I drove west on U.S. 280, savoring the sights, sounds and flavor of my adopted state—the low country marsh, rich in palmettos and live oaks, the soil, dark muck, and the water, brackish. Further west, the tangy scent of pines permeated the air. Red clay bordered the road, broad expanses of corn, soybeans and other cash crops dominating the countryside. John Deere tractors, green as the grass they were tilling, sporting huge tires like the muscular shoulders of a weight lifter, crawled the fields, casting high plumes of rusty dust over the land. The hours passed as I drove west. The pines intermingled with the lush leaves of maples, oaks and sycamores and, of course, kudzu flourished where allowed. I passed the orchards of peach and pecan trees, occasionally breathing the fleeting fragrance of honeysuckle. There was a subtle seduction to the land. I understood how roots could sink deep.

Shortly after noon I crossed the Upper Mowalgee River and entered Forrest County on a narrow state road. Forrest County was slightly different from the others I had passed through. Gently rolling hills added variety to the drive. The crop of choice was corn. Horses and beef cattle grazed leisurely in the verdant open spaces. On the outskirts of Connally I passed a John Deere dealership, Cargyle's Used Cars, Trader Jack's Mobile Homes and an abandoned red brick textile mill surrounded by a cluster of dilapidated mill houses. Servicing the mill village were a liquor store and a convenience store. The highway intersected with the main east-west street running through town. I turned west toward the center of town. The street was bordered by well-maintained homes painted in whites or pastel shades of yellow, blue, and green. Lemon-scented magnolias, lush oaks, maples and blooming dogwood trees precisely planted in the yards, hedges of azaleas, red tips and hydrangeas boasted their brilliant flora of red, pink and white. A middle-aged man tended his roses in his yard and I inhaled the rich scent of freshly mown grass. Uptown the complexion of the town again changed, with residential homes renovated into offices for attorneys, doctors and insurance agencies. One stately mansion succumbing to the same commercial indignity was now a mortuary.

The county courthouse was not located in the traditional center of the town square, but instead, was situated in a government square north of the main street. A three-story red brick structure faced west toward the Sheriff's Department and Fire Department across the street. A dense virid lawn with monuments representing the Civil War, World War I, World War II and the Viet Nam War stood on each side of the square. North of the square was the city government and utility building, east was the Carnegie Library, and south, across the main street, were the churches. I drove on through town past the finance company, the bank, Belk's Department Store, an antique shop, a dress shop, an abandoned movie theater, and a Rexall drug store. Crossing the railroad tracks, I turned into a residential area.

My apartment complex was located in an older but well maintained area of the city. The apartments were two-story brick townhouses facing inward, five units on each side and five units forming the base of a U. A semicircular driveway surrounded a common courtyard. I gathered my keys from the apartment manager, a pleasant woman who seemed happy to have me as a tenant. I spotted three open spaces and paralleled my Jeep and trailer in front of my rental. My new abode was a single bedroom apartment, a downstairs living area with a half bath and an upstairs loft with a full bath. With practice borne of my years in the army, I entered my new home to survey the barracks. The apartment, though clean, bore the dank odor of vacancy, painted in the standard off-white with beige carpet, bearing recent lines of vacuuming, and furnished with the latest in contemporary mobile home veneer and compressed sawdust fixtures. I found the thermostat, turned down the air conditioning, checked out the oven, stove, refrigerator, disposal, toilets, and fans. Satisfied, I began the task of unloading my belongings.

I unlocked the U-Haul and heard a soft, Southern feminine voice. "Are you the new kid on the block?"

A tall, lean woman in her mid-twenties, wearing a burgundy ribbed tee shirt and cut-off jeans, leaned on the doorframe. Thin dark hair draped just below her shoulders, the eyes, large, framed by thick ebony eye lashes and brows, the face, broad with high cheekbones. She seemed relaxed, and confident. I walked past her to the rear of my Jeep and opened the cooler on the back seat, next to the birdcage. "I've been driving for the past five hours. I think I earned one of these," I said, removing a dripping can of beer from the icy slush. "Would you like one?"

"Thanks," she said, accepting the second beer from the cooler. She stood just within my body space and pried open the top, staring at me with a critical eye. "You're not from around here, are you?"

"Why'd you say that?"

"Well... your accent for one. And you're drinking beer in public. Most people from around here know better. It denotes... a lack of breeding."

"Well, I guess I'm gonna have to learn," I said, pulling a box from the trailer.

"My name's Megan Rilley," she said, extending her hand.

Shifting the box to my knee, I shook her hand softly. I have never been comfortable shaking a woman's hand. With a man, the shake is solid and firm, but with a lady, too soft and she thinks I'm either a wimp or patronizing, too hard and she thinks I'm a brute or insensitive.

"Where you from?" she asked.

"Maryland."

"You're joking. Why would anyone from Maryland want to move to Connally? You're not hiding from the law, are you?"

"On the contrary," I said, walking into the apartment with my box. I put it upstairs and when I returned she was waiting on me.

"Well, if you aren't hiding, what are you doing here?"

I pulled a piece of luggage from the trailer. "If I have to be questioned, grab a box and help me."

"In exchange for what?"

I shrugged. "If you're helpful, maybe you'll get another beer and an answer to your question."

She pulled out a box and followed. "Okay, what do you do?"

I dropped my luggage beside the sofa. She did the same. "I'm Hank Monroe."

"That wasn't the question."

"I'm with the G.B.I. I'm an agent."

"Can you fix a ticket?"

I shook my head, surprised at the response. "No! I can't fix a ticket."

"Well... for a cop, you can't do much for me," she said, draining the can.

"And you, Miss Megan, why are you living in this town? You sound like you're from here."

"Don't call me Miss. That sounds too Southern. I'm from Madison, east of Atlanta. I got out of college three years ago with a teaching degree. I wanted to get my master's in early childhood development over at Columbus College but I still needed a job to pay off my college loan. So I took a job here, teaching second graders. Connally's close enough to drive to Columbus and I should have my masters by the end of the year, thank God."

"Second graders... I bet they're cute."

"They are," she smiled wistfully. "Their innocence makes them cute. Most want to learn and are eager to soak up knowledge. It's the parents

I have trouble with."

I returned to the Jeep and hefted the birdcage out of the back seat. The Major screeched his disapproval. "Shut up you ol' crow."

"I know that's not a crow, but what is it?" she said curiously, examining the bird hunched over his perch.

"It's a myna bird."

"He's cute. What's his name?"

"Major Boyd."

"Major Boyd? What is that, a play on myna bird?"

"Kind of. When I was in the military, my company had this West Point puke named Major Carlton F. Boyd. The guy wasn't a leader, he was a full-lipped butt-kisser. None of the guys liked him. Two of my sergeants came up with this great idea to get a myna bird and name it Major Boyd. They found him at a pet store and began teaching him to talk. Two days later they took the bird to the NCO Club with an extensive vocabulary. Would you like to hear him talk?"

"Sure."

"Come on Major, talk for the lady," I coaxed.

"Good morning, Major…. That's a great idea, Major…."

"See what I mean. And it gets worse," I cautioned. She nodded bemused. "When I got word of the animal, I went over to the NCO Club. I knew if the Major ever found out about the bird, there'd be hell to pay. Well, the sergeants told me if I was gonna take him, I had to keep him. So, I'm stuck with this crow. Would you like a pet?"

"No, thanks," she replied laughing.

"Well, do you enjoy living here?'

She shrugged. "It's okay. Not much different from any other town in the South."

"What do you mean? It's quiet and boring?"

"Hank, it's easy to see you're not from the South. You might be an agent, but you've got a lot more to learn than just arresting crooks." She placed her beer down and leaned back on the kitchen counter with a knowing smile. "I'll give you a short course…." And in her teacherly way, Megan offered instruction to her class of one.

"The formal Southern feudal system, known as plantations, ended in the 1860s. Over time it's been modified, but it still exists, subtly, and it's vigorously protected. Look at who owns the land, the banks, the mills, and the major franchises and dealerships. They will belong to the 'old names' whose families have lived here for generations. Their kids leave town, go to college and get their degrees, and then they return to manage the land and the businesses. They know everyone, but more importantly, they know about everyone. Especially their indiscretions and occasional crimes. They are the prominent members of the country club, the church, and they're officers in the Kiwanis and Rotary. They contribute generously to causes but not so much as to blemish their lifestyles. You'll meet them in your business, Hank, and they'll be friendly... but never your friend. You are not one of them. I am not one of them. We are merely tenants allowed to stay on their land until we become troublesome."

"That sounds kind of cynical."

"Don't get me wrong. The vast majority of people in this town are good, caring people who believe in honor, God and country, but this town ain't no Mayberry."

CHAPTER TWO

THE FOLLOWING morning I awoke early, feeling antsy. I showered and dressed in a charcoal pinstriped suit, starched white shirt, and red rep tie. I strapped on my holster and my assigned Smith and Wesson 6906, a stainless steel nine millimeter pistol. A magazine pouch with two magazines went on the left side of my hip. I examined myself in the mirror. A professional appearance on a blue-collar salary. Not bad.

A pair of squirrels scampered up a dogwood as I walked to my Jeep. The morning air was crisp, scented of pine, and patches of fog hovered in the low areas of the neighborhood. The bouncy whistle of a Bobwhite in the distance greeted the day.

I stopped at a Hardee's for breakfast and settled in a booth with the local newspaper. The weekly *Connally Citizen* ignored the national news. The front page included articles about potential candidates for the various local elections. A page was devoted to obituaries, church news and activities, and a schedule of events of local social clubs. A side article entitled "Police Activity Log" listed, I assumed, the week's crimes in the local area. Two cars were burglarized, two men arrested on marijuana possession, and someone stole gasoline from a nearby convenience store. These crimes were the most noteworthy among a smattering of domestic calls, stray dogs, and drunk and disorderly complaints.

The regional office of the Georgia Bureau of Investigation was a modest one-story brick building next door to the Georgia State Patrol Post on the outskirts of town. Had I not directions I might have mistaken it for someone's home. Only a small brass plaque next to the front door indicated that it was a State office. A single automobile was in the parking lot. The front door was locked so I rang the doorbell. The door opened cautiously.

"Can I help you?" asked a man wearing a blue dress shirt and gray slacks. He was clean cut and appeared to be in his late twenties.

I held up my badge. "Hi, I'm Hank Monroe. I'm supposed to report here."

The guarded facade disappeared, replaced by a broad smile and an extended hand. "Oh yeah, I heard we were gonna have some new blood. Come on in. I'm Dennis Lanier."

I followed him through the reception area into the neat, but austere, office interior. "I'm usually the first one here. I've got a boy in elementary school, so I help in getting him off, then come on in. Most of the guys start arriving between eight-thirty and nine. Peggy should be here in a few minutes—she's our secretary. Can I get you some coffee?"

"Sure."

He led me to a small kitchen complete with a full-size refrigerator and stove. A pot of coffee was perking on the counter. "The cream and sugar are on the table there. We should have some styrofoam cups somewhere 'round here," he said rummaging around in the cabinets.

"So you made it?" boomed a sonorous voice.

Startled, I turned to see a large figure completely filling the doorway to the kitchen. No doubt he had been a Georgia trooper. Not only tall at six foot four inches, he was also broad, weighing, I guessed, two hundred forty pounds. Though he was in his fifties, he had the sturdy mass of a tree trunk. Someone I would hesitate to challenge.

"Mr. Henry," I said, shaking the hand of the Special Agent in Charge, SAC for short. "It's a pleasure."

"I see you met Dennis. Did he show you around the office?"

"Not yet, Cobb," Dennis replied. "I was fixin' to."

"Well, get yourself a cup and come on back to my office," he said to me.

I followed him down the hall to his office. I scanned the office of J. T. "Cobb" Henry. He motioned me to a chair while he hung up his coat, taking his time so I could examine his pedigree. The dark pecan paneled walls displayed an illustrated history of the man, spanning thirty years of law enforcement. There were signed photographs of him with three governors, Senator Sam Nunn, and Herman Talmadge, a proclamation appointing him a Colonel aide-de-camp of the Georgia Militia, three local "lawman of the year" awards, and letters of appreciation from the Director of the F.B.I., the Administrator of the D.E.A., and the Attorney General of the United States.

"Did you have any trouble getting settled in?" he asked as we sat down.

"No, sir. I still need to get connected for a phone and cable."

"We'll get you fixed up. I want to introduce you around the office. Especially to Peggy, our secretary, and Johnny Cole, who you'll work with for awhile. Cole's a good agent. Been with us for about fifteen years. He knows the area and the thieves. You should learn a lot from him. I've also got you a car. It's a Ford LTD over at the Post. It's not in the best of shape, 1984, but when you're the low man you have to take what you can get."

"Yes, sir."

"I understand you were with the Rangers."

"Yes, sir."

"Well, we are a little more relaxed than the military. The guys here call me 'Cobb'. Coats and ties are required unless you have a reason not to wear one and there'll be those times. Office hours are technically eight-thirty to five but as you can see, some don't come in 'til nine or so. Trust me, we'll get the time out of you. If you're needed at night or on weekends, just like the Rangers, you'll be called. And you work 'til the job's done. Any questions?"

"No, sir."

"Well, if you have any, be it about a case or a personal problem, come talk to me. I think after thirty four-years I've 'bout seen it all."

"Sir, you're about maxed out, aren't you?"

"I've got less than two years to retirement. Then me and the missus are going to buy a Winnebago and see what's outside Georgia."

Cobb glanced out the window. "Cole's here. Come on."

Cole's desk was in the rear corner of the squad area, an area of prime real estate for any agent. This desk placement told me that he was the agent with the most seniority or that he was savvy enough to obtain the spot over the others. Cole was on the telephone leaning back in his chair, a pouch of chewing tobacco at the corner of the desk. He had a lean, rangy build with dark wiry hair and a neatly trimmed mustache. He saw Cobb and me, rose from his chair with a broad smile, and shook my hand while still talking on the phone. He raised an index finger to indicate he would be off in a minute.

"There's your desk over there," said Cobb, pointing out an unadorned dark wood desk at the front of the squad area. I inspected the desk until Cole hung up the phone. "Johnny, I'd like you to meet Hank Monroe."

"Glad to meet you," said Cole. "We sure could use the help around here."

"A lot going on?" I asked, surprised after reading the police activity log in the newspaper.

"You'd be surprised. Usually nothing big like they'd have in Atlanta, but enough to keep us busy. You'll find out."

"Johnny, I'd like you to show Hank around. What do you have this morning?" asked Cobb.

"I've got Grand Jury at ten over in Colby County. It's for that burglar I caught two weeks ago."

"Yeah, I remember. I tell you what... Hank and I'll go get some breakfast at Wingate's and maybe he can get with you this afternoon."

. . .

Wingate's was a humble diner located on the outskirts of town. Trimmed shrubs lined the brick sidewalk leading to the front door, two bay windows accenting each end of the brick building. In the lot next door were two trucks and a dozen cars haphazardly aligned in the dusty parking lot. Cobb led me into the cool interior toward the back of the restaurant to a group of six men, sitting around a pair of tables pushed together.

"Well... look what the hogs dug up!" a uniformed man blurted in greeting.

"The hogs dug up another agent to help your sorry butts," replied

Cobb. "Hank Monroe, let me introduce you to this gaggle," he said, pointing around the circle. "There's Chuck Gulespie, the Chief of Police, Dan Maddox, he's Chief of Detectives, Lynn Stevenson and Donny Proctor are with G.S.P., Parker Long's with the Forrest County S.O., and Luther McCoy, over there, is a rabbit sheriff with the Department of Natural Resources. If there is anything you need to know about what's going on around here just ask them. If they don't know, they'll make something up."

We pulled up chairs as a young full-busted waitress with lacquered hair came up to us. "Can I get you something, Cobb?"

"Hey, Carol. This is Hank Monroe. Just moved into town." She nodded at me with a hearty smile. "What would you like, son? It's on me," said Cobb.

"Just some sweet tea. I ate earlier today."

"Carol, I'll have the number three breakfast," said Cobb placing the menu back between the napkin dispenser and condiments. "Chuck. What's this I heard about Lew Hicks?"

The Chief of Police shook his head in embarrassment. "Yeah, it's true and we're dealing with it."

"What's true?" asked McCoy.

"Go ahead and tell him," said Parker Long.

"You see what you've stirred up, Cobb?" said the Chief in frustration. The Chief leaned on the table with both elbows and scrubbed his face. "Well, it was last Saturday night and Lew had the midnight patrol. Lew is riding by the Macedonian Church and thinks he sees a car in the back. He thinks it might be a burglar so he circles around back behind the cemetery with his lights turned off, and he drives up between the tombstones." The Chief notices me and continues, "You see, there's a cemetery that backs up to the church and ol' Lew figures he can sneak up and catch the burglar in the act, be some big hero and all. When he gets close, he realizes that it's Buck Crawley's pickup, and he's getting on with some gal in the rear bed." Some of the men are chuckling and that bolsters the Chief. "Lew can see the top of Crawley's head and his fat ass barely bobbing over the sides of the truck. Of course, Buck is so busy that Lew is able to drive up to the edge of the cemetery and park behind a statue.

"Lew remembered that Buck's granddaddy was buried in that cemetery and was known as Paps. So he turns on the P.A. system in the car and begins moaning like a ghost. 'Ooooohhhhhh, ooooooohhhhh, Bucky, ooooohhhh Bucky. Paps is angry Bucky.... Paps is angry Bucky.' Well, Buck's ol' butt freezes in midstroke and there's a short pause, like the two in the truck are trying to figure out what's going on. Then two heads pop up over the side of the truck, jerking side to side. 'Oooohhhh, oooohhhh. Paps is coming for youuuuu, Bucky. For yyyyyooooouuuu!' Lew told me that all he could see was assholes and elbows as the two were scrambling out of the bed. Buck is trying to flee and pull up his britches. Before they are up, he trips over his pants legs and falls out of the truck. He's stunned and the girl-friend is now in the truck screaming at him. He jumps in and guns it. Well, the truck is in reverse. It shoots backwards and slams into a headstone knocking it over. Buck rams it in first and peels out." Everyone around the table is laughing uncontrollably.

"What looked like a cute joke is now a problem. We've got a head-stone knocked over and two furrows in the cemetery deep enough to place a couple of caskets. We can't really charge Buck because Lew caused it to happen. The City's going to have to pay for it and you know who's going to catch hell from the City Council about this."

"Why didn't Lew just keep his mouth shut? No one would have known," said Lynn Stevenson.

"The Grayson family who owned the grave with the headstone that got knocked over would have reported the damage and we would have initiated a case," replied Dan Maddox dryly. "Would Lew ever been caught if he had kept his mouth shut? Probably not. But if it ever came out, Lew might have been charged criminally. Instead, he'll get some days off. He did the right thing."

"Hell, when I started out I wouldn't have dared told my sergeant about some of the things we did, and he didn't want to know," said Donny Proctor.

"Yeah, but that was twenty years ago," replied Cobb. "Things have changed."

"Generally for the worse. It's just too dangerous nowadays." They all nodded. Cobb emptied his cup and looked at me. "I'll tell you what, let's finish here, then I'll get you back to the office so you can go get your utilities hooked up."

. . .

I returned to the office precisely at twelve. Cole met me at the door. "Let's go," he ordered. "Your first case is awaiting."

We got into Cole's car. "What've we got?" I asked nervously, as we pulled from the lot.

"A burglary down at the backwater."

"The backwater?"

"Yeah. The lake over at Godwin County."

"Why are we working a little old burglary?"

"Because the Sheriff asked us to," said Cole dryly.

"Can't he work it?"

"They may have taught you Georgia law at Forsyth, but they didn't teach you diddly 'bout Georgia politics. There are a hundred and fifty nine counties in the great State of Georgia. Each county has its own Sheriff, Magistrate, Coroner, Probate Judge, Clerk, plus their County Commissioners. That adds up to a lot of chiefs, and some counties don't have a lot of finances. A large case and resulting trial can break a county. You might have a Sheriff with only one or two deputies. He doesn't have the time or the resources to tie up on an investigation. He needs us and we need him."

"What do you mean?"

"Hank, remember, we're an assisting agency, not a State Police. Generally we only get involved in an investigation when requested and we need to be asked or we're out of a job. Plus, we provide a political out for the Sheriff."

"How's that?"

"When we show up at this burglary, the victim will see that he's important enough to warrant state involvement. If we don't solve the case, the Sheriff can lay it off on us. If we do solve it, the Sheriff can step in and take the credit."

"Sounds like we're getting used."

"In a way, maybe. But our job is to enforce the law. As long as we do that, our job's secure. The Sheriff doesn't have that luxury. Every four years he has to worry about getting elected and, in the meantime, he's got to please the public, keep the peace, run the jail and the court. It's a balancing act I wouldn't have."

He turned off the state highway onto a narrow county road.

"When we get there you do the interviews, since you got on that shiny new suit. I'll take the photos and throw the dust around. Let me give you some advice. Keep two types of suits handy. Wear your nice ones to court and save the others for walking through the woods and pastures, crime scenes, and street work. Otherwise, you'll end up destroying a lot of good cloth."

As it turned out, the one piddly burglary led to five others. As we processed the first house, Cole explained that "Most of the houses on the lake are summer homes occupied on weekends, maybe six months of the year. So after a burglar hits one house he moves on to the next. Kind of like a burglar buffet, picking up whatever items suit his fancy, then moving on to the next. They may have broken into a dozen houses along this shore." An assisting deputy checked the surrounding shoreline and Cole was right; we had other homes burglarized and therefore, other crime scenes to process.

It was after six before we drove back to Connally, tired, sweaty, and dirty. Black smudges of fingerprint powder mixed with perspiration streaked Cole's face and dotted his white shirt.

"Did you ever eat lunch?" Cole asked, as the cooling air conditioning slowly dried us out.

"No. I was too busy getting phone service," I replied.

"Then I'll treat you to a seafood dinner."

"Thanks," I said appreciatively. I was hungry.

Two cans of sardines and a pack of soda crackers later, we were back at the office.

CHAPTER THREE

SARTORIALLY WISER, I was in the office the next the morning wearing a lightweight gray sport coat and blue slacks. Dennis was in the kitchenette making coffee.

"Well, how was your first day?" he asked, sitting down at the table, holding a steaming mug between his hands.

"More than I expected. I've got six burglaries assigned to me," I sighed.

"Don't tell me. You got the dreaded lake burglaries."

I nodded.

He chuckled. "That's the privilege of being low man 'round here."

I heard the side door open and peeked out of the kitchenette to see Peggy. I grabbed my cup. "She's here. Better get to work."

Peggy patiently assisted me through the initial paperwork to open a case... or should I say cases. Cole arrived later, helped me with the format of my investigative summaries, and made suggestions about the contents. Cobb breezed through the area to check on me, then retired to his office. I didn't see him until midmorning. My telephone rang, interrupting my dictation. "Hank, this is Cobb. Can you step in my office?"

I walked into his open office. Cobb pointed to a chair, motioning me to sit. "How're your cases coming?"

"Fine, sir. I was in the middle of dictation."

"You got the items on N.C.I.C.?"

"Peggy's got a list, sir. She should be entering them now."

"Good. Just got a call from Terry Knox, the Sheriff in town here. I meant to take you to meet him yesterday. Anyway, he got a call late last night from Amanda Carson. Amanda's daughter, Lydia Carson, works for the Railroad and Merchants Bank, the main bank in town. She was supposed to arrive yesterday in Atlanta for a meeting or something and she never showed. Her mother's worried and thinks maybe something happened to her. Terry convinced her to wait 'til this morning. As of this morning Amanda still hasn't heard anything. Then about an hour ago the bank called reporting Lydia missing. Terry asked us to look into it. If the bank hadn't called I don't think Terry would be asking us... but I think he's feeling a little pressure to check it out. You understand?"

"Yes, sir," I replied. I suppressed my annoyance. Here I was, saddled with six burglaries and he was pulling me off so the Sheriff could keep a bank happy. I was beginning to understand what Cole meant by understanding the politics of the community.

"You're not going to have to do much. Interview the family and some people at the bank. Call the motel where she had a reservation and confirm she hasn't arrived. Then put a look out on her if the Sheriff hasn't done so."

"Yes, sir."

"Come on. Get your stuff. I'll drive you to the S.O. and introduce you to Terry."

I grabbed my briefcase and followed Cobb to his car.

Five minutes later Cobb glided his Crown Vic into a parking space across from the Forrest County Sheriff's Department, a two-story brick building with a steep slate roof. Though it was no longer a jail, prison bars still adorned the upper story windows. A wide concrete porch welcomed visitors. Cobb led me inside

"Hi, Jenny," said Cobb, greeting a woman in a khaki uniform behind a wooden counter in the lobby. A trustee in white canvas prison garb was in the corner mopping the gray linoleum floors. The walls were just as dreary, painted a listless pale blue, with photographs of past sheriffs circling the room. "Is Terry in?"

"Yeah," she replied. "He's been expecting you. Go on back."

Knox's door was open and I followed Cobb in. The Sheriff was sitting back in his chair, cowboy boots propped on his desk, reading an issue of *Guns and Ammo*. He saw us and tossed his magazine aside. "Been reading a lot about that new forty caliber round. Hear it has the high capacity of the nines but the power of the forty-five. What you think, Cobb?"

"Heard much the same," said Cobb, dismissing the question. "Terry, want to introduce you to a new agent, Hank Monroe. Fresh out of the academy."

I stepped forward to shake his hand. Suppressing his perturbation, he lowered his boots and half rose from his chair to accept the handshake. Sheriff Terry Knox was younger than I assumed, probably mid-fortyish, slightly shorter than me, but thick and broad shouldered. The incipient signs of middle age hung from Knox, pulling on his cheeks and softening his middle, but judging from his handshake, it hadn't sapped his strength. He reminded me of a pit bulldog with an aggressive confidence, quick and alert. His sport was probably football, his position, pulling guard. His face had the wide pores of acne scars and his chestnut hair was barely long enough to part and comb.

"You bring me another new agent to train, Cobb? God, they're getting younger and younger each year," he announced.

"They ain't gettin' younger; you're gettin' older. And yeah... I bring 'em here so you can train 'em. You're the bad example. I tell them to watch Knox, and for God's sake, don't follow his lead."

"Better not say that. I learned it all from you."

"You learned how to dial the G.B.I. That's what you learned."

"Hank," said Knox, ignoring Cobb's counter-jabs, "Stick with me and you'll learn more this morning than you can in a year hanging around with this dinosaur. You know he still carries a revolver and can't even turn on a computer, much less operate one?"

"Listen, are you going to run your mouth all morning or are you going to tell us what's going on?" asked Cobb, plopping down in a nearby chair.

"There's nothing more to tell you. Perkins and two other of his employees went to Atlanta to take a computer course at their bank's headquarters. They were all staying at the Lenox Inn. When they got together this morning for breakfast, Lydia wasn't there. They checked with the front desk and she hadn't checked in. Perkins called Reed Norman in a panic and Reed checked with her mother, then called me, insisting I look into this."

"Have you done anything?"

"Put a lookout this morning along 85 and 185, thinking that maybe her car broke down or, God forbid, she had a wreck. Here's a copy of it," he said, taking a computer printout off his desk and handing it to Cobb. Cobb surveyed it briefly then passed it to me. The BOLO was for a missing person, Lydia Carson, a white female, date of birth: June 9, 1964, height: five feet, eight inches, weight: one hundred fifteen pounds, brown hair, brown eyes, two inch scar on her left upper arm. She was driving a white 1988 Honda Civic coupe, Georgia tag DMZ 114, between Connally and Atlanta, Georgia. I jotted down the description of her and the car.

"And nothing?"

"Nothing." Knox reached into his desk drawer, removed a pistol and slipped it into his waistband. "So why don't young Hank and I visit a few folks and see what we can learn."

"He's all yours. Just drop him by the office when you two finish."

I followed the Sheriff out the back of the building where his car was parked. A young trustee was wiping the remnants of water from a shining navy blue automobile.

"Just finished her for you, Sheriff," said the trustee with a proud gap-toothed grin, tossing a cleaning rag into a nearby wash bucket as if he was shooting free throws. "Got both inside and out. And she's all gassed up."

"Thanks, Billy. She sparkles," complimented the Sheriff as he got inside.

Knox took the side streets as we drove north out of town, keeping both hands on the top of the steering wheel, and whenever a vehicle passed, one of the hands popped up, fingers fluttering, in a brief greeting to the passersby.

Once we were clear of the town the Sheriff asked, "Where're you from? You ain't from 'round here?"

"I guess you'd say Maryland, sir. Graduated from college there then joined the military."

"Which branch?"

"The army, sir."

"Oh, I was in the Corps... and by the way, you ain't in the army no more, so you don't have to say 'sir'."

"Yes... Sheriff," I said.

He nodded in acceptance. "I can deal with that."

As we topped a rise a tractor loomed in front of us. The Sheriff tapped the brakes to avoid the tillers that dominated nearly the entire width of the road. The driver noticed us and pulled to the shoulder, allowing us to pass. Knox touched the horn and waved in thanks.

"What about you... have you lived here all of your life?" I asked.

"Yep. 'Cept for a stint in the Marines. Had posts at Lejeune, Okinawa, the Philippines, and, of course, on a few ships. Got to see a lot of ports. And after all that traveling, I knew that I wanted to spend my life in Forrest County. I saw it all and just wasn't impressed."

Rounding a curve, two vultures perched on a carcass in the road took flight. Knox calmly steered the car around the remains of a possum. "I believe Forrest County should have the distinction of 'The Road Kill Capital,' known worldwide for its varied and abundant road kill. Y'sir, that ought to be our touristy theme: 'We got it all, whether it runs, flies, or crawls.' From the domestic, such as dogs or cats, to the exotic, such as snakes, turtles, or frogs, to the wild, such as possums, coons, squirrels, deer, armadillos, to the bizarre such as alligators, buzzards, and wild boars. Buddy, you don't want to go bumper to butt with a boar. He'll eat your car up."

I reeled at the sharp odor of manure, saw in the pasture a herd of Holsteins lining the barbed wire fence like spectators at a parade, chewing their cud with bored indifference as they watched us pass.

"I guess living here all your life you know about everyone," I commented.

"Near 'bout."

"Do you know Lydia?"

"Know her?" He shrugged. "I know of her. See, she's not the kind anyone would really notice. She isn't bad, she isn't wealthy, and she isn't pretty. She keeps to herself, lives with her parents, and goes to work and church. Her mother, now that was a different matter."

"What do you mean?"

"Amanda's three years older than I and I remember her well in high school—very well. Talking about a good-looking woman, she was a dish of cream. Hair the color of honey and bright as goldenrod. Skin as smooth and pure as porcelain. And her breasts...." He pursed his lips, exhaling a long breath. "...they stood at attention better than a platoon of Marine Honor Guards. I spent many a night in my youth dreaming of what would never be.

"She was popular with the boys. She went to their cabins on the lake on weekends, water-skied and attended the fish fries, hot suppers and barbeques. Was a cheerleader, dated some of the guys on the football team, and was on the homecoming court every year. When she graduated from high school, though, things changed."

"What happened?"

"Well, Amanda was an average student, mostly B's and C's. . She probably could have gotten into a community college if she wanted to, but... she didn't want to. I think she wanted to get married and get away from home. And she was hoping to hook one of the boys who had money. It didn't work. During my junior year in high school she started hanging around with a rougher crowd. Dated Nate Carson, who was a mechanic at the Ford dealership here in town. Nate liked his beer and good times, and I was surprised she went for him. She and Nate had a stormy relationship, one of those love-hate affairs. He decided to go into business for himself and started a body shop. I guess that's when she thought he had a future and married him. The business lasted about two years then went under."

"What happened?"

"Nate was just too ornery and sorry to manage a business. Couldn't keep customers. Then he managed to get a job as a long haul trucker, gone for a week at a time. Apparently those absences made the heart grow fonder because Lydia showed up shortly thereafter. I won't say they have the best relationship but they've stayed together. Maybe Lydia was the cause, I don't know. Amanda raised Lydia strict and straight, probably because of the mistakes she's made in her own life. I think Lydia is her only real accomplishment in this world, so it's natural she's worried."

"What about Lydia? What kind of student was she?"

"Don't really know. But she didn't go to college. Why? I can only guess.... Nate was never a father, nor a husband. He was in love with the booze. All he has ever been interested in was screwing and drinking. Amanda wrote him off years ago and realized her only true family, her only true accomplishment in this life, was Lydia. Lydia was smart enough to go on to college, but Amanda can't live without her, and I think she's been holding on a little too tight."

"Can't live without her?"

"Sure. Lydia is her life. Amanda's afraid if she allowed Lydia to go away to college, she'd find a man and marry him. Then what would Amanda have? Nothing. She can't take the chance and have Lydia leave her."

We came to a series of bungalows set some hundred yards off the road. A tool shed in the rear and a satellite dish to the side complemented the landscape of each house. The Carson residence was a white masonite-sided home with dark shutters. A small shaggy mongrel rose from the porch and began barking as we parked to the side of the house. A woman came to the door to greet us and scolded the dog.

Walking up the concrete porch steps the Sheriff offered a sincere smile. "Good morning, Amanda. It's good to see you."

"Morning, Terry," she replied, opening the noisy screen door.

The Sheriff introduced me to Amanda and she escorted us to a small living room with worn, drab furniture. The musty odor of cigarette smoke hung in the air. She offered us iced tea and we politely declined. There were framed pictures on the mantle and I paused to examine them.

"That's Lydia." Amanda pointed proudly to a picture of a young woman wearing a graduation gown. Lydia wore the forced smile of a girl embarrassed by attention, her eyes reflecting shyness. Traces of blemishes speckled her forehead. The brown hair was orderly, each strand pulled tightly back, pinned behind the crown of her head, then falling limply to the middle of her long neck. If she wore makeup I couldn't tell, and the apparent lack gave her a bland appearance. Was she attractive? I thought she could have been.

I had known the type when I was in school. They would listen quietly in class, rarely ask questions or raise their hands, never sit in the first or last row, but instead feel comfortable in the core. They were never discipline problems, for that caused embarrassed attention. Likewise, high academic achievement was rarely sought, for that too meant singular recognition. If they participated in extracurricular activities, it would include such pursuits as chorus, band or set construction in drama. There was comfort wearing a uniform, moving in a massed formation or watching a performance from the wings of a stage.

Next to Lydia's photograph was another. I recognized her immediately. She wore a pleated navy blue skirt and a fluffy yellow Angora sweater, reflecting the style of the times. Her honey colored hair flipped in a stiff pageboy, the skin smooth and flawless, the eyes clear and amber, invitingly alluring, with a smile set in a subtle sexually challenging pose. The teeth were perfectly aligned and white, the full lips lush and the rouged cheeks set high. I could understand Terry's attraction to this high school senior. I felt a certain remorse that this woman had gambled her future solely on her looks, and that now, nearly thirty years later, they had deserted her like an uncaring suitor.

As she stood next to me I could still see the remnants of what used to be, the tinted hair dry and coarse, gray at the roots, the skin leather tan with the rough texture of a grocery bag. Lines sprouted from the corners of her eyes and traced sagging cheeks. Her teeth were dulled from coffee and cigarettes and the eyes were milky with the spirit of helplessness. Life can be an unforgiving thief of the gifts of youth. I understood why Amanda so treasured Lydia.

"Amanda? We need to need to ask you some questions," said Terry, interrupting the viewing.

"Sure," she said. "Get out of here, Scooter!" The dog, nestled in an afghan on a maroon easy chair, hesitated to leave his comfortable position until she shoved him from the chair. "He's Lydia's dog, I'll tell you, she'll take in any mongrel. At one time we had two dogs, two cats, and a goose. The only one worth a damn was the goose. Better watchdog than the watchdog. If she thought the animal didn't have a home she'd take 'em in. I'd tell her that you can't be kind to everything and everyone—they'd eventually suck you dry. But Lydia would spend all her money on these animals. She just wouldn't listen."

She sat in the easy chair and I positioned myself beside the Sheriff on the sofa with my opened notebook.

"Amanda, tell us about Lydia's activities yesterday," said the Sheriff. "Everything from the time she got up, what she packed, when she was to leave for Atlanta... everything."

Amanda took a deep breath in thought. "Well... Lydia had a seminar in Atlanta that was supposed to start today. She and Mr. Perkins and two other women in the operations center at the bank were scheduled for computer training today. Lydia left for the bank at the usual time yesterday, seven a.m., and put in a half a day at the bank. She left the bank sometime yesterday afternoon to go to Atlanta. She should have been there easily by five. Normally she'd call when she got there. By nine I began getting worried, so I called her hotel. Nothing. So I called for Mr. Perkins. At first he wasn't in, but I got a hold of him around ten. The first thing he did was ask me about Lydia. He hadn't seen her all night. We both checked with the front desk and she hadn't checked in. I knew then that something was wrong and I called you, Terry."

"I assume she drove by herself?" asked Terry.

"Yeah, in her car, the white Honda, which I gave you the information on last night."

"Do you know the names of the other two women who went to Atlanta?"

"One was Denise McClary." She shook her head. "I don't know who the other one was. You can get her name from the bank."

"Did any of them drive together?"

"Perkins drove by himself. Said he had some earlier business at headquarters. I don't know if the other two women drove together."

"Do you know the way Lydia normally drives to Atlanta?"

"Same route everyone else drives. Head out the main road to I-185, then head north to I-85, then into Atlanta."

"Where is the Lenox Inn located?"

"On the north side, in Buckhead, across from Lenox Square."

"Would she have driven straight through downtown or taken the perimeter?"

"Oh, she would have taken the perimeter 'round to the north side of town. Lydia hated Atlanta—it's too congested and mean. She never would go downtown. I remember one time, the church was planning to go to a Falcons game, you know, take a bus and go up there. Lydia refused to go, even though a group from her Sunday school class was going."

Terry paused in his questioning and looked at me.

I continued. "Ms. Carson, did Lydia always go directly to Atlanta... or did she sometimes stop off at a rest area, a restaurant, or maybe an outlet or something?"

Amanda pressed her palms together, considering my query. "Now that you mention it, there was a McDonald's where she sometimes stopped to eat. It was an exit or two north of I-185 on 85. There was also a filling station somewhere in the same area. Lil' Miser, I think it was called. Sometimes she'd stop there for gas or a cup of coffee. There's also an outlet mall near Newnan. Sometimes she'd stop there. I can't think of anything else between here and Atlanta."

"Did she have any friends in Atlanta who she might visit... then decide to stay the night with?"

"Boy friends?" she asked defensively.

"Anybody."

She considered the question. "No. I mean, there are people who she knew who used to live here, you know, like classmates in high school, who moved to Atlanta. But they never kept in touch. No, there was no one in Atlanta she'd stay with."

"Have you talked to your husband about her disappearance?"

"I haven't heard from him yet. He's supposed to call tonight."

"Where is he?"

"He's... well, you know he's a long haul trucker?"

"Yes, ma'am."

"He had a load of Japanese auto parts to pick up at the port in Jacksonville and haul them to Chicago. From there he had a load of electronics, computers I think, to take to Dallas. He's supposed to arrive in Dallas tonight and call. From there he was gonna see if he could locate something to bring back to this area."

"Do you know where Nate was last night?"

"Sure. Somewhere between Chicago and Dallas."

"Yes ma'am. But do you know exactly where he was, what motel he was staying at? Can you confirm he was between Chicago and Dallas?"

Amanda's jaws tightened in anger. She placed her palms on the arm-rests of her chair, elbows splayed outward, and leaned forward as if to rise. She ignored me and addressed the Sheriff. "Terry, I know Nate and I have gone through some tough times. But Nate would never hurt my Lydia. I know you know it and I resent this young man's questions. I'd suggest you go find my Lydia and quit wasting time and insulting people."

Terry gave me a disapproving glance. "Amanda, he didn't mean no harm. It's his job. He's supposed to ask those questions. Nothing person-al, understand?"

She silently considered his supplication, then slowly relaxed. "Yeah... I guess so. But are you gonna look for Lydia?"

"We're gonna look for her and we're gonna find her. Don't worry. That's why I brought the G.B.I. They're gonna comb the entire state."

"Ms. Carson, do you have a tape recorder you can attach to your phone?" I asked.

"I have a small recorder but I don't know how to hook it up to no phone."

"Well, just on the off chance—and I'm not saying she is—but in the event she might have, for some reason, been kidnapped..."

"Kidnapped! What makes you think she's been kidnapped? Oh, my God!"

"Ma'am," I said, interlacing my hands in front of her. "I doubt that's so, but—"

"Well if you doubt it, I don't want to hear about it." Amanda pressed her hands to her face as if to shove back tears of anguish.

"Ms. Carson, it's just a precaution. You never know, she might call for some reason and it would be best if it were taped. And I'll get you a device to connect to the phone and show you how to use it. It's easy."

She addressed me softly. "Okay. But please, find Lydia. She's the only gift the good Lord gave me that I didn't waste."

"We'll find her, ma'am."

"Do you have a recent photograph of her we can have?" Terry asked.

"Sure, just a minute." She walked to the rear of the house and returned a minute later. She handed it to Terry. "This was taken last Christmas. Everything's the same, including the length of her hair."

Terry looked at it briefly, then handed it to me, a full-length photograph of Lydia standing by a Christmas tree. She appeared essentially the same as her graduation picture. She looked more relaxed, taller and about five pounds heavier on a willowy frame, the combination giving her a more mature and confident bearing.

Amanda walked us to the small front porch and thanked us for our help. Walking to the Sheriff's car I turned back to her. "Ms. Carson, I'll get back with you today on the recorder—"

"Watch out!" warned the Sheriff, pointing to the ground.

Fearing I had stepped in dog droppings, I jerked my leg up. Instead I had walked onto a fire ant mound. Two dozen of the little creatures were already scurrying around my wing tips and socks. I briskly beat them off my leg, accepting the fate of a bite or two.

"Son, if you're gonna walk around this section of the country, you'd better learn where to put your feet," the Sheriff warned.

I sat in the Sheriff's car and examined my leg, found a few stragglers and crushed them. The tingling began on a couple of spots above my sock. Though annoying, the bites weren't serious.

Heading back to town the Sheriff asked, "What do y'think?"

I shrugged. "Don't know. When are Perkins and the women returning?"

"They're supposed to be back tomorrow, but I'll call Reed Norman and see if I can get them back this evening for an interview."

"Do you think he'll pull them out of the seminar?"

"He'd better. Remember, they're the ones that called me."

"Do you think we should have searched Lydia's room? Maybe that would turn up something."

"Hank, the girl's missing. Nothing more. We don't have any indication of foul play. Most likely she was involved in an accident or something. If this was a kid it'd be different. But we're dealing with an adult and I'm not gonna tie up my whole department based simply on the fact that her momma can't find her. And I can guarantee you that Cobb ain't gonna let you spend much time on this unless there's more to go on."

"I think I'll drive the route to Atlanta, maybe up to the perimeter. She could have ridden off the road and no one saw her."

"Good idea. I'll get a deputy to ride with you. But other than a couple of bank employee interviews, I'm not gonna push this thing."

CHAPTER FOUR

AT THE Sheriff's Department, Terry introduced me to Deputy Willie Simmons, a muscular black man with a relaxed bearing and a hearty laugh. "Willie knows the area and has good eyes. If Lydia went off the road, Willie'll find her," he assured me.

We drove the route Lydia would have taken, watching for skid marks on the highway, furrows on the shoulders, broken or bent signs and mailboxes. A couple of times we stopped to check on suspicious tracks in the grass on the roadside.

"Just don't watch the ground. Also check the sky, Hank," Willie advised. "It can help you out."

"How?" I asked.

"Buzzards."

We turned north onto 185 and drove past the green rolling country-side. Just north of the intersection of Interstates 185 and 85 we found the McDonald's Amanda had mentioned. The employees had seen nothing. The Lil' Miser was at the next exit. No one had seen her or her car. And the outlet mall was just off the interstate on Highway 34. We searched the parking lot for her Honda and inquired in every store. No luck. At the perimeter, Willie turned around and we drove back to Connally.

"I had hoped we'd find something. Anything. This afternoon was a waste of time," I complained.

"No, man, it weren't no waste. And I'll tell you this, you're gonna have a damn frustrating career if you think most of your leads are gonna be successful. Hell, most of what an investigator does is negative. You might interview ninety-nine witnesses and ninety-nine suspects and come up with nothin'. But that hun'ert person will be the one that solves your case. If there's one thing that solves cases, it's... persistence. That's right," Willie concluded with an exaggerated nod of his head confirming his philosophy, "It's persistence!"

I thanked Willie for his help, then drove out to Amanda's to deliver the recorder to her. I taught her how to operate it, and placed the suction cup of the microphone to her phone.

"Nate called," she said. "He's in Dallas delivering a load of boots to Atlanta. He should be home Friday night if you want to talk to him."

"Thanks." As I was about to leave I asked impulsively, "Ms. Carson, would you mind if I looked through Lydia's room? Who knows... it might help me find her."

"You want to search her room?"

"No, ma'am. Just kind of look around."

"I don't know. I don't like the idea of some stranger going through her stuff when she's not around."

"I'm not going to search her room. Just going to browse."

She considered my request. "Okay, but don't mess anything up."

She led me down a narrow hall to the bedroom area of the house, stopping at the second door. "This is her room," she said, opening the portal.

The room was dimly lit by a shaft of saffron light from the setting sun. The light green paint on the walls and the maple spindle bed covered by a cordovan and blue gingham quilt complemented the rays of sunlight, giving the room a cozy feeling. The theme was sunflowers: a border of sunflowers circling the upper walls of the room, sunflower pillows propped on the bed, a poster of sunflowers on the wall, a vase of them on the dresser; and bright paintings and prints of birds on the walls: bluebirds, cardinals, storks, orioles, all different types and colors.

"Lydia likes sunflowers. They're her favorite. She feels they represent hope, faith, and a better tomorrow," Amanda said to my obvious reaction.

"Why the birds?" I said, slowly examining each wall.

"She says they're 'art in motion'. She loves them."

The room was neat and precise, and I'd seen barracks during inspection that were dirtier. "Do you clean her room?" I asked.

"Rarely. She has always believed cleanliness is next to Godliness. This is her place and I don't come in here often. If I do, it's because I've misplaced something like a hairbrush and I need to borrow hers."

I turned on the clock radio next to her bed. It was tuned to an easy listening station out of Columbus. "I'm surprised.... She doesn't like country?" I asked.

"Sometimes she listens to it. Nate and I listen to it a lot, but Lydia likes classical, Christian, and what I call elevator music."

The clock's alarm was set at seven a.m.

Amanda pulled back the sliding door on one side of the closet, the dresses neatly draping on hangers, each hanger facing the same direction, four pairs of shoes sitting on the floor below, toes touching the baseboard.

"All that's here are dresses. Does she wear pants?"

"She's got a pair of jeans and maybe a pair of cotton slacks in one of her drawers, but I don't remember the last time I saw her wear them."

"What about jerseys, knit shirts, shorts?"

Amanda smiled. "She's got some. They're in the drawers too, but she only wears them around the house."

I shut the closet door. "She seems to be a very proper lady."

"We've raised her that way, Mr. Monroe. It ain't easy, but when you love someone, it's worth the effort." She looked out the window in the distance at the sun, as orange as an October pumpkin low in the sky. "I've learned the hard way, wasted so damn much. It's not going to happen to Lydia. She's not gonna make the mistakes I made."

I left Amanda with a false farewell indicating that I would continue the search for Lydia. Regrettably, Knox and Cobb were right. Other than a few bank interviews, there wasn't much more I should do.

. . .

I was tired, ready to grab a beer and hopefully catch a Braves games on T.V. I skinned a can of chili and plopped the goop heavily into a sauce pan. Chili, white bread, and beer, what a supper! Only someone who lives alone can bear such a meal. The phone rang.

"Young Hank. It's Terry Knox."

"Sheriff, how'd you get my number?" I said, surprised.

"It's a small town. There are few secrets," said the Sheriff smugly. "By the way, I've got Perkins and company here at the S.O. if you want to interview them. Otherwise, I'll take a statement and send them home to supper."

I glanced longingly at the untouched beer. "No, I'll be on my way."

I knocked on a door a few apartments down from mine. Megan answered. "Hank! What's up?" In her Georgia Southern jersey and jean shorts she was as attractive as I remembered.

"Would you like a beer?"

Her eyes narrowed. "Well... yeah."

"Good. Take this," I said, thrusting the bottle at her. "And maybe I'll join you later with another one."

. . .

At the Sheriff's Department, I was immediately escorted back to the Sheriff's office. Terry appeared weary after a long day, but maintained his poise and manners appropriately, introducing me first to Alan Perkins, then Denise McClary and Clarece Eberhart.

Ms. McClary was the eldest of the three, in her fifties, an employee of the Railroad Bank for a number of years. Her frosted hair was cut severe, Dutch boy style, just below her ears, and ornate eyeglasses hung by a gold chain on her upper chest. She had a smoker's deep rough voice. She was a supervisor at the Operations Center, just below officer status. Ms. McClary provided a statement, saying that she and Clarece, who also worked at the Operations Center, drove up to Atlanta together. They worked a half day at the Center, had lunch, then drove up in her car, arriving around three. After unpacking, they went shopping at the mall across the street. Did she know Lydia? Sure, but not very well. Lydia substituted at the Center on occasions when someone vital was sick or on vacation. She had taught Lydia the work over there. Lydia was intelligent, learning procedure quickly, but tended to be quiet and reclusive. When did she last see Lydia? Last week when she cashed a check at the bank.

Clarece was in her mid-thirties and single, I assumed, by the absence of any jewelry on her left ring finger. She was of middle height and at least fifty pounds overweight, making me think of an Eskimo who had feasted well during the winter months. Her auburn hair was teased with a flourish. She was pleasant, but had an irritating and nervous giggle that punctuated her whole narrative. Clarece confirmed Ms. McClary's statement: they worked a half day yesterday, rode together to Atlanta for computer training, and they were to meet with Mr. Perkins and Lydia at the motel. Late last night Mr. Perkins had called her, concerned that Lydia had not arrived at the motel. And when she did not show at breakfast, he called the bank. Clarece did not know Lydia well. She had worked with her a few times at the ops center and Lydia seemed pleasant, but reserved. When did she last see Lydia? Oh my, she said, she couldn't seem to remember when she'd last seen Lydia.

After the ladies left, I met with Perkins. Unlike the first two I interviewed, who were tired and nervous, Perkins was poised, confident, and immaculate. He was in his mid-forties, trim and muscular, in a starched shirt without a wrinkle from the day's wear, his dark gray suit form-fitting and obviously expensive. His dark curly hair was conservatively cut, lengthened a bit toward the back giving him the urban appearance of an Atlanta executive. "I understand we interrupted your evening?" he said with a lazy smile. "Thank you for coming." His gray eyes, however, were cold, offering no apology. His speech was not the typical Southern drawl, but soft and proper.

"No sir, thank you," I replied. "I know you're tired. I'll try to make this brief so you can go home." I flipped over a page of my notebook. "Tell me about your purpose in Atlanta and basically what you did?"

"Sure," he said, sitting back in his chair and crossing his legs. "About four years ago Railroad and Merchants was purchased by a holding company, Atlantic Seaboard Corporation. In the banking business these days that isn't too uncommon. ASC is headquartered in Atlanta and one of my duties as executive vice president of the bank is to periodically report personally to ASC's president about our bank. We discuss how the bank's doing, how we are adopting the company's policies and procedures, and present a plan of long range goals compatible with the company's philosophy. In that vein, the company is in the process of implementing a new computer and multistate ATM system. Naturally, we need to be trained in the system. I was chosen, along with Ms. McClary, who pretty much runs the Ops Center, and Ms. Eberhart as a backup. Lydia was chosen because of her versatility."

"Her versatility?"

"Oh, yes. Lydia has worked with us since she graduated from high school. Though she's classified as a head teller, she has worked in virtually every part of the bank—operations, real estate, loans, customer service.... She has even worked as a secretary. Worked for me a time or two. She's a quick study. Knows short hand, she's proficient with letters, and she's very organized."

"Why didn't you keep her?"

"The secretary I have now... well, she's been with the bank for years. Before I was even hired. Confidentially, even though she isn't as good as Lydia, she's loyal and... it would appear an insult if we moved her out of Administration. Our employees mean a lot to us Mister, excuse me, Agent Monroe. It matters in a small town like Connally.... Besides Lydia wouldn't take the job."

"Why not?"

He paused as if to correctly phrase his words. "Lydia is a shy person, but she likes people, almost to a fault."

"Oh?"

"For instance, if a person came to the bank wishing to cash a check but didn't have an account with us, or the check wasn't drawn on our bank, by policy we have to turn him down. Lydia hated to tell a person 'no'."

"I'm confused, Mr. Perkins. If Lydia is so shy, how is she able to deal with customers?"

He smiled with a knowing grin. "The counter."

"Excuse me?"

"The counter. She enjoyed dealing with customers as long as there was a barrier between them, but she has to have that barrier to be comfortable."

I changed the course of the interview, having him relate a chronology of the previous two days.

"I left for Atlanta early yesterday morning, arriving at ASC at nine-thirty. The day was spent attending meetings. After work I went out for a drink, and then I had dinner with a friend, returning to the motel around ten. I checked with the front desk to make sure that the others had registered and I learned that Lydia had not. I also had a message to call Mr. Norman, the bank president. He told me about Amanda's frantic call and her report to the Sheriff. Reed told me to call him first thing today if Lydia still had not registered, so I called Reed at his home, and I assume he called you. We attended the computer seminar, but I must confess our minds weren't on business. I pray for the best."

. . .

I pulled into my slot in front of my apartment, and got out stretching to rid myself of the knots in my shoulders and back. I was convinced there was more to criminal investigation than what I'd witnessed in the past two days. Because I was the new kid, I'd been stuck with the mundane cases that no one else wanted, and Cobb knew that I was too new to bitch about the assignments.

"Hey!" I saw Megan in the lit doorway of her apartment holding an empty beer bottle. "You left something here. I need to return it." I approached her wearily. "Man, do you always work this late... or are you just trying to impress the boss?"

I shook my head. "I hope not. Just got called out."

"Have you eaten?"

"Not yet. I've got a mound of chili resting in a pot."

"Homemade?" She read my face. "Silly question. Probably the only thing you make at home is your bed. Come inside, I've got some leftover spaghetti from tonight. Save the chili to clog your arteries some other time."

"I like your style, Megan. Do you always insult your guests or do I inspire you?"

She considered my question. "You seem tough enough to take direct-ness," she said, shoving a plate of pasta inside a microwave oven.

I sat down at the kitchen table. "Very observant. And after today I find it refreshing."

She slid a salad across the table. "What? Are you finding the Subtle South unnerving? Bet they didn't teach you that at the police academy?"

"Nope," I said, pouring a liberal portion of salad dressing on my lettuce.

"Subtlety is an art form down here. To anyone with the proper upbringing, especially women, it's second nature. Mothers pound it into their daughters. One simply must have the ability to express oneself in an understated manner. It's exhibited in our clothes, hair styles, and mannerisms. And conversely, one must be receptive to the signals. Directness is considered crude and a lack of social grace. Northerners tend to have a difficult time with it."

"What do you mean?"

"Well, for instance, the word 'sir'. In the Army you said it to a supe-rior, correct?"

"Yep."

"If he's a superior that means you're an inferior or of lesser status. Up North, who would address you as 'sir'? Someone you have authority over. Down here it's different—it's a sign of respect, not subservience."

"And is this understatement carried over into the bedroom by Southern ladies?"

The question caught Megan off guard. "Why, Mr. Monroe, I'm sur-prised you would ask such a direct question. But, speaking from hearsay, mind you, I've heard that Southern ladies fall into two categories. There are those who have been trained for so long that properness is difficult to dispel even in the intimacy of the bedroom. Then there are others who delight in shedding the inhibitions—there's a certain lure in the risqué. And appearances may be deceiving. One never knows into which camp a certain lady belongs."

"And I assume you fall into the latter."

"Hank, have you ever noticed when you're at the beach, the women who appear the most alluring are those that leave a little to the imagina-tion? Relationships are the same way. That which is given away has no value; that which is exclusive is cherished."

"Megan Rilley." I leaned back in my chair. "I can't think of anyone I'd rather spend an evening with, eating leftover spaghetti and discussing philosophy."

She removed the empty plate. "Then I'll treat that as a compliment… and as a good evening."

She walked me to the door. The entrance light brightened her face, revealing a trail of light freckles across her nose. The face, framed by hair that seemed darker in the night, didn't have or need makeup.

"Maybe next time you can join me for a meal," I suggested.

"That might be nice."

$\bullet \quad \bullet \quad \bullet$

"Hello."

"Hey. I called to give you a heads up on what's going on."

"What do you mean?"

"It's going the way we figured. Momma called Terry last night and the bank called him this morning."

"What'd Terry do?"

"He called the G.B.I."

"The G.B.I.!"

"Sure, don't worry. It was expected. You don't think Terry wants to get involved in something like this. He's gonna give it to the State."

"What do you think Cobb'll do?"

The caller laughed. "The dumb shit gave it to a kid fresh out of the police academy. All this pup's gonna do is chase his tail."

"Who is he? Do you know anything about him?"

"Don't know his name, but it's a kid just out of the army. Never done a day's policing in his life. Glad it's not Cole or Davenport. If Cobb gave this to a rookie, it tells me that even he's not taking this seriously."

"I don't think Momma is just gonna forget about this thing."

"No, of course not. At least for now. In a week or so they'll find the car. There'll be a flurry for a few days 'til they confirm that the girl left the country. Then they'll forget about her."

"Even with Momma raisin' hell?"

"Let her. Her little girl, whether she likes it or not, is an adult and if an adult wants to up and disappear there's no law against it. There's no solid evidence of a crime. And there's enough real crimes with real victims and real evidence to keep them busy instead of chasing ghosts."

"You think so?"

"Listen, everything we've done together has worked out grand, right?"

"Yeah, so far."

"Well, any time you're not satisfied you can get out. Just gimme the word."

"No... it's okay. Just let me know what's goin' on."

"I always do. Bye."

CHAPTER FIVE

THE NEXT morning I met Stan Echols and Robin Davenport, two other agents who'd returned from the Academy in Forysth. Echols was in his early thirties and had been with the Bureau for six years. He was going through a difficult divorce, forced to give up his two young children. Though he was a devoted father, he knew with the job he could not attend to them appropriately. He had lost fifteen pounds in the last year due to the ordeal. Davenport was in her late twenties, with a neatness and preciseness about her that was attractive. She wasn't overbearing, but she could give it as well as take it during the office banter. She seemed comfortable with the guys.

Cole arrived later. Since he was my training agent, I briefed him on the Carson case. "Do you think I should tell Cobb?" I asked.

He shook his head as he wadded up a ball of tobacco to chew. "No. Cobb's got five agents, a secretary, and administrative duties to attend to. Unless there's something significant, a concern, or the chance that the G.B.I.'s gonna get in trouble with Atlanta, don't bother him. And from what you've told me, you've done all you can for now, so move on. You can't dwell on cases. You're like a doctor in an emergency room. If you worry about every injury, broken bone, or death, you'll have an ulcer within three years. Stay clinical. Work your cases and do the best job you can, but don't get emotionally involved."

Midmorning Cobb wandered into the squad area. "How's he doing?" he asked Cole in my presence.

Cole leaned back his chair to stretch. "I think we've got a keeper, but we need a few more weeks to be sure."

During the week, Amanda Carson called me twice to learn of any progress in locating her daughter. "We're still working on it," was my semi-truthful statement. The case was still open, so therefore I was technically working the case. But I was no longer diligently pursuing Lydia's disappearance. Both the Sheriff and Cole were right—I was busy working cases that were actual crimes with real victims

Monday morning Cobb summoned me to his office. He was on the phone and waived me to a seat, cupping his hand over the receiver. "Lydia's car was found. Atlanta airport." He spoke into the phone. "Yes, Billy. My agent'll be leaving shortly to Atlanta. He'll be there as long as need be and will assist Lopes as long as you need him. Thanks for your help, buddy."

"Okay, young Hank," said Cobb, hanging up the phone. "That was the SAC for the Atlanta area, Region 10. He's got an agent, Bobby Lopes, and an evidence tech en route to check out the car. You need to get your rear up there to see what we've got."

"Where's the car? How was it found?" I asked, trying to organize my thoughts.

"It's at the Atlanta airport on the ground level, short-term parking on the south side. Early this morning APD ran the tag of the vehicle. It'd been sitting there for a while and just for safety, they ran the plate. APD's holding the car, waiting for us to arrive. Lopes will be handling the investigation in Atlanta and you'll work with him. The evidence tech will do a preliminary check on the car, have it towed to our office in Atlanta, then vacuum and dust it. Head on up to the airport. They'll be at the scene and should be working on the car when you arrive."

. . .

It took twenty minutes to successfully negotiate through the asphalt and concrete maze leading to the Hartsfield International Airport and find the right parking lot. A gray van, a slate blue Oldsmobile, and a white APD squad car encircled Lydia's Honda. A uniformed officer stood beside his unit and two investigators were leaning inside the Honda's open doors. The APD officer sized me up as a curious citizen or an obnoxious traveler.

I held up my credentials. "I'm looking for Bobby Lopes."

The officer pointed to the butt on the right side of the car as if he was aiming a pistol. "Right there."

"Bobby!" I hollered. The investigator withdrew from the car. "Bobby, I'm Hank Monroe."

He greeted me with a handshake, and introduced me to the Evidence Technician, Linda Killgore. "Have you found anything?" I asked optimistically.

He shook his head. "Not a thing. I've seen new cars dirtier than this one. No receipts, no trash, even the parking ticket's gone. Take a look. Be careful not to touch anything. Linda's gonna dust it later."

I looked though the window, and the interior of Lydia's car was as immaculate as her room. "Nothing?"

"Only her proof of insurance and registration."

"Have you looked in the trunk?"

"Not yet. We'll check it when Linda's ready to move on"

Patiently, she searched toward the rear of the car examining every crevice of the carpets and seats. "OK... I'm gonna hit the trunk release," she warned.

Lopes and I moved to the rear, bracing ourselves for any unexpected discoveries that should spring from the rear. The trunk lid slowly rose. Nothing.

"Was the owner this fastidious?" Linda asked. "Otherwise something this clean looks suspicious."

I nodded. "According to her mother and from what I've seen, she liked her areas neat, organized, and clean."

"Well, we've learned a little. The front seat was pushed up indicating the driver of the car was approximately five feet. How tall was the owner?"

"Five eight. But couldn't she have pushed the seat up in order to get her luggage from the back seat?"

"Possibly... but I've also checked the side and rear view mirrors, and the angles confirm the height."

"Interesting."

"Also the radio was on an FM hard rock station here in Atlanta. Does she listen to hard rock?"

"I seriously doubt it."

"So we've got a probability that the last driver of the automobile was short and listens to hard rock."

"And while Linda is processing the car, we've got work to do around here with APD," said Lopes. He turned his attention to the officer. "I understand Sergeant Haskins is pulling the parking lot video?"

The officer nodded. "Yes, sir. He's waiting for you at our airport office. It's just below Delta's baggage claim area. If you can't find it, ask one of the security people in the concourse."

We easily found the place and were escorted to the investigation area of the small office.

"Come on in, gentlemen," Haskins greeted us. "I've got the video and I was just reviewing it. It's a bit tedious."

"Did you have any luck with the Honda?" asked Lopes.

"Not much," I answered. "Hoping we can pull all the airport security videos and the passenger manifests."

"May I make a suggestion? Pulling every one of the videos and reviewing them will take a lot of time. If it's all right with you two, let's see if we can get lucky with the parking lot video. That will narrow down a time period. Then we'll pull the passenger manifest on every airliner say... for a twelve hour period from the time the Honda arrived at the airport. Then if we can put her on a flight, we'll pull the video in that area."

"That sounds logical," agreed Lopes. "Is the video time-lapsed?"

"Yeah, every three seconds. We've played around with the times and by the time someone pulls up to the gate, pushes the button, retrieves a ticket and drives into the lot we've got a plate."

"Do you have a VCR set for time lapse?"

"Yeah. If you want, you can review it here or take the tape back to your office for viewing."

I looked at Lopes for a decision. "If you don't mind, I'd just as soon stay here. If I go to my office, someone'll interrupt us."

"Fine. Come on." Haskins led us to an interview room. The VCR was resting on a table with a labeled cassette resting on top. I examined the tabs of the cassette. "They've been popped," said Haskins. "You can't record over it. I've heard horror stories about evidence being ruined because some idiot forgot to break the recording tabs."

Lopes and I sat down in front of the machine. After an hour of staring at the screen, watching cars approach the gate, identifying the make and model, and dismissing each frame, I was beginning to get a headache. I leaned back in the chair and rubbed my eyes. "I'm going to get some coffee. You want any?"

"No, thanks," said Lopes, watching the monitor.

I found a stale pot with barely enough coffee to fill my cup. The coffee, sitting for hours, resembled used motor oil. I emptied two packets of sugar into the thick expresso to cut the bitterness.

When I returned to the interview room Lopes was stretching in his chair with a grin. "There she is, buddy," he said, pointing at the image of a white Honda next to the entry gate. The tag was blurry but clear enough to positively identify Lydia's car. The gate was under the parking deck shielding the sunlight and the interior of the car was too dark to identify the occupant.

"Damn! You found it," I exclaimed. I checked the date and time on the screen: 6:25 p.m. "It's the same day she left Connally."

"Yep. We can take this to the Crime Lab and get them to sharpen up the images. Also we'll get them to identify the license plates of the previous ten cars and the next ten cars. There might be a connection with her disappearance."

"And I'll get Haskins to pull the manifests."

Haskins made the calls to the airlines for passenger manifests from flights leaving from six p.m. 'til the end of the day. I followed Lopes over to GBI Headquarters, site of the Crime Lab, on Panthersville Road in Decatur. I'd been to Headquarters before, but as an outsider, either seeking employment or as an agent in the Academy. This was my first visit since I'd become a full-fledged, gun-toting, by-God agent. It was a great feeling, the same kind I had when I joined my Ranger Regiment. After identifying yourself and your purpose to the receptionist, you were allowed into the Georgia Crime Laboratory through a door located behind her. This led to the Crime Lab evidence reception area where a secretary called for the appropriate specialist. The specialist, with the help of the secretary, would log the evidence, then take custody of it. Only in unusual circumstances was an agent allowed into the inner sanctum of the lab. In this case, the photography specialist came forward and Lopes explained to her the basics of the case and what was needed from the videotape.

Lopes bought us a Coke and we went to a desk in the investigative area of the building. "My office is actually in Conyers, up the road from here. But they leave a few open desks for times like these. We've got a while before the Lab is able to get those tags. Why don't you go ahead and make reservations for a motel." Lopes gave me the name of a motel near the office where agents got a special rate. I made my one-night reservation and returned to Lopes' desk. He was in conversation on the telephone, diligently scribbling notes.

"Thanks, man. I'll be back in touch," he concluded. "Hank, that was Haskins. He found Lydia's name."

"So soon?" I said surprised. After waiting for over a week for a break in locating Lydia, information was flowing in.

"She took a one-way flight on Delta 1851, which left Atlanta that night at 7:40 and arrived in Miami at 8:50 and then she connected to a flight to Cancun the next morning."

"Cancun!"

"Yeah. Why would she go to Cancun?"

"I have no idea. Is Haskins pulling the security video from the gate for the Miami flight?"

Lopes counted on his fingers. "He's pulling the video. Confirming that she did board the plane. He's gonna determine how she paid for the ticket, if she made reservations, and he's gonna get a complete list of passengers from Delta and their addresses, as well as their assigned seats so we'll know who she sat next to. Delta Security should be able to provide the manifest for both the Miami and Cancun flights. He's also contacting his counterpart at Miami PD to see if there's a video at MIA they can provide."

"I wonder why she flew to Cancun?"

"It's a favorite honeymoon spot. Maybe she met someone." He finished off his Coke, tossing it in a nearby wastebasket. "Hank, this is a
missing person, right?" I nodded. "If she was on that flight, I'd close out
the case. She's an adult and if she wants to fly the friendly skies, that's her
business. Why she wants to leave a garden spot like Connally for the trop-
ical gulf breezes of Cancun is none of your business. It's a family matter
and certainly not worth the effort, time and cost to the State to pursue."

"But what about the car? Why would someone five feet tall be driving her car?"

"Maybe the driver was Carson's friend who flew to Cancun with her.
Possibly a woman friend. If Carson was on the flight, it doesn't matter
who was driving the car or why. It could be a Munchkin from Oz for all
I care. The fact is Carson flew to Miami. Come on, let's go the garage and
see how Linda's doing. She should be finished with the car by now."

The garage was located in the rear of the building in the basement.
The examination area, likewise, required special access. Linda was waiting for us at the door and led us inside.

"Any luck?" Lopes asked, while Linda stored her crime scene gear in
her van.

"Yeah," she replied, hefting a plastic crate to her hip. "Got a number
of finger and palm prints. Hank, do you have any prints of Carson that
the Ident Section can use as elimination prints?"

I shook my head. "Sorry, Linda. I'll ask her mom, but I don't think
she ever had her prints taken."

"I expected that. I also vacuumed some fibers from the driver's seat.
They look to be burgundy—different from the Honda. Maybe the Lab
can identify where the fibers came from. Who knows... it might help
some day."

"Do you think the prints are clear enough to run through AFIS?"
Lopes asked. AFIS was the Automated Fingerprint Identification System
which could perform a computer search of felons in the Georgia Crime
Information Center database.

"A couple are. We'll give it try and we might get lucky. It's happened
before."

Lopes called the photo lab, scribbling on his writing tablet while repeating the tag numbers to the technician on the line. "I'll be back," said Lopes pushing away from his desk. "I'll run tag information and a criminal history on those twenty cars and see what we get."

Five minutes later Lopes returned with a disgusted look on his face. "Damn computer's down. Won't be able to get the information back 'til tomorrow." He plopped down in his chair and rubbed his face. "I'll tell you what... get with Haskins tomorrow morning. He'll be in at eight. You can review the video and get the manifest information from him. I'll drop by here tomorrow morning and run the tags and CCH, then come on down to the airport and join you."

. . .

The next morning, I joined Haskins at the airport and settled in to view the video, searching for a glimpse of Lydia on the monitor. The camera was positioned approximately fifty feet past the departure gate of Lydia's flight, so I could see the concourse and the front of the departure desk. To board the flight she had to walk in view of the lens during check-in. Knowing the times her Honda pulled into the parking lot and her flight departed, I factored in a time frame of 5:25 to 8:40 p.m. The search was tedious as I examined each frame searching for Lydia. After an hour, I had to rest my eyes. I found Haskins at his desk.

"How's it going?" he asked.

"Do I look cross-eyed?" I said, bowing backwards to stretch my muscles.

"Not yet." He pushed some stapled sheets of paper at me. "This just came in over the fax. It's the flight manifest and other information concerning your girl."

The sheet listed Lydia Carson as a passenger in seat 24A. 24B was occupied by a Leonard Johnson from Grand Rapids, Michigan and 24C was occupied Jorge Batista from Coral Gables, Florida. "She purchased the ticket through a travel agency."

"Which one?"

"Delta doesn't have that info available yet."

"When Lopes gets here, let's compare the car registration list with the manifest. Maybe we'll get a match," I said. "Does it say if she made reservations and when? Or if she boarded the plane to Cancun?"

"No. Delta'll have to run an off-line search for that information and confirm she boarded for Mexico."

"It'd be nice to know. It doesn't look like she was traveling with any-one. It's possible she just took the flight to Miami to get out of town. If this was planned, she'd made the reservation days in advance."

Haskins smiled. "Hank, you're going to drive yourself nuts playing the possibilities game. Maybe her friend was on the plane, but not next to her. Maybe she was to meet him... or her, in Miami or Cancun. But it does look like she was on the flight."

"Or someone posing as Lydia Carson."

"Well, before you start believing some elaborate conspiracy theory, finish reviewing the video. See if you can find her."

"I'll do you one better," I said, reaching for Haskins' phone. "What's the area code for Grand Rapids?"

He checked the telephone directory. "Six one six."

I dialed information for Grand Rapids and asked for Leonard Johnson at 416 Chinaberry Lane. Within seconds I was dialing the num-ber the operator provided. A lady answered.

"May I speak to Mr. Johnson please?" I said.

"He's not here. May I take a message?" she replied in a secretarial tone.

"Is this his wife?"

"Yes."

"Ms. Johnson, I'm Special Agent Hank Monroe with the Georgia Bureau of Investigation in Atlanta, Georgia. I need to speak to your husband."

"May I asked what it's about?" she asked with a concerned pitch in her voice.

"He's in no trouble. He flew to Miami through Atlanta last week and I'm trying to identify a passenger he may have sat next to on his trip. She's missing and I'm hoping he just might be able to provide some help-ful information."

I detected a faint release of air and a change in her tone. "Lenny's at work. Let me give you his number. He'll be glad to help."

I dialed the number she provided and was routed through to his office.

"Agent Monroe, what can I do for you?" greeted Mr. Johnson in a direct bold voice.

I explained the reason for my call. "Was there a woman sitting next to you on that trip?"

"Oh yeah," replied Johnson, surprising me with his answer. "The flight was packed and I was stuffed into the middle seat. I'm six foot five, two forty and it was a miserable flight. I was hoping to get a window or aisle seat. No such luck."

"Could you describe her?"

"Nothing much to say. White female, southern accent, blonde or light brown hair I believe."

"Southern accent? She spoke to you?"

"Oh yeah... small talk. Said her name was Lydia something-or-other."

"Lydia? Are you sure?"

"Yep. I'm in sales and I remember names. Lydia is the name of my secretary. But I don't remember her last name, sorry."

"Did she say anything else?"

"Oh boy...." He paused to think. "I think she said she was going to Mexico, Cozumel maybe, to meet her boyfriend. Said it was her first time out of the country and she was kind of nervous."

"So the boyfriend was already in Mexico?"

"I don't know. She said she was meeting him there."

"Did she happen to mention his name?"

"No... I don't believe so."

"There was a gentlemen sitting next to you, right?"

"Yeah, but he didn't say much. He had a Spanish accent."

"Do you recall if Lydia spoke to him?"

"No. Don't believe so. Like I said, he was quiet."

"Did you ever see her standing? I'd like to know how tall she was."

"Hmmm... I can't say for sure. Most everyone looks short to me. But I don't believe she was very tall. When we got up to disembark I was getting my carry-on luggage from the overhead compartment. I think she was standing up under the bin, but she could have been slumped over."

"What kind of build did she have? Was she heavy, large busted...?"

"Sorry I don't remember. If she was anything special I would have noticed but I can only characterize her as pleasant."

"Could you recognize a picture of her?"

"Maybe. I can't be sure. Mr. Monroe, I had other things on my mind."

"I understand. But could I fax you a photo of her? Maybe you could identify her?"

"If you like. Here's my number...."

Hanging up the phone, I handed Haskins the photo of Lydia given to me by Amanda. "Could you fax this? If he can ID her, then my problems are over."

It was midmorning when Lopes arrived. I had reviewed only an hour and a half of video without success. He grabbed a cup of coffee and we went to Haskins' office. I gave him an update on the Johnson interview.

"Here's the registration list of the twenty vehicles that pulled into the parking garage before and after Lydia's Honda," he said, handing it to Haskins. "Not much of anything. Two slight possibilities: the fourth car ahead of the Honda, registered to Tony Burton, and the seventh car behind the Honda registered to Teresa Sierra. Burton was arrested on some bad checks and forgery charges. He's from Decatur, Georgia. Sierra was arrested for bank embezzlement and was placed on three years' probation." He handed the sheet to me. "My guess is that these are coincidental."

"Probably, but let's have the Fingerprint Section compare Burton's and Sierra's prints with the latents recovered in the Honda."

Ten minutes into the review of the tape, Haskins stopped by. "Got a call for you Hank. It's Johnson."

"Mr. Johnson, I assume you received the picture?" I asked anxiously.

"Yeah, I've got it, but Mr. Monroe, I'm just not sure," he said apologetically. "If I had to make a choice on whether the photo was or was not the woman I sat next to, I'd lean toward was not. But I'm not positive."

"Okay Mr. Johnson, thanks for calling me back so soon," I said.

Haskins and I returned to the tape and continued the search through lunch and mid-afternoon. When the tape displayed 8:40 Haskins turned off the VCR.

"Well, what do you think?" asked Haskins, leaning back on the back legs of his chair. "Could we have missed her or could she have somehow gotten by the camera?"

I shook my head. "No... I don't think we missed her, but just to be sure I'd like to view the tape once more."

"And if she's not on the tape, then what?"

"Then we've got a problem."

"No, Kimo Sabe... you've got the problem. I just helped you on a lead. Tomorrow, I'm back at work on my cases. You'll be in Connally trying to convince Cobb that you've got a crime."

"You know... when I learned the car had been found, I thought that we'd solve the dilemma about Lydia's disappearance. I'm no better off now than I was yesterday."

"Come on, I'll buy you a Coke and then we'll take one more look at the video. Who knows, maybe we'll find her."

We didn't.

CHAPTER SIX

THE NEXT morning Cole and I met with Cobb in his office. I briefed him on what Lopes and I had learned, and the inconsistencies of the evidence. I could put a woman with the name "Lydia" on the plane, but I couldn't put Lydia Carson on the plane. I could put Lydia's Honda in the parking lot but I couldn't put Lydia in the Honda. I was frank with my concerns.

"I know I'm new, sir, but it just doesn't feel right," I explained. "I don't think she boarded that plane."

He listened attentively, leaned back in his burgundy executive chair, lacing his fingers behind his head and said, "Hank, don't get caught up in trying to answer every question of her disappearance. Right now you have some legitimate concerns, reasons to continue, but right now, we don't have a crime. We are in the business of criminal investigation. In other words, don't get involved in this anymore than you should.

"How many cases do you have? Other than the Carson thing, all you've got are the lake burglaries, right?"

"Yes, sir."

"Okay. If you've got some legitimate leads and some legitimate cases with real victims and real crimes then you'll work those. Understand?"

"Yes, sir."

"And if you get some extra time, then work on the Carson investigation. From now on, unless you can convince me otherwise, it's a non-priority case."

"Yes, sir."

"Okay. Next question: have you talked to the Sheriff about this?"

"No, sir. I'm meeting with him at his office at eleven. I called him this morning to set up an appointment."

"Good. I don't think Terry will expect any more than what you've already done. Hank... you're doing a good job."

I returned to my desk to catch up on my paperwork. Lopes called with the results I'd expected: both AFPIS and the comparisons of the parking lot suspects were negative. Haskins also called Lopes with the results from Miami. "Lydia Carson" was on the manifest for Cancun.

.   .   .

I found Knox in the lobby of the Sheriff's Office talking to a middle-aged black couple. The lady had tears in her eyes while her husband, grim-faced, listened to Terry. I waited at a respectful distance until the Sheriff walked them to the door.

After they had left, Knox turned to me. "Come on, let's go back to my office." He tilted his head toward the couple. "Their son got arrested last night in Savannah, driving a stolen car. They're good people and raised him up right. Mr. Holt's working two jobs to put his son through Savannah State, and the boy goes and gets involved in something like this. It's a damn shame. They wanted to see if I could help."

"Will you?" I asked.

"Sure. I'll give the Sheriff in Chatham County a call and recommend a low bond. The sad part is, you can do your best and sometimes your children are still going to go do something stupid." Entering the office he pushed the door shut with his foot and pulled out a cigar. "Do you mind?"

"Not at all," I replied, sitting down across from him.

"And speaking of children going to go do something stupid, tell me about Lydia. Cobb tells me he thinks Lydia decided to spread her wings and fly."

"Maybe... but I'm not so sure." I gave him a detailed report with the facts indicating Lydia had left and the facts indicating that someone was trying to make us think Lydia had left. I concluded with Cobb's recommendation to place the case in a non-priority status. "Cobb feels you'll agree and if you don't, he'd like you to give him a call and you two can discuss it."

"No, I agree," Knox said, exhaling a billow of smoke. "Were you planning to speak to Amanda?"

"Yes, sir. I thought I'd go by her place this afternoon."

"Good. And I'll go see Reed, the president of the bank, and explain things to him. They'll be shocked but..." he shrugged, "that's life."

Knox glanced at his watch. "Say, have you had lunch?"

"No, not yet."

"Come with me. The Country Club has a buffet on Wednesday. My treat. A thank-you for the work you put in on this case, and a way to introduce you to some of the fine citizens of Connally. With all the work you've been putting in, you haven't had much of a chance to meet anyone, have you?"

"No, sir."

"Good. Let's go."

. . .

Twin Creeks Country Club was located north of the city, its antebellum style clubhouse poised on a rise overlooking manicured fairways framed by pines and poplars. Approaching the imposing columns of the two-story structure I half expected to see Scarlet and Melanie sitting on the veranda sipping their mint juleps. I noticed a swimming pool off to the left and four tennis courts beyond.

Parking in a side lot, Terry and I followed a threesome of businessmen through a side entrance which led directly to the dining room. The bar, tables and booths were red oak. Copper pots and implements decorated the room and prints depicting hunting scenes, complete with beagles and Labrador retrievers, hung from the beige textured walls. A hunter green commercial carpet softened the sounds of the room while a half dozen brass ceiling fans gently stirred the air. Terry was comfortable in the dining room, greeting everyone he met and politely introducing me. He handed me a warm plate and I joined him in line with the others. Stainless steel serving dishes mounted over sterno contained steaming Southern selections of entrees and vegetables: fried chicken, country-fried steak, mashed potatoes and gravy, fried okra, butterbeans, squash, black eyed peas, crowder peas, greens, rice, biscuits and cornbread. I'd once read a report that Southerners had one of the highest rates of heart disease. Initially I was skeptical of the report knowing their slow, laid-back lifestyle, but then I thought of the food they ate and understood why a coronary bypass was as common as a tax audit in this section of the country. My plate was piled high. After all, meals like this didn't just appear at my apartment. We neared the end of the line and I saw Terry heading for a booth in the rear of the room. Then I sighted the pecan pie.

"I'll see you later," I said to the pie.

Terry was standing at the end of the serving line, talking with a distinguished looking gentleman in his fifties, shirtsleeves rolled half way up his forearms.

"Hank, want you to meet Ross McTimmons," said Terry, introducing me to the man. "Hank's a new G.B.I. agent. Been in town, oh, a couple of weeks. Right?"

"Yes, sir," I replied.

"He was an officer with the Army Rangers and he's still saying 'sir'."

"Well, I wouldn't say that's such a bad habit. Nice to meet you, Hank," McTimmons said, shaking my hand with a firm grip. "Civility isn't as common as it use to be."

"The McTimmons are an old family 'round here and if Ross doesn't own it, one of his aunts, uncles, or cousins probably does," said Terry. "Who're you eating with, Ross? You can join us if you like?"

"No thanks. I'm here with my kids, Graham and Hayley," McTimmons said pointing to a nearby table. "Hank, let me introduce you. They're about your age."

We weaved our way past a half dozen linen-covered tables. I spotted them a couple of tables away. Ross's son, Graham, was about my age, late twenties, trim, with coarse, light brown hair and a square jaw framing a firm face and eyes. And then there was Hayley. She wasn't merely beautiful. She was stunning, she was striking, and she looked as if she had stepped from the cover of *Glamour*. Every sense of mine instinctively sought more of her: my retinas expanded to see more, my nostrils flared seeking her scent, and I longed to hear her voice and feel her touch. Bright green eyes, the color of jade, confidently gazed at me. Her hair, the color of butterscotch, brushed from a part on the right of her head, softly rested on tanned bare shoulders. Like her brother, she had a straight nose and strong jaw, and an aura of calm assurance. She was dressed in traditional understated Southern fashion, relying on neatness and simplicity as much as flair. A teal and gold sundress accented her eyes and hung from two simple straps. A small gold ball earring adorned each ear. "Graham. Want you to meet someone," ordered Ross. "He's Hank Monroe. A new G.B.I. agent in town. Who knows, you might need him someday."

Graham rose halfway from his chair and shook my hand. "Nice to meet you," he said with respectful boredom.

"And this is Hayley," Ross said. "Finally graduated from UGA last quarter and is home for the summer. She's going back this fall to get her law degree."

"Congratulations," I said, extending a hand to her, staring at her green eyes.

Her slender fingers accepted my hand and I gave them an appropriate squeeze, wishing it could have been longer, hoping she felt the same. Her face and eyes revealed no clues.

"Happy to have you in town. Are you considering joining the club?" she asked with a smile which revealed gleaming, perfectly aligned teeth.

"Haven't even thought about it. The Sheriff invited me for lunch, that's all."

"Is Cole still working at your office?" asked Graham.

"Yes, he is."

"He worked an embezzlement for me a couple of years ago at my insurance business here in town. My office manager was forging checks and Cole investigated the matter. Did a good job, too. Tell him I said 'hello'." His statement seemed more an order than a request.

"Come on, Hank," said Knox, "The food's getting cold."

Terry and I returned to our booth and settled in.

"Well, what do you think?" asked Terry with a smug grin.

"About what?" I replied, shaking a bottle of vinegar over my turnip greens.

"I saw your face when you spotted Hayley. Boy, you can't hide nothing. I thought your little ol' eyes would leap from their sockets like a couple of bullfrogs," he said, stuffing a square of cornbread in his mouth.

"Was I that obvious?"

Terry grinned impishly and nodded. "Don't worry, son. It happens all the time with young studs like you."

"Graham said he was in the insurance business? Does he own the business?" I asked, turning to look at their table and seeing Hayley. She was in conversation with her father, but then stopped, apparently sensing she was being watched, and she turned and smiled at me.

"No, though Graham wants you to think that. He runs the day-to-day operation, but Daddy Ross owns the business." Terry rose from the booth. "Going to get a slice of pie. Want anything?"

"Yeah. That pecan pie does look good."

Moments later he returned, sliding a generous portion of pie toward me. "Son, let me give you some advice. If you can get close to her, great. Someone that good looking with a daddy that rich doesn't come along too often. Just don't get your hopes up. She's in a different league."

CHAPTER SEVEN

THE HEAT of the day was subsiding when I arrived at the Carsons'. Dark gray clouds marched toward Connally, low rumblings of thunder in the distance pushing sporadic breezes across the yard. Amanda met me at the front porch and invited me inside.

"Is your husband home?" I asked, once seated on the sofa.

"He'll be home tomorrow afternoon. Do you want to talk to him?"

I nodded. "Need to."

"I'll have him call you when he gets in."

There was an uncomfortable pause as she waited for me to report on her daughter. I took a deep breath and told her about the discovery of the car, and that Lydia apparently had flown to Mexico. While she listened to me, she would subtly shake her head in disagreement. I concluded with a question. "Why would Lydia fly to Mexico? Was she romantically involved with someone?"

"Mr. Monroe, I don't know what's going on, but my Lydia didn't fly to Mexico."

"Supposedly, Lydia purchased the airline ticket through a travel agency. We're running down the name of the agency."

"I'm telling you, that wasn't my girl on the airplane."

"Well, I'm left with two options. One, she was on the flight and I need to know why she left. Or two, she wasn't on the flight and I need to know why someone wanted it to appear she had left. Now if we assume that she left–"

"She didn't," said Amanda firmly.

"Bear with me, Mrs. Carson. If we assume that she left, it doesn't really matter why she left. She's a grown woman, and neither foolishness nor stupidity is a crime. But I may have to eliminate the first option to prove the second. I'll need to ask you some personal questions and I'll also need to search Lydia's room."

The room darkened and the rumble of thunder increased with the approaching storm. Amanda silently considered my request as she turned on two nearby lamps that cast long shadows across the room, giving our meeting a gothic atmosphere.

"Ma'am, if you want me to find Lydia you've got to help me," I pleaded.

"Does Terry know you're here?"

"Yes, Ma'am."

The rain arrived, splattering the house with an increasing staccato. Amanda rose and opened the front door as a flash of lightning lit the room, water cascading off the porch roof like a waterfall. I watched while she stared out the door as if she was expecting someone to arrive. She inhaled the rain-soaked air.

"I love the smell of the air during a storm. It's so fresh, so pure, so... cleansing."

"Yes Ma'am. But about Lydia. How is your relationship with her?"

"It's fine. Even though I'm her mother, I think our relationship has become more of a friendship."

"Does she confide in you?"

"She does."

"In other words, if she had a boyfriend you'd know about it."

"I think so. I mean, that's not something you can easily hide."

I shrugged. "Did you ever have a boyfriend you hid from your mother?"

She gave me a hard stare. "I see your point, Mr. Monroe. But my relationship with Lydia is nothing like I had with my mother."

"What do you mean?"

"Is this really pertinent?"

"It could be. I don't know, Mrs. Carson, until I hear the answer."

Amanda paused, carefully phrasing her words. "My mother was a meek individual, completely subservient to my father. She'd been raised in the old school, where the wife's job was to raise the children and take care of the husband. To be blunt, Mr. Monroe, I didn't really respect my mother or her opinions. She was not one I would have confided in."

Lightning flashed again and lamps flickered.

"What is Lydia's relationship with Nate?" I asked.

"They get along fine. She's not as close to him as me. He's gone most of the time and, of course, he's a man."

"Has he ever been... abusive to her?"

"Has he ever hit her? He spanked her at times when she was little, but he never beat her."

"What about... sexually abused her?" Her eyes flashed, as angry as the outside storm. "Mrs. Carson, please, I have to ask these questions."

"The hell you do," she quickly countered. "If something like that was going on I'd tell you. You wouldn't have to ask. You'd be interviewing me for Nate's killing."

"If something like that had happened, do you think you'd know?"

"Yeah, I'd know. Between Lydia and Nate, I'd figure it out. Nate may have had his problems in the past and he may have strayed at times, I don't know, but I know this much about Nate, that ain't his way."

"Had you and she had any arguments recently? Did you notice a change in her attitude or health?"

She sat back in her chair pondering the question, searching her memory. "No, not really. She had the flu about a month ago, throwing up and all. Six months ago she was having some female problems, but that cleared up. How far back should I go?"

"That's enough. Any arguments with you or Nate?"

"She'd occasionally argue with Nate especially 'bout some of his racial attitudes. She hates it when he uses racial slurs. They've gotten into some heated discussions about that. Especially when it comes to interracial marriages. Or when they disagree on the government's involvement in welfare." She shook her head. "I just stay out of it.

"As far as Lydia and I are concerned, I can't think of any big arguments we've had. Certainly not one that would cause her to pack her bags and leave. About two months ago she was considering moving out to an apartment in town. I talked her out of it."

"Why did she want to leave?"

"She said she wanted her space. But I convinced her to wait. Her salary at the bank wasn't enough to afford the cost of an apartment, food, utilities and a car payment. Living with us she was able to put away a tidy sum to pay for college or use as a down payment on a house. She understood and agreed, but she seemed disappointed. Really that's about the only disagreement we've had recently, and I wouldn't call that an argument. Oh... and a couple of months ago we had a discussion about predestination."

"Predestination?"

"Yeah. In other words, does God already have your life laid out for you? No matter what you do, it's already planned by God."

"And what did you think?"

"I could tell that Lydia was thinking serious about it. Kind of like that maybe she was gonna do something God had planned for her."

"Do you think leaving the country might have been it?" I asked.

"No. Lydia wouldn't have done nothin' like that. Sometimes she had questions like that. She's always been a deep thinker. But she'd never leave home," said Amanda with certainty.

"What about friends? Does she have any friends that she might confide in?"

"A couple. I am her best friend, but she has Jenny Tisdale and Leslie Autry. Leslie works with her at the bank. Jenny's a friend who attends church with her."

"What about boyfriends?"

"Not really. The ones that are interested in her are trash." She read my thoughts. "Mr. Monroe, you don't understand Lydia's situation here. I grew up in this county and I know the rules. Like it or not, they are the rules you live by around here. When I was growing up everyone went to public schools and I was able to meet some attractive guys, guys who were going somewhere and would end up able to take care of a wife and raise a family. I couldn't go to college, and every eligible man went off, met his wife and most didn't return. And even if someone worthwhile came back, he wasn't about to consider someone whose parents were 'lint heads.'

"It was no different with Lydia. The guys with promise went to private school, so she never got a chance to meet them. Sure, there were some in public school that went off to college and will probably do well, but they didn't return to Connally. So the only fellows that show any interest in her are the same type of scum I hung around with when I got out of school. I know what they want and I know why they're here. I won't let them through the door.

"I was kind of wild growing up and I made some bad choices. Leaving my parents to get away from their discipline was one of them. I won't let Lydia make the same mistake I made."

The storm passed, the thunder booming in the distance like artillery.

"Let's take a look at her room," I said softly.

She considered my request, then led me down the hall. Nothing had changed since my last visit. I began at her dresser sifting through socks, underwear, bras, jerseys, and t-shirts. I checked her closets, reaching over the top shelf and pushing aside hats, caps, and scarfs.

I moved to her student desk, with notebooks, pens, paper, and ledgers neatly arranged in the drawers. I sat at her desk and looked into each drawer. I found her checkbook.

She wrote few checks, mostly for cash. There were the monthly payments for the car and to the savings account. There were her deposits. I was surprised to see that she was making less than I. No wonder she had to live at home. The other checks were miscellaneous, for groceries, car insurance, or to Sears, Penney's and Belk's. No checks to Delta or a travel agency. No hint of a boyfriend or any outside interest. I searched each drawer examining every piece of paper for notes or a clue as to her intentions or character.

I moved to her bookcase, containing an interesting mixture of classics, poetry, and self-help books. There was *Little Women* and *Anne of Avonlea*. I flipped through the pages of *Angels* by Billy Graham, and *Dr.*

Dobson Answers Your Questions by James Dobson. The lower shelf was lined with *People* magazines and *Reader's Digests*. Flipping through the magazines I noticed inked circles around each *Reader's Digest* "Word Power" test, and each time she scored no lower than "exceptional." I checked behind the bookcase, leaning it forward, hoping that Lydia had hidden a clue behind it.

I looked under her bed. *The Living Bible* was tucked behind the draping bedspread. I rummaged among a couple of empty shoeboxes and a dusty wire clothes hanger. Stretching my arms between the box springs and the mattress, I felt papers, and I removed a *Playgirl*, displaying the buffed figure of a male posed provocatively.

Amanda's hands shot to her face. "My God, I don't believe it!"

I nonchalantly handed her the magazine and continued the search, probing through Lydia's bedside table, a cedar chest, and curio cabinet. Nothing. No letters, no cards or diary, no indication that she had a lover worth leaving home and country.

I looked up to tell Amanda I was leaving. She was gone.

I found her at the dining room table, hunched over, appearing almost shrunken, staring at the magazine. "I'm through," I announced softly.

"I tried to protect her," Amanda said with a resigned quiver in her voice. "I raised her the best I could. Why God, oh why?"

I didn't have an answer to the question. I wasn't sure what "why" meant. Why was the magazine in Lydia's room? Why would her daughter want to succumb to natural urges? Or, in discovering another side of her daughter, had Amanda begun to realize that Lydia might have a lover and that she would willingly leave her mother's protective nest for a new life? That afternoon a part of Amanda Carson died.

I considered going home, then remembered that a Braves game was going to be on television. I stopped off at the Piggly Wiggly, purchased a six-pack of beer, a jar of salsa and a bag of Doritos. I needed to relax and visit the Expatriates.

.   .   .

"Hello."

"Hey. It went as predicted."

"What do you mean?"

"They found the car. They can put the girl on the flight to Mexico. There's nothing more they can do. Case closed. Now we can get on with our lives, get on with business."

"What about that agent? Did they take him off the case?"

"No. The young pup's gonna chase his tail for a few more days probably, get tired, then go on to other things."

"I hope so. I didn't want it to happen this way, but...."

"Oh yeah, the agent met Ross, Graham, and Hayley today."

"How'd that happen?"

"Sheriff took him to the Club, ran into Ross and he introduced him to the kids."

"Do you think that'll be a problem?"

"No. Who knows, in some ways it might help. You worry too much."

"Maybe not enough."

CHAPTER EIGHT

I WAS introduced to Katie Bostick and her boyfriend, Roy Dutko, one evening, while over at Megan's apartment. Katie was a fellow teacher and close friend of Megan's. Roy worked as a surveyor for a local engineering firm. Roy was a free spirit who saw wonder and delight in every moment.

Roy's passion was not Katie. It was Georgia football. He had attended his beloved school for five quarters before he was rejected by his true love. Those who enjoy and eventually graduate from Georgia quickly learn that there is a fine balance between the social and the academic aspects of university life, the latter requiring a discipline that follows the graduate throughout life. Roy never realized that he actually should attend class if he wanted to remain in the institution. For two football seasons he operated under the myth that the rest of the school was a life support system for the Georgia Bulldog football team. His belief in the "Dawgs" approached a religious faith. Roy was too good a person to ever hate anyone. If one wasn't a Bulldog, that was all right with Roy; it was, instead, an opportunity for him to evangelize.

Through Roy I met the "Expatriates," a group of six friends ranging in age from twenty-four to twenty-nine, who met over at the home of Mitch Sivak and Joe Hudson, a couple of high school buddies. Their house was an informal sports bar, where friends had an open invitation to meet during the summer whenever the Braves where playing. The unofficial price of admission was common beer and a bag of munchies. Though I very much enjoyed Megan's company, the home of the Expatriates was a perfect venue for self-exile from the norms and pressures of society, a place to burp, be bawdy, and tell jokes. Baseball was a perfect backdrop to the good-natured bantering, when you never knew when it would be your turn in the pit.

The fact that I was from Maryland qualified me as a Yankee. While there was no malicious intent, my origin was always a source of harassment. "I've always wondered why the nation considers us a bunch of bumpkins, but for every Southerner moving to the North, there are five Yankees coming south?" said Donny James. "When are they gonna leave us alone?"

"Yeah, we ought to have some sort of immigration laws set up," growled Jason Morton, a two hundred and fifty pound, burly-faced member who had played football for two years at Georgia, before a knee injury destroyed any hopes of a pro career. "There's more Yankees here than fire ants. Hank," said Jason, leaning toward me with a mock sneer, "Do you know the difference between Yankees and fire ants?"

"Northerners marry outside their family," I answered smugly.

"Wrong! The ants are easier to reason with, they're not as obnoxious, and it's legal to poison them."

After visiting Amanda, I needed a place to unwind and forget the image of Lydia. I drove by Sivak's and Hudson's house, a small brick bungalow in the older section of town. Cars were stacked in the driveway. The gathering was in session. I parked my car on the curb, gave the front door two hasty raps, and went inside.

"Hank!" greeted five guys, arranged in a loose semicircle around the television.

"What's the score?" I asked, heading for the kitchen.

"Nothing to nothing. Game just started," answered Hudson.

Opening a beer, I shoved my remaining six-pack in the refrigerator, popped the bag of chips I was carrying, dumped the salsa in a bowl, and returned to the group. The living room, an interior decorator's nightmare, was dominated by a twenty-seven-inch television, and the furniture was chosen with two questions in mind: was it cheap, and could it withstand beer stains? Two overstuffed sofas, upholstered in a beige burlap fabric, formed an L, and two naugahyde easy chairs completed the semicircle around the T.V. A mismatched collection of end tables with circular water stains and warped veneer supported cans, bags, and bowls of snacks.

"Where's Roy?" I asked, laying the chips and dip next to a bowl of popcorn.

"He's supposed to be here. Late as usual," said Jason, scooping some popcorn in his massive hands.

"Didn't you and Roy go to a Braves game last weekend?" Mitch asked Donny.

"Yeah... and a word of advice. Never, and I mean never, go on a trip in Roy's car," warned Donny, shaking his head in dismay.

"What do you mean?" I asked. "He asked Megan and me to go along, but Megan had a school project. What happened?"

"You're lucky. We went with Katie and Lynn. Roy offered to drive— he has that old hatchback that has at least two hundred thousand miles on its carcass. Well, we drove up to Atlanta Sunday morning. We're gonna tailgate. We're heading up Interstate 85, crammed in that car like sardines, when all of a sudden it sounds like the engine is about to fall off. I hear metal scraping underneath the car and it's growling like a pit bull, scaring the girls to death, and I'm thinking the car's broke down, we'll miss the game. Roy's as calm as a fighter pilot. He pulls over to the shoulder of the road, reaches into his glove box and, get this, pulls out two oven mittens. Everyone's starring at him like he's crazy.

"Roy gives us his patented shit-eating grin and shrugs. 'It's the muffler, folks,' he explains. 'Happens about every hundred miles.'

"'A hundred miles!' Katie screams. 'What's going to happen when we're on the interstate in downtown Atlanta and the muffler drops again?'

"Roy gives her a wave of dismissal and says, 'Don't worry. Done this a thousand times.' He's calm and he shimmies under the car. I hear this *thunk* and within seconds he's back in the car, handing the mittens back to Katie. We make it to the stadium okay and begin unloading the gear. As I'm setting the cooler on the ground I notice this glint underneath the car. I look closer and I can see the sunshine reflecting off portions of both of the rear tires. Guess what it was?" Donny paused for a few seconds. "It was the friggin' steel belts on the tires!

"'Roy!' I hollered, 'What in the hell is this?'

"I get this grin like he's been caught screwing the sheep. 'Well, Donny... you know... I've just been busy. Ain't got around to buyin' tires. Don't worry, the steel belts are in good shape and I got a spare... I think.'

"Well, the game is shot to hell. I'm watchin' Glavine pitch and all I can think about is, 'How we're going to make it home in this roving death trap?' Roy is next to me, stuffing his face with hot dogs and swilling beer. Not a care on this earth."

Suddenly the door sprang open. "At ease, gentlemen," Roy Dutko somehow announced, even while clutching the corners of two bags of chips in his mouth and balancing a paper bag in the palm of each hand.

"Oh boy, it's Roy," the group chorused. "Hide your women and pets!"

Roy hobbled into the kitchen amid the flurry of Fritos and popcorn thrown at him. "I know you love me," he shouted as he dashed through a swinging door. Moments later he burst through the door with a large mug. "What have I missed?" he asked, plopping down on a sofa.

"Donny was telling us 'bout your trip to Atlanta," I said.

"Great game. Great game."

"Have you got those tires replaced?" Donny demanded to know. "Or should I report you to the State Patrol?"

Roy grimaced and lowered his head in feigned misery. "Haven't had a chance to get them replaced. Will do it next week."

I would always remember the Expatriates with fondness. The gatherings were a place where one was accepted with no preconditions. For me, it was a place to remove the mantle of "agent" and for an evening, forget a responsibility that I took seriously.

• • •

The next morning was clear with a sky as blue as robins' eggs. The passing storm had lowered the humidity and I hoped that the day, with me trapped in a coat and tie, would be bearable. I parked in the near-empty lot of Dr. Favor, D.D.S., and a cooling breeze ushered past the scent of gardenia as I opened the car door. The office, a converted brick ranch framed by live oaks and wisteria, was located in a mixed residential area that was slowly succumbing to commercial property. The waiting room was small with a half dozen chairs lining the wall, and dominating the room was a round coffee table covered by *Highlights*, *Woman's Day*, and *Good Housekeeping*. I made a note not to use Dr. Favor as my dentist. Any doctor who wouldn't pop for at least a *Newsweek* or *Sports Illustrated* wasn't going to put his hands in my mouth. A small frosted glass window adjacent to the office area was closed. With a loud ping I rang the bell that was sitting on a ledge beside the window.

The window slid aside almost immediately and a startled young girl said, "Sorry, sir. We weren't expecting anyone."

"I don't have an appointment," I said, presenting my credentials. "I was looking for Jenny Tisdale. I was told she's the dental hygienist here." The receptionist's eyebrows arched when she saw my badge. "She's a friend of someone who disappeared recently. I'd like to speak with her."

She nodded with relief. "It's about the Carson woman, eh? Jenny was just talking about it." I nodded with a brief smile. "Just a minute, I'll get her for you. She doesn't have an appointment for the next twenty minutes... Mr. Monroe."

While I was flipping through one of the magazines I heard the office door open. A faint voice anxiously called me. "Mr. Monroe?" A woman in a light blue smock was standing in the doorway. She was broad shouldered, in her late twenties, with short sandy blonde hair cut in a wedge.

"Ms. Tisdale?" She nodded. "I'm Hank Monroe with the G.B.I." I held up my badge. "You are a friend of Lydia Carson?"

"Yes."

"I'm sure you know she's disappeared. Could I have a few minutes of your time to ask you some questions?" Though it was a question, it was spoken as a directive. I led her to a pair of chairs and balanced my notebook on my legs.

"Can you tell me what's happened to her?" Jenny asked. "I heard her car was found in Atlanta."

"Yes, ma'am. It was. And I was hoping you'd be able to tell me what might've happened to her. You were close friends, right?"

She shrugged. "I guess so. We knew each other from church. We both go to First Methodist, y'know."

I nodded, prompting her to continue.

"We're in the same Sunday school class, took a Disciple's class together, we're members of the Altar Guild and we help in various church projects such as yard sales, bake sales....." Her voice trailed quiet as if she couldn't think of any further comments.

"Do you have a boyfriend?" I asked.

"Sure," she replied, accented as if she was offended.

"What about Lydia?"

She paused, considering the question. "None that I was aware of."

"You said you were close. Didn't you ever socialize with her... say, double on dates with her?"

She smiled and shook her head. "No, Agent Monroe. We knew each other through church. A couple of times we met at the movies and went to the Dairy Queen afterwards. But we never dated together. In fact, I don't think Lydia's mother allowed her to date."

"Allowed her to date?"

"Uh-huh. Her mother was very oppressive. Lydia talked to me about it a number of times. Even though Lydia was a grown woman, she had to clear each of her suitors with Momma. And Momma didn't approve of nobody.

"Agent Monroe, I don't know what you've heard about Lydia. She needs what every woman needs. I know what her mother's been through, and maybe her mother's doing this out of some misguided love. But Lydia needs to meet others, even if it means that she's gonna get hurt. Hey, that's life... that's a part of growing up.

"I heard a rumor that Lydia's left the country, is that true?"

"I'm not sure. What do you think? Did she ever talk to you about leaving Connally?"

She licked her lips. "Not that I can recall. But I think she's left."

"You think she has a boyfriend. Is that why she left?"

"Yes sir, I do. Why do I think so?" She paused, contemplating her own question. "Call it woman's intuition. Small hints I think only a woman would pick up. During the last days before she disappeared, she seemed more relaxed, more confident, more directed... like she finally had a future, a purpose in life, like she just wasn't hanging around, growing old, gaining weight, and collecting wrinkles."

"But she never said anything. You're just talking about your feelings."

She pursed her lips together. "About a week before she left, it was after a Bible study class, she asked me a philosophical question about God's commandments and meanings: if a motive is pure, can the result be sinful?"

I gave Jenny a questioning glance.

"In other words, Agent Monroe, if you shoot and kill someone, did you commit a sin?"

"It would depend on the circumstances," I replied.

"Exactly. What was your intent or purpose in shooting? Was it to stop a crime, to save someone else's life, or maybe your own? Or was it revenge, or anger, or hatred toward someone? In both cases the result is death. But what was your motive when you pulled the trigger? It is not the result that causes the sin; it is the motive of the act."

"And that's what you told her?"

"Of course."

"What were her hobbies, what did she enjoy doing?"

"Well... she enjoyed reading," recalled Jenny, "especially romance novels. I think it was a way for her to escape life. And romance novels always end happily. That's what she was searching for and, I believe, has finally found.

"There's another thing that I always found interesting about Lydia. Though she was shy, she was always searching for ways to help people. She'd visit the nursing home and if someone had a tragedy in their family, like a death or illness, she was there for them, whether it was to help them with errands, or food, or simply an understanding heart. She didn't necessarily go through the church. If it was something she felt was important she'd go handle it herself and without any fanfare."

"Well, you've been very helpful, Miss Tisdale. Thanks for your time," I said rising.

She escorted me to the front door. "Agent Monroe, I don't know what other cases you have, but you don't need to look for her any longer.

In fact, and don't take this wrong, I hope you don't find her. I don't believe Lydia was ever a happy person. I think that's one of the reasons she was so active in church. She's an intelligent woman who's been held down. A social woman who's been cloistered. I pray she's happy now."

. . .

The lobby of the Railroad and Merchants Bank was decorated in Early American, soft creams accenting the mahogany woodwork, a lush burgundy and slate carpet in the business area. The tellers' windows were on the right as I entered, and a series of offices with facing glass walls formed a U around the floor.

I met the manager, Rick Brouder, a young man who looked no older than I. He had thinning straw-blond hair combed in a futile attempt to mask his encroaching baldness, and wore the traditional Southern male business uniform: khaki slacks, a blue oxford cloth shirt with heavy starch, and penny loafers. The only allowance in such a uniform was in the color and pattern of the tie. Yellow had been popular for a number of years, but the power reds and greens were in vogue now. He'd chosen green.

"Mr. Brouder," I said, shaking his hand. "Hank Monroe, G.B.I. I wanted to see if I could speak to one of your employees, Leslie Autry. It's in regard to the Carson disappearance."

"Oh yes," he replied nervously. "Glad to help. She's a teller. Let me get her for you. Cindy, please take Agent Monroe to the kitchen. It'll be a good place for him to conduct his interview." His speech was smooth and refined with a soft measure cadence.

"Also is it possible to check on Lydia's accounts?" I added. "If Lydia were planning on leaving the country, you'd think she would take her money. She did have a bank account here, didn't she?"

"Yeah. Checking and savings."

"Would you mind checking to see if she had any large withdrawals prior to her leaving?"

"Sure."

"Did you ever do an audit on the areas where she was working? I hate to think she may have embezzled some money, but it's a possibility, considering she left the country."

"That's been done. The President, Mr. Norman, ordered it and the results were negative."

"That's good to hear."

Cindy led me behind the teller's counter to the back of the bank, where the opulent surroundings took on a more austere motif, as if passing from a Hollywood set of rich carpet and exotic hardwoods to a business area of paneling, linoleum and plywood. Dented gray file cabinets lined the walls, stacks of computer papers were shoved in the corners of rooms, three-ring binders in different sizes stacked across make-shift shelves. The small kitchen was clean with a white medium-sized refrigerator, stove, stainless steel sink, and a black microwave oven and coffee maker tucked under the cabinets. I sat down at a small round table and declined Cindy's offer of a Coke or coffee.

Brouder rapped on the door and entered. "Mr. Monroe, this is Leslie Autry," he said, introducing me to the young woman trailing behind him. Leslie Autry was thin-boned. Everything about her was thin, her legs, arms, lips, nose, even her teeth appeared malnourished. Her thin wiry reddish brown hair resembled an ocean sponge, with stray strands sprouting in various directions.

I stood. "Ms. Autry."

"Mr. Monroe, if you need anything just give me a call," said Brouder, pointing to a telephone on the kitchen counter. I pointed her toward a chair. "I'm sure you understand why I'm here," I said, scooting my chair under the table.

"Yes, sir," she said meekly.

"I understand you were good friends with Lydia Carson?"

She shrugged. "I'm not sure what you mean by 'good friend.' I mean, I was probably the closest friend she had at the bank. But she wasn't my closest friend. I guess Jenny, who works at Dr. Favor's, was her closest friend."

"What did you think of Lydia?"

"I felt sorry for her. She had a mother who wouldn't let her grow and once you got to know her, you could see it was creating a pressure in her. It was like her mother was this balloon and Lydia was the air. The air was expanding, growing in the balloon and the balloon was trying to contain it. I think the balloon finally burst."

"So you think she fled the area to get away from her mother?"

"Yes sir, I do."

"Did Lydia ever speak or hint to you that she would be leaving?"

Leslie leaned back in her chair in thought. "Can't say that she did. She was a very private person. A couple of weeks before she left, I did notice small changes in her. She was more talkative, quicker to laugh, and she seemed more relaxed."

"Do you think she had a boyfriend?"

She nodded. "That'd be my guess."

"If you had to guess, where do you think she'd met him? In church?"

"Right here."

"What do mean 'Right here'?"

"Good Lord, there're men coming into the bank all the time. They're easy to meet, plus..." she smiled mischievously, "you get to know how much money they have. If they're worth getting to know."

With A sharp rap on the door, Brouder poked his head through the door with a look of concern. "I've got something for you, when you're finished with Leslie."

I wrote my name and address on a sheet of paper. "Is there anything else that you can think of that might help?"

"No, sir. Can't think of anything."

I handed her the paper. "My business cards haven't arrived yet. If you'd keep my name and number, I'd appreciate a call if you think of anything at all that might help."

She folded the paper. "I'll call," she said, tucking it into her purse.

I turned my attention to Brouder. "Problems?"

Nearly penitent, he presented a printout to me. "Her checking account is the same. But last Monday, all but one hundred dollars of her seventy-eight hundred dollar savings account was withdrawn."

"What! Seventy-seven hundred! How come no one called us? Four friggin' days and no one knows about it? Jesus!"

"It was a bank draft drawn on a bank in the Cayman Islands, the Caribbean Gulf Stream Bank. Everything's legitimate, I assure you," he pleaded. "I've spoken to the operations officer and everything's in order. Mr. Monroe, you don't understand. Our employees working in the operations center are only high school graduates, making barely above minimum wage, and they are reviewing literally thousands of checks each day, encoding the amounts and comparing signatures eight hours a day. They can't be expected to recognize a legitimate signature that comes across their desk. It's simply not fair."

I backed away composing myself. "So you're saying she withdrew practically all of the money from her account using a Cayman Island account? And the withdrawal is proper?"

He appeared reluctant to answer. "Yes, sir. I've personally checked. I'm truly sorry."

I thanked Brouder for his assistance and returned to my car. I glanced around to make sure I wasn't being watched, then slammed my fist against the dashboard. I'd been convinced that she was abducted. The interviews today and the withdrawal convinced me she'd fled. The Lydia Carson that I'd seen in the photographs and the high school annual was gone.

Less than a hundred yards away, a figure watched my tantrum with relief, rubbed his chin in satisfaction and chuckled softly. It had happened just as they had predicted.

CHAPTER NINE

PASSING COBB'S office I heard his booming voice. "Hank!" Cobb was on the telephone, waving me inside with his large beefy hand. He motioned me toward a chair as he concluded his call.

"Morning," he greeted, as he hung up. "How'd your interviews go?"

I told him of the two interviews, what Jenny and Leslie believed, and then the withdrawal from Lydia's account.

Cobb leaned back in his chair. "So you think Lydia's question to Jenny, 'If a motive is pure can the result be sinful?' was Lydia's way to justify leaving her parents and running away with a guy?"

"Yes sir, I do. I thought I'd run over to the Carsons' place and interview the father just to tie things up."

Cobb smiled. "Well... how does it feel to have solved your first case?"

"It's not quite what I'd hoped," I replied with a dejected grin.

"Welcome to the real world, son. Don't worry, you'll have many more cases with real perpetrators. The Carson thing was something we had to check out and you've done a thorough enough job to satisfy anyone who's objective... including the Sheriff and the D.A. And they're the ones that count."

Peggy intercepted me in the hall. "Got a couple of messages for you,"

she said handing me the pink slips of paper written in her elegant flowing script. The first was from Amanda Carson: *Nate will be home late
tonight. If it's convenient, you can interview him tomorrow morning at nine.
Thanks for your help.* The other message simply read, *"Hayley,"* with a
telephone number. I stared at Hayley's message dumbfounded, then suspicious of the propitious occurrence. I was becoming too wary, especially after today. I went to my desk, studying the faces of Johnny, Dennis,
Stan and Robin, looking for body language indicating that they were
playing a prank on me. Or maybe it was a legitimate call regarding insurance fraud or another embezzlement. Nah... if it was a business call, I
would have heard from Graham.

"Cole," I said nonchalantly. "Someone named Hayley called me.
Peggy said she didn't know who it was. You know a Hayley 'round here?"

Cole was reading a newspaper. He thought for a moment. "Nope, can't
think of anyone. Only Hayley I know is Hayley Mills. She was in those
movies *The Parent Trap* and *Moon-Spinners*. Fell in love with her in *Moon-
Spinners*." He retrieved his cup, spit into it and returned to the paper.

No clues from him.

I found the cross-reference directory and checked the number she'd
left. It was listed to Trulock, McTimmons, and Associates. The possibilities were simply too inviting to ignore. I had to make the call.

"Trulock and McTimmons," the soft feminine voice said. A nervous
jolt passed through me, the hairs on my arms rising. It was her!

"Hayley? Hank Monroe," I said, trying to sound as calm as possible.

"Hey, Hank," she said brightly. I could envision her sitting at the desk
twirling that silky blonde hair as she spoke to me. "I hope it was permis-
sible to call you at the office."

"Certainly. Don't give it a second thought." *Come on, woman! Why did
you call?*

"Well... the reason I called... Graham and his wife are having their
second anniversary this Saturday. My family's having a get-together at
our house for them, and I wanted to invite you as my guest. Daddy's
going to barbeque some ribs and the dress is casual."

"Sure, Hayley, I'd love to come. What time should I be there?"

"It begins at seven."

"Sounds great. See you then."

I returned the telephone tenderly to the cradle. *Thank you, Lord. Thank you.*

That night Megan and I met at Katie's apartment for dinner. Roy, as usual, was late. We grilled chicken, drank white wine, and played Sorry. I watched Megan, her long tapered fingers bouncing the colored game piece around the board, her shimmering mane gently swaying across her shoulders, her bright smile, and quick giggle. I enjoyed her company and, slowly, she was becoming a part of my life. We'd begun using phrases and quips with the hidden meanings that only close friends understood. She was comfortable with her femininity, with the need to socialize and know others, but she was independent, slow to anger, and firm in her resolve. She was a joy to all my senses including my heart. Was I stupid to risk this relationship by seeing Hayley? My head thought no, my heart felt so.

After the game was over and the dishes were cleaned, I walked with Megan to her apartment. We strolled, holding hands, so near to each other that we'd bump our shoulders if we stepped out of stride. The sky was clear and an engorged yellow moon hung over us.

At her door she tilted her face invitingly toward mine. Her kiss was soft and lingering. She sighed softly when we parted lips and smiled sensually.

"I may have had too much wine," she confessed. "Would you like to come in?"

"That's very tempting, but I don't take advantage of inebriated ladies," I said, hugging her and kissing her on the forehead. "See you tomorrow," I said, breaking the embrace, leaving reluctantly.

I fed the bird and took a hot relaxing shower. While I was brushing my teeth the telephone rang. "Please, don't be the office," I said to myself, walking to the phone. "Hello."

"Uh... Hank Monroe?" a feminine voice asked.

"Yes." I didn't recognize the voice.

"Uh... are you the agent on the Lydia Carson case?" the voice asked nervously. From the sound of the voice I guessed she was white, probably between thirty and forty-five years old. Maybe it was Megan, but I didn't think so. This voice wasn't acting.

"Yes. Who are you?" I demanded.

"I'm a friend of Lydia's. I heard you were going to quit looking for her. You shouldn't stop, you mustn't stop," she pleaded.

"How did you get my number? It's unlisted." I was trying to determine the character of this woman. She sounded lucid and intelligent, but her mysteriousness made me uneasy.

"Mr. Monroe. There are no unlisted numbers in Connally."

"So I've heard. Well then, why do you insist I continue my investigation?"

The line was silent. For a moment I thought she'd quietly hung up. "Because, Mr. Monroe, Lydia's dead."

Her statement was said with certainty. Stunned, I slowly sat on the edge of my bed. "Why would you say that?"

"Mr. Monroe... I know you're going to think I'm crazy, but I assure you I'm not. I know she's dead because she told me."

I shook my head, confused. "Because she told you. Lydia told you?" I asked, trying to confirm what I thought I'd heard.

"Yes."

"What... did you have a dream or something?" I said cynically.

"No. I'm... I'm an angel. Actually, I'm her messenger. When it was learned you were going to quit looking for her, Lydia contacted me for help. She wanted me to help you catch whoever killed her."

"Killed her?" I interrupted. "Not only is she dead but she was killed by somebody?"

"That's correct."

I was tempted to hang up on this loony, but I was intrigued. "Well Miz..., what do I call you?"

Pause. "You may call me Celeste."

"Celeste," I said, tasting the name. "Cute. I guess that's short for Celestial? Well... Celeste... why don't you just ask Lydia where she is and who killed her? That could save both of us a lot of time and trouble."

"I don't think she can answer those questions. That's why she needs your help."

"What does the Bible say? 'The Lord helps those who help themselves'."

"That, actually, is not in the Bible. Mr. Monroe, I know you think I'm probably some disturbed, lonely person who has nothing better to do than to call you on a Thursday evening. I'm not. I'm Lydia's angel and I'm asking for your help."

"Celeste, let's assume what you're saying is true. I don't have any evidence. Unless you or Lydia can provide me with some evidence, I've got no justification to continue. Good evening, Celeste."

"No! Please! Don't hang up! You want evidence, I can help you find it."

"And how is that?"

"Tomorrow, go see Judy Moon. She can show you the evidence. I promise."

"You promise?" I said, trying to hold back a little of the mocking tone. "I didn't know angels made promises. And who is this Judy Moon?"

"She's a root doctor."

"A what?"

"A root doctor. She's an advisor and makes up poultices for illness or for special needs," Celeste explained.

"She's a fortune teller."

"Not exactly. People go to her to help them with a variety of problems."

"You wouldn't happen to be Judy Moon needing some business and thinking maybe you can con a new agent?"

"Please, Mr. Monroe. Go out of town on the Old Quarry Road approximately ten miles. When you get to Winslow's bait and tackle store, take your first right onto Nesbitt Road. It's a dirt road maintained by the county. Then take your second left, that's Judy Moon's driveway. If she can't convince you with the evidence, then I'll never call you again."

"How much is she going to charge me?"

"Tell her you work for Cobb. She won't charge you anything."

"Cobb? How does Moon know Cobb?"

"They've crossed paths in the past. But don't talk to Cobb about this."

"Why?"

"Cobb has too much history in this city. It's not to his benefit to solve this case. He just wishes to retire quietly."

"I find that kind of hard to believe."

"Oh? Then why did he assign the case, a potential murder, to an agent just out of the police academy?"

A cold clamminess crawled across my skin as I considered her question and the absurdity of the call. Here was an anonymous caller, an *angel* no less, telling me she was in contact with a murder victim and she wanted me to drive alone out into the boondocks and seek guidance from a voodoo doctor. And to top it all, not tell my supervisor because somehow he might be involved in the cover-up.

"Celeste I'm not sure–."

"I'm telling you, Lydia was murdered," she said with conviction. "Some day, Lydia will be found. It'll probably be years from now. But when she is, you'll know that you could have found her sooner and probably caught her killer. You'll have to live with that for the rest of your life. And there's another reason you should see Judy."

"Which is?"

"Because in your own heart you also know Lydia's dead. Good night, Mr. Monroe."

CHAPTER TEN

I SLEPT late the next day, heading straight from my apartment to the Carsons' house. The morning fog was reluctant to burn away, hanging tenaciously in the hollows. The farmers were already in their fields on their tractors, harvesting early corn. I arrived five minutes early and noticed a red Diamond Rio tractor looming next to the bungalow. Nate was lounging on the front porch reading the newspaper. He lowered his paper as I approached.

"Mr. Carson?" I asked in a cheery tone. "Good morning."

"Morning," he replied in a rough gravelly voice that sounded like a cross between Bear Bryant and Kris Kristofferson. He was in his early fifties, but the smoking and drinking made him seem aged beyond his years. A gray morning stubble sprouted from his tanned, craggy face and his thinning hair, also graying, was slicked back with Vitalis. He was barefoot and wearing a white tank tee shirt and gray scuffed work pants that barely contained his belly.

I stopped at the steps and displayed my badge. "Did Mrs. Carson mention I needed to talk to you about Lydia's disappearance?"

He nodded. "Said some G.B.I. agent might be stopping by this morning. Said you were trying to find Lydia."

"Yes, sir. Like to ask you a few questions. Mind if I sit down?" I said, pointing toward a nearby chair.

"Sure, have at it. But from what Amanda tells me, sounds like you have already found her... or least you know what happened to her." He rose abruptly, grabbing his coffee cup with surprising swiftness. "Need to top off before we start talking. Want some?" he asked, lifting his cup.

"Sure," I said, pulling out my notebook.

He returned moments later handing me a chipped souvenir cup from Rock City. "Drink too much of this crap. It's gonna destroy my prostate," he said as he slurped. "But what the hell. Don't have much use for it anyway." He folded his newspaper and tossed it aside. "Go ahead with your questions."

"Well first, what have you heard about Lydia's disappearance?" I asked, pen at ready.

"Just what Amanda's told me. That she disappeared last week, the police found her car up in Atlanta, and found out she'd flown to some god-forsaken place in Mexico. Then yesterday the police came over, I guess that was you, and found a porno magazine in Lydia's room."

"What do you think happened to her?"

He shrugged. "I dunno. Guess she took off for Mexico. Well, part of me thinks she left, but part of me feels she didn't. Lydia and I were real close when she was little. We did everything a daddy and his lil' girl could do. We fished, we went camping, and I even taught her how to shoot a rifle. But she wasn't a hunter."

"Really?" I asked intently.

"One night... she was, oh, 'bout nine, we took the dog and went rabbit huntin'. Nighttime is the best time to shoot a rabbit. The dog would point the rabbit and you'd freeze it with a light. Then while the rabbit is still, you take the shot. Dang, if she didn't get one on the first shot. But it wasn't a clean kill and the rabbit flopped around a bit before dying. It broke her heart, taking a life. She handed me the rifle and never picked it up again."

"Yes, sir."

"As she got older she started wantin' to do things girls do. I was... hell, still am putting in a lot of hours on the road. I was only seeing her a day or so on weekends and..." he lowered his head in regret, "I guess she was developing other interests. Lydia is a pretty girl, just like her mother. Smart too. Where she got that, I'll be damned. But we began to drift apart. Sometimes we'd talk politics but she'd get mad at me when I'd speak my mind. When Lydia began going through puberty, Amanda got real protective of Lydia, suspicious even. Like Lydia was some bitch in heat and was going to jump in the sack with every boy she met. I knew better. Lydia was smart and disciplined. But Amanda kept her on a short leash.

"Amanda and Lydia are a lot alike. They're both strong willed and independent. Most people don't know that about Lydia, but I think she just got fed up with Amanda and...." Nate bit his lip and looked away. He took a couple of ragged breaths and coughed. "Damn cigarettes." He stood up, leaned on a porch column, staring across the field away from me. "Yeah, my guess is she left. I hope it's not forever. I understand why she did it and I forgive her. I just hope... I'll see her again."

"Mr. Carson, you also said part of you didn't feel as if she left. Why?"

He composed himself, then turned to me. "It doesn't seem the way Lydia would have left us. She would have done it differently instead of runnin' off like that."

"Did you know any of her boyfriends?"

He thought for a moment. "None in the last year. Amanda had a way of either discouraging her or running the boys off."

"Did she seem different in the last couple of months?"

"No," he said with a wave of his hand. "Seemed like the same person to me."

"When was the last time you saw her?"

"The morning I left on this last run. I kissed her goodbye and she told me Godspeed like she always does."

"Did you call her while you were gone or contact her in any way?"

Nate flashed a cynical grin. "I know what you're leading up to, son. Did Daddy molest his little girl and she fled the country to get away from him? I understand you got to ask those questions." He shook his head. "I'd never done nothin' like that. Be glad to take one of those lie detector tests. Ain't afraid of it one damn bit. Hell, if you'd like you can take a look at my driver's log, weight slips and fuel receipts. They'll show I've been everywhere I said."

"No sir, I believe you. But if you think of anything that might help me find Lydia, please give me a call. Amanda's got my number, okay?" We stood and shook hands. "Oh, one more question. How do you get to the Old Quarry Road from here?"

. . .

The Old Quarry Road was a narrow, rough paved county road you couldn't find on a standard issue state map. The landscape along this stretch was overrun with kudzu, and the only human structures were mobile homes and rotted abandoned houses. I'd driven the road for over twelve miles without passing Winslow's. I mentally limited my search for two more miles. If I hadn't passed it then, I'd cancel my search. *Celeste, sorry, you should've given better directions.* Roughly a mile later I came upon a faded yellow cinder block building with two antiquated gas pumps in front. "Winslow's" was painted on the side of the store. "Bait and Tackle, Deer Processing," it read further down the side. A warped plyboard sign hung from a post advertising "Today's Special: B B Q Goat." Hoofed creatures didn't last too long at Winslow's. I turned right a hundred yards later on Nesbitt Road and took the second left onto a narrow rutted dirt driveway. Weeds and briars grew tall along the road and I passed some tires strewn in the bushes. This place looked more like a garbage dump than a homestead. Rounding a curve I drove into a clearing. Under two expansive oaks, a dingy white clapboard house in dire need of painting rested on cinder blocks. Two mongrels slithered from under a wooden front porch to bark at me, scattering chickens in their wake.

Off to the side I noticed a white pickup, gray primer spotting the body, with the hood opened. A young black man bent over the fender heard the barking, then lumbered toward me cautiously. "Can I do you something?"

"I was looking for Judy Moon. Does she live here?" I asked with a disarming smile. "I work for Cobb."

The name evoked a brief smile from the impassive face. "Just a second," he said, walking to the house, shooing the dogs back under the porch. Nearly five minutes later he returned. "She's waiting for you."

I walked up on the sagging porch and peered through the screen door into the dimly lit room. A vague figure sat in a distant chair. "C'mon in, bwa," a tired, wheezing voice instructed. As I opened the screen door, its rusty hinges groaned as if warning me not to enter. The room was smoky, smelling of sweet pipe tobacco, and the little sunshine that managed to enter the living room was scattered by the smoke, giving the area a soft hazy appearance. "Come inside and sit over yere, s' I kin get a look at ya," the figure encouraged, using a stick to point to an opposite wooden chair.

I sat across from Judy Moon. She was a diminutive black woman, shrunken by the years. Her matted gray hair was pulled back tightly into a bun. Her face seemed disproportionately small, her mouth tiny with deep vertical lines intersecting dry lips. A half dozen errant whiskers sprouted from a weathered face so deeply lined it seemed her face might split apart. Her eyes were a dull milky white from cataracts, and one gnarled hand rested on a shillelagh. In her other hand she held a wood-briar pipe perched close to her lips. She wore a wrinkled gingham dress and cotton stockings.

She leaned forward and studied me for a moment, allowing an uncomfortable silence to settle between us. "So you work fer Cobb," she said, finally breaking the silence.

"Yes ma'am. I'm working a case and was told you might be able to help," I said respectfully. "Did you hear about a young lady, Lydia Carson, who recently disappeared?"

"Lyja... Lyja," she said, slowly repeating the name. "Is she da baby of Manda Tate?"

I recalled that Tate was Amanda's maiden name. "Yes ma'am. Amanda's now a Carson, married Nate Carson a while back."

"Oh yeah... yeah. I 'member. Manda wuz a good looking girl. Every'un thought she'd be da next Miss Georgia. But she wuz like so many young'un... thinkin' dat looks and life is gonna last forever." She pointed the stem of her pipe at me. "Now, I be one of da lucky 'uns. I managed to hold on to my looks," she said seriously.

"Yes ma'am."

"Come on, bwa," she cackled. "I's just funnin wif ya. Jus cause you a po-lees, ya don have to be all serry eyed."

She had caught me off guard. Embarrassed, I returned her smile.

She coughed, took several puffs on her pipe and leaned back in her chair. "Tell me all 'bout it," she ordered.

She listened intently as I told her about Lydia's disappearance: the interviews, the car, the withdrawal from Lydia's savings account. I didn't mention Celeste.

She leaned back in her chair digesting the information I'd given her. The only sound was the soft pop as her dry lips sucked on the pipe. "Well... da first thing we need t' do is 'cide whether she's live or dead. Do ya feel she's dead?"

I didn't feel comfortable so I wanted to choose my words carefully. "I think—"

"Son! I dinnin axed ya 'bout thinkin'. I axed ya, what ya feelin'?"

"Ms. Moon, I don't know. That's why I'm here."

She nodded, accepting my answer. "Okay, let's 'dress da idea: is she live or dead? Agent Monroe, Lyja's dead," she said with certainty. "From what ya telling me, Lyja, she be smart and all. Plus, she loves her family and believes in loyalty. If she wuz gonna take off, she'd done alot of thins she just dinnin do. She'd written a note to her momma saying she wuz leavin'. She'd given her close friends a final peck. And she woulda takin' da money wif her when she lef'. She be too smart to go to Mexico and din call for da money. No, she woulda gotten da money first. Which means she dead." She pointed the pipe at me. "You felt she wuz dead. Dinya?"

"Yes ma'am," I confessed.

"Go wif ya feelins," she insisted. "Now, next question.

"Wuz she kilt?"

"Yeah," I nodded following her logic. "The Honda at the airport, the mysterious woman on the airplane, and the money missing from her account after Lydia left. It couldn't be accidental."

Judy smiled. "Now ya gittin' it."

"Finally, why wuz she kilt?"

"I don't know," I answered.

"Well son, did ya go to da po-lees school?"

"Yes ma'am."

"Din ya know why people commit crimes, don' ya?" She reminded me of a college professor, asking questions, never satisfied with the answer, which only leads to other questions.

"I don't remember covering that subject."

She snorted with disdain. "No wonder. People commit crimes for only one reason: dey wan' what ya got!" she said leaning toward me. "Thin' 'bout it. Mos' of it 'volves money. Dey rob a sto' cause it got money. Dey break into yo house cause it got somtin' to steal. You get raped 'cause dey want to take ya dignity. Even a ser'l killer got somtin' he wants—yo life. Lyja's dead cause she had somtin' som'body wanted."

I rubbed my face accepting her judgment. As primitive as she might appear, the logic was as tight as a decision of a Supreme Court Justice.

"Next, let's deal wif why she be kilt. That's why ya came here, right?"

"Yes, ma'am."

"Wuz she kilt for her sex or cause she got grabbed by some ser'l killer? Either one might haf hidden da body but dey wouldn't haf gone to da trouble of makin' up tickets to Mexico. An' dey wuddin haf stollin her money outta her account. Dat means dat dis be planned. Now son, what did Lyja have dat day wanted?"

She was tearing my investigation apart with questions I couldn't answer. "I don't know."

She shook her head in disgust, lifting her stick and poking it at me. "She had knowledge, dammit!"

"Yes, ma'am," I replied, recoiling back from the stick.

"She knew somtin' dat dey dinnin wan' her to know. Have ya looked at dat?"

I shook my head. "No ma'am."

She nodded sympathetically. "You new, bwa. Find out what she knowed, din ya fin' da killa."

"Ms. Moon, do you have any ideas where I might look?"

She looked toward the ceiling. "Lawd, where do dey get dese youn'uns. Ain't got a lick o' sense. Thin' bout it, son. Wha do she haf knowledge of?"

"The bank?"

"Might be a good place t' start. Could be a customer, could be some-one who works wif her, or it could be a boss. Y'might wanna nose 'round dere. Or mabbe ya need to look at h'church."

"Can you tell me anything about her killer?" I pressed.

"Damn son, do ya wan me go find 'em, 'rest 'em, and cuff 'em fo ya, too?"

"No, ma'am," I conceded. I was afraid to ask any more questions.

"By da way, how's dat rascal Cobb? I ain't seed him in a month of Sundays," she asked.

"Oh, he's fine. Going to retire soon."

"You don' mean it. Lawd, I 'member back in da sixties when he jes got on wif G.B.I. He was a young buck. Full of piss and vinegar, he wuz. He'd been on 'bout two years when a couple of bwas came here t' rob me. Dey took my money and thumped me 'round a bit. I was kinda feisty back den and thought I could take 'em. Lawd, dey whooped my ass, den stole my money. Everthin I o'd."

"How much?" I asked, thinking it was a couple of hundred dollars.

"Round thirty thousand."

"Thirty thousand dollars!" I said, shocked at the sum.

"Yep. Knowed better now. 'Sperience can be a cruel teacher. Well, Cobb met me at da hospital and axed me some questions 'bout da rob-bery. I could tell it did'n bother him 'bout da fact dey robbed me, but somtin' rubbed him raw dat dey would beat on a lady." She paused as if to catch her breath. Then I noticed her cloudy eyes, glazed with tears. "You probly were a baby back den, but da black folks were goin' thu some tough times den. A lot of white po-lees did'n wanna help us. Dey considered us trouble and if we got hurt and robbed dat wuz jus too bad. Most of us did'n want any problems. We jus trying to get by and feed our fam'ly. Well, as I said, Cobb came to da hospital, saw what dey did to me, and promised me he would catch 'em." She paused and coughed up some phlegm into a handkerchief. "Two days later he had 'em in jail, and found all da money 'cept fer a hundert dollars dat dey drunk up. I found out later what he did to 'em once dey wuz in jail." She smiled a devilish grin. "But I'll never tell.

"To Mr. Cobb, it did'n matter what color I was. It mattered dat I was a lady and dat dey hurt me. I wuzzin a white lady, I wuzzin a black lady. I wuz a lady who'd been thumped and Cobb wuzzin gonna allow it where he worked." She bit her lip and a single tear escaped, flowing down her lined face. "He treated me wif respect. And I've never forgotten dat."

CHAPTER ELEVEN

THE MCTIMMONS estate was three miles north of town, next to the country club. An expanse of lush pasture bordered by a white wooden fence alerted me to the approaching entrance. A modest mailbox with a quarterhorse painted on the side was posted next to the entrance. Underneath the horse, the name "McTimmons" was stenciled in Old English letters. I turned onto the gravel driveway under the gaze of two of the McTimmons' beautiful horses.

The house was located a quarter of a mile off the highway under a half dozen spreading oaks. I had expected a large plantation house or at least a two-story Georgian with a broad porch and rocking chairs. Instead, Ross's home was a single story wood framed white house, with hunter green shutters and a cedar shingled roof. The porch contained six rocking chairs and a swing and stretched across the entire length of the house. An amalgam of vehicles from pickup trucks to Lexuses were parked haphazardly around the front yard. Approaching the front door I could hear laughter and the boisterous hoot of someone already soused. I rang the door bell and before the dong had died, a handsome, well-dressed lady wearing khaki jodhpurs and a white cotton blouse answered the door.

I took a gamble. "You must be Ms. McTimmons. I see your features in Hayley."

"Well, thank you," she said. "And you must be a friend of Hayley's. I don't believe we've met. Are you from Georgia?" Implying the University of. While her smile expressed friendly welcome, a glint from her eyes betrayed that she was studying me with the same analytical detachment of a breeder inspecting a thoroughbred.

"No, ma'am. Just moved to town. Met her and Mr. McTimmons Wednesday at Twin Creeks. She invited me to the anniversary celebration."

At the mention of her husband's name, the jaundiced regard vanished. "Well, come on inside and let me see if I can find Hayley. I'm Patty."

"I'm Hank Monroe," I said, returning the courtesy.

She led me through the house to the kitchen. The interior of the house was decorated in French country, mahogany beams crossing nine foot ceilings and oriental carpets covering heart of pine floors. The common theme of the many wall hangings was horses. There were scenes of jumpers, fox hunting, and steeplechases, a print of Robert E. Lee astride Traveler, and drawings of Civil War cavalry scenes. We found Hayley talking to a couple in the corner of the kitchen.

"Hayley, one of your guests has arrived," Patty said.

In a tight pair of jeans and a blue and green calico blouse, she was as stunning as I remembered.

"Hello, Hank," she said, greeting me with a bright smile. She gave me a light hug, surprising me with her familiarity, and I inhaled the scent of her hair, her skin, her perfume. She introduced me to the couple. I smiled sincerely, shook their hands, and immediately forgot their names. "Can I get you something to drink?" she offered.

"What are you drinking?"

"White wine," she said, holding up a clear plastic tumbler.

I considered the choice. "Do you have a beer?"

"Good Lord, we're in the South. There's always beer at a party...." She smiled mischievously. "Unless it's a church function."

"A church function?"

"Of course. Have you been to church here yet?"

"No... not really."

"Listen, we go to First Methodist, here in town. The main service is at eleven. If you'd like, why don't you meet me there?"

"Sure," I replied. "Hayley, did you ever know a woman who went to that church named Lydia Carson?"

She thought for a moment. "That was the woman that's disappeared isn't it?"

"Yeah. Thought you might know her or maybe some of her associates in church."

"I knew her only in passing. She was older so we really didn't cross paths much. I believe she attended a midweek bible study at somebody's home and she might have been involved in some community outreach projects."

"She would have been about Graham's age, right?"

"She was probably a year or two older. Why?"

"I don't know. Maybe he might know some of her friends."

"He might. But Reverend Pheim could answer those questions."

"Who?"

"Reverend Pheim. It rhymes with hymn. Nice name for a preacher, don't you think? If she was active in the church, he would know who her friends were. Come on," she said, grabbing my hand. "Let me show you around and introduce you to some of the guests."

She led me out the kitchen door to a rustic brick patio shaded by magnolias and oaks. There were at least three dozen guests spread across the back lawn, an even mixture of ages and personalities. Some appeared to be friends of Ross and Patty while others were buddies of Graham and Hayley. Ross, strapped in a denim apron, was manning a barrel-shaped grill, slathering barbeque sauce on sizzling slabs of ribs, the distinctive smoky aroma dominating the air. Stereo speakers were playing country music. Hayley waved to Ross as we approached.

"Hey, Hank," greeted Ross, wiping his hands on a towel before he shook hands with me. "Hayley said you might come. Glad you did." He turned to three middle-aged men standing in a rough semicircle around the grill. "This is Cliff Jacobs... Ron Newhouse... and Robby Hester. Cliff's a builder, and Ron and Robby are real estate developers. Robby's the carpetbagger," Ross said, chastising one of the men. "He's joined forces with a bunch of Yankees out of Chicago in developing some property on the lake. Ron's working on some property adjacent to the county club. Hank's with the G.B.I. Moved here a couple of weeks ago."

"Daddy, could you get Hank a beer?" asked Hayley.

"Sure," said Ross, reaching into a large cooler brimming with ice and canned drinks. "Don't feel you need an invitation to get another one. Lord knows, these beer piranhas around here will have this ice chest chewed up inside two hours."

Hayley gave me a slight tug on my arm. "Let's get away from these folks. They'll get you into trouble."

"Nice to meet you," I said to the men as Hayley pulled me away.

We walked along the side of the pool where a group of eight folks our age had gathered around a cluster of patio tables and lounge chairs. I spotted Graham sitting next to an attractive willowy brunette.

"Hi everyone," said Hayley, interrupting their conversations. "Want to introduce you to someone new in town –Hank Monroe. Moved here two weeks ago."

I shook hands with those nearest to me and nodded to the others as they introduced themselves. After Jim, Lyle, Ashley, Beth, and Linda, I lost track of the names and relationships. The smiles were pleasant, the greetings seemingly sincere, but I was being scrutinized by each individual as either an ally or a threat, an asset or a liability. My association with Hayley brought a certain air of reverence. But was I worthy of that association, or should I be merely graced with the perfunctory, "Hey, how y'doing?" and a "Y'all come back now, y'hear?"

"Evening, Graham," I said, shaking his hand. I turned to the brunette next to him. "Congratulations. I understand it's your second anniversary."

"Yes, it is. Thank you," she said, extending her hand, staring me straight in the eyes. "I'm Linda. A pleasure to meet you."

"Well, is the honeymoon portion of the marriage over with?" asked Jim, leaning across the patio table with a leer.

"He should be the one to talk," said his wife, Beth. "A week after I'd lowered his testosterone level, he was more interested in Georgia's rankings than me. Feed him every night and bed him twice a week, and there's nothing I can't get from this guy."

The group laughed in derision. "Only twice a week," laughed Lyle.

"Yeah," said Ashley, "It's the other way around with Lyle. Bed him every night and feed him twice a week."

The group roared in again in ribald laughter.

"Well, have you finally gotten to know the real Graham?" another member of the group asked Linda.

"Yeah.... I think after two years you know both the good... and the bad about someone," replied Linda with an embarrassed grin.

"I hope so. But I believe it takes a lot longer," I said with certainty. The group, even Hayley, looked at me in silence, as if I'd broken the frivolity. "I believe it takes years, if not decades, before a couple truly knows each other. Too often, the dark secrets seep up into the relationship long after the marriage has supposedly settled."

"Well... that might be the case where you're from," Graham retorted. "Linda and I have known each other since we were freshman at Georgia. That's nearly ten years. I don't think there's anything to hide."

"Hey, everybody," said a voice behind me. "Sorry I'm late."

"Rick!" someone said. "Don't tell me you were working late at the bank."

Brouder sauntered toward the table with a beer in each hand. "Just finished the back nine. The Brewsters were playing in front of us. Y'all know how slow they are and they won't let a soul play through."

"Well, pull up a chair. We're grilling Graham and Linda," informed Ashley. She put an arm around Linda and asked in a conspiratorial tone, "Now, that y'all've been married for the appropriate number of years, when is the little bambino arriving?"

Linda grimaced and shook her head. "I don't know."

"Oh, sure you do. Tick... tick... tick. Hear that?" teased Ashley. "That's your biological clock. There's not a better time."

"Ashley, why don't you keep your mouth shut?" demanded Graham. "I don't need you stirring things up."

The repetitive brass clang of a triangle sounded. "Chow time!" announced Ross. "Get your plates over here and go through the line."

As we went down the line, Brouder sidled next to me. "Hey, Hank," he said. "You with Hayley?"

I nodded.

"I'm impressed. You're involving yourself in the community very quickly. By the way... how's the Carson disappearance coming along? You gonna close it out?"

"Not yet. I spoke to Nate Carson yesterday and developed some leads. I'd like to talk to some of your other tellers, and I need to interview you, and maybe the bank president."

"Me?" he said with a hint of alarm. "You can if you want, but I don't have anything that can help you."

"Maybe you don't think so, but something that might seem trivial to you might mean something to me. So if you don't mind I'd like to come by, maybe the first of next week."

We ate at long tables under the magnolias. Hayley was the consummate host, drawing me into conversation, asking questions when there was a lull. I feasted on a slab of ribs, corn on the cob, cole slaw, and iced tea. Initially, I tried to maintain some sort of decorum as I handled the succulent ribs. I soon realized it was hopeless but others, including Hayley, were not so self-conscious, as they tore at the meat and then wiped their fingers on paper towels placed in the middle of the each table. Hayley caught me watching her as she licked her fingers and smiled mischievously. The sun was lying low over the horizon, the shadows extending, when we finished the meal to the music of Reba McEntire.

"Graham and Linda have a few gifts to open. Why don't I show you around?" said Hayley, picking up our plates.

"Should I have brought a gift?" I asked.

"No, of course not," she said with a wave of dismissal. "Most people didn't bring anything." She opened a French door leading into the house and took my hand. "Come on." Holding her hand was arousing, and as we walked into the coolness of the house I silently prayed I wasn't obvious.

The house was not as large as I expected. What was lacking in size was compensated for in quality. On the walls were trophies, plaques and other memorabilia. There were footballs autographed by Herschel Walker, Lindsay Scott, Vince Dooley and Wally Butts.

"The house was built around 1890 by my great-great-grandfather shortly after he moved to this area," Hayley explained.

"Was he a farmer?" I asked.

"No, not initially. He was a civil engineer and helped rebuild the railroad system in the South after the war. Working on lines that went to West Point and Columbus from Atlanta, he discovered this area of the country and fell in love with it. He was a young man with a great job in an area that was dirt poor."

"Where was he from originally?"

"Virginia. Graduated from VMI, fought in the Indian Wars out West, then got a job in the South. He was one of those sorts who needed very little money and had saved most of it. So he bought up the land around here, married a local lady by the name of Connally. They built the center of the home and since then it's been added on to as the family grew and needs changed. Let's go to the stables."

The air had cooled considerably providing a refreshing respite to the day's mugginess. Lightning bugs flickered and glided by us as we strolled, holding hands, to the distant stable.

"You're a senior in college?" I asked.

"Not anymore. I graduated a couple of months ago. I'm going to go ahead and get a law degree at Georgia."

"That's right," I said, recalling Ross's introduction at Twin Creeks. "Will you come back here or leave Connally for good?"

She smiled. "I have no idea where it'll lead me. I could go to Atlanta if I wanted to, or possibly come back here."

"Can I ask you another question?" I said, stopping our walk.

She looked at me curiously. "Sure."

"Why me?"

"What?"

"Why me? Hayley, you're a beautiful woman and you could have any man out here with you this evening. Let's just say I'm not used to such good fortune, so I wonder, why me?"

She smiled and pushed a strand of flaxen hair back from her oval face. "I bet you're the oldest child in your family." She turned and continued walking toward the stable.

I nodded following her. "Yeah, I am. But—"

"Read an article about birth order. The oldest child is usually the cautious one, more introspective, and studious. The second child tends to be more social, street wise, and rebellious. Being the second sibling I like to try new things, meet new people. I found you interesting and I wanted to get to know you. You, on the other hand, are wary. This was the second remark that indicated your cynicism. The first was your comment to Linda about getting to know someone. Were you speaking from personal experience?"

"Yeah... maybe I was."

"Have you been married before?" she asked anxiously.

"No... it's just... well, I've been on this case of the woman who disappeared and...."

"That Carson lady?"

"Yeah. And in looking for her, her mother's learned some things about her she didn't know. Unsettling things. Things that destroyed the image of her daughter for her. Even if she's found, the relationship between the two will never be the same."

She nodded with affirmation. "That's why you sounded so skeptic when everyone was discussing Linda's and Graham's relationship."

We stopped at the stable door. I flashed a broad grin, then put my arm around her squeezing lightly. "No more depressing talk, okay? Let's see your horses."

She surprised me with a peck on the cheek. "Good idea."

She flicked a switch, lighting the dim interior of the stable. I heard a couple of animals snorting, surprised by the light. The stable was neat and swept, with stalls for a dozen horses, and had the complex earthy scent of hay, manure, leather, and liniment.

"What kind of horses are these?" I asked, as we passed the stalls.

"Jumpers, mostly."

"You do horse shows?"

"Used to, but I enjoy the steeplechases. That's what these horses are trained for. Here," she said, stopping in front of a proud bay. "This one's my baby." The horse took two heavy steps toward her and she stroked his long nose, talking to him as if he was an infant. "Yeah you mine, aren't chu? I gonna take good care of my baby and you gonna win every race, right?" She turned to me. "Y'know what I named him?"

"Mister Ed."

She gave me a look of disgust. "I should've known better than to ask. His name's Hayley's Comet. Cute, huh?"

"Cute."

We continued down the stalls, stopping before each horse while she told me about the animal, every one with his own character, strengths and foibles.

"Is it true what they say about women and horses?" I asked.

"Which is?" she said, feigning ignorance and placing a hand on her hip.

"Oh... that they enjoy the feeling of having a large muscular animal between their legs, and they savor riding and controlling the beast? They find it, uh, very stimulating."

She pondered the question for a moment. "Of course I can't speak for other women, but personally, if the animal doesn't have an I.Q. above a horse I don't ride him, and thus far... I can't think of any I've ridden."

"Ooooo.... well said."

It was dark now, the sky clear and the stars twinkling like brilliant diamonds. A cool breeze stirred the air as we walked back to the house. Hayley moved closer to me, tilting her head to rest on my shoulder. I turned to her and kissed her lightly on the crown of her head. Her perfume, the texture of her hair, her softness and curves were overwhelming. I found her face, then her lips, marveling in the moment, restraining my passion. I kissed her softly and let the contact linger... then pulled her close to me.

She exhaled a soft breath. "Thanks for coming, Hank. This is why I invited you." We composed ourselves, letting the tension and nervousness ease. "We'd better go back," she suggested.

We returned to the group. If anyone had been aware of our absence, it wasn't mentioned. A half hour later I excused myself and thanked the McTimmons for their hospitality. Hayley walked me to my Jeep and I kissed her goodnight, hoping it would be a memory she would carry to her dreams. It definitely would for me.

As I drove away I felt an exuberant bliss I'd never before experienced, even with Megan. Megan! As I approached town the bliss was dissipated by guilt. I remembered that Megan had gone to Columbus College to work on a research project. She would notice my missing car and probably think I was visiting the Expatriates. But whether she found out or not wasn't the issue. I inhaled deeply, considering my quandary.

I pulled into my parking space. The lights were out at Megan's, so I slunk quickly inside my apartment. I fed the Major and was cleaning his cage when the phone rang.

Please, don't let it be Megan, I silently prayed. "Hello."

"Hank?" said a voice that was familiar, but I couldn't place.

"Yes."

"Evening. This is Celeste," she said, speaking softy with assurance. "I hope I didn't disturb you. I called a number of times today and you weren't in. Been busy?"

"Hey, you're the angel. You're supposed to know what I've been doing."

"Come on, Hank. I'm an angel, I'm not omniscient. Whether you believe it, I am limited in what I can and cannot do."

"Sounds like a frustrating life. I mean, what do you do for fun? Do you and a bunch of your angel friends get together for a basketball game? And how high do you set the basket? I bet there's a lot of dunking."

"Very funny. Ha, ha, ha," she replied, unperturbed. "By the way, what did you think of Judy Moon?"

"I didn't go see her."

"Oh, sure you did. It's not nice to lie to an angel, especially one who's on your side."

"What makes you so sure? Like you said, you're not omniscient."

"No, but I'm not stupid either. I know you went for two reasons. One, it was a lead you had to follow if there was a chance of helping Lydia, and two, she must have convinced you that Lydia's dead and hasn't left the country because you're not talking to me in that skeptical tone of our first conversation."

"Well, you're wrong. I'm not convinced, not really. But she made some good points. Brought up some areas that need to be examined, so I'm going to do a few more interviews."

"Do them everywhere, Hank."

"What do you mean?" I asked.

"Let everyone know you're still working the case. I think the results of your interviews will assure you that she's dead and you need my guidance."

"What do you think the interviews will show?"

"The interviews will probably reveal very little. It's the fact that you are continuing the investigation, still digging, that will be telling. If she's not dead and really in Mexico, nothing'll happen. If something did happen to her, as Lydia has told me, someone, somehow, will let you know you're an annoyance."

"And what does that mean? Someone's going to slash my tires or toss a Molotov cocktail through my window?"

"I don't know, but Hank, be careful."

CHAPTER TWELVE

I FOUND a parking space in the lot across from the First Methodist Church, five minutes before the eleven o'clock service. One block from the courthouse on Main Street, the church was a multifaceted building with weathered bricks accented with an occasional cobalt blue. Stained glass windows lined the outside of the sanctuary, and, unfortunately reflecting the times, each frame was protected from vandals by plexiglass. English ivy clung to the shaded areas of the church and under an expansive oak off to one side, giving the sizable building the cozy appearance of an Anglican chapel. The warm morning had forced many of the men out front to abandon their coats in favor of their short-sleeve white cotton shirts and ties. Hayley was waiting outside the double front door and her face brightened when she spotted me approaching. As usual, she was beautiful, in a black shift with a white diagonal stripe across her chest

"Did you think I'd come?" I asked.

"I hoped so," she said, taking my arm and leading me through the narthex and down a side aisle where Ross, Patty, Graham, and Linda were sitting.

The organist was playing a soothing prelude as we slid into the pew beside Ross and Patty. Watchful eyes immediately began evaluating the visitor sitting with the McTimmons. Smiling, Patty handed me a bulletin, and Ross shook my hand. Graham and Linda, sitting opposite Hayley and me, acknowledged my existence with a perceptible nod. I searched the bulletin looking for names of employees I might interview about Lydia. At the bottom of the front page were the listings: Pastor: The Reverend Shelby M. Pheim; Director of Music: Martha Godwin; Youth Director: Jennifer T. Mentions; Church Secretary: Opal Lockhart; and Custodian: Albert Miner.

I felt Hayley's shapely calf rubbing against my leg. I glanced at her as she nonchalantly thumbed through the hymnal. Hayley, with those full lips and the flawless face. She was teasing me, in church and right beside her parents, and I was trying to contain myself, trying not to show my desires, but hoping that she wouldn't stop.

The choir, wearing light blue robes, filed into pews behind the altar and two men dressed in blue-trimmed black robes reverently strode to chairs on either side of the single pulpit. The organist concluded her music and one of the men, bent with age, walked unsteadily to the lectern.

Hayley leaned to me and cupped her hand over her mouth. "That's Horace Wright. He's the opening act. He's been doing this for forty years and no one has the courage to force him off the position. Other than an Irish greeting and a Georgia cheer, no one knows what he's gonna say."

"Top o' the morning to ya," Horace said in a crusty voice, peering through bottle-thick glasses at notes he held in his trembling hands. He had to be at least eighty years old, barely a strand of hair on his shiny head. Dark eyes encased in swarthy circles were accentuated by his glasses, and gave him the contemptuous appearance of a nineteenth-century college professor who knew you weren't prepared for his class. "We have been blessed by the Lord with another beautiful morning. Getting enough rain for the crops. We had ninety-eight in attendance at the early morning service and one hundred sixty-one in Sunday school. This morning. Mira Newberry and Franklin Jellin are in the hospital. Please remember them in your prayers. As most of you have probably heard, Ken Brunning was killed in a car wreck two days ago. Drove straight into a tree. He was drunk, as usual, and he was a sorry S.O.B., but his wife and kids are good people, members of this church, and they could use our financial support and prayers during this very difficult period. Though you couldn't have drug Ken into church, he'll be toted in here tomorrow morning for a memorial service. I trust God will deal with him mercifully." There were some uncomfortable stirrings at the candid comments.

"See what I mean," murmured Hayley, stifling a chuckle.

Horace continued. "Wednesday night Women's Circle meeting has been canceled. Ms. Coxwell will be out of town to care for her sister, who'll be having surgery at Emory. There'll be a meeting of the Building Committee following this worship service. Those of you on that committee, please stay around for a very brief meeting. Shouldn't take more than ten minutes. Yeah, I know, the Baptists will beat you to Wingate's but we have to have this meeting. So be there. That's an order! Any other announcements?" No one dared speak. "Very well. Go Dawgs." And he returned to his seat.

"Good morning." Reverend Pheim greeted the congregation from the pulpit. "It's nice to see each of you here on this day that the Lord has made." The Reverend Pheim appeared to be in his late forties, slender, with a ruddy complexion and the thinning hair that is common at that age. Though his eyes were soft they were confident, alert, and as he spoke, he looked at the parishioners. He appeared to be truly content and joyous to be standing before the congregation and speaking to them about the message.

Pheim opened the service with a brief prayer, then returned to his seat while the music director led the congregation in "Holy, Holy, Holy, Lord God Almighty." A couple brought up an infant for baptism. Pheim blessed the child, then walked down the aisle to introduce God's newest member to the congregation. Hayley and Patty perked up and the congregation oohed as they watched the gleeful child cradled in his arms. "This is what it's all about, folks," Pheim said as he returned from the aisle.

After the Affirmation of Faith, Pheim held an entertaining children's sermon telling about the grace of God. He led the congregation in an extended prayer; there was an offertory where I tossed in a couple of bucks; and a hymn of presentation.

Pheim reverently approached the pulpit and read from 1 Corinthians

13, the famous love passage of Paul. I listened with indifference, more concerned with stealing a glance at Hayley, than his spoken words. "In the same way, we can see and understand only a little about God now, as if we were peering at his reflection in a poor mirror; but someday we are going to see him in his completeness, face to face. Now all that I know is hazy and blurred, but then I will see everything clearly, just as clearly as God sees into my heart right now."

The Reverend held up the Bible saying, "The word of God for the people of God."

"Thanks be to God," the congregation replied in unison.

"To God," I blurted out, trying to learn the ritual.

With an appropriate pause Pheim surveyed the assembly, then began. "In describing the majesty of the Lord, he has been characterized as omniscient, omnipotent, and omnipresent. All knowing, all powerful, and all present. Pretty powerful adjectives, I'd say. If I wanted to create a deity I would think this would be all I'd need, agreed? If one would examine history's dictators these are exactly their goals: to know everything, to have complete power, and to have their influence present throughout the land. Hitler, for example, through the Gestapo, established an efficient and ruthless intelligence operation, the dreaded SS maintained his power as Chancellor, and Goebbel's propaganda department controlled the country with the Youth Movement, the swastikas, and the media. But in every historical case, whether the dictator was Hitler, Stalin, or Caesar, their influence failed.

"We worship the same God as the Jews and Muslims. And each religion sees God in the same fashion. However, as Christians, we acknowledge one other power in God. And to me, personally, I find it the most majestic of all, dwarfing his infinite power, his infinite knowledge, and his infinite presence. It's his power of limitless and unconditional love. I find it utterly awe inspiring that God can view the humanity in this world and see the avarice, the greed, the selfishness, and perversity in each of us. To see how we waste and abuse the talents, the blessings, and the gifts the Lord has given to us. And in spite of all this, he loves us and was willing to send his son to die for us...."

The sermon was interesting and provocative, but I found myself drawn to the vision of Hayley, glancing at her legs merely inches from mine, studying the profile of her face, the long elegant neck accented with a demure gold chain, and blonde flaxen hair precisely coifed. Was the sin of lust amplified if committed in a house of worship?

"Please turn in your hymnal to page..." interrupted my reverie as the congregation stood and took to song.

After the benediction we filed toward the front door with the others. Ross and Patty greeted those merging into the throng from the surrounding pews. Ross shook hands with a slender gentleman in his forties with a silver shock of hair. His fleshy face appeared swollen and ruddy, indicative of someone who might have had one too many the night before. Ross pointed to me and waved me over.

"Hank, this is Emory Vance," introduced Ross. "He's the District Attorney. Apparently y'all haven't met yet."

"No, sir," I said, shaking Vance's hand. "Nice to meet you, Mr. Vance."

"How long you been in town?" he asked in a smooth southern tone.

"Moved here, oh, about two weeks ago."

"I'm surprised Cobb hasn't brought you by my office," he said. Vance exuded a casual charm, but his eyes were quick and alert, missing little.

"Well... Cobb has had me running since the first day I got here," I apologized.

"I can understand. We've got a lot going on 'round here," he said, not pressing the issue. "If you get a chance, stop by, let me show you the office and introduce you to my assistants and the office staff. Have you met the judge?"

"No, sir."

"Come on by next week and I'll show you around."

"Thank you, sir. I'll do that."

Hayley lead me to the front door and Reverend Pheim.

"Good morning, Hayley." The Reverend greeted her with a sincere smile. He smiled at me and extended his hand. "And did you bring us a visitor?"

"I'd like you to meet Hank Monroe. Just moved to town."

"Welcome. Are you here in town to visit Hayley?"

"No, sir. Just moved here. I'm with the G.B.I."

"Really? That must be interesting. Hope you will visit us again."

"Well sir, I'd like to know if I can meet with you, maybe tomorrow or early this week?" His brow creased with anxious curiosity. "I'm trying to locate Lydia Carson. I'm sure you've heard she's disappeared. Thought you might be of help?"

"Of course. I have meetings tomorrow morning but I'll be in my office tomorrow afternoon at one. Would that be convenient?"

"That would be fine. Thank you, sir."

Hayley and I walked under an oak to escape the noonday heat. I lightly squeezed her hand.

"Thanks for inviting me," I said. There was an awkward silence as she waited for me to continue. "Would you mind if I called you?"

"No, Hank," she replied, flashing an endearing smile. "I'd like that. Listen, we've got a place on the backwater, a boat, dock, and cabin. Maybe when you call we can try to work out a time to go there."

"Sure. Sounds like a great idea. I'll call you... soon," I promised with a point, taking a couple of backward steps then turning to leave.

Before returning to my apartment I stopped by the Piggly Wiggly and purchased an *Atlanta Constitution* and groceries. I'd considered visiting the Expatriates, but decided to invite Megan over for a dinner and spend a quiet afternoon reading the bulky Sunday paper. Maybe there was some guilt in my heart. I hadn't spent time with Megan since Saturday morning. Instead, I'd seen Hayley twice. I hadn't had sex with Megan, committed myself to her, or vowed not to see others, but I had this gnawing feeling in my gut that seeing Hayley was wrong, and worse, it was a betrayal of Megan. Hayley was, simply put, beautiful. Her looks, her voice, her laugh, her smile—were beauty personified. Plus her daddy owned most of Forrest County. But Megan... It was difficult to put into words. She tugged at my heart, she made me laugh, she made me think. She was comfortable. She fit and molded to me. Whether she lay across my lap on the couch or folded into my arms during a dance, she fit.

"Hello," the familiar but weary voice said.

"Hey, Megan. Hank. How's your research paper coming?"

"Hank!" she said, her voice lifting. "Oh, fine. Should have it finished by tonight. It's due tomorrow. Not a moment too soon. Buy the way, how did your case go Saturday morning? Haven't seen much of you lately."

"All right, I guess. I stopped by Roy's place and watched the Braves game with him," I said, laying out my alibi. "Have you ever seen his place?"

"Only from the outside. Kate drove me by once. How is the inside?"

"Let me put it this way: if Martha Stewart is doomed to hell, she'll be forced to live with Roy. I've known cockroaches with more pride and better housekeeping skills."

Megan burst into a laugh that cheered my heart.

"Listen Megan, I know you're busy, but if you want, come over tonight around six and I'll cook up some sausage and peppers. You could probably use a break, and afterwards you can go back and finish your paper, or hang loose with me."

"Thanks, Hank. That sounds good," she said gratefully. "See you at six."

Megan arrived twenty minutes late. She was wearing a navy blue jersey and jeans that gave her a comfortable and relaxed attractiveness. I greeted her with a warm hug and kiss.

"Sorry I'm late. Just finished the paper, completely," she said with an exhausted sigh. "Hank, you called at the right time. Thanks."

"Don't be sorry. I just finished the rice," I said dismissing her apology. "Tell you what. Since you're finished with the paper, let's run out and rent a video for tonight?"

"Good idea."

We rented *The Secret to My Success* and ate a meal of Italian sausage, onions, green and red peppers, smothered in stewed tomatoes and poured over rice. Even Megan was impressed with my culinary prowess. Afterwards I made some popcorn and we retired to the living area, dimming the lights to watch the movie. We played silly games, tossing popcorn in each other's mouths and seeing who could throw the popcorn highest and still catch it in their mouth. I sat on the sofa and she lay on the couch with her head on my chest. I stroked her ebony hair and smooth, soft cheeks, running my fingers along her neck and strong jaw. She relaxed, contented to be in my arms. This was the way Sunday evenings were supposed to be. Halfway through the movie I detected her breathing was deeper. I leaned around to look at her face. She was sleeping.

This weekend I had been graced with the company of two special and unique women. But my thoughts drifted to the coming week, the interviews, the questions, the search for a missing person. This week my thoughts would be occupied by two other unique women, two different visions. I thought of Lydia, her delicate, innocent face in her graduation photograph. And I pondered the image of Celeste, forming a composite from her voice. This week, with luck, I would find them both.

. . .

After clearing up some Monday morning paperwork, I returned to the Railroad and Merchant's Bank. When I entered the bank I saw the way the tellers were murmuring among themselves, and I knew I'd been immediately recognized. Apparently Brouder had alerted them that they might be interviewed.

"Morning, Wanda," I said, greeting the lady who had opened my account. "Is Rick in?"

"I believe so," she said, reaching for the phone. "I believe he was expecting you this morning?"

"Yes ma'am."

"Mr. Brouder?" she spoke into the phone. "This is Wanda. Hank Monroe is here to see you. Yes, sir. All right." She looked at me hanging up. "Do you know where his office is?"

"No ma'am."

"Go down the that wide hall at the back. Mr. Brouder's office is the first door on your left."

"Thank you."

Brouder's office was neat and precise. The walls were lined with framed diplomas, awards, and certificates for achievements varying from collegiate degrees to seminars attended. He stood from behind his desk as I entered the open door.

"Morning, Hank. Have a seat," he said, motioning to a nearby chair. "Could I get you some coffee?"

"Sure. Thanks," I said.

Brouder spoke briefly into his phone, ordering the coffee. "I was surprised to see you at the McTimmons' Saturday. And with Hayley at that. I'm impressed. Are you two dating?"

I shrugged. "It was just a date. Nothing serious."

"Well, a word of advice. Don't let that slip away if you can help it. Hayley's a good girl. I've known her since second grade and she was pretty then. God, she's probably been an evening of fantasy for half the guys in this state."

"Mr. Brouder, here's your coffee," said a young lady, holding a tray with two mugs.

"Thanks, Jane. Just set it right here."

"Thank you, Jane," I said reaching for a cup. I declined the sugar and creamer. "I drink it black. A bad habit I got in the Army." I took a cautious slurp. "Hmm, good."

"You mentioned that you wanted to interview some of the bank personnel including me. Who would you like to see first?"

"I'd like to interview the tellers Lydia worked with, you, and Mr. Norman. Didn't you say she also did some work over at operations?"

"She did, but that was a while ago. At least six months. If you really need to interview them, I guess I could arrange that for you," he said with obvious annoyance.

"Well, let's see what we turn up here."

"Okay. Mr. Norman's available now but he's got a meeting at ten. He should be back by 11:30. Do you want to talk to him now or wait?"

"Why don't I talk to you now and see him later. In between I can speak with the tellers."

"Then let me notify Mr. Norman," he said, touching an extension number on his phone. He spoke briefly and reverently, using more "sirs" than a second lieutenant at the Pentagon. He nodded, cradling the phone. "He'll see you at 11:30." Brouder leaned back in his burgundy executive chair, holding his hands up as if to surrender. "Now Agent Monroe, ask your questions."

I began by obtaining background information on Brouder—his address, date and place of birth, and Social Security number. Gathering these little bits of information is an unobtrusive technique to ease into the more pointed questions.

"So you've grown up in Connally?" I asked.

"Born and bred. It helps when you're running a bank. I know most everyone who comes in here and whether they're trustworthy and reliable or not. When you're loaning people money, personally knowing their background and character is much more accurate than a loan application. Sometimes, though, a customer may not see me as a bank manager, but as a child they knew twenty years ago, and they don't take me seriously. But, all in all, it's an advantage. It's good for me and good for the bank."

"So that's how you know Hayley?"

"Yeah. I'm two years older than Graham. We went to school together, and played sports together. She was like a typical little sister, proud of big brother and wanting to tag along." His eyes stared in the distance, reliving the past. "Even when she was eight, still gawky and willowy, all arms and legs, you could tell she was going to be a looker."

"And when you graduated from high school, where did you go to college?" I asked, not taking notes. I wanted the interview to appear more conversational.

"Went to West Georgia College in Carrollton and got a degree in accounting with an emphasis in finance. Then I came back here and got on with the bank."

"You didn't want to go anywhere else?"

He considered the question for a moment. "No, not really. I wanted to join a bank or a brokerage firm, but I didn't want to get caught up in a monolithic institution, shoved into a cubicle, and forgotten. I mean, I'm not putting down others who want to do that, but I'm happy with my decision."

"When did you become manager?"

"About six months ago. I initially was hired as an assistant operations manager. It wasn't very glamorous, but it gave me a chance to learn the nuts and bolts of the business. Then I was promoted to an officer and then assistant manager. Then we were purchased by Atlantic Seaboard Corporation, a holding company. The manager moved to Atlanta and I was promoted."

"How is it working for Atlantic Seaboard?"

"Oh, it's got its advantages and disadvantages," he said, carefully choosing his words. "We're in a much better position for servicing the customer throughout the Southeast. For instance, say you're low on money in Virginia and need some extra cash. Soon, you'll be able to use an ATM through our member banks. Plus we now have huge reserves to loan money. As a small bank we might get a little nervous loaning large amounts of money, but not now. And people who travel a lot are able to use our services without losing the personal services of a small bank. "

"And the disadvantages?"

"Nothing major. Just some different areas of policy and oversight. Decisions that were traditionally made here now have to be referred to headquarters."

"In what areas?"

"Major physical improvements or purchases, upper personnel hiring or dismissals, operation policies, the assignment of loan limits, training...." His voice trailed silent as he thought of other areas. "Can't think of any others. But we've generally been given a free hand. We've been successful and profitable and I don't think Atlanta wants to tinker with a prosperous formula."

"How long was Lydia with the bank?"

"Hummm... Maybe ten years. I was hired after her. I could pull her personnel file if you wish."

"If you don't mind, I'd like to look through it. There might be something in there that might help." I sipped on my coffee while he called the personnel department.

"The file will be here in a minute," he said after hanging up.

"You're about the same age as Lydia, right?"

He nodded. "Right. We were in high school together."

"What kind of student was she?"

"Bright, but very quiet. She was the type who when the teacher asked a question, she'd know the answer, but was too shy to raise her hand."

"Did she date much?"

"Heck, no. I don't recall ever seeing her with a date or a boyfriend. I don't think she ever went to the prom. She could have been attractive if she'd spiffed herself up, but her hairstyle was drab and she never wore makeup. It was as if she was trying not to be attractive. No, let me take that back," he said, leaning forward as if an idea had occurred to him. "It was as if she was trying not to be noticed."

"And her grades?"

"They were always good. The only times the boys paid her any attention was when they wanted help on their homework or needed tutoring."

"Did she have a teacher she was close to? Maybe someone who took a special interest in her and saw her potential?"

Brouder pursed his lips and inhaled deeply. "Let me think.... There was a Mr. Lymens. Taught Spanish. At the time he was in his mid-twenties, and he looked kind of like Mark Spitz, remember him? A lot of girls had a crush on him and I think Lydia did too. A lot of girls, including Lydia, joined the Spanish club just to be near him."

"Is he still around?"

"Don't think so. He moved away about five years ago. He had an account here and I recall he got a professor's job at some college here in Georgia."

"Do you have a forwarding address for him?"

He shook his head. "I can check and let you know, but customers don't normally leave one. I can give you his last address. Maybe the post office can help."

"When she worked here, what kind of employee was she?"

"Exemplary. I wish all our employees were like Lydia. You know the Boy Scout code? 'A scout is trustworthy, loyal, helpful, friendly, courteous' and etcetera.... She was like that. She had a lot going for her. The only thing that held her back was her education and herself."

"Did she ever have any special relationship with any of the customers?"

Rick suppressed a smile. "A couple. But I don't think they'd be anyone you'd be interested in."

"Why?"

"Well, there's Bucky Staples. Whenever he came in she was always delighted to see him. Of course, he's sixty-seven and walks with a cane. But he's a major flirt. If the woman is younger than he is, he's hitting on her. The guy's a master with the sexual innuendo. I'm still learning from him. And there's Harold Spahn. He's in his late fifties and fighting prostate cancer. Lydia was friendly to any man who wasn't a sexual threat."

"During the last few weeks or months did she seem frightened or concerned about her safety?"

"Nope. I don't recall any change in her attitude or demeanor."

"Mr. Brouder," said a young lady at the door. "You requested a file from personnel?"

"Thank you, Alice," Rick said, accepting the folder. "You want to look at this before you speak with the tellers?"

I scanned the file noting Lydia's performance appraisals. It reflected Brouder's opinion of Lydia: versatile, reliable and efficient. Lydia was in her tenth year with the bank beginning as a teller shortly after the graduated from high school. Her current annual salary was $26,760.

Brouder provided the conference room to interview the tellers, and a fresh cup of coffee. As I arranged my papers there was a firm knock on the door.

"Are you Agent Monroe?" asked a neatly dressed middle-aged black lady.

"Yes ma'am. I am," I replied, extending my hand to her. "I assume you are one of the tellers?"

She nodded. "Nancy Griffin."

"Please have a seat," I said, sliding back a chair for her then sitting in my own. "I guess you know why I'm here?"

"I heard talk. It's about Lydia. I thought she'd left for Mexico."

"Well, it's a possibility, but I'm wanting to make sure. Did you know her?"

"Humph. I don't think anyone really knew Lydia. Now, don't get me wrong. It wasn't that I didn't like her. She just was a distant kind of person."

"Did you work with her?"

"Sometimes. I worked next to her on occasions at the window and sometimes when she was in charge of the vault."

"Did she have any friends, either in the bank, or maybe customers?"

She leaned back in her chair. "Leslie Autry is the only one I can think of in the bank. As for customers..." she paused in thought. "I believe there was a guy. About a year ago, could be longer. His name was Shepherd... Larry Shepherd, I think. Was an electrician, kind of a good looking boy in his twenties. He'd come in and flirt with her. Course he'd flirt with all of us. But he seemed to enjoy messing with Lydia and while she acted embarrassed, I could tell she enjoyed the attention."

"You say he's an electrician?"

"Yeah. Works for Georgia Power."

"Is he still here? Has he closed his account?"

She shrugged. "I honestly couldn't say."

"Have you seen him recently?"

"No. Not lately."

"Were there any others?"

She sat back in her chair rubbing her chin. "No. Can't think of anyone else."

"One more question. Did you notice anything about Lydia that was different during the last few weeks? Was her makeup different, her hairstyle? Her attitude. Did it seem different, like maybe she was happier, more open, more talkative, uh... did she seem more preoccupied with other things?"

Nancy bit her lip in thought. "You know, I did notice a slight change in her attitude just before she left. It wasn't something I'd really have thought about unless you'd mentioned it."

"What was it?"

"Now really, I'm not trying to make more of it than it is. But she did seem a lot livelier, more animated. And I did notice a little more makeup, not much mind you, but a tad more than normal. Her lipstick was a little brighter, and I think I remember seeing a little rouge."

"Anything else?"

"No... I can't think of anything else right now. But you've got me thinking."

"If you think of anything else, please give me a call."

During the next hour I interviewed three other tellers who replicated Nancy Griffin's information. They all agreed that Lydia was bright and the description of her personality ranged from cold to aloof to shy. Her only friend at the bank was Leslie Autry, a kind lady, who befriended her. All noticed subtle differences in her attitude before she disappeared. She didn't seem so intense, she laughed easier, and her features took on a softer texture. Were there any customers she seemed to be close to? No.

Brouder queried the account of Larry Shepherd. It was active with a balance of $232.15, with the most recent transaction, a a twenty dollar ATM withdrawal two days ago.

I had a little time to kill before interviewing Mr. Norman so I ate a lonely meatloaf lunch at Wingate's, and promptly returned to the bank at 11:30.

The bank's administrative offices were located on the second floor. The nondescript stairs opened into a tastefully decorated secretarial area with thick aquamarine carpet. The walls were expensively decorated with glossy chair rails dividing the painted part of the wall from the fabric-covered part. Prints of quail, wild turkey, and pheasants decorated the walls. Cherrywood desks for three secretaries occupied the space. Brass and marble lamps and accessories completed the professional appearance.

When I arrived, Alan Perkins was giving a secretary some documents with instructions. He spotted me out of the corner of his eye when I came through the door.

"Agent Monroe, isn't it?" he said, with a toothy smile that didn't match his cold eyes.

I nodded. "I'm here to see Mr. Norman," I announced, half to him and half to the secretary.

"Excuse me. Connie Morgan, this is Agent Monroe with the G.B.I. He's investigating the disappearance of Lydia Carson."

The secretary, a middle-aged lady impeccably tailored and wearing half moon spectacles, smiled and extended her hand. "Nice to meet you," she said with the cultured Southern accent that always ends with the high-pitched accent on the next to last syllable. "How are you doing?" Peering at her calendar she continued. "You have an eleven-thirty appointment."

"Yes ma'am."

"I'll tell him you're here."

"I'd heard Lydia's mysterious disappearance had been solved. That she'd found some greaser down in Mexico. Why do you need to talk with Reed?" Perkins asked.

"Well... that's a possibility, but I'm not convinced. She still might be around here," I replied, watching his eyes, hoping for a reaction. "And until I'm satisfied... I'm going to keep searching and I'm going to keep asking questions."

"Huh!" he exclaimed, spurting a puff of air. "I think everyone around these parts knows she left to escape her mother. That's no big secret and I can't really blame her. I just find it kind of silly that the State of Georgia's going to spend my tax money on a wild goose chase. I think there'd be other crimes to investigate."

"I bet if she was your child you wouldn't feel that way."

He grinned. "Doubt it."

I suppressed a knot of anger rising from my gut and reached into my pocket, retrieving a dime. "I'll tell you what Alan... considering what you pay in state taxes and the amount of your money that filters down to my meager salary...." I flipped him the dime. "Here, I've returned your money. Now, you won't be wasting your taxes on my wild goose chase."

He reeled back. Apparently such a bold retort made by a young man to a pillar of the community caught him off guard. Connie returned at that moment. "Mr. Monroe, he's expecting you."

Reed Norman's office was expansive, clearly reflecting his position in the bank. It was decorated in a vein similar to the secretarial area. As the secretary led me into the office, I noticed a private bathroom to my right and a sitting area complete with a sofa, wing back chairs and a Chinese oriental rug to my left. Norman was talking on his telephone and refer-ring to his computer located on a credenza behind his antique desk. An oak wall unit displayed golf trophies and plaques of appreciation from the United Way and the March of Dimes.

He waved me to a nearby chair and covering the mouthpiece of the phone, whispered, "I'll be off in a second." Norman appeared to be in his late forties, rail tall, and physically fit with the healthy tan of someone involved in outdoor sports. He had a full head of hair with a touch of gray at his temples, and steel gray eyes. A tailored gray suit and the hint of Aramis cologne completed his polished appearance.

When he finished he stood up offering his hand. "Good morning, Mr. Monroe. I was on the line with Atlanta. A persnickety bunch, never satis-fied. Now what can I do for you?" he asked, settling in his executive chair.

"Lydia Carson," I said ponderously.

"Knox told me the matter had been concluded. Y'all had found that she had cleared out her checking account and had it transferred to Mexico."

"It's possible. But I'm not convinced. There's a chance that she was set up."

"Set up?" he questioned. "Mr. Monroe, it appears you've been watching too much T.V. I don't believe that some deep dark conspiracy exists in Connally. This is not Washington."

"And you're probably right. But...." I shrugged. "I just have to be sure. I'm sure you understand."

"Certainly," he said begrudgingly, leaning back in his chair and pushing away from his desk. "Go ahead with your questions."

I opened my notepad. "Mr. Norman, did you personally know Lydia Carson?"

He smiled. "Of course. This is a small bank. I know all my employees and strive to know every customer. I've learned that, especially in today's financial climate, it's a tremendous advantage to provide personal service."

"I noticed in her file that you hired her."

"Sure did. I knew her mother, Amanda. We were in the same high school class together and she worked at the bank for a short time. Amanda called and asked me if I'd give Lydia a chance at the bank. As a favor, I said sure. Glad I did. Lydia was one of the most reliable and versatile employees we've had. Sorry she left, but I can understand why."

"You can understand why? What do you mean?"

"Mr. Monroe, you can conduct whatever investigation you wish. I mean, I'm certainly not going to tell you how to do your job. But I think it's obvious to most everyone in town who knows what's going on, that she found a lover and left to escape Amanda."

"You said she found a lover. What makes you think that?"

"From talking to the tellers. That's what they seem to think. I invite you to talk to them."

"I already have," I replied. "Mr. Norman, you said she was versatile. In what ways?"

"Good Lord, in most every way. She worked as a teller, head teller, worked in the vault, worked in operations in the check clearing section, dabbled in the loan department, and even worked as Alan

Perkins' secretary. Frankly, she could have been a bank officer if she'd wanted."

"Why didn't she?"

He laced his fingers behind his head. "I don't really know. She was discreetly approached about it, but she shyly declined."

"Did she ever work for you?"

"Never did."

"So you can't speak directly to her abilities?"

"On a day-to-day basis, no. On occasions, when she was working for Alan, I might ask her to do some typing for me. She never complained and did her job thoroughly and accurately."

"How would you describe her character?"

"I already have: shy." I waited without comment for him to continue. "I could go on, but my characterizations would only be variations of the same word. Shy, reserved.... I believe she had the potential to be attractive, but she chose not to be. She didn't take compliments too well."

"What do you mean?"

"Well... I remember one day I had to get a letter out in a hurry to an attorney regarding a loan default. I had her come in and I quickly dictated the letter. Within ten minutes she had the letter on my desk in immaculate condition, improving on my diction and phraseology. I thanked her and told her that the bank was fortunate to have her working for us. She turned beet red and said it was luck. Imagine that, luck! There's no luck involved in good work. But I've heard other similar stories when she was complimented and deferred to another, or to good fortune. It was as if it was a sin to accept recognition for a job well done."

"Did you know of her being close to anyone at the bank or any customer?"

"You mean 'close' as in a girlfriend?" he asked.

I nodded.

"Let me think...." He slowly shook his head. "I can't think of anybody offhand. The people on the first floor would know better than me."

"You said Amanda worked here at one time. Did you hire her also?"

"No. She was hired when I was in college. Worked here a couple of years, then left."

"Why'd she leave?"

"Officially, to take an office manager's job at Lucas Diesel. Unofficially... she just wasn't able to handle the paper flow of a teller. She never was in balance and I think she got frustrated with the job."

"You said you knew Amanda in high school. What kind of person was she?"

"A knockout, to put it bluntly. She was good looking, she knew it, and she used it to her advantage."

"In what way?"

"If there was something she wanted, she wasn't above flirting, or maybe more, to get what she wanted. And that included a guy, a class position, or even a grade."

"Did that include you?" I asked, hoping I wasn't being offensive.

He smiled, thinking back. "Yeah, I must admit I went out with her a couple of times. There was only one problem. There was no cake under the frosting. There was no substance to her, only looks. In a way, it seemed she was the antithesis of Lydia. Maybe she raised Lydia compensating for her own shortcomings."

"Mr. Norman, you mentioned that Lydia didn't have any friends. Did she have any enemies?"

His brow creased. "What do you mean? Were there people jealous of her and her abilities?" he asked, seeking an explanation.

"Was there anyone who would want to hurt her?"

He seemed startled by the question. "No! Of course not. Lydia was a hard worker. I can't imagine anyone so jealous of her to want to harm her."

"Is there a possibility that she might have learned something about a customer, or... maybe within the bank where..." I stumbled, searching for the proper word. "....where someone might want to hurt her?"

He shook his head firmly. "Mr. Monroe, I'm afraid you're tracking the wrong possum."

"No sir," I replied frankly. "I think I'm tracking someone more like a fox. Someone who is good at confusing his scent."

CHAPTER THIRTEEN

I WANDERED into the church precisely at one and found the church offices. I caught the secretary, Opal Lockhart, leaving for lunch. From the appearance of her office and mannerisms she struck me as fastidious. She was a slender, middle-aged lady who wore half-lens reading glasses hanging from a gold chain around her neck.

"I have an appointment to see the Reverend," I said. "I'm Hank Monroe."

"Just a moment," she said, referring to her appointment calendar, watching me with cautious, questioning eyes. This lady obviously saw herself as the guardian of the gate, a constant between a continuum of Methodist ministers who entered and left the Connally church. While they might bring fresh ideas and visions for the growth of the church, she knew they would ultimately leave. She would remain, protecting her turf, protecting her church. "Oh yes, I see it. Please come with me." She escorted me to Pheim's office.

"Come on in. Hank, isn't it?" he said with a serene smile. He was dressed casually in beige cotton slacks and a navy blue knit shirt. His office contained the expected religious accoutrements. His seminary diploma and a twelve-inch wooden cross hung on the wall behind his desk. A large bookcase to his left contained various religious texts and references, with authors ranging from Norman Vincent Peale, Billy Graham, Robert Schuller, Josephus, and C.S. Lewis to the Torah, The Wesleyan Bible Series and various versions of the Bible. I found the office more disheveled than I expected, with stacks of papers and manuals on his desk and side tables. The office was cool and I was thankful, for a change, to be wearing a coat.

"Yes sir."

He glanced at a brass wall clock. "And right on time, I see. Punctuality is a lost virtue, I'm afraid." I smiled in agreement. "I understand that you wanted to talk to me about Lydia?"

"Yes sir. No doubt you are aware of her disappearance."

"Of course. It's been the talk in the church. But I thought she'd left town."

"Those are the rumors. And if she's left I need to know why. That's why I'm here. She was active in the church, I understand?"

"There's a saying, that in any church roughly five percent of the members do ninety-five percent of the work. Lydia was in the five percent. She was in the choir, in a Bible study class, active in Sunday school, and also helped in various outreach programs. She visited nursing homes and hospitals and delivered meals to members that had a death in the family or some type of tragedy."

"Did she have any friends?" I asked.

Pheim inhaled and rubbed his chin thoughtfully. "Lydia was friendly but she had few friends. It was as if there was this barrier of intimacy that couldn't be breached. The only friend I can recall is Jenny Tisdale. They were in Sunday school and a Bible study together. You ought to speak with her."

"I have. Were there any male friends?"

"No, Hank. I never saw her with any, and she never mentioned it. I believe that Jesus was her male friend. Not in a sexual way. The church and her relationship with Christ was a way for her to cope with her loneliness. In a way it's sad, but I was glad we were here for her."

"How was your relationship with her?"

"What do you mean?" he asked with a hit of defensiveness.

"Did y'all talk on more than just a superficial level? Did she confide in you?"

"Superficial? I wouldn't call it that. Because she was active in the church, many of our meetings and discussions concerned the various projects she was involved in. She might seek my counsel on the best way to approach a problem or what member might be able to assist her."

"Apparently you think she fled the area with a boyfriend."

He shrugged. "It seems that way. Why? Is there something you know that might indicate otherwise?"

I considered telling him about Celeste, but I wasn't sure how he'd react. "Reverend, I ask that what I'm about to say be kept confidential. I think she's dead."

His eyes widened in astonishment. "Dead! My Lord!"

"Is there a reason anyone would want Lydia dead?"

"No! Lydia was a beautiful person, a loving person. No one would want to kill her, no one would want to hurt her."

"Could she have learned some... dark secret about someone who attends this church that would've caused them to hurt her?"

"None at all. Can you tell me why you believe this?"

"Not right now. I hope I can someday."

"Hank, I can't think of any reason why someone would want to hurt her."

"Well, that's what I'm looking for. There's a reason out there and as soon as I find that reason, I'll find her killer."

. . .

It was early Monday evening when Billy Nash ordered his two Brittany Spaniels into the back of his Ford F-150 pickup and drove to a bird field he leased. He loved this time of day when Mother Earth provided respite from the oppressive heat and humidity of the day. The sun, looking like a large ripe orange, was slowly sinking in the west, painting the clouds with varying pastels of purple, aqua and turquoise. And as if she was sighing from the day, a light breeze rustled the tall grass, bathing the field with the scent of pine. His dog Sheba was seven years old and he loved her as much as he had ever loved a woman. The younger male was named Mohawk, due to a two-inch streak of dark brown fur running between his ears. Billy loved to hunt. It was in his blood, answering a primal urge. He could identify with his hunting dogs, who had the same passion for the hunt as he. Sheba would work a field until she dropped from exhaustion. And when Billy called, she was ready to hunt. No matter what day, no matter what time. With a quick whistle, Sheba was in the bed of his pickup ready to pursue God's purpose for her.

Billy truly believed that God had bequeathed dogs to be man's life mate. A dog didn't growl if you came home drunk. A dog didn't care if you had others dogs. A dog didn't care if you had other dogs in the past. When you bought a dog, you didn't get her mother and father. A dog could be trained. You could talk to a dog knowing you wouldn't be judged, criticized, or scolded, and your dark secrets would forever remain with a dog. A dog showed more affection. A dog was unconditional love. Two failed marriages had taught him that.

But Sheba, God bless her, was getting old, and she was missing the little things. Not as sharp on the point and her endurance wasn't as it used to be. Billy realized it was time to pass the mantle and a buddy sold him another Brittany, with a solid pedigree, at a good price. Mohawk was ready to search the fields, but needed Sheba as his mentor.

Billy dropped the tailgate on his truck and sent them off. Sheba, with Mohawk following, immediately lowered her nose, covering the area in a loping trot. She was meticulous as she worked the area slicing through the tall dry grass. Mohawk knew his place in the pack and obediently followed his mentor. Billy reached into the bed of the pickup, opened a small cooler, and grabbed a beer. Sitting on the tailgate, he watched the dogs run the field, occasionally disappearing in the taller grass. A half hour and three beers later he whistled them in. Sheba returned, her long tongue lolling across her white incisors.

"Where's Mohawk?" Billy asked, as if he was truly expecting an answer from her.

She sat, panting in front him, awaiting his release.

Bill whistled again. Longer and louder. No answer.

"Damn dog," he spat, flinging his empty can into the bed of the truck and stomping down the middle of the field. "Come on, girl. Let's find him."

He walked at least a hundred yards when, off to his right, he noticed movement, a small tail twitching like a metronome at the edge of the field.

He quietly approached Mohawk wondering what he'd found. Ten yards away he could see the pup digging in the soft sandy soil.

"Mohawk!" he yelled. "Get over here!

The startled dog lowered his head in submission and slunk toward his master, dropping a small meaty bone.

"God! You stink!" Billy reeled back, smelling the fetid dog. "What kind of carcass you find?"

He glanced at the depression, his eyes widening suddenly. "Oh Jesus, Mohawk." he murmured softly.

Protruding from the khaki sand, as if it was a plant to be plucked from the earth, was the remainder of a rotting right hand.

. . .

"Good evening, Major," I greeted my bird, setting my gym bag down on the sofa.

"Aten-chut!" the bird responded.

"Bought myself a gift," I said, laying a bag on the coffee table. "With a little luck I'll be able to catch myself an angel."

After the interview with Pheim, I'd gone to the Bell South office, signed up for caller I.D., and purchased a caller I.D. display. I was shown how to install the device and how it functioned. Was it a hundred percent accurate? Unfortunately no, I was told. If a number is unlisted, the machine will display "Private Name." Other times the telephone computer doesn't pick up the number, such as a long distance number in another state or a mobile telephone. On those instances, it will display "Unknown Number." Then there is the occasional electronic glitch, that will read "Data Error." But in the case of local numbers the machine is reliable, displaying the name of the subscriber and his—or her—telephone number.

Installation was a simple process, running the telephone line directly from the wall to the machine, then plugging a similar line into the telephone from the machine. Voila! I decided to run a test.

"State Patrol. Burke," the operator answered.

"Dan, Hank Monroe. How you doing?" I said.

"Hey Hank. It's nice and quiet," he said, his voice changing from official to amiable.

"Can you do me a favor? Just bought one of those Caller I.D. machines. Would you call me back so I can see if it's working okay?"

"Sure. Do it right now," he said hanging up.

Five seconds later the telephone rang. The display read, "State of Georgia," with the Patrol's phone number.

I answered the phone. "Hey, Dan. It works fine. Thanks." *Now call me, Celeste.*

And she did, shortly after nine. The phone rang twice while I anxiously watched the small display window. It flashed, "Unknown name." I silently cursed. "Hello."

"Hank," said the demure voice. "It's Celeste."

"Good evening. How thing's going up in the heavens?"

"Come on, Hank. Don't be so crude. Thought I'd call to see how the case is going. Learn anything from the interviews?"

"No, not really... except maybe, I'm beginning to look like a fanatic, looking for a dead woman who's really in Mexico."

"Don't let that concern you. Too often a fanatic is a person that doesn't move with the herd. St. Paul was considered a fanatic and look what he accomplished."

"Were you there back then or did you just recently become an angel?" Since I'd wasted money with a clever attempt to identify her with a machine, I was now forced to use the old fashioned method: a subtle interview.

"What do you mean, 'recently become an angel'?" she chided.

"Well, I thought you died, then became an angel. What did you look like back before you died?"

"Everyone thinks that angels are former humans that go through some type of initiation, then 'win their wings' and spend their time lying on clouds. Hank, we are spirits who assist God in his mission."

"So you don't have any physical form?"

"I take whatever form is necessary."

"Interesting. What kind of physical form are you taking now?"

"I'm a guiding voice. Do you need to know more?"

"It'd be nice. People like to put a face with a voice."

"Sorry, I can't help you."

"Well, if you were going to take a physical form, what kind of person would you put with the voice? You sound like a lovely white female in her, say, early forties? How am I doing?"

She laughed. "Nice try, Hank. Visualize me any way you wish. Make me as young or as old as you like, blonde or brunette, short or tall. I'm here to help you find Lydia, not help you find me. You need to stay focused on her."

"You were never a human? Never a young milkmaid in southern France or a Polynesian princess? You've never experienced the joy of childbirth or had a lover, smelled a rose, swam in the ocean, or ridden a roller coaster?"

"No Hank, never have," she said with a tinge of regret in her voice. "And in a way, we angels envy that aspect of your life and are jealous that y'all don't revel in the blessings that God has provided you."

"Celeste, if you were planning on meeting me, face to face, what type of form would you take?"

"I don't know. I'll consider it if we ever do meet."

"Well, I think we should meet. How about tomorrow?"

"Sorry, Hank, I can't do that."

"Why not?" I insisted. "If you truly care about finding Lydia, you'll meet with me. Then I'll know you're an angel and we can work together to find her. Right now I can't completely trust you. This entire situation is just... too bizarre."

"Hank, I really do wish I could meet with you, but I can't. It's not possible right now. If you don't trust me now, I hope you will over time. Just because I'm not something you understand, it doesn't mean I'm not real. Look elsewhere for your enemies.

"I'll call again in a couple of days. You take care."

I stared at the dead phone for a moment, then disgustedly replaced the receiver. I sat on the edge of the bed considering my options in locating Celeste. I could go to the phone company and get a trap and trace on the line. But that would require a court order and a court order would require me to give Emory Vance a reason for the trace. Obviously I couldn't say I was trying to find an angel, but I could say someone was calling me, passing on clues to the whereabouts of Lydia. Celeste referred to St. Paul, indicating that she was a well-read Christian. Maybe she was affiliated with the Methodist church, maybe a friend of Lydia, and she knew what had happened to her, knew where she was. Maybe she was involved in her disappearance and this was her way of working through her guilt. I had to talk to Cobb and get the trap and trace. Celeste was the key to finding Lydia.

The phone rang again, the display reading, "Private Name." Damn! My first two legitimate calls and I've learned nothing from the cursed machine.

"Hello," I said, hoping it was Celeste.

"Hank," said the gravel voice. "It's Cobb."

"Yes sir."

"A body's been found over in Adams County."

"Is it Lydia?" I asked anxiously.

"Don't know yet. I've got Cole en route and I'm sending you to help, just in case it's the girl. The body's buried, partially dug up by a dog. I don't have all the details yet. If the body's been buried, it ain't no accident. So I'm sending Stan Echols who's a crime scene technician. He'll handle the scene. Any questions?"

"No, sir."

"Got a pencil? I'll give you directions."

· · ·

Twenty minutes later I was driving down a dark county road searching for the landmarks that would lead me to the crime scene. I drove through a blizzard of bugs that turned into a staccato of pops and smeared my windshield with blobs of black and yellow. In my rear view mirror I noticed the flickering of blue lights. It had to be an officer rushing to the scene. I slowed, and when the car passed me, I saw the word "Sheriff" emblazoned on its side. I kept pace with it, traveling nearly ninety miles per hour until it turned onto a farm road. I saw other lights up ahead. This had to be the place. I drove slowly through the unfamiliar trail until I was stopped by a uniformed deputy blocking the trail. I rolled down my window.

"Sorry, sir," the burly deputy said as he approached my car. "This place is sealed."

"I'm looking for Cole. Is he here?" I asked, presenting my badge.

He examined my credentials with his flashlight. "Yeah. Been here about ten minutes. The Sheriff and him are parked over there," he said, pointing with his light.

I parked beside Cole's car and retrieved from the trunk of my car a nylon windbreaker with "GBI" stenciled on the back. Slipping it on, I grimaced at the annoying insects and the thick humid air.

A deputy walked by. "Excuse me," I hollered. "I'm looking for Johnny Cole."

"They're down yonder with the body," he said, pointing down the field.

I walked through the field toward flashlights, briars and burrs snagging and tugging at my pants. Cole was kneeling beside a slight depression, with three other men. They appeared to be examining a limb protruding from the ground. Walking closer I recognized the remnants of a darkened gnarled fist, closed as if in defiance. The group heard me approaching and stood up.

"What we got?" I asked Cole.

"All I can tell you is that it's a body. That's all."

"Think it might be Lydia?"

He shrugged. "Don't know. Let me introduce you to the Sheriff." He turned to the other men. "Sheriff, this is one of our agents, Hank Monroe. Hank, Sheriff Tyler Webb, his Chief Deputy, Ward Dickson, and the Coroner, Micky Dowell.

We exchanged greetings, then Cole continued. "We've got a problem here, but won't make a decision 'til Echols gets here. Exhuming can be tricky business. One has to be slow and methodical because body parts can come apart and evidence belonging to the perpetrator could be with or near the body. Usually this is the type of job done in daylight, not at night. It's obvious that whoever did this is long gone, so there's no rush in gathering the evidence. Unless Stan differs, we need to wait 'til morning to dig up the body and check out the immediate area."

"Do the Sheriff and Coroner agree?"

He nodded. "This also means that someone has to maintain a vigil on the grave. The Sheriff will leave one of his men. Would you mind standing guard with him? I know it's a shitty job, but I need to do some interviews and Stan needs to rest so he can do the exhuming."

I reluctantly agreed. I'd done enough sentry duty in my time, but Cole was right. The body next to us belonged to Cole unless there was evidence it was Lydia. And Cole would also be up all night interviewing the owner of the property, neighbors and whoever had access to the field.

Stan arrived and met with us, agreeing that a more thorough job could be done in the daylight. "After all," he said, "the victim ain't going nowhere and whoever did this is long gone. So there's no rush. Let's do it right.

"When I get back to the house, I'll call Atlanta and get Dale Ludwig, another crime scene tech, to help. I'll have him here at six-thirty. And I'll advise Atlanta to have Dr. Bohnoff on standby."

So I spent a night suffering with the beefy Deputy J.T. Price who smoked Swisher Sweet cigars and regaled me on every subject ranging from how the Atlanta Falcons could win the Super Bowl to the trilateral conspiracy of acid rain. And as I sat beside J.T. watching the grave, breathing secondhand smoke and listening to his pontifications, I recalled an instructor in the academy addressing the new agents class, stating that for every G.B.I. agent hired, one hundred were rejected. Wasn't I the lucky one?

. . .

"Hello."

"Hey. Monroe, or as you called him, the little puppy, isn't chasing his tail like he's supposed to. He was at the bank and the church today interviewing everyone who had anything to do with the girl. Apparently he's not convinced she left town for Mexico and he's going to keep digging 'til he's satisfied."

"Are you sure?" he said, his voice laced with concern.

"Damn right I'm sure! This little ruse isn't turning out like you expected."

"A couple of days ago he believed she'd left. What made him change his mind?"

"Cobb?"

"I doubt it. The word is that Cobb thought this was a simple disappearance and instead of tying up an experienced agent, he assigned it to Monroe to appease Knox and the bank. He was overheard at Wingate's saying he'd assigned the case to Monroe so he'd learn his paperwork."

"Well, someone's talking to him and we need to know who."

"Don't worry. I'll handle it. Just don't make more of this than it is."

"What do you mean? You got me into this."

"Got you into this? Bullshit! You got yourself into this and because of your stupidity you only made it worse. Made it worse for everyone and I'm trying to pull your sorry ass out of the fire. Don't you ever blame this on me."

"Well," he said, more meekly, "do you have any suggestions to resolve this dilemma?"

"Yeah... I believe so." The line was silent while the caller considered his options. "Let me make a few calls. Collect on a favor or two."

"Well, do it quick... before he turns up something."

CHAPTER FOURTEEN

THE EARLY morning darkness surrendered itself to the new day's sun and the robins, larks, and cardinals greeted the morning in song. The sun rose, quickly warming the earth and painting the sky. I stepped out of the patrol car into the dewy grass and stretched my legs. I felt stiff, greasy, and smelled of cigars. J.T. was grumpy, having exhausted his supply of stogies.

They began arriving at six-thirty in a straggled line. Echols was followed by Ludwig in a white van, then the Sheriff. Cole pulled in a minute later with a brown sack of coffee and sweet rolls.

"Thanks, man," I said gratefully, accepting his gifts. I carefully removed the top of the cup and slurped cautiously. "You didn't happen to bring a change of underwear?"

"Hey, don't push your luck," he warned. "I've only had three hours sleep. Just enough to make me ornery."

"Well, did you learn anything last night?"

He shook his head. "Not much. Spoke to the fellow that owns this land. Sheriff knows him and says he's as straight as they come. I don't think he had anything to do with it, but just the same, I was thorough. He leases the land to a hunting club. I got the names of the members.

But anyone who knew the road could have driven onto the property. He's the nearest person to this area and he lives two miles away."

"What's he doing with the land?"

"Growing pines and taking a tax write-off."

Echols and Ludwig had slipped on navy blue coveralls. Ludwig was setting up a three-foot-square strainer next to the grave and Echols was photographing the area.

Echols walked over to us. "When y'all finish your coffee you need to do a crime scene search of the area. Walk the edge of the road and the area around the gravesite. Other than that, Dale and I will handle everything else. Is the Coroner coming?"

"Should be here 'round seven," Cole replied, then turned to me. "Ready to take a morning stroll around the area?"

"Yeah, why not?"

We walked the farm road, Cole taking the right side of the trail and me taking the left. We found the usual litter, beer cans, plastic bottles, snack wrappers, and a single boot. We walked the county road finding the same kinds of discards, as well as the carcass of an armadillo. Returning to the gravesite we walked the area in the thicket of pines and the field of briars and burrs. An hour later we joined the Sheriff and the Coroner who were watching the two agents slowly excavating the body. As Ludwig lay on his belly next to the grave, he meticulously brushed away the soil from the body. Echols gathered the dirt and filtered it through the strainer. They had uncovered the front of the body. It was nude and lay on its back. Insects and maggots had infested the corpse, but not so much as to completely distort the features. It was a female.

"I'm going to let the M.E. make the call on this one," Ludwig announced, sitting back on his haunches. "All I can tell you is it's a female, probably white, but that's it. Bohnoff's going to have to give you an age and other particulars. With a little work we'll be able to tell you how long the body's been here."

I looked down at the rotting face, flesh and cartilage missing from the nose, front teeth exposed in a hideous grin, and knew it wasn't Lydia. Cole elbowed me. "Look," he said, pointing past the grave. "What do you see?"

I looked where he was pointing and saw nothing, only sand and footprints where we had walked during our search. I frowned at his question, not sure I understood him. "What?"

"Dammit, Hank," he said, the pitch of his voice rising in a mixture of excitement and dread. "Look at the ground!"

I looked again. Then I saw it. A thousand needles pricked my skin, the hairs rose on my arms. It reminded me of a three-dimensional image hidden in an obscure picture which could only be seen if viewed in a particular way. There was no undergrowth, no grass, no briars, only soft soil. And I counted four other depressions, all in a row.

"Jesus, Johnny," I whispered.

. . .

The work on Grave One ceased while Ludwig turned his attention to the depression five feet away, working the soil gingerly like an ordinance technician would dismantle a mine. "If we get a body on this..." he said, the voice trailing into thoughts we all feared. Serial killer.

He continued his painstaking process for another ten minutes, then stopped and leaned back, exposing a gritty patch of skin the size of a saucer.

"My God," said the Sheriff softly, immediately realizing the political and public pressure he would be facing.

"Let's check the other sites first before we make any decisions on what needs to be done," Ludwig suggested.

"I agree," said Cole. "But I'm calling Cobb right now. He needs to be here. If we've got multiple bodies he's gonna need to call in some troops."

Cobb arrived within an hour. He was dressed to work and assembled Cole, the Sheriff, and Echols immediately. "Okay. Tell me what's going on," he said with aplomb. They briefed him while the rest of us stood almost reverentially on the fringe of an imaginary circle. They showed him the two graves and their suspicions. He paused, considering the multitude of decisions to be made.

"Okay," he said as if to issue an edict. "The first thing that needs to be done is to call the Director. There's going to be a hell of a lot of press looking into this and he needs to be advised. Because of that, we'll get all the support we need from Atlanta. Stan, do you need any additional crime scene support?"

Ludwig spoke first. "Yes sir. We need Alice Coultrane. Next to me, she's the best."

Cobb smiled. "You got it. And what about profilers? Who do you recommend?"

"Ralph Merrit's the best."

"All right. I'll get him. I want him here to view the scene and the bodies, and get his opinion of what we've got. Next, where's Bohnoff?"

"He's on standby," said Cole. "He was expecting one body."

"Well, now he may have five. Make arrangements to have all of them shipped to Atlanta," ordered Cobb. "He's gonna be up to his ass in bodies. We need him to examine all five, ASAP, as soon as we can get them to him. Also, have Robin accompany the bodies and witness the autopsies."

He noticed me. "How long have you been awake?"

"All night, sir. I was watching the grave."

"Go home. Right now, you're worthless to me. Get some sleep and page me at three. Trust me, I'll have some work for you to do. Cole, get Robin and Dennis over here to help. Next, Tyler," Cobb said, turning to the Sheriff, "can you get some more of your men over here. It appears we've got five graves, but let's be sure. And we're gonna need help in keeping reporters and gawkers out of the area. Can you help us on that?"

"Sure, Cobb," the Sheriff responded.

"Let's focus on the crime scene and the bodies. Then we'll all meet to evaluate what we have and where we need to go with this thing. Any questions?" There were none. "Good. Let's do it."

• • •

At two-thirty the annoying buzzing of my alarm clock woke me out of a deep dreamless sleep. I felt lethargic and had to think through even routine tasks such as shaving and dressing. I made myself a sandwich and paged Cobb. My phone rang back promptly.

"Afternoon, Hank," said Cole. "Ready to join us?"

"Sure. Were any of the bodies Lydia's?"

"Not a chance. Been there too long—too much decomposition."

"Oh well What do you need me to do?"

"Nothing yet. We've got a total of five bodies. Three males, two females. We're on the last one now. And we'll be shipping her to Bohnoff as soon as the techs pull her out. We should be finished by five, then we're going to have a meeting in the courtroom and discuss what we've got. So meet us there at five thirty."

I arrived at the courthouse fifteen minutes early. The building looked less like a courthouse and more like a small granite church built in the early twentieth century. The layout was typical rural Southern court-house: the county offices, Probate Court, Clerk of Court, Licensing Bureau, and Sheriff's Office, were located on the first floor; the court-room, Judge's Chambers, District Attorney's Office, and a makeshift office for visiting attorneys was on the second. The courthouse was near-ly vacant and I scampered up the steps without notice. The second floor was dark and musty, and the mahogany floors echoed my footsteps as I walked down the hall. Dark brown benches, slick from decades of wear, lined the walls. I sat in the dim light and waited for the others.

Shortly I heard sharp, crisp taps of heels from the stairwell, then saw the silhouette of a woman at the end of the hall. Once her eyes adjusted to the darkness she proceeded toward the courtroom, and noticed me.

"Hello," she said. "Is this where the meeting is supposed to be?"

The woman was in her early twenties, dressed conservatively in a checkered print suit. Her light brown hair was cut just under the ears, flipping inward, giving her a scholarly appearance.

I nodded. "In a few minutes, I believe."

"Thanks," she said, flashing an easy smile. "Do you work here?"

"I'm out of Connally. What about you?"

"Atlanta."

Then it struck me. I had assumed she was an agent or at least some-how connected with the case. "Who're you with?" I asked suspiciously.

"AJC."

"What agency's that?"

She laughed, placing her slender hand over her mouth. "I'm sorry. You're not a reporter, are you? I thought you were a local reporter cov-ering the serial killings. I'm Nita Humphries, with the *Atlanta Journal-Constitution*. AJC for short. I was sent here to cover the discovered bod-ies. And you?"

"I'm with the G.B.I."

"Oh?" she said, as if she had found a new love interest. "How's the investigation coming? I heard they had five bodies unearthed?"

I shrugged. "Can't really say. I haven't been involved in the investigation today," I replied, semi-truthfully. "That's why I'm to attend the meeting. How did you learn about it?"

"I was at the Sheriff's Office trying to get some details on this story. Overheard a deputy mention. it." She pushed a strand of hair from her face. "A rather reticent group. I couldn't get the time of day from them. And there's no way to get photos at the scene. It's as if they were unearthing the remains of King Tut."

I heard the heavy clunks of approaching footsteps from the stairwell. The large dark frame of Cobb loomed, rising from the staircase, followed by smaller profiles.

I pointed toward Cobb. "That's the man you need to talk to, if you want to get 'the story'."

She rushed toward him. "Sir, I'm with the *Atlanta Journal-Constitution*. How many bodies were uncovered?"

Cobb gave her a disinterested glance. "Ma'am, let me have this meeting, then I'll get to you and the other reporters, or excuse me, I mean journalists," he said, jerking his head to a half dozen others following him up the stairs. He stopped at the entrance to the courtroom and announced to the press, "Ladies and gentlemen of the press, please allow us a moment to meet and assess what we have and then the Sheriff and I will answer your questions! If you'll return to the first floor a deputy will let you know when we're finished!"

Like he was herding a gaggle of geese, a deputy forced the reporters toward the stairwell. Nita resisted, pushing against the arm of the deputy. "I have a right to remain in this hall," she shouted to Cobb. "It's public property!"

The Sheriff smiled. "No ma'am. I'm in charge of the courthouse and its security. Right now, the public is not allowed on the second floor. Don't force this issue or the *Journal* will be posting your bond. Not a good career move."

She considered his comments, then with a contemptuous glare

retreated downstairs.

"Spunky little lady," chuckled Tyler, unlocking the courtroom door.

The investigative team filed into the courtroom. The darkened pews were as sturdy as they had been when they were first built. We all occupied the right side of the room while Cobb and Tyler went to the prosecutors table to address us. Someone flicked on the lights.

"Good afternoon," began Cobb, unfolding a sheet of paper. "It's been a long day for most of us. Some of us have been assigned to various duties and need to have an overview of this case. So I thought it best for everyone to assemble here, discuss what's been done, what's been determined, and where we need to go from here. After that, the Sheriff and I will discuss what needs to be released to the press. Okay?" The group nodded.

Cobb looked around the room. "Has anyone heard from Robin or Dr. Bohnoff?" Cole spoke. "She called me just before we got here. They're finishing up on the last body. Should be calling us any time."

The Sheriff pointed to a telephone on the prosecutor's table. "I've arranged to have a speaker phone installed for this meeting. When they call, we all can hear them."

"Thanks, Tyler. All right, Johnny, why don't you give us a brief summary of the initial call and the discovery of the first grave, then continue with what your investigation has learned thus far? When Robin and Dr. Bohnoff call, we'll talk to them, and we'll also hear from Ralph Meritt."

Cole walked forward and told of the discovery of the first body, the crime scene search, and spotting the pattern of depression. He gave a summary of his interview with the landowner. "He's growing pines which he plans to harvest in a couple of years," said Cole, "and he's leasing the area to a hunting club that uses the land to hunt birds and deer. I got the names and addresses of the club members. Some are from around here, some are from the Columbus, Macon, and Atlanta areas, and a few are from Alabama. It's a total of fifty members. We need to do a background check on each one and interview them."

The telephone chirped and the Sheriff quickly answered the phone. He handed it to Cobb.

"Doctor, we're in the Adams County courtroom with the investigative team," advised Cobb. "You're on speaker phone so you can address the group. You ready to brief us on your findings?" asked Cobb.

"I assume everyone here is somehow involved in this matter. There are no press or interested citizens?" the speaker blared.

"You assume correctly," Cobb assured him.

"Good," he said softly, smacking his lips in satisfaction. There was a rustling of papers. "Gentlemen, and ladies. Today I examined five bodies. I must remind you that my statements and findings during the examinations are preliminary and are subject to revision. I speak to you so you may use these findings to assist you in the near future.

"Today I examined two white males between sixty-five and eighty years of age, I examined one white female between sixty-five and eighty years of age, I examined a black male between sixty-five and eighty years of age, and I examined a black female between seventy and ninety years of age. The general cause of death in each case..." Bohnoff paused for effect, "was natural causes." A shocked murmur vibrated throughout the group. "Now, these findings are not one hundred percent conclusive. No evidence was found of any trauma. There were no cuts, no incisions, no apparent bruisings, no broken bones, no asphyxiations. No evidence that anyone was beaten, stabbed, shot, strangled, or drowned. Nothing. I examined the bodies for possible injections but due to the deterioration of the bodies I can't be positive. However, I did recover some body fluids and organs and a toxicology examination will be made.

"Let me explain the evidence that supports my opinion. White male number one had severe liver damage due to sclerosis; white male number two had severe heart damage indicative of a massive heart attack; the black male had one lung removed and the other lung contained heavy deposits of carbon and tar which is evidence of a heavy smoker; the black female had undergone several amputations including a right foot and all her toes on her left foot, indicative of diabetes. Both of her kidneys appeared to have suffered damage. And the brain of the white female had severe hemorrhaging indicative of a massive stroke. I might have been suspicious if all had similar causes of death but this is a diverse lot here. Once again, I need to conduct tests on the fluid and organs to ensure that they weren't, say, poisoned, or injected with a bacteria or virus. But my preliminary cause of death is of natural causes. Any questions?"

"Doctor, would you give an estimate length of time each has been buried?" asked Ludwig.

"Certainly. Now, this is a general estimate mind you, based merely on the examination of decomposition of each body. There are, naturally, various factors that influence the rate of decomposition, such as heat and humidity. But a general estimate would be from nine months, which was the white male found in grave one, which you found first, to three months which was in grave five containing the black male in the last grave in the row. I will be able to provide a better estimate based on the samples of insects recovered from the bodies."

"Doctor, you touched briefly on the one corpse that had several amputations," noted Cobb. "This would be helpful in identifying the body. You mentioned another that had a lung removed. I would assume he would have had a scar on his chest. Would you go through each of the bodies and identify any unusual scars, marks, tattoos, etcetera, that might help us to identify each person?"

"Of course, Cobb. I'd be happy to. In regard to the black female and her amputations, she also had a golf-ball-size external tumor under her left upper arm. The white female had an eight-inch scar on her abdomen, indicative of either a cesarean section birth or a hysterectomy. The black male was missing the tips of his second, third, and fourth finger on his left hand. The cuts weren't precise enough to indicate a surgical removal. It appeared like it may have come from a knife or saw. He also had a gold left incisor tooth. One white male had tattoos on his arms. On his left arm was the tattoo of the 101st Airborne Screaming Eagle and the on the other arm was a rose with the name Dorothy under it. The other white male had dentures and he had a scar on his chest, indicative of heart surgery.

"Cobb, I don't know what your plans for a press release are, but if these characteristics were made known to the public it might help in identifying the bodies."

Cobb, leaning on the armrest of the chair, nodded in agreement. "We probably will. Thank you doctor. Now let's hear from Ralph."

Ralph Merritt was a slender, slow-talking Southerner from north Georgia. A veteran investigator with over twenty years experience, he had participated in hundreds of murder investigations including the Atlanta Children Murders and the Columbus Strangler. He had a relaxed, easygoing style that belied his attention to details and thoroughness. With his experience in homicides he was one of the first G.B.I. agents to attend the F.B.I.'s Criminal Profilers Course at Quantico.

"Hello, everyone," he said, glancing at a list. "Some of my initial conclusions tend to confirm the good doctor's findings. I'll explain in a moment. All of the recovered bodies were nude, void of clothing and jewelry. No earrings, bracelets, watches, or rings. Each body was laid on his or her back, each facing the same direction."

An agent raised his hand. "Ralph, was there any evidence of necrophilia?"

"Doctor?" asked Ralph, deferring to Bohnoff.

"No evidence," Bohnoff curtly replied over the speaker. "But due to the decomposing, I'm not positive."

Merritt paused for any other questions then continued. "The second interesting aspect is that the deceased were buried beside each other in an orderly fashion, not merely dispersed around the area. It's as if this was a private graveyard. And from examination of the graves, the perpetrator didn't simply dig a hole, these graves were neat and squared, which indicates that our suspect is a fastidious individual.

"Based on the doctor's conclusions of natural death, this confirms my opinion that we have a burial plot. Meaning they died somewhere else and were transported to the crime scene. The fact that no clothing or jewelry were on the bodies indicates that the perpetrator did not want the dead identified. Why? Probably because once they are identified then there's a good possibility of tracing them to him.

"Therefore, I believe you'll be looking for a male between eighteen and thirty five years of age."

"Why not a female?" asked Dennis.

"It's doubtful that it's a female unless it's a very strong woman or she had an assistant. One of the males weighed over two hundred pounds.

"Next, because of the respectful way they were buried and, as I've previously mentioned, they were stripped of any obvious identification, I believe that he knew the victims. The perpetrator could have been a relative, but that's doubtful, or a member of a religious group that doesn't believe in formal burials, also doubtful. More likely the person was associated with them somehow. Meaning that he works in the area where you will find the elderly of different races. This could be a funeral home, a morgue, retirement facility or an association that works with the elderly such as Meals on Wheels or an ambulance or handicap transport. And as I have previously mentioned he is comfortable with the area which also means he will be from this general area."

"Just because he's familiar with the area doesn't necessarily mean he's from around here," interrupted the Sheriff. "Why would you rule out someone from the hunting club from, say Atlanta or Montgomery?"

"It's possible, Sheriff, nor should it be overlooked," replied Merritt. "But if you had a body in the trunk of your car would you drive down here from Atlanta or over from Montgomery. Not just once, but five times? I doubt it. I think the question is, why would he surreptitiously bury five people who died of natural causes? Once the bodies are identified I believe you will find a common denominator that will lead you to the perpetrator."

Cobb rose from the table. "Thanks, Ralph. And that question leads us to the next topic of discussion: how to identify the bodies. Doctor, don't you have an artist at the crime lab who can do a rendering from the photographs of the bodies?"

"We've got someone excellent on contract. I'll contact her right away," responded Bohnoff.

"Good. Until we get positive confirmation that these deaths were due to natural causes we need to investigate this matter as a homicide. Ludwig, keep your evidence tight and chain of custody in order. Dr. Bohnoff, I'd like you to keep me current on your findings. Cole, put together an interview team made of agents from our office. I want everyone who has any association with that property. That includes anyone who hunts, works, or pisses on the property. As for anyone from out of our area, such as Alabama or Atlanta, I'll coordinate with A.B.I. and our Atlanta office. If there's anything any of you here need let me know. I'll see that you get it.

"Now press coverage. Sheriff, if reporters think they're writing about a clandestine graveyard, they'll bury the story in the rear of the paper. If they think they've got a serial killer investigation, they'll put the story on page one. And since we can't positively conclude at this time that the deaths are natural, I think we should tell the press that we can't yet confirm the causes of the deaths and we're treating the discovery as homicides. We won't be lying and we'll get a lot of press coverage. We'll ask for the public's help in identifying the bodies and get the artist's renderings to the press as soon as possible. Any questions?"

Most everyone was tired and ready for the day to end. Everyone was silent.

"Okay then. Dr. Bohnoff, thanks for your help. I know it's been a long day," said Cobb, terminating the call. "Atlanta agents, you're dismissed. Have a safe drive home and thanks. As for my agents, everyone except Cole is dismissed. Go home, get a good night's rest and be ready to work first thing tomorrow." Cobb motioned Cole over to the table. "Draw up the interview teams and assignments. I'll be with Tyler on a press release and outline."

Walking down the courthouse steps, Nita Humphries sidled up to me. "The Sheriff and SAC will be with you in a few minutes," I said, hoping to thwart her questions.

"Thanks, how'd the meeting go?" she said with her best disarming smile.

"C'mon Nita. I can't talk about it. You know that," I said, walking to my car.

She stepped closer to me. "What can you tell me? Off the record," she whispered in a conspiratorial tone.

I glanced around, making sure no one could overhear us, then half covered my mouth. "I can tell you that I think you're a cute young lady and if I didn't have so much work to do tomorrow, I'd ask you out for a drink."

Her disarming smile vanished and the eyes hardened. "Cute. It'll be a cold day in hell before I have a drink with you. Well, if I can't get any straight answers, I won't guarantee the accuracy of the story."

I paused at my car, unlocking the door. "A reporter worried about the accuracy of a story? Now that would be news."

. . .

The last remnants of light smoldered in the west as I drove by the modest wood frame house just off Main Street near the church. A light flickered in the front rooms of the house so I parked on the street. Stepping onto the front porch I heard the unsteady plinking of a piano and through the sheer curtains of the front windows I saw a young girl sitting on a piano bench and an elderly lady wearing a flowered polyester dress sitting beside her. I rapped softly on the glass paned door. The lady at the piano rose and I heard the muffled cadence of approaching footsteps.

Ms. Godwin peered through the glass. "May I help you?" she asked properly with a breathy Southern accent.

I held up my credentials. "Yes ma'am. I'm Hank Monroe. G.B.I. I'd like to— "

"G.B.I.! Good heavens! Is something wrong?" she exclaimed, eyes widening in alarm.

"No ma'am. I'd like to speak with you about Lydia Carson. She was in your choir, wasn't she?"

She opened the door then looked around hesitantly. "Sir, if you could wait for about ten minutes. I'm in the middle of a piano lesson. You may sit here in the parlor if you like."

I sat in a corner chair across the room from the piano. The room was decorated in Victorian antiques and the aroma of a nearby bowl of potpourri reminded me of a tea room.

"Kathy," Ms. Godwin said to the child, "this is Mister — I'm sorry, I forgot your name."

"Hank Monroe," I chimed.

"This is Mr. Monroe. Would you mind if he listens to you play?"

"No ma'am," the child said with a demure smile, biting a fingernail.

For the next ten minutes I listened patiently as the young girl plodded through a familiar piece by Beethoven. Ms. Godwin coached her with encouragement and assurance. After the girl left with her mother, Ms. Godwin turned her attention to me.

"She was a little nervous playing in front of a stranger, but the experience is good for her," she said. "May I get you something to drink?"

"No ma'am, thank you."

"Well if you would pardon me for a moment, I have some mint tea brewing. I've got a sinus condition." Shortly she returned to sit next to me in a velvet wingback chair. "I thought Lydia had..." she paused searching for the diplomatic words as she sipped her tea, "left town."

"That does seem to be the rumor. I want to make sure that it's not just a rumor, but a fact. She was a member of the choir, wasn't she?'

"Yes sir. A devoted member. She was at every Wednesday night practice and at every Sunday service. I'm going to miss her," she said pensively. She pointed a slender finger at me. "I remember when she first began coming to practice. She was no more than twenty. I don't believe she had a car and she talked her mother into lending her the car. Well, when she walked in to the choir room you could have heard a pin drop.

"Why is that?"

"Because she just showed up. No one had asked her to join and she hadn't mentioned it to anybody. It was as if she had been moved by the Spirit. Since that day I don't believe she ever missed a practice or a service unless she was out of town."

"Was she a good singer?"

"Lydia was an enthusiastic singer. While she was solid," Ms. Godwin shook her head, "I wouldn't have ever featured her in a solo."

"How many are in the choir? I was at your service Sunday. It looked as if there was nearly thirty."

"Well I hope you enjoyed it. Do you sing Agent Monroe? We could use some additional male voices."

"No ma'am, I'm not a singer," I said, dodging recruitment. "They'd issue a noise ordinance against the church if I was in the choir."

"Oh pshaw," she laughed, waving a hand at me. "I'm very proud of our choir. We have thirty-five members. But we average between twenty-seven and thirty-three members at a time."

"Were any of them close to Lydia?"

"No sir, not really. Lydia was friendly, to a point. She'd talk to you if you spoke first, but rarely would she initiate a conversation. Some tried at first, but gave up when she continued to keep her distance."

"Did the choir ever have any social gatherings?"

"Certainly...."

"But Lydia never attended," I said, finishing Ms. Godwin's sentence. She nodded taking another sip of tea.

"Some of the people around town that I've talked to said they noticed a change in Lydia's attitude before her disappearance. Did you ever notice it?"

She gazed toward her lap, almost embarrassed to answer the question, then nodded. "Yes sir, I did. That's why I think she's gone."

"What did you notice, Ms. Godwin? Did she say anything to you?"

She took a deep breath, as if she was unloading a burden. "During the month before her disappearance, her singing was livelier. It had more bounce and projection. I might be an old lady, Agent Monroe, but to me she looked like a woman in love. It' s something a lady can't hide."

"What do you think happened to her?"

The question surprised her and she thought for a moment. "I think she left the country with a man that her parents would not have approved of. Maybe someone who was divorced or had a menial job?"

"What makes you think that?"

"It was something she said to me one night."

"Go on," I urged.

"Well... the choir was taking a break and I noticed Lydia, as usual, sitting alone. So I went over to her and complimented her on her singing. She smiled and thanked me and said things in her life were taking shape, going very well. The twenties can be a very difficult time for a single woman if they don't see any future. Anyway, she asked me how long I had been a Christian. I told her, 'Over fifty years.' Then she asked me the most curious question. She asked, 'If the motive is pure, can the result be sinful?'"

"And what did you tell her?"

"I told her I thought the results may not be sinful, but they could be harmful or hurtful. I used the example of someone who would send all their money in to a shyster televangelist. The motive of sending in the money was pure, but having no money to feed the family could be hurtful to them."

"What was her response?"

"Well... there wasn't one, really. She just nodded indicating she'd heard the answer and stared straight ahead. I think I gave her an answer she didn't want to hear."

"Ms. Godwin, I've also heard a rumor that she might be dead."

"Dead! You mean, accident dead... or that someone killed her?" she exclaimed, placing her cup to one side.

"Ma'am, it's possible that someone killed her."

She shook her head in denial. "I can't believe anyone would kill her. She's a wonderful girl. For the life of me I can't think of any reason for anyone to kill her."

"I don't know either. That's why I'm asking questions."

CHAPTER FIFTEEN

"GOOD MORNING, everyone," resonated Cobb's authoritative bass voice. "I trust everyone had a good night's sleep and is ready to hit the ground running?" The agents assembled in the squad area nodded, mentally preparing for another exhausting day. "Good. First order of business for the Connally office is to interview every one of the hunt club members. Not only as suspects, but also to determine if they might have seen something suspicious or unusual.

"Of the fifty members in the club, we have thirty-eight in this area we need to interview. The rest are scattered in other areas and I'll see to it that they are interviewed. You will be divided into four teams with two agents to a team. Johnny and I have divided up the assignments as equitably as possible and tried to keep the leads in the same area so you aren't going to have to go driving to one end of the region, do an interview, then drive to the other side of the region. Johnny, go ahead and hand out the packets."

Cole walked through the room and dealt large manila envelopes to the agents. He passed by me and said in a low voice, "You're on my team. I'll get our assignments later."

"Basically you're going to find in each envelope a list of those to be interviewed, a G.C.I.C., N.C.I.C. and local records checks on the person you're to interview," Cobb explained. "As I said yesterday, until we get a confirmation that these people died naturally, they are to be treated as victims of a homicide. In other words, be suspicious and be careful. Each team has either nine or ten interviews. Unless there's a damn good excuse, I expect them done by close of business tomorrow. We'll have another get-together tomorrow morning to compare notes and see how everyone is progressing. Also, by tomorrow morning I should have, with luck, the results of Dr. Bohnoff's toxicology test and also the artist's rendering of the bodies. Any questions? Good. Have at it."

As everyone separated into their assigned teams, Cole handed me our packet. "Ready to go?"

"Sure. Anything special we need to take or know?" I asked, reviewing the lists of club members.

"Nothing unusual with our group or any of the groups." He looked over my shoulder at the list. "This one's a dentist, this one's a pharmaceutical sales rep, this one's a farmer, this one's a real estate broker, this one's retired military, this one owns a building supply house, this one's a plumber. Stock broker, attorney, and, last but not least, an accountant," he said, pointing to each name on the list.

"How'd you know that?"

"The landowner, my boy," Cole answered in a poor imitation of W.C. Fields. "Let me get my spit cup and we're out of here."

We headed west in Cole's dark blue Crown Vic, gliding over the twin lane country roads lined with purple verbena, daisies, and black-eyed Susans.

Cole shoved a wad of Red Man behind his cheek and muttered, "You know what this is all about?"

I didn't understand his question. "What?"

"This massive manhunt. You're looking at Cover Your Ass, CYA, on a grand scale."

"What do you mean?"

"Tomorrow Bohnoff is going to report natural deaths. And when the report comes in, this case will become a backburner case. You'll see agents abandoning this case like passengers on the Titanic." He could tell I was still puzzled. He spit into his cup and continued. "Instead of a serial killer, what do we have? Probably some religious cult or political group that doesn't believe in reporting a death to the government. Instead of a capital felony, we've got a misdemeanor. Hardly worth justifying burning hundreds of man-hours. But right now Cobb can't afford to take that risk, so he's going full bore on this investigation. And the Director can't afford to take the chance either, so he'll give Cobb anything he wants."

"Do you think we'll catch whoever did this?"

"Oh yeah," he replied with certainty. "We're not looking at some career criminal here. We're going to find some misguided soul who'll confess, and the jury will feel sorry for him. So the District Attorney will plead him out to probation and a fine." He drew the cup to his lips again. "Hank, you'll find after a while that the best way to keep your sanity in this job is to not take it seriously. Don't save the world. When we catch this guy, throw him in jail, forget about him, and let the courts sort it out."

"Are you telling me that it doesn't matter to you whether this guy, or any guy for that matter, gets any time?" I asked incredulously.

"That's right. I used to take it serious and I'd go home worrying about it, taking my frustrations out on my wife. Nearly ruined my marriage. Then during plea day, I was watching the masses appearing before the bar, so many of them, the same people I'd jailed before. It was like dealing with fire ants. I'd destroyed the mound and it would sprout up a day later, three yards away. I'd chase them but they'd return. It dawned on me that I'd one day retire. I'd leave this job. But my wife and children would or should still be a part of my life. My family should be where I needed to place my focus and my worries. Now when I go home, I leave my work at the office."

We found the dentist easily enough at work, but had to wait forty-five minutes until there was a lull in his schedule. The pharmaceutical rep was out of town. Wouldn't be back until Friday. The farmer was in town at a Deere dealership; Cole left his business card and pager number. We caught the retired military officer, Colonel Dennison, in his driveway loading golf clubs. He was nice enough to allow an interview. The real estate broker wasn't in, but his secretary called him on his mobile and he quickly returned to his office. After the interview with the broker, Cole was paged by the farmer and off we went to interview him. The attorney was concerned about our visit, until we explained the nature of our call. He'd read the article in *The Macon Telegram* and was happy to talk to us. It was late afternoon when we interviewed the stockbroker, whose mind was more on the Dow Jones average than on us.

As we got back in Cole's car he asked, "Well, what do you think?"

I pointed my thumb down. "The whole day's been a wash. I hope someone else had better success. Who's next?"

Cole referred to the list. "I'll tell you what. It's nearly... " Cole referred to his watch, "five-fifteen. It'll be a quarter to six by the time we get back to Connally. We've got four to do tomorrow."

"I thought we had ten interviews. We've done five," I reminded him.

"The rep's out of town 'til Friday, remember?"

"Right."

"So tomorrow we'll do the remaining four. My wife wants to go to Wednesday night supper at the church. We should get back in just enough time."

"Sure. That's fine with me," I relented.

While driving back to Connally I thought of Cole's interview technique. He was masterful. Normally respectful and as accommodating as possible, he knew when to press, knew how to ask accusing questions without being confrontational. But most of all he listened. He listened to the words, the phrases, the tones, the inflections, and observed the body language. He drew a person out of his shell, urging him to talk, tossing in questions requiring additional explanations. He was professional with the attorney in a relaxed sort of way, he was a good ol' boy with the farmer, interested in the rainfall and harvest, and he talked of the discipline that used to be in the military before a bunch of liberals turned it into a social organization.

He noticed my silence. "Something on your mind?"

"I was thinking about the way you were interviewing. I learned a lot."

Cole thrust a fresh wad of tobacco into his mouth. "Thanks, but it's an art form. The only way to learn interviewing or interrogation is to talk to people yourself. I've been doing this for fifteen years and I'm still learning. There is no pat way to interview or interrogate. You have to mold it to your own style and personality. And you can attend all sort of classes and read all types of books, but it's like swimming... unless you jump into the water, you ain't gonna be worth a damn.

"There are some classic retorts, though. When you ask someone a question and he responds with a question, like 'Who told you that?' or 'Why would you say that?', he's not denying the fact, he's wanting to know who snitched on him or how did you figure that out. Another response is simply not to acknowledge the question, but instead give an answer to something completely different. Politicians are masters at that one."

"You make it look easy."

"Thanks. But it's not so easy for me. I've rarely left an interview or an interrogation where thirty minutes later I wished I had asked another question."

As we drove through the rolling hills of western Georgia, he walked me through each of the interviews of the day. None of the interviews were serendipitous; they were planned based on Cole's intuition and evaluation of the person interviewed. I didn't anticipate any breaks in the case tomorrow, but I looked forward to learning more from Cole.

But before going home that night, I'd conduct one more interview.

• • •

No one answered the door at Opal Lockhart's house, a modest vinyl-sided house in a modest vinyl-sided neighborhood at the edge of the city limits, a barrier between a mobile home park and a neighborhood of brick ranch homes. I drove over to Albert Miner's residence, an aged brick ranch located in a racially mixed part of town. The door was answered by a cute black girl, no more than five, with errant pigtails tied in bows. She barely cracked the door, coal dark irises surrounded by clear whites, peering innocently at me.

"Is your Mommy or Daddy home?" I asked, kneeling down to her level.

The door suddenly widened and a large woman in her sixties with a cautious glare asked, "May I help you?"

I understood her reasoning. White males appearing at her door usually were a poor foreboding. Except for the occasional turkey at Thanksgiving or a gift during Christmas, a white man on the doorsteps meant trouble.

"Good evening ma'am. I'm Hank Monroe with the G.B.I.," I said. "I'm looking for Albert Miner. I wanted to talk to him about a member of the church."

"Who's that?" she demanded.

"Lydia Carson. You know her?" I asked with my best disarming smile.

Her features softened. "She's been here a couple of times. When Albert had appendicitis and was laid up the hospital, she brought over some meals for the family. She was a good person. She warn't no turkey dropper. She'd come here not for show, but because she really cared about us."

"Then I guess you know she's disappeared?"

"I knowed."

"Do you or Albert know what might have happened to her?"

"I knowed she ain't gone down to no Mexico. I also knowed that's what someone wants you to know."

"And who might that be?"

She shook her head resolutely. "You the po-lice. I reckon you the one that needs to figure that out."

"If Lydia was such a good person, can't you tell me for Lydia's sake?" I pleaded.

"Wouldn't help Lydia no way. What is, is what is."

"Well, maybe Albert will talk to me? Is he here?"

"Naw. He's at the church. Wednesday night supper. You can catch him there if you hurry."

. . .

I parked behind the church and found the rear door to the kitchen unlocked. Wednesday night in the rural South is still a midweek pause. As recent as the seventies, retail businesses would close for the afternoon, and on Wednesday nights the Christian stalwarts would congregate at their church for the service. No conflicting little league or civic meetings were scheduled for the same time. In the more economically competitive times of the following years, businesses remained opened all day on Wednesdays and some were bold enough to open on Sundays. As a result, church attendance on Wednesday evening plummeted, until some resourceful soul examined the problem and countered with an innovative solution: appeal to the stomach. The heart of any social gathering tended to be food, and the lure of giving Mom a break from the drudgery of kitchen duty by providing a low-cost, wholesome meal was a sure-fire winner, bringing the congregation back to church on Wednesday night. The technique proved successful, doubling, tripling, even quadrupling Wednesday's attendance, and providing an informal setting for members to meet and greet each other.

I slipped into the commercial-style kitchen, which was a hubbub of activity. I was surrounded by a large black iron oven, stainless steel pots, pans, utensils and work tables. There was a mixture of blacks and whites cleaning flatware, washing pots, and stacking glasses in the cabinets.

"Excuse me," I said to a man carrying a gallon jar of mustard past me. "I'm looking for Albert Miner. Is he here?"

The man gave me a brief nod as he cradled the jar and pointed to a black man at the stainless steel sink. "That's Albert."

I backed against the gas stove as a woman passed by, then scooted over to Miner. He was scouring out a steel pot.

"Albert," I said, "I'm Hank Monroe, G.B.I. Could I have a word with you?"

Miner was a broad shouldered, squat guy whose beefy face gave him a permanent smile and caused his eyes to squint.

"Sure," he replied with a gravelly voice. "Mind if I finish up in here? Don't want to leave these fine people with all the dirty work."

"Of course, I understand."

"Should take, maybe, ten minutes," he said. "By the way, there should be some cake outside in the fellowship hall. Get yourself some and by the time you're finished, I'll be with you."

I was surprised at the number of people in the fellowship hall; it had to be a hundred people. Most had finished their meal and were talking and drinking iced tea. Four long tables ran the length of the expansive room which seemed to have subtly divided itself into specific social groups. In the back of the hall to the left were the families with small children who had politely segregated themselves as to not disturb the other families. Many were still eating or trying to coerce Junior to eat his string beans. To the right were the teenagers who had socially partitioned themselves from their own families. The group seemed relaxed as they teased and flirted with each other. The group closest to the kitchen were the elderly, numerically well represented. An unusually large number of women, neatly dressed with impeccably placed hair, surrounded the area. But there were a few couples who, over the years, had managed to cheat the specters of infirmity, death, and divorce. They stayed close to each other, as if they were in a life boat, out of familiarity, out of need, and out of fear. The remainder were the various members of the church.

I selected a slice of chocolate cake and scanned the group. Then I saw Hayley. She was sitting with Ross and Patsy, talking enthusiastically with a young couple across the table from her. I watched as she sipped her tea, running her tongue across her lips.

"Excuse me. Can everyone hear me okay?" said someone from an address system at a podium to my left. The devotional was beginning.

I walked behind Hayley and lightly pinched the trapezius muscles on either side of her neck. She winced slightly, turning around.

"Hank!" she said in a surprised greeting, but somewhat confused. "Did you eat here?"

"No. Believe it or not, I'm here on work. I need to interview some-one who's here." I realized my manners. "I wanted to let you know how much I enjoyed the other night. You made it special."

"Thanks," she said, seductively brushing aside a strand of hair. "I hadn't heard from you. I wasn't sure."

"Don't even think that. It's that... I've been so busy lately. I was think-ing of calling you for Saturday night, but I've got to work," I shameless-ly heard myself say.

"Oh yeah. I heard about those bodies they found over in Adams County. Were you on that?"

"Oh yeah," I said. "Everyone is. We're still working on it."

"No, you don't need to apologize. I understand. Listen," she said, clutching my hand. "This weekend we're gonna be at our house on the backwater. If you can get away, come join us. We'll be skiing. I know you'll enjoy it. But if you can't make it, I understand."

I squeezed her shoulders. "If I can, I will."

I heard Reverend Pheim's voice. "I want to thank everyone for attending tonight. I hope you enjoyed your meal. It was hosted by the New Beginnings Class." Everyone around me clapped in approval.

Miner entered the hall and waved at me.

"I need to go," I said, lightly touching Hayley's shoulder.

"You know the McTimmons?" Albert asked as I approached him. I nodded. "High cotton, my man. C'mon, we can talk where I work."

We walked down a half flight of stairs to the brick basement, turned left to a small room containing a work bench, basic tools, cleaning supplies, a cot, chair, and wooden table. A thirteen inch television with aluminum foil hanging from the antennae like a silver flag sat in the corner, and a stack of magazines rested neatly at the foot of the cot. "This is where I hang out. When my wife kicks me out of the house, this is where I end up. Have a seat," he said with a chuckle, directing me to a chair at the table.

"I met your wife, or I believe she was," I said, giving him a brief description of her.

"Oh yeah, that's her. Not one to be messing with." He set himself across from me. A checkerboard lay between us. "I can move this if you wish," he said, pointing at the checkerboard.

"Oh no! Leave them there."

"Checkers is my game. Ain't too many around these parts that can take ol' Miner," he said proudly. "Now what does the ol' G.B.I. want with Miner?"

"Wanted to talk with you 'bout Lydia Carson. I understand you knew her?"

"Knew her?" he said repeating my question. "You talking about her like she's dead."

"Might be," I replied. "Your wife seems to think so."

"Addie," he said, shaking his head. "She sees conspiracies everywhere. Thinks Kennedy was kilt by the Mafia, the Cubans, and the C.I.A. Can't you imagine those three sitting across the table from each other, planning an assassination? That'd be a hell of a meeting. Whoops, better not be any cussing in His house. Sorry Lord, I slipped up."

"Well, let me rephrase the question. Do you know her?"

"Oh, yeah." He tilted his head toward the checkerboard. "She used to come down here and we'd play checkers. Wasn't worth a tinker's dam when she started, but lately she'd been giving me fits."

"Really? Tell me how y'all began playing checkers together."

"Oh, about two years ago, right after I had my 'pendix taken out, Lyjia brought some casseroles over to the house. I don't believe it was part of some organized function from church. She just showed up at the door with some food. Shy, but she was insistent that we take it. Now, don't get me wrong, the people at the church were generous, in both their prayers and food. And I was still getting my salary. So it wasn't that I was in a hurting way. After about a week I was well enough to walk around the house, but I was going nuts inside those four walls. I decided to try doing some light work. I was right here at the workbench one night sharpening a mower blade when I heard a knock at the door. It was Lyjia. She'd been at a Bible study and just stopped by to see how I was doing. Even brought me a carrot cake. The girl can bake a cake, let me tell you. She noticed the checkerboard, just like it is right now, and commented on it. I challenged her to a game. She refused at first, like a girl being asked to dance and was too shy to get on the floor. But there was something about her that I saw inside her that really wanted to play. So I insisted. Threatened not to take the cake or no more of her food. At first, I thought I'd pushed too much, kinda gotten uppity. She had this stern look on her face and I thought she'd leave. Then suddenly her face broke into this daring smile and she said, 'Okay, maybe one game.' The one game became three. I let her beat me on the last, cause... well... I enjoyed her company and wanted her to come back. And she did. Nearly every week." His lips tightened in a tight grin and his eyes moistened.

"I think she played checkers with me because I didn't want nothing from her and we could just talk about the game. It's like two guys at a sports bar watching a football game. They don't have to know a thing about each other, don't even have to know each other's names, but they can join in a common activity with a common goal. That's the way it was with us. She wasn't forced to talk about her life, her likes, her dislikes. Didn't have to talk about religion, politics, work, or social life. We bonded through checkers."

"But you got to know her?"

"Oh yeah. You don't play with someone and not learn something about them. Lyjia was sharp, only made the same mistake once. You could only use the same trap once on her. Then she'd be ready with a counter. Very competitive and though she knew it was a game, she hated to lose. Once when we were playing, she had her chin propped on her hand while she was trying to figure out a problem. She ended up losing a man. Later I noticed the palm on her hand, you know that meaty piece on the edge under the little finger. She had bite marks there. She'd been biting herself, either out of anger or punishment for making a poor move."

"Interesting. Did she ever talk about any of her friends, her social life, her parents, or work?"

"Naw, can't say she did. If fact, she asked me a lot about my family. About my kids, my wife. What it was like having children and the demands they make. We talked about Addie, why I married her, why we never divorced. You know, I remember once, she asked me a kinda curious question. Wanted to know if I was glad I got married and did I ever have regrets."

"What did you tell her?"

"I told her getting married and having a family was the best thing that ever happened to me. They say you can't take it with you. Well, maybe you can't. Everything you made, bought, and have, are of this world and will forever be left behind. But with God's blessing, you will eventually be in heaven with your wife, your parents, your grandparents, and your children. That's the only thing worth working for in this world."

"What did she say?"

Albert laced his fingers, placing them under his chin in a modified prayer. "She didn't say nothing. She...." His voice cracked briefly, then he took his shirt sleeve and wiped his eyes. "She smiled at me as if I had confirmed her feelings. She leaned across the table and she gave me a soft kiss on my cheek."

"You think she's dead, don't you?" I asked quietly.

"I pray it's not so. But I fear it is, don't ask me why, I just do. I've prayed that her killer's found. I truly believe that if the good Lord wants it so, he'll find a way. The Lord can conquer the strong with the weak."

"Mr. Miner," I said rising from my seat, "I think the Lord will answer your prayers."

That evening I rented *Ghost* at the video store. Then I called Megan.

"Hey stranger. Where you been?" she cheerfully greeted me.

"Work," I replied honestly. "They've been keeping me busy. I guess you heard about those bodies found over in Adams County."

"Yeah. I read about it in the papers."

"You busy tonight?" I asked. "I rented a movie."

"No. Come on over. I'm a cheap date. I'll make us some popcorn."

We prepared popcorn and iced tea. I sat on the couch with Megan comfortably formed next to me. We talked about her studies and her new school year. Megan expressed concern with the relationship between Katie and Roy. They both thought that Roy was drinking too much. She asked about the Adams County case and I feigned chagrin when I told her I couldn't discuss it.

As we watched the movie I gazed at Megan, the downy fine hair at her jaw line, the delicately shaped ear, the flawlessly expressive face. I understood what Albert meant and maybe what Lydia was searching for, when she asked him about marriage. A relationship wasn't the mere physical union of two biological creatures. It was the bonding of souls through mutual experiences, ideas, hopes, goals, successes, tragedies, and support that transcends time and space—an emotional interweaving so tight that when one is removed, it rips at the fabric of the other. I now understood how a mother could look with unconditional love at a baby so ugly it would make you shiver, or how an elderly couple, wrinkled and spotted with age, could love each more than when they were first married. I was bonding with Megan, passing through a portal I wasn't comfortable with, but it felt right. Before I left I asked her out. I was treading on unfamiliar ground. The Expatriates were having a mixed evening tomorrow. The Braves were playing, of course.

CHAPTER SIXTEEN

"GOOD MORNING, all," greeted Cobb. "Ready for another day of good old fashioned detective work?"

"Yeah, yeah," the squad answered in a surly chorus.

Cobb ignored the impertinence. "All right. Let's hear from the team leaders. Robin?"

Robin gave a dry report of the five club members she'd interviewed. Nothing unusual. The other team leaders, including Cole, gave similar reports, nothing to raise the hackles of suspicion with the investigate teams.

"Well, we got the renderings Fed-Exed to us this morning. I think the quality is good enough for your interviews. Johnny, would you hand them out?" he asked, handing him a thick stack of paper. I examined the five charcoal drawings. They were excellent, and gave life to what before had been mere antiseptic names. "Also, Bohnoff has assured me that the forensics and toxicology reports will be available by tomorrow. Are there any of you who don't think you can finish your interviews, except for those persons out of town?" No one replied. "Okay, finish your leads." As the group broke Cobb shouted above the crowd, "Monroe, I need to see you in my office."

I looked at Johnny as he finished distributing the pictures and shrugged. "If I'm not back in thirty minutes, come looking for me," I joked.

Cobb was prepared for me when I entered his office. "Have a seat," he said cordially, indicating the chair in front of his desk.

"Am I in trouble?" I asked in jest.

Cobb's demeanor was serious. "I uh... got a call from the Director this morning..... It was about you."

"Me!" I said alarmed.

Cobb nodded. "Apparently, a state representative from the district here, who happens to be on the Appropriations Committee, called him with a concern. There was an allegation made by one of his constituents that you've been running around Connally accusing members of the community of being involved in Lydia Carson's death. He wanted to know the story."

"Who made such a charge?" I angrily demanded. "That's absurd."

"I don't know. Apparently you've accused someone of Lydia's death. Is that true?"

"That's bullshit," I blurted. "I haven't accused anyone."

"So you've been interviewing people about Lydia's disappearance?"

"Yes, sir. I believe I told you that there were a few more people to be interviewed before I felt comfortable enough to close the case."

"And have you interviewed those people?"

"Some," I answered. I felt a pressure closing in on me. Was I being forced to quit the investigation? Suddenly, like a howl from the grave, I recalled Celeste's words: *"It's not to his benefit to solve this case. He wishes to retire quietly,"* and *"Someone, somehow, will let you know you're an annoyance."* The hair rose on my arms.

"When will you be able to close this matter?"

"This is asinine," I suddenly blurted, catching Cobb off guard.

"Excuse me?" he replied, preparing for a verbal assault. I felt Cobb's cold gray eyes burning into me like a laser.

"Sir, I say with all due respect," I said, referring to my officer's training. "I find this ironic that we have eight agents and support personnel involved in an investigation with bodies that died from what appears to be a natural death. At the same time, I'm catching heat and no support about a case where there's no body, but a homicide has been committed.

You don't see something strange about that, sir?"

"I would if you can present evidence that a homicide has been committed." Cobb retorted. "But so far, all I've gotten is suppositions."

There were no doubts now about Celeste. Her prediction had proven true.

"Give me two weeks," I promised. "I'll have your proof."

Cobb reluctantly shook his head. "Sorry, Hank. I can't keep the dogs at bay that long. The Director's insistent. Politics is involved in this now. I'll give you three days."

"Three! How can I work with Cole and finish this in three days. Give me at least a week. Please," I pleaded.

Cobb leaned back in his chair, rubbing his chin. "All I want to do is retire. First Office Agents will be the death of me. I'll give you five, and that's laying my butt on the line. And you better have some evidence of a death or the investigation's over, understand?"

"Thanks, boss," I said, leaping from my chair before he changed his mind.

Cole was waiting in his car for me. I leaped in and said, "Let's get these interviews over with. Who's first on the list?"

Cole cranked the car and referred to his list. "Wayne Kearse. He's the owner of a builders' supply store. No record." We pulled out onto the highway, heading east. "Everything between you and Cobb okay?"

"It's the Carson case. He's given me five days to resolve the thing or he's gonna shut it down. Seems I've hurt someone in town's itty bitty feelings," I mimicked in a whiny voice. "And they're putting the heat on in Atlanta."

"Hank, mind if you get some advice from an older but wiser agent?" Cole asked.

"Nope."

"You remember I told you to look at your cases in clinical terms, don't get attached to the victims or the suspects. If you want a long lasting career in law enforcement, you don't stick your neck out. Oh, you'll probably get away with it for a number of years, then you'll take a risk for the right reasons, then suddenly you get your little pee-pee whacked. If they don't want you looking for the Carson girl, screw it, go on to another case. Whether she's found or not, in the big scheme of life, it won't matter.

There are other people to be killed, other businesses to be robbed, other homes to be burglarized, and other drugs to be purchased."

When I didn't answer he continued. "I guess I sound like one of those cynical old farts."

I chuckled. "Well, I'd say you're approaching the zone."

"Maybe I am, but one day you'll see what I'm saying."

Twenty minutes later, with the advantage of Cole's heavy foot we pulled in Kearse's Builders Supply located on the edge of Thomaston, Georgia.

"It's your turn to write," said Cole, gathering the portraits. "I expect copious notes."

Stacks of railroad cross ties, pressure treated beams and wheelbarrows sat underneath the low overhang of the long wood-sided building. It was an old family-owned hardware store with worn, hardwood floors that had managed to survive the corporate encroachment of the large volume national chains.

A young salesman approached us as soon as we entered. "Can I help you?" he asked.

Cole flashed his badge. "Is Wayne Kearse in?"

"Yes, sir!" the young man said, his eyes widening.

"Could I speak with him for a moment?"

"Just a minute," he said, darting off to the office area.

In a few minutes a middle-aged man wearing khakis and a blue Duck Head knit shirt approached us. He had an oval baby face, with clipped black hair and a neatly trimmed mustache. He was surprisingly young for the owner of a building supply business. "Gentlemen, I'm Wayne Kearse. Can I help you?"

Cole again produced his credentials. "I'm Johnny Cole and this is Hank Monroe. We're with the G.B.I. Are you a member of a hunt club in Adams County?"

"Yeah."

"I don't know if you've heard, but there were five bodies discovered on that property and we're interviewing everyone associated with the land. Is there a place we can talk?"

"Of course," Kearse replied. "Let's use my office."

We walked through a panel-lined corridor to his panel-lined office, which contained various photographs of sponsored little league teams, and plaques of appreciation. Stacks of computer printouts were scattered around the office.

"Can I get you something to drink? Coffee maybe?" he asked.

"Thank you, that'd be nice. Black," Cole replied, looking at me.

I nodded. "Same way."

"Just a second," Kearse said leaning out in the hall. "Martha. Could you pour a couple of coffees, please? Black. Thanks."

Cole used the same low-key approach as he'd used in the previous interviews: respectful but official. "You are a member of the hunt club on the Brewster property?"

"Yeah, been a member for the last five years," Kearse replied, appearing more relaxed.

"How often do you go hunting on the property?"

"Hmmm... maybe three, four times during deer season, and... I guess the same amount during bird season."

I was studying Kearse's body language, the position of his body, the inflection in his voice, his eye contact. There was nothing to indicate deception.

"Do you normally go by yourself or do you go with others?"

"I never go alone. This day and time it's too dangerous. Besides, it's no fun hunting by yourself. I always take someone with me. Normally I go with Don Holton, who's a member and lives here in town."

"Have there been times you've gone alone or with someone other than Don?"

Kearse blew out a breath of air. "I can't think of any. Now there were times Don and I met with other members of the club, or we invited some local people as guests. But, to the best of my recollection, we always went together."

Cole reached into his brief case, producing the drawings. "These are sketches of the people found buried on the property. Do you recognize any of them?"

I studied his eyes, looking for any indication of recognition. He studied each picture, carefully placing one behind the other when he had finished. While he was looking, an elderly lady softly knocked on the door with the coffees.

"Hey, Martha," Kearse said, indicating with a waive of his hand that the coffees were for us. "These two gentlemen are with the G.B.I.

"I'm sorry, sir," he said, shaking his head in regret. "I don't recognize any of these people. Martha, you've been here awhile. Take a look at these pictures. Recognize any of 'em?"

Martha walked behind Kearse's shoulder to look at the drawings. She shook her head at the first. She looked at the second and suddenly inhaled sharply. "My God, that's Mose!" she said with certainty.

Kearse turned toward her with alarm. "Who?"

"Moses Beal. He worked here about five years before your daddy brought you on. Your daddy hired him about thirty years ago, back when you were a toddler." She directed her comments toward Cole and me. "I'd been working for Mr. Kearse for maybe five years when Mose showed up wanting a job. Mr. Kearse hired him on a whim to work in the lumberyard, cutting wood and making deliveries. Ol' Mose had a habit of hitting the sauce," she said, holding an imaginary glass and titling it up at her mouth. "Mr. Kearse had to fetch him from jail a time or two on weekends following pay day. But come Monday, Mose was at work at eight o'clock."

She pointed toward the drawing. "Did this guy in this picture have the tips of his fingers missing from his left hand?"

I caught my breath. That was him, it had to be!

"Yes ma'am," replied Cole calmly.

"He lost them one morning cutting lumber. The rip saw cut them so fast he didn't even know he'd lost them 'til he noticed blood on the wood. And I also believe he had a gold tooth in the front."

"Ms....?"

"Barnett, Martha Barnett."

"Ms. Barnett. You say he used to work here for Wayne Kearse's father?"

Wayne spoke. "My grandfather started the business back in the thirties. It was passed down to my father, who passed the direction of the company to me about seven years ago. Moses wasn't here when I started to work."

"What happened to him?" Cole asked.

"He retired, oh, about fifteen years ago," said Martha, enjoying the rapt attention. "Every now and then he'd stop by here to visit. Last I heard of him he'd gotten ill. Emphysema I think. Mose had always been a heavy smoker. Used to smoke those smelly Camels, with no filters. He was in a nursing home here in town." She turned to Wayne. "You know, the one run by your hunting buddy."

"Don Holton?" he spurted.

"Yeah, that's him."

I recalled Merritt's briefing. The suspect could be associated with a nursing facility.

"It appears we need to speak with Mr. Holton," said Cole stoically. "Mr. Kearse, Ms. Barnett, I'll ask you not to call or mention our discussions until we've talked to Mr. Holton, please."

They shook their head in unison. "Of course not," they chorused.

. . .

The Quail's Roost Nursing Care Facility was a sizable structure stretching nearly one hundred yards. The white brick ranch was perched on a rise a quarter of a mile off the highway to provide privacy, and boasted a wide terrazzo porch that ran the length of the building with benches and rocking chairs. A number of the tenants were making use of the porch, enjoying the warm morning until it would become too stifling under the humid noonday heat.

Cole parked in the visitors' parking space and gathered his papers. "Since Holton is on the list of club members, let's treat this as a cold call. Don't let on that we've seen Kearse. We'll show him the picture of Moses and see what happens. If he ignores the picture we'll continue the interview, but keep a close watch on him in case he gets froggy."

Don Holton was the nursing home's administrator. In his late thirties, five feet ten inches tall, he had piercing, challenging eyes behind his tortoise shell glasses.

"Let's go to my office," he said, greeting us in the foyer with direct eye contact. We walked past the traffic of the elderly, moving slowly along the halls in wheelchairs and walkers. Some were alert, with a quick greeting, but too many were slumped in their chairs with sunken, life-less eyes. Others reached out as I passed, simply wanting attention or someone to talk with. I felt a pang of pity, wishing I could help, but I had to move on.

"How may I be of service?" asked Holton, once Cole and I were seated in his well-appointed office. I noticed a diploma from the Citadel that explained his forthright demeanor.

Cole gave him the standard spiel of the previous interviews, confirming his membership in the Brewster Hunt Club. "We had an artist produce some renderings of the bodies we found. Would like you take a look at the drawing; see if you might recognize anyone?"

"Sure. Be glad to," he said, casually taking the drawings. He leaned back in his chair, laying the eight by ten sketches on his crossed leg. "No," he said, placing the first drawing to the side. He straightened with a start. "That looks like Shirley Martin! She was a patient here about a year ago."

Cole tried to maintain his composure but I could tell he was excited. "Look at the others please," he calmly urged.

"My God! That's Moses Beal." He examined the fourth illustration. "This is Taylor Duckworth. And I, I'm not sure about the last." Holton was pale and visibly shaken. "Would you mind if I call my head nurse? She's been here twelve years. She may be able to recognize these two and confirm the others."

Cole nodded. "Go ahead."

Holton quickly dialed a number requesting that Mrs. Beggs come to his office immediately. "I don't understand it. If I'm correct, the ones I identified died within the last year. Ol' Mose used to work here in town. He died maybe four months ago."

There was a firm knock at the door.

"Come in," Holton called.

A middle-aged woman in a nurse's uniform opened the door. "Don, you need to see me?"

"Jean," said Holton, respectfully standing. "Please come in and shut the door. These gentlemen are with the G.B.I. Take a look at these sketches, see if there's anyone who looks familiar."

She furrowed her brows, suspicious of the circumstances. Holton handed them to her. She carefully leafed through each portrait, minutely nodding. "They look like pictures of former patients: Moses Beal, Shirley Martin, Judy Gilmore, Rosa Richey, and Taylor Duckworth."

"They were found buried in a shallow grave a few days ago in a field in Adams County," said Holton.

"Impossible. I'm sure each one died here. There's no way something like that could've happened," she insisted.

"Would you please pull their files," Holton softly asked. "Maybe there's something in there we should know about. And Jean... keep this quiet."

"What are the normal procedures when someone dies here?" Cole asked, after the nurse had left.

"Well, we have a doctor on call, as well as Jean, our head nurse, who's an RN. An LPN is on duty for each shift and qualified attendants do most of the work. When a patient passes away, the physician is immediately notified. He examines the patient and formally pronounces him or her dead. In cases such as these, death was not unexpected. Taylor, I believe, had sclerosis of the liver. He was jaundiced and eventually died. After the patient expires, the family is notified so arrangements can be made for the body. However, in these cases I don't believe any of them had family."

"No family?" repeated Cole. "How were their burials handled?"

"We have a contract through the county with Crawford Funeral Home. They're called and the body is disposed of according to state and county laws. Unless there is a religious objection, the body is cremated and buried in a county plot. If the deceased had a religious affiliation we'll contact a local minister to handle a burial service."

Jean rapped on the door and returned with the files. She walked behind Holton's desk and set the files in front of him. "I scanned through them briefly and didn't see anything unusual. In each case they had no next of kin and their only means of support and care was Social Security, Medicare and Medicaid. Oh yeah, there was one other interesting item. They all allowed one of the nurses, who worked here, to handle their financial affairs."

"Oh really," said Cole, raising his eyebrows. "And who was that?"

"Chris Spadalin."

"Is she working here now?"

"Chris is a he. No, he left about six weeks ago to work at the Medical Center in Macon."

"Why would they do that?"

"Chris was a great guy. Everyone around here liked him. He was very competent and caring for the patients."

"Would you hire him back?"

"In a second if I could," replied Jean. "He got a better offer in Macon, and well... he was single and there wasn't much in the way of a social life around here for him."

"In what ways would Chris handle their financial affairs?"

"Nothing major. He could cash their checks, maintain their checking accounts, pay their bills, and file their tax returns. I think he also handled their burial."

"May I take a look at one of the files?" asked Cole, extending his hand.

"Sure," said Holton, handing him Beal's.

"I know what you're thinking," Jean said to Cole. "If I didn't personally know Chris I might have suspected something myself. But as far as I know, Chris handled all their affairs honestly. He was like a son to each one of them, always bringing them desserts and a gift on their birthday and Christmas. Besides, they didn't have any money to be cheated out of."

Cole slowly turned the pages of the file. "Should there be a copy of the death certificate in here?"

"Should be," said Holton. "You can't find it?"

"No," said Cole, handing the file to Holton and Jean.

They leafed through the pages in the file. Holton picked up another file and examined it, flipping through the pages. Then the third, the fourth, and the fifth. He turned to Jean, eyes wide in concern. "There's not a copy of the death certificate in any of these files."

"How are death certificates normally handled?"

"We have blank certificates provided to us by the county. The administrative office fills them out and forwards them to the physician who verifies the accuracy, signs them, and forwards them to the Health Department."

"So they should be on file with the Health Department?"

"Yes, sir."

"Why would anyone want to withhold a death certificate?"

"Chris would have a reason," Jean answered with the pained tone of certain betrayal. "Once the certificates are received by the county, the state is notified. Also HHS is notified so that Medicare and Social Security payments are discontinued. If they aren't notified, the checks would keep coming to Chris and since he has power of attorney he can legally cash the checks."

"Let me call the Health Department to see if they were filed," volunteered Joe. He dialed a memorized number and spoke quietly to a familiar person, giving her the names of the deceased. In a few minutes he had the answer. "No Certificates of Death have been filed at the Health Department," he announced solemnly.

"Oh no," sighed Jean. "I would have never thought...."

"Assuming Chris was involved, Mr. Holton, how would he have gotten access to the certificates? Does he complete them?"

"No, but we're a trusting group around here. Let me call Administration. Doesn't Kelly normally handle those?" Holton asked Jean.

"Yes, sir."

He dialed the extension to Administration. "Kelly? Don Holton. You normally handle the death certificates, right? Got a question for you. Do you remember completing the certificates for Moses Beal, Shirley Martin, Taylor Duckworth, Judy Gilmore, and Rosa Richey? Did you send the certificate to Dr. Winston? Excuse me? Are you sure? Okay, thank you." Holton carefully cradled the phone. "According to Kelly, in each case, Chris came to the office after they'd died and told her since he was the administrator of their estate, he'd handle the burial, the death certificates and such. He said he wanted to personally handle it because he felt a sense of responsibility for them."

"If Spadalin is still collecting checks, how much Social Security do you think he's receiving?"

"They probably each averaged around eight hundred dollars a month. For five people, he would be collecting four thousand dollars a month, tax free. Not a bad stipend."

"Impressive," whistled Cole. "But I have another question. If Chris was involved in this, how would he have known about the Brewster property?"

Holton rubbed his eyes. "I began running this home about four years ago. As a way to promote a team concept we had some parties at various locations, such as at the country club and at my house. Because I like to hunt and fish, I invited some of the employees on some trips with me. I invited Chris on a deer hunt on the Brewster property a couple of years ago. Told him it was a great site. That the game wardens never showed and that it was pretty much an abandoned area." He lowered his head in shame. "God, I'm so sorry. I never knew."

"What about the bodies? You said you had a contract with Crawford?" asked Cole.

"Yes sir. Sometimes someone with them would come in the hearse and retrieve the body. Other times if they weren't available, Dennyson's, an ambulatory service, would handle the call."

"Would that be reflected in the files?"

"Should be," said Holton, as he and Jean began examine the files. They compared the files and handed them to Cole. Holton shook his head in a mixture of disgust and suppressed anger as each of Cole's questions tended to confirm their suspicions. "As you can see, there was a receipt of the bodies. In each case it was accepted by Dennyson's for delivery to Crawford. And in each case it was signed for by Charlie Jarette."

"It seems like the same people are involved in the same ways," noted Cole.

"But why would Spadalin bury the bodies?" I asked. "Why not go ahead, send them to Crawford, and let them bury the bodies appropriately? Why does he have to dispose of the bodies in a field?"

Holton answered my question. "Because Crawford would require a copy of the death certificates signed by the doctor before they would bury them. If Spadalin gave the doctor the certificates to sign, then he'd forward the certificates to the Health Department—and the checks would cease coming."

"Can you provide us these files so we can positively identify the bodies? And Jean, you may be needed for identification."

She nodded solemnly.

"Could you get me an address for Dennyson's? And we'd like to review Spadalin's file and his current address, if you have it."

"I'm sorry. I know there's not a current address for Spadalin in our files except for the hospital. He told me that he would be staying temporarily at a friend's apartment and once he was settled, he would provide a forwarding address, but...."

"He hasn't yet," said Cole, completing the statement.

"Bingo," she replied through clenched teeth.

We examined Spadalin's file. There was nothing unusual in it, but we did obtain his identification data which included his Social Security number, date of birth, and next of kin. They were also nice enough to allow us to borrow an employee photo of him that was in the file. We thanked them for their courtesy and requested that they keep the interview confidential. Once we were in the car I asked, "What do you think?"

Cole reached into his bag of Red Man and grabbed a pinch of moist leaves. "I think lil' Chris decided that there was more in the nursing business than just nursing. Suck up to a bunch of lonely abandoned geriatrics, give them gifts, time, and a helping hand, and lure them into giving you the power of attorney. I think it was a worthwhile investment. Once they're dead, you're collecting a substantial salary for doing squat. This guy's making between forty-eight and sixty thousand a year simply collecting and cashing their checks. If the bodies hadn't been found, he could have carried out this little scam for decades."

"What do we do now?" I asked. "Go see Charlie Jarette?"

"I'm tempted," said Cole with an evil smile. "But we can always squeeze him. After all, we got him receiving the bodies. All we have to do is check with Crawford and see if they received them. If not, what is he gonna say? My bet is that Chris slipped Charlie some bucks and took the bodies. Knowing about the hunting preserve, he drove over to Adams County and buried them. For now, let's go back to the office. I've got a contact with the Inspector General's Office at HHS. I'll give him the Socials and he can tell me if the checks are still being sent to Spadalin, to what address, if they were cashed, and by whom."

. . .

The office at the First Methodist Church of Connally could have with-
stood the inspection of a Marine Drill Instructor — it was meticulously
cleaned, dusted, and vacuumed, with every bulletin, notice, manual,
pamphlet and paper in its proper place. It was obvious Opal Lockhart
ran a tight ship. And because she was so organized there was no reason
to include another worker into her bailiwick. Miss Lockhart, and she
definitely was a Miss, greeted me with a restrained smile when I entered
the church's office.

"Good afternoon. May I help you?" she asked rising from her desk.

I wasn't sure she recognized me from my previous visit with the
Reverend. "Yes, ma'am, I'm Hank Monroe, G.B.I. I was here a few days
ago to speak with the Reverend."

"Oh yes, of course," she replied. "I'm sorry, but the Reverend isn't in.
Did you have an appointment?"

"No ma'am. Matter of fact, I was hoping to speak to you."

"Me?" she said, arching her eyebrows. "What about?"

"Lydia Carson."

"Sorry, Mr. Monroe," she said, setting aside some church bulletins. "I
didn't know Lydia very well and, besides, I've made it a hard and fast rule
not to discuss members."

"That's not a bad rule. I can understand. Discretion is very important
in your job."

"Then if you'll excuse me," she said in an apparent dismissal.

"I'm sure you won't mind if I go in to the Reverend's office and look
around?"

"I most certainly would," she replied, startled I would ask the question.

"Well, what are you going to do? Tell the Reverend or the police? As
you said, you make it a rule not to discuss members. I believe I'd fall
under that category."

"Sir, you are not a member. Please leave now!" she insisted.

"You would discuss it because I'd be breaking the law. And since
Lydia's dead—"

"You don't know that! I've heard the rumors you've been spreading.
But I don't believe it."

"You've been gossiping, Miss Lockhart? Not very becoming, nor very Christian."

"And you've been slandering. Not very professional."

"Miss Lockhart, please listen to me. If I'm wrong, I look foolish. If you're wrong, you may have allowed a murderer to escape."

Opal bit her lower lip. "I don't know...."

"Please, Miss Lockhart," I pleaded. "It'll be confidential if you prefer. But I have to know about her. She was a special member of your church. She needs your help. Don't abandon her."

She exhaled a surrendering breath. "What do you wish to know?" she said sitting behind her desk.

"Do you know her well?"

"No, not at all. Lydia, as you already probably know, was a private person. I had some dealings with her in church functions but it was strictly business. She rarely smiled and I don't recall ever seeing her laugh."

"Would you describe her as intense?"

"Generally, like around town when I saw her. But here, at the church, it was as if she was in a safe haven. She seemed more relaxed."

"Did she have any friends that you know of?"

"The only one I knew of was Jenny Tisdale. And..." she hesitated, "I heard that she was friends with our janitor, Albert Miner. The word was they were playing checkers, but I wonder if that was all that they were playing. I don't approve of such things."

"Was she open with Reverend Pheim?"

"What do you mean by that?"

"Did she ever seek his counsel, his advice?"

"Yeah, they talked sometimes... about different functions she was involved in."

"Did she ever seek his advice of a personal nature?"

"Why don't you ask the Reverend that question?"

"Because he's not here. A month before she disappeared did she make an appointment with Reverend Pheim?"

"What does this have to do with a criminal investigation?"

"Because whatever was troubling her might've been a reason for her death. Please, check your schedule. Did she have an appointment a month before her disappearance?"

Miss Lockhart stiffened. "I'm sorry, I can't tell you."

"Or you won't tell me."

"Phrase it any way you wish."

"That's okay, Miss Lockhart. The fact that you won't say, tells me she did have an appointment. Have a good day," I said leaving.

"I told you nothing. Keep up your slander, but I told you nothing!" she shouted as I shut the door.

. . .

I returned to the office to find Cole inundated with paperwork from the previous days' investigations. I slumped down in an office chair next to his desk.

"Did you get in touch with the HHS fellow?" I asked.

He nodded. "Yep. He's running down the information now. Should have it back by tomorrow morning. If it's positive, he might get involved in this. When you think about it, the only state crime Spadalin's committed is the concealment of a death. He'll never get any state time. At the most he'd get a few months in a county facility washing the Sheriff's cars. And if he pleads guilty in Federal court, he'll probably get probation and have to pay restitution."

"Have you told Cobb?"

"Just did. While we were talking, the Crime Lab called with the official results of the autopsy."

"And?"

"All natural. That's why I know all we've got is concealment of death. Cobb's going to let the others finish their interviews just on the off chance someone comes up with something more promising. We'll hold off on our other leads 'til we follow this lead out. Oh yeah, he's also going to hold off on sending leads out of state."

"What's next, then?"

"We'll get the mailing address from HHS and confirmation of payment, then pay the boy a visit."

"Any criminal history?"

"He's clean. Nothing on record. So catch up on your paper and go home at a decent hour."

"Are the Braves playing tonight?" I asked. Then I remembered. "Oh man! I've got a date tonight."

. . .

The party was scheduled for tonight for only one reason: the Braves were playing, and were off on Friday preparing for a road trip. I was to bring the hamburger meat and the buns, Roy and Donny were in charge of the drinks, Mitch would make his infamous jalapeño highway salsa and provide the chips, Joe was cooking up his baked beans, and Jason would bring the coleslaw. Megan and I agreed to double with Katie and Roy, so if Roy got blitzed, he'd have a driver.

I called Megan as soon as I got back to my apartment. "Hey, Megan." I wanted to add "honey" or "sweetheart" but I couldn't form the words and make that verbal commitment of affection. There was still this impenetrable emotional barrier that wouldn't allow me to voice that endearment. I could tell her that she was pretty, cute, and I enjoyed her company, but I couldn't tell her that I cared. "You haven't forgotten about tonight?"

"No, not at all," she said relieved. "I was afraid you might have to work late."

"And miss an evening with you? Never!"

"You're such a liar, but it's nice to hear. Roy's coming over to Katie's and we'll all go over together. We'll just walk over to your place."

"No, I'll pick you up. That's the proper thing to do. And I am a proper kind of guy," I said with a swagger in my voice. "We'll all meet at your apartment."

We arrived at the party as Skip Caray was announcing the line-up. "Ahoy, it's Roy!" the group chorused. "Hide your pets and uncooked meats!" Some of the group were at the television while others were at the dining room table with the snacks.

"What do they mean?" Katie asked.

"Ignore the cretins," warned Roy. "Greatness is never appreciated in its time."

I carted the meat to the kitchen.

Mitch came through the back door. "Great. Glad you're here. Started the coals five minutes ago. Megan, would you check on the number of burgers everyone wants?"

"And if they want cheese on them," I added, washing my hands.

"Sure," she said, heading for the living room.

"Here you go," said Roy, opening a bottle of beer for me as I patted out the meat.

Mitch assisted me as I cooked the hamburgers. Megan and Mitch's date, Joanne, joined us at the picnic table. Breathing deeply the mixed scent of pine trees and hickory smoke, we relaxed on the patio comfortable in our conversation, not needing to impress or entertain. The women, as if drawn by a maternal urge or frustrated with our culinary inefficiency, insisted on preparing the table.

We feasted on baked beans, potato salad, chips, coleslaw, and burgers piled high with cheese, tomatoes, lettuce, and onions. We joked, laughed, and took no one seriously. Joe brought out his portable stereo, turned to an oldies FM station, and as the sun set, we listened to The Four Tops, Gary Lewis and the Playboys, Sam and Dave, and the Temptations.

"Uoo, now that's a tune," swooned Megan, when she heard the lead-in to "You've Lost That Lovin' Feelin'" by the Righteous Brothers.

"You want to dance?" I asked, extending my hand.

Megan, caught off guard, glanced around, unsure.

"Come on," I said, tilting my head to an open area on the patio.

She grinned broadly and took my hand.

"Whooaa!" the crowd hooted when they saw us embrace.

"Careful, Megan," warned Jason hoisting a beer. "When a man's willing to take a woman to the dance floor, he's got serious late night plans."

"Jealousy," I said, my face inches from hers. "They don't have the guts to get up here."

"And make a fool of yourself?"

"Maybe... but you're worth it," I replied, pulling her close.

Megan took a deep peaceful breath. "I love this song."

"Why do women get all gooey when this song's played?"

"Romance and feeling. Something you Neanderthals don't understand."

"Well, maybe you can teach this Neanderthal something."

"It'd be a labor of love," she said, drawing near to me.

"See what we've started?" I said, pointing to the others. Bolstered by drink and the insistence of their dates, the Expatriates reluctantly joined us in the dance.

"Thanks, Hank. I could be watching the Braves now," growled Jason as he joined the dance.

But the dancing didn't stop with one song, as the tune was quickly followed by the Rolling Stones' "Satisfaction." And the Braves game was soon forgotten in the cool breezes of the evening as we shagged to the music of the Tams, Jay and the Americans, the Supremes, the Beach Boys and countless others who provided music that was simple, yet timeless. The fireflies flew just outside our ring of light and seemed to keep time with the music. I danced awkwardly with Megan during the fast songs, thankful that the others were too stewed to notice my gyrations. But it was during the slow dances when we swayed in each other's arms, our fingers intertwined, our bodies molded together and moving as one, that I felt the closest to Megan. I nuzzled in the nape of her neck smelling her light perfume, feeling the softness of her powdered skin. She pressed close to me, straddling my leg as we danced. The memories of the evening blended into an emotional kaleidoscope of foods, friends, fun... and Megan.

It was near the end of the evening. We were dancing to "Hold Me, Thrill Me, Kiss Me," one of my favorite songs. Whether it was the time of the day, the stress of the week, or the beers, I don't know, but as we danced, I tilted her head up to kiss her and looked in the face of... Lydia. I was looking at her brown searching eyes, dark eyebrows, and clear alabaster skin. Megan's lips were parted to accept my kiss, but I drew back, startled.

"Are you okay?" Megan asked.

"Sure," I replied, trying to recover my composure. I kissed her softly and again drew her close to me. I closed my eyes and held her tightly, feeling her warmth... then finished my dance with *Lydia*.

CHAPTER SEVENTEEN

FRIDAY. I had four days remaining.

Cole was already at the office when I arrived, reading the sports section of the *Atlanta Constitution* and nursing a cup of coffee.

"Have you heard anything from your IG buddy?" I asked, slumping down at my desk.

He shook his head. "No. We won't be hearing from him 'til at least nine o'clock."

Cobb walked into the squad area. "Morning, gentlemen. Heard anything?"

"Should hear something in about thirty minutes," said Cole.

"I've got the media clamoring about the bodies. I've been able to put them off, telling them that we haven't anything conclusive and that we're conducting a routine investigation."

"Have they asked you about the causes of death?"

"Yeah. I told them that I wasn't going to comment on the causes 'til I received the lab report."

Confused, I asked, "Didn't you tell us that the lab called and—"

"That's right... the lab called. I haven't received the report. But I'm going to have to tell them something. If it's not that Spadalin fellow, then

I'm going to have to disappoint them with the natural cause verdict."

"We'll know something by the end of the day," Cole said reassuringly.

"Good. I've assigned Robin the task of positively identifying the bodies. She's armed with a subpoena and pulling the files of the suspected John and Jane Does at Quail Roost. Also Holton's been nice enough to supply a nurse who knew all five of the victims. Robin's going to take her up to Atlanta today and hopefully get a positive I.D. on the bodies."

"Tell Robin, 'Thanks.'"

"Young Hank, how's the Carson case going?"

I shrugged. "Haven't had much time to work on it."

He smiled and departed with a wave. "Well, it's good to know you aren't bored."

I grabbed a tape recorder and began to dictate the numerous investigative summaries from the previous days of interviews. I was on my third summary when Cole's phone rang.

He snatched it before the second ring. "Hey buddy, how's it going.... Good..... Great." Cole wrote on his pad. "Uh-uh.... Yep.... Sure, I should be able to let you know this afternoon.... I don't see a problem getting you a copy of our report.... Well, let's see what he says first. Can you fax me a copy of the checks? Okay, that'll be fine. It'd be nice if I could show him a copy of the checks, but we can make do.... Let me give you my fax number. Okay, thanks for your help. Good-bye."

Hanging up, Cole tore the paper from the pad. "Mr. Spadalin, as of last month, is receiving five Social Security checks in the names of our recipients for a total of $4,228.81 per month. All five checks were endorsed by Spadalin and deposited into his account at Nationsbank in Macon. He gave me a breakdown of monthly payments to each person and he's going to get me the total dollar value of fraud based on the date of each person's death. Hank, I think we'd better go pay Mr. Spadalin a visit."

· · ·

The Medical Center of Central Georgia, situated in the historical section of Macon, was an imposing monolith built of brick and concrete with a splash of glass and contrasting bricks and pipes. Cole chose to forgo the parking garage and parked near the entrance on Hemlock Street, placing his blue light on the dashboard.

"Hemlock. That's a poison. I believe Socrates committed suicide by drinking it," I commented.

"Really? That would give me a lot of confidence, knowing I was about to receive treatment at a hospital located on a street named after a poison."

We entered the hospital through the main door. I noticed that valet parking was available. I pointed out the sign to Cole.

"Nice touch," he said. "I wonder if they have a concierge."

The lobby was smaller than I expected, but stylishly appointed with plush carpet and cracked marble on the wall behind the reception desk. I fell a half step behind Cole and followed his lead. Cole approached the receptionist.

"Good morning," he said with a cheerful smile, "Could you point me toward the personnel director's office?"

"Certainly," she said with a soft raspy voice. "It's on the main floor. Go down this hall to your left and follow the signs."

Like a couple of rats in a mauve painted maze, we weaved through the corridors until we found the office.

The secretary greeted us immediately as we entered the office. "May I help you?"

Cole displayed his badge and took on an official air. "Ma'am, we're with the G.B.I. We'd like to see the Director of Personnel."

"Just a moment," she said, her eyes expanding in concern. She dialed a four-digit number and spoke softly. "Mr. Robinette? I have two gentlemen here with the F.B.I. "

"No. G.B.I. Georgia Bureau of Investigation," Cole corrected.

"Excuse me, G.B.I.," she nervously repeated. Pause. "Yes sir, they've shown their identification. Yes sir." She cradled the receiver. "He'll be with you in a minute. You may be seated," she said, gesturing toward a row of chairs.

"He's probably calling the hospital administrator trying to find out if the hospital's been padding the Medicaid bills," whispered Cole as we sat down.

I was perusing an outdated *People Magazine* when I heard, "Gentlemen, I'm Jules Robinette. How may I help you?"

Robinette was a middle-aged fellow with a generous gut and the harried, exasperated look so often seen in managers who've been worn down by the politics, regulations, policies and infighting of a cumbersome bureaucracy. He wore a drooping mustache and his hair was combed as if to cover a receding hairline. This combination emphasized his apparent desperation. The fact that two state agents were now at his office door had to be a harbinger of a miserable day.

"Good morning, Mr. Robinette. I'm Johnny Cole and this is Hank Monroe," he said, presenting his credentials. "Could we speak to you privately?"

"Sure. Come on." We followed him to a meticulous office. "Have a seat," he said, directing us to a couple of chairs across from his desk. "Now, what can I do for the G.B.I.?"

I wondered what tack Cole would take in approaching Robinette. He could low-key his approach, saying he simply needed to interview an employee of his and hope Robinette would pull him for an interview, or he could mention that Spadalin was somehow involved in the death of five people and hope the pressure would force Robinette to cooperate. He chose the latter.

"We need to talk to an employee of yours, a Chris Spadalin. I understand he was recently hired by your hospital?" Cole said in an almost soothing approach.

"Spadalin? Oh, yes. I didn't hire him. One of my assistants did. Came highly recommended as I recall. Is there a problem?"

"I don't know if you've heard about it, but there were five bodies discovered earlier this week—"

"And he was the serial killer?" Robinette asked, eyes wide in alarm. Cole had subtlety introduced a new concern to manager. If Robinette wasn't cooperative and it was later learned that Spadalin was a serial killer, imagine the backlash on the hospital. Cole was approaching Robinette, not based on the goals and concerns of the State of Georgia, but on the goals and concerns of Robinette.

"We don't think he was involved in their death, but we think he might have been involved in the disposal of the bodies," Cole replied casually. It was masterful. In just as few short sentences Cole had Robinette's complete and fearful cooperation. Cole had been truthful, playing on Robinette's assumption that the deaths were by a serial killer. Robinette was willing to help Cole anyway possible, not because of any civic duty, not because five bodies were found, and not because his help could lead to the solution of five deaths, but because of a standard bureaucratic dread of being second-guessed. This was not a good morning for Jules Robinette.

Robinette leaned back in his chair. "Whatever you need, we're willing to help."

"We'd like to speak to Spadalin, but before we do, we'd like to take a look at his personnel file."

"Of course!" was the immediate reply. Robinette grabbed the telephone and ordered the file.

Within two minutes the file was before us.

The file revealed nothing new except that Spadalin was working in the respiratory section of the hospital.

"Do you have an area where we can interview him?" asked Cole.

"Certainly. One of my assistants called in sick today. You can use her office if you'd like. It's right down the hall," Robinette said. "I checked and Spadalin is on duty today. I'll call Security and have him escorted over here."

"No. I'd rather not alert him. If you'd simply have him come down, we should be able to catch him off guard," Cole recommended. "If you have Security get him, he'll know something's wrong."

Robinette nodded in agreement. "That makes sense. I'll call the nurse's station." He dialed the phone and spoke briefly to someone. "He's on his way down. I told the nurse it was a personnel matter. Now, let me show you the office."

He led us down the hall to a smaller office, with ample room and three chairs for the interview. The room was neat, decorated with statuettes, pictures, and assorted bric-a-brac. "I hope you find this acceptable."

"It's fine," said Cole.

"Do you want to meet him in the reception area?" Robinette asked.

"Hank, why don't you greet him and bring him back here?"

I nodded.

"Oh, by the way... are y'all planning on arresting him... here...

today?" asked Robinette hesitantly.

"No, sir. We just want to talk to him. But if we learn something that might have bearing on his employment, we'll let you know," assured Cole.

Robinette's secretary knocked on the door. "Mr. Robinette. Mr. Spadalin's here."

"Hank," said Cole, stopping me before I followed Robinette. "I'll sit here behind the desk and you sit over there. I'll ask the questions and take the notes. I don't think we'll have any trouble with him, but if he disposed of five bodies he might be a little wacko. So make sure you keep an eye on him."

I held a thumb up. "Sure. Let me go get him."

Robinette led the way to the reception area. Spadalin was sitting in a chair calmly reading a magazine. Though I had read his personnel file and seen his picture, he was smaller than I expected, with a lean compact build. His brown hair was short and combed forward. He wore wire-rimmed glasses and a neatly trimmed beard. Dressed in the standard hospital scrubs, he noticed us approach him and stood up.

"Mr. Spadalin, this is Hank Monroe. He's an agent with the G.B.I.," introduced Robinette. "He'd like to talk to you and I gave him permission to do so." I shook his hand. It was dry and I felt the fine grit of talcum powder, presumably from the latex gloves the nurses often wore.

"Is there a problem?" he asked, frowning with concern. His movements were steadied and direct and his voice was precise and confident. I noticed the natural anxiety but no fear that he was about to be interrogated by agents.

"No, we just wanted to ask you a few questions about when you were employed at Quail Roost," I replied, trying to make the interview sound routine. "Please, come with me."

I led him to Cole who stood up when we entered with an engaging smile. "Mr. Spadalin, I'm Johnny Cole." Johnny presented his badge. "Please have a seat."

I sat to the right of Spadalin, studying his body language and spotting nothing unusual. Johnny leaned back in his chair in a relaxed pose and laced his fingers below his chin. "I don't know if Agent Monroe mentioned why we asked to speak to you, but you might have some information that could help us on a case." Cole was approaching Spadalin in an indirect method, not immediately confronting him with our suspicions. He would solicit his cooperation, giving Spadalin the impression that he was helping the authorities. "I understand that you used to work for Quail Roost Nursing Home. Is that correct?"

"Yeah," replied Spadalin, obviously knowing we knew the answer. "I quit a couple of months ago."

"Why?"

"Come on, look around. The opportunities and pay here are much better. Plus Macon has a little more social life than Thomaston."

"Chris, I don't know if you heard about it, but earlier this week we recovered five bodies over in Adams County. They were found on a tract of land called the Brewster Hunt Club." Cole slid the sketches across the desk to him. "Do any of these people look familiar to you?"

Spadalin studied each of the renderings then handed them back to Cole. He leaned back in his chair and crossed in legs. "Of course they do. And you know that I know them. No doubt you've been to the Roost and they've identified each of these people. And from there you tracked me here."

Cole maintained his composure. "What was your relationship with them?"

"I was their friend."

"Nothing more?" Cole pressed.

Spadalin gave Cole a puzzled look. "No."

"Didn't you have power of attorney in their business and financial affairs?"

"Yeah, but it was to help them out. Listen, those poor people had nobody to help them. Sure, I had power of attorney, but they had no money. I paid their taxes and took care of their personal affairs. I suppose you know they had no relatives, no one to help them. In a way they were like orphans. Most people think of orphans as children who have no parents to help them grow up. These were people who had no children to help them grow old. They needed me."

"And you knew when they'd died?" If Spadalin knew they were dead, he had no reason to cash their checks. It would be his duty to return the checks to the government.

"I'm not sure."

"What do you mean?" insisted Cole. "If you were their protector, you knew when they died."

"Possibly," he replied coyly. "But I'm not sure if I was present when each one of them died."

"Really? Then why did you sign off as the attending nurse on each of their records?"

Spadalin sat back in his chair. "Why don't we cut the B.S. Every question you've asked me you already know the answer."

This guy was clever. He was attempting to control the tempo and direction of the interview.

"I'm trying to find out how honest you are."

"And?"

"I think there's room for improvement," countered Cole. "You buried those people, didn't you?"

I was surprised at Cole's directness. Maybe he was trying to upset Spadalin.

"Yeah. But that's not why you're here. You've already interviewed Jarette and you know I kept the bodies."

"Why?"

"You think you know the answer to that one too, don't you?" he replied with a smirk.

"Humor me. Why?"

"Come on, Mr. Coleman."

"Cole."

"I needed their checks," he answered bluntly.

"What did you do with the money? Spend it on drugs?"

Spadalin gave him an unrepentant stare. "Yeah. I spent the money on drugs." He looked up at the ceiling in thought. "I assume there're no more checks coming?"

Cole nodded sympathetically.

"Then am I to be arrested?" he asked formally.

"Not now. The only state laws you've broken are the concealment of a death. The violation's a misdemeanor. And with your cooperation and clean record you'll probably get probation with restitution from the Feds."

"That's too bad."

The curious reply alerted me. Then, in one fluid motion he reached into his pocket and came out with a syringe containing a dark burgundy liquid, its needle glistening. He adroitly removed the protective plastic tip and stabbed across the desk at Cole. I couldn't believe what was happening. Where was the logic here? He had just learned he would only receive a state misdemeanor charge and now he was assaulting an agent. Cole recoiled from Spadalin's thrust, falling backwards in his chair. I leaped from my chair grabbing Spadalin's right wrist, carefully avoiding the needle. Spadalin, fighting my grip, shoved the plunger forward, spewing the serum at Cole. Just in time, I managed to shove his hand away from Cole as the plume of crimson arced harmlessly to Cole's right. Using my entire body as a lever, I twisted Spadalin's wrist and hand in a counter-clockwise motion. I heard the wrist snap and felt Spadalin's hand go limp. He screamed in pain and involuntarily dropped the syringe. I continued with the motion forcing Spadalin to the floor.

"You son of a bitch!" screamed Cole, rising over the desk with his pistol pointing at Spadalin. "I'm gonna blow your fucking head off!"

"No! I've got him Cole. Don't do it!" I insisted. Spadalin was cradling his right wrist and was now submissive. I rolled him face down on the floor and reached for my cuffs.

"I think my wrist's broke," he hissed through clenched teeth.

Robinette burst into the office, his face ashen in fright. "What's going—?" Then he saw me on top of Spadalin, cranking the cuffs around one of his wrists. "Oh my God!"

"Son of bitch tried to kill me!" Cole angrily explained.

"I'll call Security," said Robinette, quickly slamming the door.

I loosely placed the other cuff around the broken wrist that was now swelling. "You really screwed up, buddy," I chided as I rolled him into a sitting position. "With your clean record you probably wouldn't have gotten any time. Now you're looking at prison. What's wrong with you?"

He smiled at me contemptuously. "You idiots think you know it all, but you know nothing. I have AIDS." I reeled back, half expecting him to infect me with a bite or with his sweat. "I needed the money for the medication to stay alive. You asked me if I used it for drugs. Yeah, I did. Drugs like AZT, not marijuana or cocaine, but that's what you assumed. Cops always think the worst. I knew if I filed with my insurance, sooner or later, Quail Roost would've found out and I'd be fired. Yeah, I hid the bodies and tried to cover their deaths, but only to get the Social Security money I needed to buy my medication. If the government isn't willing to find a cure for this plague, I figured that they should at least subsidize my medication."

"Was that blood in the syringe?" I asked.

"Yeah, my blood. Infected with the virus," Spadalin replied with no remorse.

"Why did you do it?"

"When I read in the papers that you had discovered the bodies, I figured you'd be showing up here before long. And you'd probably learn about the checks. I had to have a way to get my medication and if the government wasn't going to pay for my medication through Medicaid, they would pay for it while I was in prison." He gave me a sinister stare with cold reptilian eyes. "You see, just by assaulting an agent, I've taken care of myself. I had nothing to lose."

Robinette returned with a couple of officers.

"He says he's got AIDS. And his wrist is probably broken," I warned the officers as they took him into custody.

Robinette shut his eyes in despair. "I've got to call the Administrator."

"Mr. Robinette, we have to seal this office and have a crime scene unit examine the office."

"I understand," Robinette agreed, and left to make his call.

Cole collapsed in the chair behind the desk and called Cobb. They spoke for nearly five minutes as Cole reported Spadalin's confession and assault. After he hung up the phone he expelled a long breath. "An agent will be coming from Perry to work the assault.". He shook his head. "You know Hank, something like this just ruins your whole friggin' day. I expected an interview, then the confrontation, then the confession, and end the meeting with a little touchy-feely, 'I'll help you out the best I can, Chris,' conclusion. That's the way it used to be, but not any longer. There's no remorse with this new crop of criminals. And what's scary... it's like what Spadalin said, they have nothing to lose, or so they truly believe. So they don't care what happens to them, as long as they hurt you."

· · ·

I blew a long breath as I unlocked the door to my home. Hey, I said home. Before it was an apartment, now I was thinking of the space as a home. Major Boyd greeted me with the usual entreats.

I was exhausted. It was after two a.m. I grabbed a beer from the refrigerator and took a long gulp from the bottle. It had been a productive day. I checked my answering machine. Roy had called. He needed company, and he sounded drunk. I wished I had been here for him. Hayley had called, reminding me of the party at the "backwater." And Megan had called. Though there was no message I knew she'd called. There were the two rings and the hang up. That was her style: no messages. I finished my beer. It was two-twenty, time for one more. Then the phone rang. It had to be Megan.... Please, I wanted to be with her tonight. I wanted the closeness.

"Hank?"

I instantly recognized the voice. "Hey, Celeste. What d'you want?"

She ignored my briskness and spoke in her reassuring mellow tone. "I was worried about you. Haven't heard from you in a while."

"I've been busy. Matter of fact, I just got home from my second case of the day."

"Bet you were involved in those bodies that were found in Adams County."

"Yeah, so if you don't mind...."

"Sure I understand. Have you had any luck in finding Lydia?"

"Nope, none at all. Like I said, haven't had much time. Plus the case will be closed on Monday."

"Monday!" she interrupted in dismay. "Why? Is something wrong?"

"Cobb said he got a call from the Director. Apparently I've offended some of the fine citizens of Connally. Cobb told me if I couldn't come up with any firm evidence of a crime, then he was closing the case."

"That's not right, Hank." I could detect desperation in her voice. "This is what I predicted, that they would try to stop your investigation. Don't you see, Hank, that's what's going on. You must be getting close, so you can't stop now," she pleaded.

"Celeste, I don't see where I have much choice. The order came from the Director."

"How do you know?"

"Know? Know what?"

"Who said that the order came from the Director? Cobb?"

"Yeah. We discussed it in his office."

"Was anyone else present?"

"No, we were alone."

"I warned you about Cobb, didn't I? They've gotten to him and he is shutting down the case, not the Director."

"Celeste, you're grasping."

"Think about it. You just said you've been busy on other cases. Did he assign you to those cases?"

"Sort of."

"Come on, Hank. Think about it and don't get involved in personalities. Cobb gives you a reasonable time to work the case. It appears he's being magnanimous and if the case is ever audited, the file will reflect he gave you enough time. In the meantime, however, he's keeping you busy so you can't solve the case."

"Well, what am I going do? You're the angel," I said half sarcastically and half frustrated. "You come up with an answer."

There was silence on the line while she considered a solution. "Tell me what you've learned, who you've interviewed and what they told you."

I told her about my interviews at the bank with Rick Brouder, Reed Norman and Nancy Griffin. The encounter with Alan Perkins. The employees at the church: Reverend Pheim, Mrs. Godwin, Albert Miner, and the obstinance of Opal Lockhart. And finally, the two remaining leads: the customer Larry Shepherd, and the Lydia's former teacher, Mr. Lymens. My briefing lasted twenty minutes. She listened intently, asking questions only to clarify.

"You are learning she was a wonderful, giving person," she noted when I finished. "You have to find her killer."

"Then tell me how," I demanded.

"First, I have a question. Why do you consider Shepherd and Lymens suspects more than anyone else around here?"

"They're possible boyfriends—"

"Who may have left the country with her. But she didn't leave the country, Hank."

I was about to argue my case but paused. "You're right. Judy Moon told me, 'Find out what she knows, then you'll find the killer.' Who would Lydia have confided in?"

"Reverend Pheim."

"Pheim? Why? I've talked to him and he didn't have much to say. Are you implying that the good minister was lying?" I asked skeptically.

"I'm asking you to look at what you have. You touched on it when you interviewed Ms. Lockhart. She wouldn't tell you if Lydia had an appointment with Pheim."

"I thought of that, but he told me that they often discussed various matters because she was active in church."

"He told you that in case you learned she had an appointment with him."

"So, what if she did? What's the big deal?"

"Hank, think about it. Even though she was active in church, she was not on a committee or a leader who would require a meeting. She was in the choir, Bible studies, and helped with charity work, but she wasn't in the position that would require a meeting."

"Celeste, you sound as if you knew her personally."

I caught her off guard. "Personally? No... no. As her angel, I know her now." Her flustered retort was too defensive to be genuine.

"Then what do you suggest? Go see the good Reverend?"

"I think so. She had a conference with him and sought his counsel. You've got to find out what was discussed."

"I don't think he'll tell me. He didn't tell me before; why should he talk to me now?"

"Because he honestly doesn't believe she's dead. You've got to convince him she's dead and he can help you find the killer."

She made sense—too much sense. She was quick to put the information I'd given her into a logical format with a certain feel for the people in this town.

"Who are you, Celeste? I find you very intriguing. For a mere angel you are very wise of this world. Are you certain you don't have a past, or maybe a present, in these parts?"

"You pry too much, Hank. Instead of considering the facts, you study the one who presents them. Hank, have I let you down or led you astray?"

"No," I conceded.

"Then let's find Lydia."

. . .

"Hey, did I wake you?"

"No, just got back from the club. Made fifty dollars off Davis tonight. He's a pretty decent gin player 'til he gets a few drinks in him, then he'll take stupid risks. What's up?"

"Just wanted to know if you were able to silence the pup."

"Of course. Made a few calls and he's been pulled off the case. It should be closed by now. Is he still nosing around?"

"No, not that I know of. I was... just thinking. You know, I've been concerned."

"Forget about it. It's history. Maybe not pleasant history, but it had to be done and now it's over."

"How were you able to take care of the pup?"

"Don't ask the question if you don't want to know the answer. Just like the girl, you're too concerned with the means. Just be satisfied with the results. The means with the girl and the means with the boy aren't your problem. The results have been achieved and that's all you need to know and should want to know. Right?"

"Yeah, I guess so."

"Listen, gotta go. I'll talk to you later."

CHAPTER EIGHTEEN

SATURDAY. I had three days remaining.

I awoke at eight, exhausted from the previous day, but anxious about the present. In the shower, I rehearsed my approach to Reverend Pheim. I was determined he would tell me the substance of their meeting.

The parsonage, located two blocks from the church, was a single story home with neatly trimmed hedges. At precisely nine, I knocked on the dark oak door. It was opened by a middle-aged lady with a genuine smile and bright blue eyes. She wore jeans and a navy blue cotton sweater.

"Mrs. Pheim?" I asked, standing back a respectful distance under the portico.

She slowly nodded, wondering who I was.

"Good morning, Ma'am. I'm Hank Monroe with the G.B.I. Is the Reverend available? I need to talk to him; it's kind of important. I hope I'm not interrupting anything?" I said with my best disarming smile.

"No... uh, no," she replied hoarsely, then turned away to sneeze. "Excuse me. I've this dreadful cold. All this pollen, you know. Uh, please... come in. I'll get him." She left me in the foyer and headed toward the rear of the house.

Pheim, dressed in casual clothes, greeted me. "Good morning, Agent Monroe. What brings you here?"

"I need to ask you a few more questions, if you don't mind?"

"Of course not. We can sit in the living room. May I get you some coffee? My cup's in the kitchen."

"No, thanks," I declined, and sat at the end of the sofa.

Pheim returned from the kitchen with a mug of coffee and sat across from me in a wingback chair. "Now what can I do for you?"

"First of all, Reverend, I want to thank you for your time. I understand Saturday mornings tend to be the restful times for preachers and I wouldn't have come here if it wasn't so urgent. As you know, I've been conducting a number of interviews around town and I've learned that prior to the disappearance of Lydia, she had a conference with you and sought your counsel on a matter." As I spoke, I scrupulously studied his facial expression hoping that my bluff would spark a reaction, and when I mentioned the meeting with Lydia with certainty and confidence, his eyes flickered then perceptively expanded. "I need you to tell me what the meeting was about."

Pheim remained silent, twirling the wedding ring on his finger. He was considering his options, what was to be said and how to phrase it. Then he sat back deep his chair. "I can't discuss the matter you, Agent Monroe," he said firmly, his eyes locked on mine. He was not going to relent.

"And why is that?"

"It's privileged," was the curt reply. "I will not discuss matters of discretion. My parishioners have to know that when they discuss concerns with me, I will not repeat them to others... including the authorities. I took an oath to uphold that trust."

"I understand, sir. But in this case, Lydia's dead."

"You don't know that. Others feel that maybe she left town."

"No, sir, she didn't just leave town. If you know Lydia like I do-."

"Like you do. That's rather presumptuous Agent Monroe. You never met the woman," he said, the cadence in his voice quickening.

"Reverend, I do know Lydia. Probably better than most. To me, she just wasn't one of the worker bees in this town. She was a loving, caring, and sensitive person. Unfortunately, she never received any of that in return. And she is dead. I'm certain of that."

"That's your opinion, Agent Monroe. Do you have any facts to support it?"

"Yes sir, I do. I was told by someone."

"And who might that be?"

I paused before answering, fearing I was going to be labeled a kook, but I was deplete of leads. If I didn't get the answer it was over. "An angel told me."

His jaw dropped. "Excuse me."

"An angel told me. According to her, she's with Lydia now." I could feel my face flush and I looked away from his jaundiced gaze.

He chortled. "Well, I have to admit that wasn't the answer I was expecting. Do you really expect me to believe that?"

"You don't believe in angels?"

"Yes... uh, yes... of course," he replied defensively, "but I wasn't aware they assisted in criminal investigations. If you don't mind me asking, how did she appear to you?"

"She spoke to me over the phone."

"She spoke to you over the phone," he repeated skeptically. "So you've never seen her, right?"

"No, sir." I knew where this conversation was leading. He was not going to tell me about the meeting, plus he would think I was loony. I leaned forward hoping to emphasize my point. "Sir, what if she is dead? Then you would not be violating a trust, true?"

"That's correct. But I'm not convinced she's dead. When you show me some proof, I'll discuss it with you, but not until then."

"Reverend, you've got me in a dilemma. What you tell me might lead me to the body, but you won't tell me 'til the body's recovered."

"I don't think you understand my position. I took an oath, a vow. It would be against the policies of the church if I violated that trust. I couldn't help you even if I wanted to... unless there's proof of her death. I'm bound by that vow."

A knot of anger rose from my gut. Pheim held the answer to Lydia's death and refused to cooperate. Had he been compromised by her killer? "You know I could subpoena you to testify before a Grand Jury?"

A wry smile grew across his face and he set his mug on a nearby table. "Nice try Agent Monroe. You must have been sleeping during your law class at the academy. My communications with Lydia are privileged. By Georgia law I can't be compelled to testify. So don't try to intimidate me. He stood up in dismissal. "I think you'd better leave. There is nothing more to discuss."

I paused at the front door. "One day, sir, I hope you will realize that today you made a grave error. Would you be violating an oath, a policy of the church? Possibly. But rules must be tempered with judgment. The right thing to do would be to tell me. The cowardly course is to hide behind your laws, your rules, your policies."

Pheim's jaw clenched. His lips formed to speak, and instead he held up a finger and forced a smile. "I'm glad you stopped by today, Agent Monroe. You have truly tested my Christian temperament. Please leave my house... and have a good day."

. . .

I maintained my composure until I entered the confines of my apartment. Today, it wasn't a home, it was an apartment. I removed my coat and loosened my tie.

"Good morning, sir," greeted the Major.

I grabbed the coat I had just draped across the chair and flung it at the bird. The force knocked the cage from its stand, falling to the floor with a metal clang, spilling water, bird seed and droppings all over the linoleum. The Major squawked and fluttered about the cage in confusion. I shook my head at my stupidity and replaced the cage on the stand.

"Sorry, fellow. It's not your fault. It's just that... " I searched for the words, "you're beginning to sound like everyone else in this town, cheery and completely insincere."

The floor was a mess. Bright move, Monroe. Now you've got to clean up this trash. Remember what Cole said, "Don't get involved in your cases. It'll ruin you." He was right. If the people in this town didn't care if one of theirs was dead, screw 'em! I opened a beer and chugged it, did the same with a second, and settled on my third. So what if it wasn't noon yet.

I cleaned the floor which needed mopping anyway, replaced the water and seed, and cleaned the cage. I checked my message machine. The first was from Megan and I was surprised she'd left a message. She had to go to the Columbus College library. Did I want to go along? We could have lunch and maybe take in a movie. The second message was from Roy. The Braves had an afternoon game and he was heading over at one to the Expatriates. I called Megan's place and didn't get an answer. I checked outside; her car was gone. Damn! This was turning into a rotten day. Maybe I should go watch the game. Then I remembered Hayley's invitation.

"Hello. McTimmons residence."

"Hello. May I speak to Hayley?"

"I'm sorry, she's not here." From the formality of the voice I could tell it was the housekeeper.

"I was hoping to speak to her. She invited me to her place at the backwater and she didn't give me her number out there. Could you provide it to me?"

"I'm sorry, sir. I'm not sure where she's at. If you'd leave a number I'll see if I can locate her and have her call you back."

I recognized the dodge, but understood her position. I gave her my number. If she didn't call I'd spend the afternoon with Roy and the Expatriates.

I slipped on a pair of jeans, a knit shirt and sneakers, then found some leftovers and mixed them with chili into a concoction that I wouldn't dare serve to a friend.

I was washing my dishes when the phone rang.

"Hank?" said the perky feminine voice. "This is Hayley. How you doing?"

"Great. I hope I wasn't intruding."

"Intruding? Of course not! When I saw you Wednesday I wasn't sure you thought my invitation was real. Thanks for calling and you're certainly welcome to come out here. We're just about to head out on the boat. Do you ski?"

"Not very well. It's been a while."

"Oh, you'll do fine. It's like riding a bike. Get your swim trunks or a pair of cut-off jeans and head on over here. Let me give you directions and the phone number, just in case you get lost."

I wrote down her phone number and instructions, silently cursing myself at my deprecating manner. I sounded like some bumpkin who had never been skiing, much less on a boat. I needed to sound more confident. Good lord, I'd been to Grenada and Panama. I had to reflect more sophistication.

The McTimmons' lake house was a rustic cedar-sided ranch nestled under beautiful evergreens and elms on the point of the lake. At the point was an L-shaped boat dock with a gazebo at the end. Five people lounged in the shadowed shelter. When I got out of my Jeep, one of them waved at me—it was Hayley. A cool pine-scented breeze blew across the lake rustling the leaves and branches as I walked down the slope to the dock.

"Come on down!" she hollered, and my heart quickened as she walked toward me. She was wearing frayed jean shorts, a faded green tee shirt and flip flops. She made the ensemble look perfect.

Come on, Monroe. Sophistication and composure, remember?

She flashed a warm smile and moved close to me. "Did you have any problems finding the place?"

"No, not at all. You give great directions," I answered, giving her a quick one-armed hug, with the hopes I wasn't being too bold.

"Ready to go skiing?"

"I'm ready to do anything if you're with me."

"Great," she said with a quick confirming nod. "Graham and the others are already out in the boat. I'll call them on the radio and have them pick us up. Can I get you something to drink? We've got some soft drinks and beer in the cooler down there. Come on."

She moved close to me while we strolled to the gazebo. I felt comfortable when I put my arm around her.

"You must have been busy. Didn't you say you were involved in those Adams County deaths?" she asked.

"I was involved in the investigation, not the deaths," I teased.

"Come on! You know what I mean," she said with a fake pout. My mind froze the endearing look, like a snapshot that I still remember in wistful moments. "Was it a serial killer?"

"No. In fact we got the guy, yesterday, and he didn't kill a single box of cereal," I deadpanned.

"I'm going to drown you if you continue with the corny jokes," she threatened, punching me lightly on the arm. "Seriously, did you really get the guy?"

I held up my arm as if to vow. "Yeah, we got him. I thought it'd be in the morning papers. I'd like to tell you more, but I'd better wait 'til it goes public."

"Deal," she said with a firm nod. "Let me call Graham and get him and the rest back here."

We arrived at the gazebo. "Mr. McTimmons. Mrs. McTimmons," I said, shaking his hand and nodding respectfully to her. "Thanks for having me out here. You've got a beautiful place."

"Thanks, Hank," Ross said. His hand swept toward another couple approximately the same age as Ross and Patty. "Have you met T.J. Budreau and his wife, Betty Sue?"

"No, sir. Don't believe I have. Nice to meet you."

"T.J. owns the Ford dealership here," Ross explained. "He never comes close to giving me a deal on a car, except back in the seventies, on those Pintos. Those were cars, Hank, not beans. And I think I'd have done better buying beans instead of that sorry excuse of a motorized vehicle."

"Oh, come on Ross. I've done a damn sight better for you than you've ever thought of passing me."

"Please!" insisted Hayley. "You two quarrel like you're kin. Daddy, could you call Graham and get him back to pick up Hank and me?"

Five minutes later a twenty-foot open bow boat sporting the sleek profile of a two hundred horse power Mercury outboard approached the dock. Graham sat on the top of the driver's seat. It looked as if his approach was too fast and I backed from the edge of the dock. At the right instant he turned the boat parallel to the dock and hit reverse. The vessel lightly scrubbed against the tires nailed to the side of the dock, the wake rocking the dock. Graham shot me an arrogant smirk, as if that was a standard berthing maneuver.

"Dammit, Graham!" yelled a lady in a one-piece bathing suit, a wide brim straw hat and sitting in the open bow of the boat, "I told you to quit those stunts." She grabbed a nearby ski jacket and threw it at him. He ducked behind the windshield. "You scared the dog shit out of me. Do that again and I'll whup your ass with one of your skis."

Hayley leaned closed to me. "That's my Aunt Lucy. She lives in Marietta. She was the baby in Dad's family and spoiled rotten. Thirty-eight and twice divorced. No man can handle her." I looked closer at this hellion. Maybe meanness suited her because she looked closer to twenty-eight instead of thirty-eight. Her features and physique resembled Hayley's, but the eyes were sterner, the hair shorter and darker, and the freckled skin coarser. "Oh, by the way, never call her 'Aunt. '"

"Any children?" I whispered.

"Not that I know of. I don't think any child would claim her."

"Don't listen to her!" Lucy ordered. She pointed a brightly painted fingernail at Hayley. "You warning him, aren't you?"

"No ma'am."

"Don't ma'am me. You should ma'am your elders and I ain't one of them yet."

Hayley was flustered. "I just wanted to introduce you to a friend of mine. Lucy Breedlove, Hank Monroe."

Lucy flashed me a wide genuine smile. "A pleasure to meet you." She turned to an older, middle-aged man behind her." And this is a friend I brought down from Atlanta, Ken Murtry. Ken, this is Hayley McTimmons and Hank... hell, something-er-other." We exchanged greetings. "Ken just moved here from Chicago. Wanted to know what it was like dating a southern belle. Hope he finds out one day." She extended a hand to me and I helped her from the boat. "Graham, wait here for me. Got to use the toilet. Ken, you need to go?"

"Uh... no," Ken said, obviously embarrassed.

"Suit yourself. Then grab me another beer, will you honey?"

I assisted Hayley into the boat and followed her.

Graham's wife, Linda, sat on one of the rear seats shaking her head. "She's not so bad once you get used to her bluster. She's really got a heart of gold."

"Or brass," suggested Graham.

I greeted Ken. "First time to this part of Georgia?"

"Yeah," he said enthusiastically. "It's beautiful country down here. I've already been in the lake and compared to Lake Michigan, it's like bath water. You're not from Georgia." He recognized my accent.

"No, Maryland."

He smiled. "I thought so."

"You work with Lucy?"

"Yeah, we're both in the insurance industry. She's an actuary. Very good actually."

"Alrighty mates, let's cast the lines. I've released my ballast," announced Lucy, walking down the dock.

Graham cranked the engines that gurgled with pent-up power. I tossed off the lines and he flawlessly guided the boat from the cove into the open waters.

Once we were out in the middle of the lake, Graham cut the engines. "Lucy and I have already gone. Who's next? Linda?"

She squinched her face. "I don't know. I'm not that good."

"Oh, come on," everyone urged. Lucy forced a ski jacket on her and I helped her cinch it.

"I'm always afraid I'll fall into a nest of water moccasins," Linda confessed, just before she jumped into the murky water.

"Just don't fall," encouraged Graham, "and you'll never have to worry about the snakes."

She bolted upright and Graham shoved her overboard.

"Graham! I'll kill you," Linda threatened.

Graham tossed her a pair of skis. "Come on, up first time. You can do it."

He went back to his seat and waited for her signal. Linda awkwardly put on the skis and grabbed the rope.

"Okay, stretch out the line," said Hayley. Graham nudged the throttle forward. The engine clunked into gear, the boat creeping forward until the line went taut. "The line's okay." Linda nervously nodded, indicating she was ready. "Okay, hit it!"

Graham shoved the throttle forward and the engine growled while the bow rose with the acceleration. Like a submarine ascending from the depths, Linda slowly rose from the lake, her skis wobbling until she found her balance. Her face was locked in determination until she leveled out in the protective wake of the boat, then she grinned proudly. We all held up our drinks in a salute to her. After a mile she decided to venture out into the open waters, leaning left. Going over the outer edge of the wake she nearly lost her balance and I held my breath. She jerked her rope over her head, was snatched to the right and somehow managed to maintain her balance. We cheered her again.

I looked over at Hayley. She was involved, as I was, with Linda, but she caught my eye and gave me a confident wink. There was a purity to the moment and I wanted to kiss her right there, but refrained so as not to embarrass her.

A bass boat passed in the opposite direction. Linda didn't notice its wake as it combined with surface chop on the lake. A swell surprised her and she overreacted, lifting the rope too high over her head. She fell backwards, tumbling into the water.

"She's down!" yelled Hayley. Graham turned the boat tightly toward Linda.

Linda's skis were floating beside her and as we puttered alongside her, she shoved them toward the boat. "That's it for me," she announced.

"Okay, who's next?" asked Lucy.

"Your turn," said Hayley, handing me a ski jacket.

"No, you go first. I need you to set the example," I said, returning the jacket.

"All right," she said with feigned reluctance. "But if I'm to set the example, I expect good things from you." In a smooth motion, she slipped her shirt over her head then took off her jeans, revealing a neon green bikini. I tried to appear nonchalant as she wrapped the jacket around her, but I was drawn to her raw beauty like a moth to a light. Lithely, she leaped over the side of the boat.

"Throw me the slalom," she ordered. Lucy found the ski and tossed it to her. The ski hit the water with a slap and flowed to her. While she slipped on the ski, Graham started the boat, creeping ahead so that the rope looped to her. She grabbed the rope and waited with the tip of the ski poking out of the water until the line tightened. She gave us a thumbs-up signal.

"She's ready, Graham," I said. "Hit it."

The boat roared to life. Hayley broke the surface of the water like a hooked marlin and immediately was in control of the ski and line. She leaned left, easily slicing the wake of the boat and dancing across the small waves. She turned right as if she was going to shoot across the wake but instead turned sharply left, digging the rear of her ski deep into the water. A plume of water arched twenty feet. She smiled, which I knew was directed to me, then turned right using the rope as a catapult and darted across the wake lifting briefly in the air. I could see the definition in her shoulder muscles as she worked the line deftly. When she was focused on a difficult maneuver she stuck her tongue in the side of her check, causing it to bulge a mite, and her hair flowed behind her like a horse's mane. She just didn't ski the waves, she attacked them and dominated them. The ski was one of her jumpers and the waves were the fences. As she pulled on the rope, I could imagine her working the reins; as she jumped the wake I could visualize her leaping a hedge. She was so... beautiful. Such a dull, simplistic word, but I couldn't conjure a better description without diluting her effect... and I was lucky to be here, a part of her world for an afternoon.

I awoke from my thoughts. Hayley was gesturing, running a finger horizontally across her throat.

"Cut the engine," Lucy ordered Graham. "She's had enough."

The high whine of the engine went bass and the bow dropped as the water's drag quickly slowed the vessel.

Using the rope, Hayley pulled herself to the boat. She accepted my extended hand and I pulled her into the boat. Droplets hung in her damp hair, around her ears and cheekbones, as if they were jewels and crystals.

"That was great! I'll be sore tomorrow," she predicted. "Okay, buddy boy. Your turn."

While buckling my jacket, I stole a glimpse at Hayley's long supple legs then looked away, trying to concentrate on my task, but like an alcoholic needing one more drink, I looked again. She reached for her shorts.

"Aw, leave 'em off," exhorted Lucy. "Hank's enjoying the scenery." I blushed. Had I been that obvious? Hayley ignored her aunt and slipped on the cut-offs. "Why can't the sexes be comfortable with their crotches?

Women think it's special and want to hide it; men think it's special and want to show it off."

Linda lowered her head in shame. "Hank, Lucy doesn't spell her name L-U-C-Y. It's spelled L-O-O-S-E-Y."

"Good one, Linda," Lucy replied. "Hank, you know why I enjoy coming down to Connally? To shake up these hypocritical tight asses. You see, they don't know how to deal with me. They can't buy me, I've got too much money; they can't intimidate me, I know too many of the powerful; they can't con me, I know who they really are, and they sure can't manipulate me because... I've never given in to their weakness. When I walk into Twin Creeks, the sphincters tighten so fast around there, you can feel the wind rush from the room. I don't paint on a happy face. 'Oh hieee. How are you?' Kissy, kissy. 'I've missed you soooo. You look so pretteeeee.' I make them uneasy because I'm quick to let them know who they truly are."

No one replied. Maybe it was the embarrassment for Lucy, maybe it was the awkwardness of the moment or... maybe it was the truth which, like a cancer, few wished to confront.

"Anyone for a beer?" asked Lucy, popping a can. She'd said her piece; it was time to move on.

I jumped into the cool refreshing water. "Two skis, please."

Hayley handed them down to me and I wrestled the things, trying to cram my feet into the rubber forms. Graham began the rituals, turning the boat so the rope glided along beside me like a water serpent. Remembering the routine from years before, I tucked my knees to my chest and leaned back so that the tips of the skis protruded like a pair of fins from the water. I grabbed the ski handle as it passed me and placed it between the skis. The slack line stiffened and I was slowly pulled through the water. The group watched me, waiting for my sign. I nodded and Hayley spoke to Graham.

The engine roared with a puff of gray exhaust and the water churned. My knees pressed against my chest as I cautiously sought my balance and slowly allowed the rope to pull me upright. I remained low, allowing my bent knees to act as shock absorbers and remained in the soft waters of the wake, until I felt confident enough to venture further.

Putting pressure on my right ski, I veered toward the outer edge of the wake, the wave rising a foot over the water. I topped the crest and lost my balance as I dropped to the undisturbed surface of the lake. I pulled on the rope and leaned left, trying to find my equilibrium. That caused me to ski back into the edge of the wake and my left ski went into the wave, peeled down into the water, and I went tumbling. So much for first impressions.

I came up spitting and saw the boat coursing a wide arc in my direction. One ski was still attached to me; the other was ten feet away. I was replacing the ski when the boat puttered next to me.

"Nice tumble," teased Hayley. "I'd give you a 9.3 on degree of difficulty, but only a 9 on artistic interpretation. You gonna give it another try?"

"Sure. I need to improve on my form," I said, paddling to the rope.

Grab the rope, tuck the knees, tips up, give the "go" sign and I was up. This time I weaved back and forth inside the wake until I felt I had the feel, then I headed for open water.I approached the edge with an attitude, no doubt that I would cross and conquer that pesky wave. I hit the wave solid and shot into the open waters. The boat crowd saluted me with cheers and beers. Confidently, I pressed my luck leaning right, extending as far to the right as I dared, the skis bouncing lightly over the waves.

Graham made a wide left turn and I held the course, my speed increasing, whipping along the outer circumference of the rope, popping over the waves. The crew cheered me on as the boat slung me around the turn. I bent my knees, which cushioned the waves, and sat back on the skis, clinging to the rope and to the hope that I could survive the whip. Gradually the boat straightened and the speed decreased. I steered back to the sanctity of the wake and rested. The muscles in my legs ached and began to tremble. I'd had enough, gave the cut sign, and let go of the rope. Better to go out a winner. The boat lowered its pitch and came around toward me.

"Had enough?" asked Lucy.

I nodded, exhausted, shedding the skis and shoving them at the boat.

We spent the remainder of the afternoon cruising along the verdant banks of the lake, enjoying the weather, the water, and the views. As we passed by the docks and the boats on the lake we were greeted by each individual with an welcoming wave and smile, not based on our station in life, but on the mere fact that we were God's creatures and thus worthy of courtesy. Occasionally one of us would ski, but most of us were spent and relaxed, enjoying the sun, the scenery, and the suds. Hayley leaned back into my chest and I gratefully accepted her, nuzzling her and smelling the saltiness on her skin. I couldn't imagine a hope, a fantasy, or a dream that could compete with the reality of the afternoon. Even Lucy settled into the arms of Ken, as we cruised along, breathing in the cooling breeze with the setting sun.

The sun hung like a large orange orb just over the tree line when we approached the dock. Lucy stroked a nearby ski and glared at Graham as he properly brought us next to the dock. Graham knew how to pick his battles, and Lucy was not among them. Ken and I jumped from the boat and tied off the lines, then helped the ladies from the craft.

Ross was up at the patio near the house. He was tending to a large stainless steel pot setting on a cast iron cooker. A propane burner was hissing under the pot.

"What's for supper?" I asked Hayley.

"Low country boil," she replied, snuggling next to me.

"What's that?"

"Why don't you go change and then take a look," she suggested.

With his hands covered in cooking mittens, Ross picked up the pot and poured, or more accurately, slung the contents of the stainless steel pot over a newspaper covered picnic table.

"Chow time!" he hollered.

I changed into a pair of jeans and a navy knit shirt, and walked out on the screen porch into the coolness of the evening as he made the announcement. A bug zapper cast its dull ultraviolet light in the outside corner of the house, electrocuting the persistent mosquito, gnat or moth that ventured toward the grill. Occasionally, one of the larger insects touched the electrodes producing a jolting, sizzling sound and a wisp of smoke, as the wings were toasted and the creature cooked.

Hayley had already changed into white shorts and a sorority tee shirt. A cooling breeze drifted from the lake, carrying the scents of outdoor grilling from nearby homes.

Foregoing the temptation of another beer, I chose instead a glass of iced tea and took a plastic plate, fork and knife from the table. I stared at the steaming low country boil on the table before me—a concoction of shrimp, red potatoes, Vidalia onions, corn on the cob, and sausage, dumped together and boiled in a pot.

"It's all great, but I'm partial toward the shrimp," said Hayley, picking the choice pieces from the pile of food.

I chose a little of each and joined Hayley and the others at the table on the screened porch.

"Interesting combination. It's kind of like a clam bake," I commented as I slathered margarine onto my vegetables.

"It originated in the low country of Georgia and South Carolina. I'm surprised you never had it in Savannah," Hayley said, running a shrimp through a puddle of cocktail sauce at the edge of her plate.

Graham and Linda sat across from us.

"You looked good out there, Hank," complimented Graham, looking over a partially eaten corn cob he was holding. "You were whipping along on that wide turn. I thought you were a goner, but you hunkered down. Nice going."

"That wasn't skill," I said in a deprecating tone, "That was fear. I knew if I fell I'd be skimming like a stone across the lake."

Ross and T.J. passed the table, their plates piled with food. T.J. paused when he saw me, "Hank, saw the news tonight on the T.V. Cobb was with your G.B.I. Director talking to the press about the killer in Adams County."

"He didn't kill them," interrupted Ross. "Remember what they said. It was some nut who had AIDS. Cobb said y'all arrested him in Macon. Was that you?"

"Yes, sir." I didn't feel comfortable about discussing the issue. I wanted to relax, enjoy the evening with Hayley, and forget about everything else.

"They said he tried to stab an agent with a syringe of his blood. Was that you?" asked T.J.

"No, sir. He tried to stab my partner and I stopped him."

"It was you that saved him!" said Hayley, astonished.

"Yeah, it was me."

"Wow, you're a hero," sighed Hayley.

"You don't understand," I tried to explain. "When something like this happens, you just react. I was lucky."

"Well, congratulations," said T.J., extending his hand. "You done good, brother. If you need a car, come see me," he said with a confirming nod.

"You know, you've got a tough job," said Graham reaching for the margarine tub. "You're not like us, in that everyone sees you as a cop... not just a regular guy."

"What do you mean, 'not like us'?" challenged Hayley, with a tinge of anger in her voice.

"Graham, why would you think I'm any different from you?" I asked. "Personally, I have the same hopes, the same goals, the same desires as you." I intentionally looked away from Hayley.

"I mean, well, you're a cop. No matter what, no matter what you do, you're forced to be a cop. It doesn't matter whether you're off duty, in church, or walking up the street, you're still viewed as an agent. And if you see a crime you have to do something about it." Graham took a long swig from his beer and looked at me with a hard stare. "Let me ask you a question: How do you deal with the gray areas?"

I wasn't sure what he meant. "Gray areas?"

"Yeah." He paused to run his shrimp through the cocktail sauce then plopped it in his mouth. "Suppose you went to a party with your date. And people were smoking marijuana. Would you arrest them?" He had that same smirk I'd seen when he'd docked the boat. "If you were a good cop, you would arrest them, wouldn't you?"

"An interesting question, and Graham, while I was at Forsyth at the academy, I thought about it. I would do what is legal and what is moral. If I walked into a party and they were smoking marijuana, I'd turn around and leave. I'd tell my date that I wouldn't—no, I couldn't—be involved in such antics. I'd leave the party."

"Why wouldn't you arrest them? They were breaking the law."

"I wouldn't arrest them anymore than if I walked into a bar and there were a couple of rednecks smoking dope at the bar. It's not worth my time. I'd do the same thing as I'd do at the party—leave. Sure, I'm a cop.

But it's not something I live and breathe whenever I'm awake. If someone drove from here with a beer too many, do you think I'd arrest them for D.U.I.? Of course not. I might try to stop them or get a designated driver, but you've got to be flexible in this job and use your common sense."

Linda patted Graham's hand. "That makes sense to me. Let it rest."

After supper, we all helped in cleaning up.

"Whew, I'm stuffed," I said to Hayley, clutching my stomach.

"Then let's go for a walk and work it off," she suggested.

I smile and nodded. "Sounds good."

"Hank and I are going for a walk, Mom."

"Don't go too far," admonished her mother. Then she lowered her voice. "And you know what I mean."

She led me up the gravel driveway and I took her hand. A cooling breeze flowed from the lake, catching the scent of honeysuckle from a nearby hedge.

"I've had a good time, Hayley. Thanks for inviting me. I really needed to get away."

"Oh. I hoped you wanted to come because of me."

"You know I did. It's just... I had a frustrating morning. I'm still working on the Lydia Carson thing. I thought I had a good lead and it fizzled out. I spoke to a person I hoped would help me and he refused to."

We stepped from the road weaving between the saplings and dodging briars.

"You know where you're going?" I asked, pushing a branch away.

"Know? I've grown up in these woods. I could walk this area blindfolded. I've got a place to show you."

She nimbly negotiated through the brush as we walked down a slight incline toward the lake. Suddenly, it was as if the trees parted, inviting us to their secret sanctum. Below us was an intimate cove, the moonlight shimmering off the glass surface of the lake, and the water lapping softly against the shore.

"It's beautiful, Hayley," I said.

"Over there's a tree with a swing rope that Graham tied when he was ten. He planned to throw the rope over the branch, then tie a slip knot and slip it up to the branch. He was in the Boy Scouts and thought he knew how to tie a rope. I didn't know a thing about that stuff, or so he thought. Well, he might have known about knots, but he didn't know squat about rope tossing. He spent the entire afternoon trying to get that rope over the branch. He wouldn't let me throw. Finally, in frustration and nearly in tears, he let me try. I got it on the fourth try. Instead of being happy about having a swing rope, he was angry that I'd gotten the rope over the branch. He wouldn't use the swing for nearly a month." She sighed. "Sometimes he lets that ego of his screw up his judgment."

As we walked along the shore, I picked up a flat pebble and flung it sidearm across the cove. It skipped four or five times.

"Hey, not bad," commented Hayley, kneeling down, searching for a stone.

"The lake's just right for skimming."

She picked a rock. "Check this out," she said, whipping a throw. The rock danced across the water."

"Nice. Four times."

"Five," she corrected with pride.

"Okay, five," I conceded. "I'll just have to go for six."

"And if you don't—you have to remove an article of clothing," she demanded.

The proposition surprised and flustered me for an instant. Was she teasing me or was this nymph actually serious? Well, she'd seen nearly as much and so had I when we were skiing.

"All right. Then it'll be your turn."

She leered. "No prob, Bob."

My first throw was five. I removed a shoe.

Her throw was four. She removed a shoe.

I threw a six.

"Lucky throw," said as she retrieved another pebble. She threw a five and removed her remaining shoe. "I'm getting the hang of it."

I threw another six. "Some people have the touch," I said, breathing on my finger tips.

"Well, smarty... let's go all or nothing," she challenged.

Her boldness stunned me. My throat was too dry to answer, so I nodded.

"You first," she insisted.

I searched for the perfect rock and found a piece of shale. "Are you sure about this?"

"Not a doubt."

I took a step, leaning low so the angle would be close to the lake and threw the stone with as much force as I could muster. It bounced once, twice, again, and again, and for a fifth time. An unforeseen wave rose and, like a fish, swallowed the rock.

She crossed her arms in a defiant stance. "Mr. Monroe, I seem to have counted only five. Do your duty."

"You... you were joking?" I hoped for a reprieve. Then I thought of a defense. "You've got to throw too."

"That wasn't the deal."

"How about four skips. You've got to get just four skips," I pleaded.

She took a moment to consider my offer then nodded slowly. "You're on." She adroitly snatched up a rock, then walked to the edge of the lake. There was a purpose in her movements, she knew she could throw four, but I was desperate. Maybe that same wave would foil her throw.

"Are you ready?" she said with a strange calmness in her voice.

I nodded nervously.

She reached out over the lake and opened her hand, palm up. She tilted her palm until the rock tumbled and I watched it, falling, as if in slow motion, to the water with a soft plop. What had she done? My heart skipped a beat. There was that now familiar devilish grin and glint. "Oops. I guess we both lose."

Before I was able to protest she was shedding her clothing. My dreams, my fantasies, didn't do her loveliness justice. In the coolness of the night I flushed with desire, each of my other senses alerted to the carnal rush. The moonlight reflected off the lake and created an aura that surrounded and moved with her. Though she was nude, she approached me with confidence, obviously knowing what she was causing. "Your turn," she said, as she pressed herself against me.

The evening became a swirl of textures, tastes, sights, sounds, and exploration. One part of me wanted to passionately consume the moment that I had only dared dream; the other part insisted I slow down

and savor the time because it would too soon end. Afterwards we went
swimming. We teased and touched each other then moved together,
enjoying each other's warmth, which again enflamed our desires. I
wished we could have stayed all night in the cove and watched the
morning sunrise. This was a moment in time and space that would never
be recreated and I didn't want to lose it, but Hayley said her parents
would soon come to look for us if we didn't return. We kissed deeply
and walked back to the cabin.

· · ·

It was after midnight when I returned to my apartment. Megan's car was
parked in her space and a faint light showed in an upper window. I
hoped she hadn't seen me arrive. So many complex feelings were bub-
bling inside me after such an emotional day: the incident with Reverend
Pheim, the day with Hayley, the night with Hayley, my feelings for
Megan. As I drove home that night I had a bittersweet taste in my mouth.
I remembered the phrase, "Be careful what you wish for, you might get
it." And I had wished for Hayley, wished for such a moment as I'd experienced tonight. And from a purely physical level it was wonderful, it
was passionate, it was something out of a romantic movie, but... It was
that "but" that disconcerted me. There was a part of me that was satisfied, but a part of me that was still needing. And I felt a sense of betrayal concerning Megan. Why? I didn't know.

While feeding the bird, I heard someone's door shut and I looked
outside, concerned that it might be Megan coming to see me. It was
Megan. She was walking to a car... with a man. It was too dark to tell
much about him, but the security lights revealed enough that there was
no doubt. They paused by the driver's door, spoke briefly, and kissed on
the cheeks. It wasn't a long embrace, more like a peck, but it sparked a
pang of jealousy and hurt.

It didn't make sense. Tonight, I'd fulfilled a dream. I had Hayley and
an evening of romance that I would never forget. I was to enjoy the trap-
pings and benefits that went with the McTimmons family. However,
watching Megan with another man made all that seem trivial. I stood peering out the window, watching Megan return to her place, and felt empty.

The phone rang. It had to be Megan. She had spotted me watching her.

"Hank?" the voice said.

"Yeah, uh, hey, Celeste," I said, relieved but, in a way, wishing it was Megan.

"What's wrong? You sound down."

"I am. You could tell?"

"Of course," she said in that soothing voice. "What's wrong?"

"I just got back from a date. And well, let's just say that, maybe dreams should sometimes never be fulfilled."

"Especially in the areas where motives aren't pure. Sounds like you've been with a woman... in the Biblical sense."

"And it was great."

"But there's this emptiness, right?"

"How would you know? You're an angel," I said defensively.

"Because I know about love and the lack of love. What do you think the core of the Bible is about? The love of God for his people and the love he wants you to have with others. Love your God with all your heart, mind, and soul, and love your neighbor as yourself. What makes people different from animals is that animals have sex while humans have the capability to love. Too many, unfortunately, never rise above the level of animals.

"Hank, sex is like a spice. It's like salt, pepper, sage, or oregano. Have you ever had a spice by itself?"

"Yeah."

"Did you like it? It was kind of empty, wasn't it? Void of nutrition and not at all filling. You have to put it on food, on substance. Love is the substance and sex is the spice that makes love more flavorful, more enjoyable. Tonight you only had the spice and you feel empty."

"You have an amazing knack for making the complicated simple. Lydia has a very wise angel."

"Thanks. Now, how'd your meeting with Pheim go?" she asked with hopefulness in her tone.

"It was a waste of time. Except I did confirm what we expected. Lydia did have a conference with the good Reverend. But he won't talk about it. Says, 'It's policy, I must respect the confidence of my parishioners'," I mimicked in a whining mock. "It's a damn shame that a preacher is more interested in the discipline of the church than in a moral right."

"I'm sorry to hear that," she said regretfully. "I truly thought he'd talk to you."

"There's not much more we can do, Celeste. Especially with only two days remaining. I could go interview that college professor in Atlanta, or that customer of the bank that took a shine to Lydia, but I don't think there's any chance with those leads."

"Are you going to church tomorrow?"

"To listen to that pompous hypocrite preach? Not a snowball's chance in hell."

"Please, Hank, go to church. Sit up front so he can see you, stare at him so he'll know you aren't afraid of him, remind him with your presence of his shortcomings. And tonight, pray for him."

"And you think that's going to work? Do you also work miracles?"

"Miracles are not as rare as you think. And as you said, there's not much more you can do. You're short on leads, you're short on time. It's about time for prayer."

"I'll go. But only because I have no choice."

CHAPTER NINETEEN

SUNDAY. I had two days remaining.

I awoke with the lethargic feeling of a hangover, not as a result of drink, but with the dread of a futile day ahead. For church, I selected a worsted wool, gray pin striped suit, normally reserved for court, a freshly starched white shirt, and a red tie. I would look my best for the good Reverend.

I arrived early to get a front row seat. There were only a few people seated already. I searched for Hayley, but didn't spot her. She and her family were probably at the lake. I selected an aisle seat on the second row, not too aggressive, but obvious enough to make my presence known to the pastor. Gradually the pews began filling. I had apparently selected the senior citizen section where each one had what he or she thought was a reserved seat. One elderly gentleman shuffled up to me. From his expression I was well aware he took exception at my seating. He cleared his throat, staring at me, gave me a backward wave of his hand as if he was shooing his cat off his favorite chair. I pressed back in the seat to let him pass.

"Sir, you are sitting in my seat," he formally advised me.

"I'm sorry, sir. I have a purpose here," I insisted.

"We all have a purpose here. This is my seat. I sit here every Sunday.

I don't mean to change."

I considered if this was a battle worth fighting. "Then may I sit beside you? I have to stay in this area."

He deliberated for a moment. "I would enjoy your company." I scooted down one seat and he sat down next to me. "My wife can find a seat elsewhere. That'll teach her to lollygag."

In a few minutes a small, frail lady with stooped shoulders stopped at our pew. Her eyes narrowed at the curious situation.

"Elsie," the man explained, "I've invited this young man to sit next to me." He cocked his head down the pew. "You may sit next to him."

She wedged her way past us and sat next to me.

"Hi, I'm Hank Monroe," I said, extending a hand to her.

"Elsie Sheffield. It's nice to meet you. Are you visiting?" she asked, sorting the situation.

"Yes, ma'am."

"Oh, it's a wonderful church. I've been attending for nearly fifty-five years."

Here I was, sandwiched between two septuagenarians, for a staring contest with a minister, based on the advice of a so-called angel, with the hopes of solving a murder case. Not standard police procedure.

The choir filed in, followed by Horace Wright and the Reverend Pheim. I noticed a flicker in the minister's eye as he spotted me. I returned the gaze, determined it would not leave him.

Horace labored to the lectern and gave his gruff greeting. I watched Pheim. Horace gave the announcements, which I ignored. I watched Pheim. He soon realized my tactic and returned the stare for as long as he dared, then broke when the minister of music announced the first hymn. Everyone stood and Pheim sang from his hymnal. I watched Pheim. If it were possible, I would have, like Superman, burned a hole through him with my eyes. And the more I watched, the angrier I got. Because of this man, this supposed man of God, Lydia might never be found.

After we sat down Elsie leaned over to me. "You must really be impressed with Preacher Pheim. You didn't take your eyes off him during the whole song."

"Yes ma'am."

The Confession of Faith was given, the offering taken, the scripture read, and Pheim rose for the sermon. I didn't listen. What was to be gleaned from this man? The final hymn was sung and the benediction was given.

I joined the congregation as they filed out past the Reverend. "A very nice sermon. You said what they wanted to hear and that's what matters, right?"

He ignored my comment. "Would you please meet with me in my office, Mr. Monroe? I have a matter to discuss with you. Give me about five minutes, please."

He was probably aggravated with my antics and wished to berate me. I looked forward to it.

I was waiting outside the hallway that led to his office when Ms. Lockhart dropped by the office.

"Mr. Monroe," she said stiffly. "What brings you here?"

"You may go on about your business. It's not anything that concerns you. As you said, 'There are some things you don't wish to know'."

She bristled at my reply and abruptly entered the office, slamming the door.

Reverend Pheim appeared. "Mr. Monroe. Let's have a talk." He opened the door allowing me to enter. "Ms. Lockhart, what brings you here?"

"Morning, sir. I'd misplaced some papers and the thought of it was grating on me. I thought I'd drop by to see if I could locate them."

"It's Sunday. Enjoy this beautiful day that the Lord has made," he ordered.

"But sir—"

"No buts. Go on."

She lingered, wanting to know about our meeting. But he remained in place waiting for her to leave.

"Yes, sir. You're right." She gathered her pocketbook and shut the door behind her.

"Please," he said, motioning me toward his office with a wave of his hand. I didn't notice any anger in his voice and his demeanor seemed relaxed, almost confessional. He motioned me toward a chair.

"This has been a busy week for you," he said, hanging his robe in a nearby closet. "You were involved in solving the Adams County deaths?"

"Yes, sir," I replied defensively.

He sat behind his desk and laced his hands in front of his face. "You have a very difficult job, very similar to mine in that way. But do you know who has the toughest job?"

"You?"

"A predictable answer. But wrong. I would wager, if allowed to do so, that the toughest job would be... the wife of a minister." He paused to let the answer settle.

"I've chosen to answer the call of Christ. I've chosen to bear the burdens that come with the job. As a minister, I wear many hats: an orator, a counselor, a civic leader, an administrator, a mediator, a fiscal expert, an evangelist, a recruiter, and a motivator. I'm prepared to move on the average of every six years and to live in a fishbowl existence. I live under the scrutiny of every parishioner and I am held to a standard that no one else in the congregation is held, because I have accepted the leadership position.

"But as difficult as a minister's job is, the wife's is more so. She must have complete faith not only in God, but also in her husband. She must move with her husband, deal with criticism of her husband, living in that same fishbowl existence that she did not ask for, but must accept. And it is the wife, who usually has one other very important role: she is the minister to the minister. When he is frustrated, angry, fearful, and at times doubtful, who does he turn to? His wife. To whom does he turn for solace and companionship? When he is hurting, to whom does he turn for true understanding and comfort? The minister bears the burdens of his church; the wife bears the burdens of the minister."

He paused to compose himself. "Yesterday, my wife, Sarah, heard our debate regarding Lydia. I must admit your points had merit, and she strongly pointed that out to me. Mr. Monroe, ministers are human and do err. And we, from time to time, tend to become so caught up in the day-to-day tediousness of our works that we fail to see what our true mission is. When we spoke yesterday, maybe I was too hardened to my position. Or maybe it's that Sarah explained it in a way I would understand. Church policy is a guide, which must be tempered with reason and the guidance of Christ. Sometimes, I can't see the forest for the trees, and Sarah has that ability to bring her unique perception to an issue. Last night I prayed for such guidance, and as a result of prayer, I wish to discuss with you my conference with Lydia.

"Lydia came to see me about a week before she disappeared. She was very disturbed and had nowhere to turn." He paused at the precipice. "She was pregnant. The father wanted her to have an abortion. But she refused to, as she phrased it, 'kill' their child. She said he was willing to marry her, but he couldn't do it immediately. He had,'obligations'."

"What kind of obligations?" I asked.

He shook his head. "She didn't elaborate. The father and she argued about it. He was willing to marry her, but needed six months. This carried on for weeks and she knew she couldn't hide the secret for long. As a compromise, he suggested if she'd leave the area for six months, he would join her. They would marry and have the baby."

That meant the father could still be in the area. I thought of the electrician from Georgia Power. What was his name? Shepherd. That was beginning to make sense. "What did she want from you?"

"She was in love. Apparently the first time she had ever had a real relationship. She was concerned about the sin of such a relationship. When we first met, she posed the question, 'If a motive is pure, can the result be sinful?' She emphasized that the love between her and the father was pure, and if they weren't married, why should the love that resulted be sinful? And if a child was produced from such purity, it had to be right. It had to be brought into this world."

"So you think she left and she's with her lover, or is awaiting his arrival?"

"Yes, sir. That's why I don't think she's dead. I think she's in Mexico."

"Who was the father?"

"She refused to tell me. Trust me, I asked, but she wouldn't say."

"Did she mention who her physician was?"

"No. I asked her if it was local. But she said she was going to an out of town obstetrician."

Great. That could be Columbus, Macon, or Atlanta. There was no way to cover that area in two days. My only lead was to confront Shepherd.

I rose to conclude the interview and we shook hands. "Thank you, Reverend... and to your wife. I've already interviewed Lydia's close friends and I believe they were truthful with me. They might have suspected she was pregnant, but that was all."

"One other thing, Mr. Monroe. Was one of her friends Libby Rudeley?"

"Who?"

"Libby Rudeley? She's an old member of the church. They initially met when Lydia was delivering meals to the elderly. They developed a close friendship. I believe that Libby was the accepting mother that Lydia never had. Later, Libby developed Parkinson's disease and had to be placed in a nursing home. In fact, during our counseling session, Lydia mentioned that she had sought Libby's advice."

"Why haven't I heard of her before now?"

"I wasn't aware of their relationship 'til Lydia came to see me. Apparently, they'd become very close. More than I realized. I didn't tell you because I felt that, too, was confidential."

"Where is she now?"

"At Forrest Manor. You know where it is?"

"Yes, sir." I rose and extended my hand. "Thank you, Reverend. I confess, I was angry at you."

He chuckled. "And I was angry at you too. But you said you had an angel advising you. Is that true?" I nodded, not wishing to admit more. "Then who am I to argue with one of God's assistants?"

$$\cdot \ \cdot \ \cdot$$

Forrest Manor was nestled in the hills west of the city with a four-acre pond in the rear. The facade had a remarkable resemblance to Twin Creeks, but once I entered the double front doors all similarities ceased. A large round reception desk manned by a gracious black lady greeted me.

"Good afternoon, may I help you?" she asked. Visitors were always welcomed at the Manor, especially on weekends.

"Yes, ma'am. I'm here to see Libby Rudeley."

"Are you a relative?" she asked.

"No, just a friend."

She referred to her chart. "Do you know where her room is?"

I shook my head. "This is my first time here."

"Then let me call a nurse to show you," she said, dialing the phone.

In a few minutes I was approached by an attractive woman about my age, wearing navy pants and a checkered smock, a smile framed by streaked blond hair, a smattering of freckles, and an upturned nose and full lips. She extended a hand to greet me. "I'm Angela McCall, Libby's nurse. You're here to see her?"

"If I can." I presented my identification. "I'm Hank Monroe with the G.B.I. I'm working on the disappearance of Lydia Carson and I understand Ms. Rudeley was a friend of Libby's. Do you recall Lydia stopping by?"

"Oh, Lydia. Of course, I remember her. She was here almost every weekend. At least, the weekends when I was on duty. If I didn't know better, I would have thought Libby was her mother, the way they carried on and talked. During every holiday, Lydia would show up with some type of treat. Not only for Libby, but for everyone on the floor. But Libby and her, yeah, they were very close."

"I need to talk to her about Lydia."

"Sure, let me show you her room." As we walked down the alcohol-scented corridors, Angela confided in a low voice, "You are aware Libby has Parkinson's?"

"I heard."

"If you had wanted to talk to her a month ago, you would have understood her. Now, you may have some difficulty." She released a regretful sigh. "I don't give her much time." She sneezed and coughed into a handkerchief. She paused at a doorway and I peered inside a private room. Sitting in a wheelchair beside the bed was a slight woman with wiry gray hair askew, wearing a green housecoat, and watching a Spencer Tracy movie on a wall-mounted T.V.. Her eyes were alert, following the scenes unfolding on the television. But her ashen face was frozen with a sickly grin, reminiscent of a skull, and her curled hands were trembling as if she was playing the piano.

"Is she watching the movie?" I asked, wondering if Libby knew what she was watching.

"Oh, yes. She knows what's happening. She loves old movies, especially the musicals. Though her muscles are static, her mind is alert. She may not be able to answer your questions clearly, but she does understand you. Believe me, at times, she is as frustrated as you."

She knocked on the door. "Hey, Libby. I've brought you a visitor."

Libby turned stiffly toward the sound. Though her facial expression didn't change, her eyes lit up, and her trembling right hand rose an inch from its rest.

Once we were in front of Libby, Angela introduced me. "This is Hank Monroe. He's a friend of Lydia's." When Angela said "Lydia," Libby's eyes brightened.

"Liiiiiiyaaa," Libby slurred. "Sheee ma freeen."

I knelt next to her, clasping her hand, the skin so soft and thin you could see the blue vessels and milky tendons. "She's my friend too. Libby, I'm looking for her. She's has disappeared and I need to find her. Did she tell you she had a boyfriend?"

There, a perceptible shake of her head. "Cann tell... cannn telll... nooo."

"Please, Libby. He might know where she is. Lydia has disappeared and if I can't find her, she may never come to see you again."

"Noooo! Liiiiiyaaa cummmm."

Angela, realizing the importance of the moment, joined me, placing a reassuring arm around her. "Libby, if you know something, please tell this man. He wants to help Lydia. You know me. I'm your friend. Tell him."

Libby dropped her head. Then from the mask of frozen muscle, a lone tear trailed down her cheek. "Kay. Ah telll. Buuu brinn baaa Liiiiyaaa."

"He'll bring back Lydia," Angela promised.

There was an eternal pause, then she spoke. "Eeeeees eeeees Noooomaaaa."

"Is that Lydia's boyfriend?" Angela asked.

"Uhhh huhh. Eeeee Nooomaaaa."

"I'm sorry Libby. I can't understand you. Would you repeat the name?"

"Eeeee Nooomaaaa. Eeeee Noooomaaaa. Eeeeee Nooomaaaa!" There was a flash of anger in Libby's eyes. She was frustrated.

I pulled Angela to the side. "Is she able to write the name?"

She shook her head. "No way. Look at her hands. What you're hearing is exactly what you're going to see on a sheet of paper."

I walked out of the room, silently cursing. I was so close. Lydia wasn't stupid. She'd had entrusted her confessions to someone who couldn't repeat them.

Angela joined me. "I'm sorry, Mr. Monroe. Libby's trying, believe me. She's doing her best to tell you."

I exhaled an exasperated breath. "I understand. And I appreciate your help." Then an idea struck me. I beckoned to Angela. "Let's give it one more try."

I turned off the television and sat on the bed next to Libby. "Libby," I said softly, "I might not be able to understand you very well. It's not your fault. But I do understand you a bit. I'm going to say some names. If one of the names I say is Lydia's boyfriend, let me know. You can do that, can't you?"

"Yaaaaaa."

"Okay, here we go." Slowly and distinctly I stated the name of everyone I knew in the case, young and old, male and female. She sat stoically in her chair as I pronounced each name. Then on the twelfth, she stiffened, her eyes flashing.

"Himmm. Himmmm. Himmm," she repeated in an excited garble.

I was astonished and looked at Angela who instantly recognized the name and was also stunned. I repeated the name. "Are you sure?"

"Yaaaa. Himmmm," she said with such force, spittle drooled down her chin.

"Angela, please don't repeat what you heard," I asked. "This might not be true and we can't let something like this get out."

Wide eyed, Angela nodded.

"Ahhh teelll. Pees breen Liiiya."

Angela gave her a hug. "You did well, Libby."

"Ahh deeeeee?"

"Yes ma'am, you did," I said, clasping her hands and kissing her on the check.

The mask stiffened along her lips and her eyes welled with tears. "Liiiiya. Pees. Breeeeen Liiiya."

. . .

Now, I had a name but no proof and certainly no connection with the death of Lydia. I had one day remaining, not enough time, and I wasn't sure if Cobb would give me a reprieve. No, I was certain. It was now clear how the cease and desist order came. I needed Celeste's thoughts, I needed Celeste's guidance. Damn it, I needed Celeste's phone number. There was nothing to do now but return to my apartment and wait for her call.

"Hello."

"Hey Megan, it's Hank."

"Hank? Hank? The name sounds familiar... I'm trying to place it."

"Come on, Megan. Don't give me a hard time. I've been busy."

"Oh, really?" she said skeptically.

"Yeah, really. It fact I've been working today," I confessed.

"Today. On Sunday." She still was unconvinced and had good reason not to be.

"Yes," I said, nodding to the phone as if she could see me. "I had two interviews."

"And they couldn't wait 'til tomorrow, I suppose?"

"No, they couldn't. Why don't you come over? I'll make us some popcorn loaded with butter, just the way you like it. We'll watch a movie, and I'll explain. Once you listen, you'll understand."

"You know, I'm a very busy woman too. I've got career aspirations. I'm not sure I have time for you."

"Please, Megan," I begged. "I've missed you and... your absence has made me know how much you mean to me."

There was a full ten seconds of uncomfortable silence and for a moment I thought the line was dead, or worse, she had hung up on me. "All right. Give me fifteen minutes and I'll be over."

And to the minute she was knocking on my door. I greeted her with a peace offering of popcorn and we sat on the couch. She was wearing tight jeans and a ribbed knit pullover that clung to her curves. Apparently she wanted me to know what I was missing.

"Is this what they mean by the term 'buttering up'?" she asked, tossing a kernel in her mouth.

"I don't know. Just as long as it works." I went on to explain in general terms my work on the Adams County case and the deadline I had been forced to accept on the Carson case. All of this would be over tomorrow, one way or the other, I promised.

She listened stoically and when I finished there was no reaction. "Do they pay you overtime for all of this?"

"No. I get nothing but my measly little salary."

She shook her head. "Lord, why do I always end up with those who have no financial aspirations?"

"Does that mean you'll stay?"

She tossed another kernel in her mouth. "Yeah, why not?" She snuggled close to me. "What movie are we going to watch?"

"It's a John Wayne flick."

"Wow, you do know how to treat a woman."

The classic John Wayne bar fight broke out when the phone rang. I snatched it off its cradle.

"Celeste!" I said enthusiastically. "I was hoping to hear from you." In the excitement of the moment I realized I'd forgotten about Megan. I held up a finger. "Megan, this call's important, excuse me while I go to the bedroom."

Her eyes flashed red. "Don't bother! You can have all the privacy you need." And she darted out the door.

"No! Megan, don't leave!" I tried to stop her, but she was out the front door trotting to her place.

"Hank, is something wrong?" I could hear Celeste's concerned voice in the ear piece. "Hank?"

"Son of a....." I sighed a frustrated breath. "Celeste? I've got a little problem here. I need your help."

. . .

After hanging up I went to Megan's apartment, knocked on the door, and rang the doorbell.

"Megan! I'm going to keep this up 'til you at least give me the courtesy of answering the door."

A curtain fluttered upstairs and the window went up. "Go away!"

"No, I will not. Please open the door. We need to talk."

She shut the window and in a moment the door slowly opened. She stood in the doorway with her arms crossed. "What do you want?"

"To talk."

"Is Celeste the woman you've been seeing?"

Somehow she knew about Hayley or at least knew I had another interest. I dodged the question.

"Can I come in and explain who Celeste is?"

"Why?" she asked firmly.

"Because...." I licked my dry lips. "Because you aren't going to believe who she is. In fact, she's going to call you in..." I checked my watch, "five minutes."

Megan's head tilted and a skeptical smile spread over her stern face. "She's going to call me?"

I nodded. "Yes. Ask her anything you want."

"Well, I'll grant you this, Agent Monroe, you've got cojones."

I reached for her and squeezed her hand. "Please, may I come inside?"

Once we were seated, I told Megan about how Celeste first called me, telling me she was Lydia's angel; about the advice Celeste had given me; and the events of the day. "Celeste is a voice on the phone. She will not meet me and I'm not able to call her. I know virtually nothing about her and, so far, she is controlled enough that I haven't been able to tell much about who she really is. And while I hope to solve Lydia's disappearance, I fear that once I do, Celeste's job will be done and I'll never speak to her again."

"Do you love her?" Megan asked.

I pondered the question. "Love her? Yes." My answer surprised Megan, so I quickly explained. "But... it's not like a love I can explain. I don't want to be with her, spend time with her, or touch her. I... I wish I could describe it. It's a love borne of respect and of honor. Megan, whoever Celeste is... she's a good person, and if she's not already an angel, she will be someday. But to me there is someone more valuable in my life. It's you. Megan, it's you I want to be with... and it's you I really love."

Her lips tightened, then quivered. "That's nice to hear. I—"

Her phone rang. We looked at each other.

"When you finish talking with Celeste, I have to talk with her, okay?"

"Okay." She lifted the receiver. "Hello? Hello, Celeste. Hank's here and we were discussing you.... Sure." Megan turned to me. "I'm going to my room. Celeste and I are going to have an angel to woman talk. Excuse me."

She stayed in her room for a half hour. When she emerged she was relaxed, almost happy.

"She's ready to speak to you," she said, handing me the phone.

I covered the receiver. "What did you talk about for so long?"

"You," she said with a smirk.

I looked puzzled. "What did she ask?"

"Well, one of her many questions was, were you a good kisser," she said bemused.

"If she asked that, she's no angel."

"I don't know, I think she's legit."

"So you believe me now?"

She kissed me on the cheek. "Yeah, I do. Go on in my bedroom so you can talk to her in private. And when you return," she raised her eyebrows mischievously, "I'll make an appropriate apology."

I took the cordless phone to her room.

"Celeste, now don't get me in trouble with Megan," I warned.

"Nonsense, she's adorable. She wasn't the one you were with last night." It was a statement not a question.

"No, she wasn't."

"Megan doesn't strike me as that type, but she does care about you. In my humble angelic opinion, you ought to hang on to her."

"I'll take your meddling under advisement," I said, dismissing her editorial. "Now let's get down to business. I spoke to Pheim."

"And?" I could almost hear her optimism.

"Lydia told him she was pregnant, but she wouldn't tell him who the father was. The father wanted her to have an abortion. She refused. She was very in love with him, but he wouldn't marry her, at least, not immediately. But she did tell Pheim the name of her confidant, Libby Rudeley, sort of a surrogate mother. So I went to see her. With coaxing, Libby gave me the name of her lover." I told her the name. There was dead silence on the line. "Celeste?"

"I'm sorry. I would have never thought. I'm... just... stunned. I would have never believed it to be him." She sounded hurt and betrayed.

"The problem is that I've got only one more day to get enough evidence on him"

"Or to get him to admit to the crime."

I laughed. "Get him to admit it? Oh, get serious. He's not stupid; there's no way I could get him to admit that. The moment I accuse him, he'll ask for a lawyer."

"Hank, hang around at this number for about thirty minutes. I might have a way."

She called back twenty minutes later. Way too soon, for when I returned from the bedroom, Megan took to apologizing in such a delicious way.

"Hank, I thought about the best way to handle this," advised Celeste. "I believe you can get him to talk to you. Go see him first thing tomorrow morning. But this is how you have to do it...."

Tomorrow was Monday. I had one day remaining.

THE FOLLOWING morning was overcast, and thick clouds hung like gray cotton batting. At eight-thirty I parked across the street from his business, waiting for him to arrive. I wasn't sure the strategy would work, but I had to trust Celeste's advice. She'd been right too often to reject her counsel.

He arrived five minutes after nine, parking his Mercedes in his personal slot. I followed him into the bank, trying to catch up to him with a half trot. He was out of sight when I entered. I knew his route and quickly climbed the stairs, with a calm but deliberate gate.

"Good *morning*, sir. May I *help* you?" his secretary asked, when I topped the stairs. I smiled and slowed just enough to lull her, then quickly turned right and walked into his office. "Hey, what are you—?" I shut the door behind me.

Reed Norman was hanging his coat on a tree and adjusting his suspenders.

His secretary burst into the room behind me. "I'm sorry, sir. He walked past me. I tried to stop him." Her cutesy accent was gone.

He dismissed her with a wave of his hand. "It's okay, Connie. Go ahead and bring me my coffee. Mr. Monroe, would you like a cup?"

"No, sir."

"I'll have your coffee shortly." She gave me a hard angry stare and shut the door. I was losing friends real quick in this town. And before it was over I was afraid I'd lose many more.

"Mr. Norman," I said strolling to his desk. "I apologize for bursting in like this, but I've come across some important information I want to discuss with you."

He raised his eyebrows. "It must be very important for you to come shoving your way into my office in such a rude manner."

I bit my tongue. "If you'll give me a moment, I think you'll agree my actions were appropriate."

He motioned me to a seat across from him and sat down.

I inhaled in anticipation. "I have one simple question. Were you the father of Lydia's baby?"

The directness of the question had its desired effect. His eyes widened and his nostrils flared. I'd touched a nerve. He quickly composed himself. "What are you talking about?"

"You and Lydia Carson were having an affair. That is the reason behind her disappearance. I'd like you to tell me about it," I said with calm assurance.

"Mr. Monroe, I think that matter has already been discussed. I don't have any idea of what you're talking about. Is this more of those rumors that you are spreading throughout the city? If that's so, then I may have to take some civil action against the G.B.I. and against you personally for libel." Norman was regaining his bearing. "I don't believe that question bears the dignity of an answer."

I shrugged. "I understand. I have no more questions. Thank you." I continued with Celeste's directions. "Then I guess I need to let Amanda Carson know what I've learned." I rose to leave.

"Just a minute!" he exclaimed, standing up quickly. "You have nothing to tell Amanda."

"Oh, yes sir. I do. She needs to know you not only were having an affair with Lydia, but you impregnated her."

"If you spread such lies, I'll sue you for everything you have. You'll be fired. Your career will be over," he sneered, his face livid with rage, his eyes squinting so tight he looked like a serpent.

"I'd look forward to taking this to open court. Please, Mr. Norman, don't bluster. I'm not bluffing, I've nothing to lose." I headed for the door.

As I reached for the doorknob he shouted, "No... no.... don't leave!"

I paused, wishing he would call me back, but I couldn't show my eagerness.

The door opened. It was Mrs. Morgan. "Sir, your coffee." "Thank you, Connie," he said, coming from behind his desk and accepting the mug. "Hold all my calls. And I mean all." She could tell there was a major problem brewing. Once she had retreated from the office, he guided me back to the chair. "We need to talk."

He returned to his chair and I returned to mine. He took a cautious sip, then leaned back and closed his eyes as if in prayer, the room quiet, save for the ticking of an antique clock. Slowly his body softened, as if his muscles were dissolving beneath the skin. When he opened his eyes to address me it was as if he had aged ten years.

"I think this interview calls for a morning libation," he said, heading for a wall unit off to the side of the room. "Care to join me?"

"No, sir. And I'd rather you not have anything either."

"Ah. Yes. You fear that in court it might be ruled that my statements were made while inebriated." He opened a cabinet door, removed a tumbler and a quart of Jack Daniels. "No, not this morning. I think today calls for something a little bolder." He replaced the Jack Daniels with a bottle of Wild Turkey.

"Sir."

"Hush, boy. Sit down and listen." He poured himself a half a glass of whiskey with a splash of water. "You know, you've been a boil on my butt since you arrived here."

He took a long draw of the whiskey, then drew in a long breath and shivered. "Wow. Good stuff." He sat the glass down with a loud clunk and said, "Where're you from? You're not from around here."

"Originally, Maryland."

He nodded. "Thought so." He took another swig. "You know how I knew?"

"No, sir."

"'Cause you don't have any appreciation for Southern culture and especially for the goings on in a small town like Connally. You don't really give a shit about what you say or who you hurt." He took another drink.

"I'm only interested in finding Lydia," I retorted.

He shook his finger at me. "You don't have any idea what a Southern man has to deal with. He has to be everything to everybody. A Southern man has to have the charm of Ashley Wilkes, the honor of Robert E. Lee, the boldness of Stonewall Jackson, and the flair of Jeb Stuart. He should be as humble as Billy Graham and as savvy as Ted Turner. He has to be familiar with the arts of fishing, hunting and golfing. Know his college football team and support his high school football team. Indiscretions are acceptable as long as they aren't flaunted. The wife will normally stand by her man, as long as he maintains her lifestyle. Social drinking is acceptable, which merely means just don't drink alone. He'd better take care of his wife and family and be able to live up to the expectations and legacy of his dad." The last phrase was spoken with a hint of sarcasm.

He swirled his glass, the ice tinkling. "I can tell from your expression that you don't understand. Like I said, you're simply culturally ignorant. I say this not to offend you or to bore you, but to set the stage for what I'm about to say."

Though difficult, I remained silent. He was talking. *Let him continue,* I thought.

"I am the third generation in my family to run this bank. Back in the late seventies and early eighties I was Vice President of Operations. The farmers were going through some very difficult times then. As a result of rising land values, banks had loaned the farmers exorbitant amounts of money and when the notes became due, the farmers, due to various circumstances, weren't able to pay on the notes. A lot of farmland that had been in families for generations was lost due to foreclosure. It happened around here and it was a very distasteful time for us. There was one such farmer who had a loan with us and it didn't look good for him.

"Around 1980 there was a crop duster who'd flown for this farmer. This duster had ferried planes all over the country and in Central and South America as well. The duster was having similar money problems because the farmers couldn't pay him. So the duster approached the farmer with a lucrative proposition. He had some contacts in Miami, Colombians who were looking for a clandestine airstrip. Would the farmer be willing to use his farmland for a strip? The crop duster would fly the load, the farmer would operate the strip and get the load to Atlanta. The farmer had two choices: reject the offer and lose his family's farm, or take the offer, accept the risks, and pay off of the loan. He chose the latter.

"I don't know how many loads were flown into his place but soon, the farmer was flush with cash. He paid off all of his mortgages. Once the debts were paid, the flights ceased. Whether it was due to the fear of discovery or some moral affliction, I don't know. But I think the wily farmer knew it was best to cash in his poker chips while he was ahead in the game." Norman took another drink and smiled. "I remember when he'd walk into the bank with a gym bag full of cash. Back then there were no CTRs, oh, excuse me, Currency Transaction Reports, that needed to be filed. He'd report the money to the IRS saying it was gambling winnings, so they couldn't touch him."

"Who was the farmer?" I asked.

He gave me a condescending look and said, "In good time, son," then continued. "In 1984, Dad retired, but retained controlling interest in the bank. The Board of Directors appointed me President. I really wanted to prove I could run the bank." He paused as if he was searching for appropriate words. "I wanted Dad to be proud and know I could exceed his standards. But two years later Atlantic Seaboard approached Dad with an offer and... he sold out. Sold my bank. It was as if he didn't believe in me. He just... gave them the bank." Norman looked down at the desk, his jaws and fists clenched. He finished off his drink and rose for another.

"But ASC wasn't stupid or cruel," he said, pouring another round. "They kept me on as President. I knew the business, I knew the customers. But I knew I was under their scrutiny and my position depended on the profits I brought in.

"Meanwhile, my farmer friend was on a golfing vacation at Doral and met with his former Colombian colleagues. Business in Miami was good, but the Colombians had a large problem. Because of the newly enacted money laundering statutes, banks in Miami weren't taking the drug money. Violators, including bank officials, could have their assets seized and receive twenty-year sentences. There weren't many takers. They wanted to know if the farmer knew someone who would launder their money. Here I was, up here in lil' ol' Connally, betrayed by my dad, and under the gun from ASC. The farmer knew I was ripe for an offer." He leaned back in his executive chair and shook his head regretfully. "Of course, if I'd known the way it was going to turn out I would have never done it, but the money was too tempting. I knew that with the money flowing in, I was assured the presidency as long as I wanted it.

"Soon the money began rolling in, hidden in front accounts, moved off shore, and back again. The farmer came in with briefcases, suitcases of money."

"Weren't the tellers suspicious?" I asked.

"Yeah, but I insisted they fill out the CTRs and the farmer did too. He told them it was winnings from Vegas. I instituted a rule that I had to sign off on the CTRs so if there was a potential problem I would be able to notify the appropriate authorities. When the tellers completed the forms, they were sent to me. Then I destroyed them.

"Soon there was so much money coming in I was afraid it was going to become too obvious. I told the farmer that I couldn't take additional money. If we were to continue we had to bring in other businessmen to launder the funds, probably people who were either greedy or desperate. We found one of each. These businessmen ran their accounts through me so the bank's bottom line continued to grow. Not only was I the darling of the corporation... but," Norman paused and bit his bottom lip, "Dad actually told me he was proud of me."

He finished his drink with an audible gulp. "Now for the names of the players. The farmer is Rooney Pate, the greedy businessman is T.J. Budreau, and the desperate businessman is..." he paused for effect, "Graham McTimmons."

"Graham!" I was astonished. "Oh, no. Not Graham."

"Now, are you happy about nosing about? You wanted to know, son," he cynically said. "T.J.'s scheme was the false sales of high end autos. Graham's was a little more sophisticated. He'd sell million dollar life insurance policies to 'executives' of offshore front companies, wait a year, then 'loan' them the cash value on their policies. A beautiful ruse, I have to admit.

"We were doing well. Taking five per cent off the top. The businesses made money and the individuals made money. I kept track of the accounts with my personal computer."

"But what did this have to do with Lydia?"

"Very good question. One that calls for another drink." He stepped, with deliberate bearing, back to the bar. A half glass of Wild Turkey, a shot of water. I watched him closely. He was drunk and, I feared, desperate enough to do something rash.

He settled in his chair."About six months ago, Lydia was subbing as a secretary for Perkins." He closed his eyes, reliving the event. "I asked her if she'd stay late to type a letter for me that had to get out by FedEx. Of course, she said yes. While she was typing the letter, I pulled up the money laundering accounts on my computer. Some of the cleaning crew, working downstairs, accidentally set off the burglar alarm and I got a call from the police department trying to confirm the robbery. Of course I knew it was an accident and I told them so. Then I ran downstairs to reset the alarm, chew out the cleaning crew and also, personally confirm everything was okay to the officer who had been dispatched to respond to the alarm. All in all, it would take about ten minutes to clear up the mess. In the excitement I'd forgotten to close out the account information and it was still on the screen.

"Meanwhile, Lydia was typing and needed some figures to complete the letter. She went into my office to check my desk for the information and saw the accounts on the screen. If it had been anyone else, they wouldn't have known what they were looking at, but Lydia had been involved in so many aspects of the business and she was sharp. She knew immediately what was in front of her. I don't know what went through her mind when she saw what was before her, but she grabbed a disk from my desk and copied the data. I can only imagine her terror as she waited those desperate seconds to load the documents.

"By the time I returned she was back at her desk. She told me she didn't feel well and needed to go home. The letter she'd written was on my desk, complete and immaculate. I didn't piece together her discovery, but the following day she asked to have a private conference with me."

He laced his fingers and looked down at his lap as if he was praying. "She told me about the discovery... and what she knew. She told me she was confused. I didn't realize it then, but I was her idol. She had always admired me and now, she didn't know how to deal with what she'd learned. It was a conflict of emotions. How was she to deal with someone who was a thief, an authority figure, and who was someone she always thought highly of? In her heart she knew she had to go to the Sheriff.

"I questioned what she saw, hoping to convince her that maybe she'd made a mistake, and had nearly convinced her when she told me she would review the disk she'd hidden. Then I knew there was no way to weasel out.

"I remember her sitting there in the same seat you're sitting in now, wearing a navy blue pleated skirt and a white blouse. I came around from the desk, trying to explain to her what she'd seen, the way life really was. She was adamant. She knew what she'd seen was immoral and against the law. She tried to convince me to talk to the Sheriff." He grinned, suppressing his anguish. "Looking back, I should have taken her advice. But no, I'm Big Daddy- too wise to take advice. I tried to convince her to forget what she'd seen. She knew what she'd seen was wrong and that she needed to report it. I knelt before her, taking her slender hand in mine and I pleaded with her. As I spoke to her our eyes met. I stared at her large brown eyes and I could see that need in her. I couldn't tell Knox, I needed a way to win her, to convince her not to tell. I slowly approached those full lips, then kissed them softly. She recoiled, but when I approached her again she suddenly met me with a kiss of unexpected force and passion.

"It was as if Lydia was unleashing a newly discovered source of energy, a need that had been suppressed inside her, building pressure for years. It happened so fast, as if we were caught in a tide, having no control in the direction we were going. At first my attraction to her was phony. I was using her, compromising her, so she wouldn't go to the Sheriff. Once this happened I knew she'd never tell. The scandal would be devastating to her. But to her, it was something different. I believe it was the first time she'd ever been in love, ever opened herself up to someone. We both needed each other in different ways. She told me that she had always felt a special bond to me, like a schoolgirl crush, and had dreamed of being with me. To me, there was a confirmation of desirability and of adventure that I hadn't felt in years. I was her coach, her mentor... I brought out her passion and revealed to her pleasures she'd never known. At first she was inhibited, then relaxed, then bold, and before long she was brazen. She had this unquenchable desire and I suspect a lot of it was a rebellion against her mother. This office liaison continued for months with an occasional fling in Atlanta, using training or seminars as an excuse.

"Then one day she walked into my office...." His voice became quiet, almost repentant. "She was beaming as if she had this joyous secret. She confided that she was pregnant and she was going have our love child. Needless to say, I was stunned. But Lydia was optimistic, mapping out our future. First, I needed to get a divorce, she instructed me. I lied, telling her that my marriage was on the rocks, and that I'd soon leave my wife to marry her. She believed me, because she wanted to. Next, we'd marry. Oh yes, there would be a scandal, but only for a while. Meanwhile, we'd have each other, and when the town saw our love, they'd eventually understand."

I was flabbergasted at the story and was tempted to join Norman in a drink.

"Something had to done and it had to be quick. I told her that I couldn't leave my wife right away and I didn't want Lydia to have a child out of wedlock. The only solution was for her to have an abortion. She refused, crying and saying she wouldn't destroy our baby. But I couldn't let her have the child.

"I met with Pate and the other two out at Pate's place and we discussed what to do. Something, no doubt, had to be done or this would explode in our faces. We knew we could lose everything, our careers, our businesses, our freedom. Budreau posed the idea of having someone assault her, like they were trying to rob her, then beat her in the belly and cause a miscarriage. I vetoed the idea. I feared that Lydia might hemorrhage and die. We didn't need a murder and I didn't want her hurt. That's why she had to have the abortion. Then Pate said he had a farmhand that could convince her to have an abortion. I wanted to know how, but he told me not to ask any more questions. Something had to be done and unless I had a better idea, we would have to go with his suggestion. I knew Lydia had a training course in Atlanta. I told Pate how and what time she would travel to Atlanta, what motel she'd be staying at, and when she'd return. He told me he'd handle everything. I was to shut up, keep quiet, and he'd be back in touch after she'd had the abortion.

"I remember the last time I saw her. It was the Friday before her trip. She tried to talk me into sneaking up to Atlanta. She loved being in the city together. We could go out there, walk the malls, go to movies—we didn't have to hide. Here in Connally we couldn't do any of that. I told her that I had a wedding I had to attend in town, that there was no way I could leave. She began touching me playfully and exposing bits of herself. She said now that she was pregnant she wanted me even more, then started telling me what she would do to me if she could get me up to Atlanta. I told her it was impossible. God, it was hard, knowing that she was about to leave for Atlanta and about to lose the essence of her life. The last memory I have of her was as she was leaving. She looked over her shoulder and blew me a kiss." Norman paused and with tears in his eyes, shook his head regretfully.

When he seemed to regain his composure I prompted, "Then what happened?"

"Monday night, Pate called me and said he needed to see me immediately. I went to his house and he told me something had gone wrong and that Lydia wasn't coming back. I went berserk. He told me not to worry, but to expect a call from Perkins or someone in Atlanta when she didn't show up to her computer class. Then I was to call the Sheriff and report her missing. I didn't have to worry about anything. I had a rock solid alibi and no one would talk." Then Norman looked at me. "Until now."

"What happened to her?"

"I don't know. I swear. Pate said the less I knew the better."

"Who was the farmhand that he was going to use?"

"I don't know. That was all Pate's doing."

I leaned forward, placing my hands on Norman's desk. "Why did she have to get an abortion? Couldn't she have just gone off somewhere and had the child?"

His pained expression slowly dissolved to disbelief. "You don't know.... You really don't know."

"Know what?"

"You said you were going to tell Amanda. But you didn't know.... Someone told you. Who told you to talk to Amanda?" he demanded.

I wasn't about to confess that I'd been advised by an angel. "What am I supposed to know?"

Norman poured himself another drink, this time avoiding the water. He took a strong gulp, shivered and slumped down in his chair. He appeared to be aging by the minute. His face was puffy and there was a hint of slur in his speech. He was bent low, his chin nearly touching his chest.

"Norman, what am I supposed to know?" I repeated.

He clenched his fists to his temples and wailed. It was an outpouring of grief by a man the likes of which I'd never before witnessed. He looked up at me and in a raspy voice that didn't sound like his said, "Lydia was my daughter! I impregnated my own daughter! Oh God... oh God, please forgive me.... Please forgive me!"

It was as if an unseen force slammed me back in my seat. I didn't know what to say. I didn't know what to do.

In short breaths he explained. "It was during my senior year in college. I was working during the Christmas holidays at the bank. Amanda was working here as a teller. She and Nate had been married a couple of years and he'd just gotten a new job as a trucker. Gone most of the time. Amanda was fabulous looking and I guess if Dad had approved I might have married her, but I knew it was hopeless. Because she was married I didn't think she was interested in me, but I was wrong. I met her after work at a bar, we had a few drinks and, well, first we started talking about old times, old feelings. But those old feelings were still there. Maybe we'd had too much to drink, but afterwards we snuck out to the country club to the back nine. It was cold, but I had a couple of football blankets in the back of the car and we took them with us, and did it on the fifteenth green of Twin Creeks. That's where Lydia was conceived.

"I didn't know 'til I went home on spring break. Amanda was still working at the bank and she was showing. Nate thought Lydia was his and Amanda never told him any different. Amanda hoped that if Nate thought he was having a child it might settle him down a little.

"So now you know." He turned around in his chair, starring out the window. "Please leave me now."

I silently shut my notebook and left the office. Leaving the bank, I felt like I was walking out of a narrow tunnel framed in haze. Once I was in my car, I exhaled a long breath. I hadn't been prepared for anything like this and I had to think this through. I needed to talk to Celeste, but I didn't have time to wait for her call. I couldn't talk to Cobb; he wasn't to be trusted. Who was Pate's farmhand? Maybe Knox would know. I headed for the Sheriff's Office.

. . .

Norman watched me from his window. After I drove off, he called the Atlantic Seaboard office and told one of ASC's vice president's that he had an urgent matter to discuss with them. He needed to drive up immediately and speak to them. Then he finished off the bottle, deleted all the money laundering files from his computer, put on his coat, adjusted his tie and left. "Connie, cancel all my appointments for today. I have to go to Atlanta," he instructed her on his way from the office. His secretary would later report that something about him was not right. He had this distant stare and anemic tone in his voice. He looked ill, she reported. She thought he should have gone home.

A Home Depot truck heading south on Interstate 185 delivering inventory to their Columbus store spotted Norman's Mercedes coming from the opposite direction at high speed. "That's bear bait for sure," he thought. Approaching an underpass, the Mercedes swerved and like a guided missile, appeared to lock onto one of the concrete supports. "My God," cried the driver as he watched in horror as the Mercedes closed the distance at a hundred and twenty miles an hour, slamming into the pillar. "No!" The driver's scream was drowned out by the explosion of metal, glass, and rubber, parts arching in varied directions like a metallic fireworks display. The driver notified the State Patrol over his CB radio and pulled into the emergency lane. There was no chance for survivors.

It could not be proven that Norman had committed suicide, so his family would receive double the amount on his life insurance policy under the accident indemnity clause. Since his death occurred on official business while driving to Atlanta, his family would receive another sizable insurance settlement through ASC. Like a good Southern man, he had died honorably, taking care of his family.

CHAPTER TWENTY-ONE

JENNY WELCOMED me with a warm smile as I entered the lobby of the Sheriff's office. "Hi, Hank. What's up?"

"Nothing much. Is the Sheriff in?"

"Just left for court. He'll probably be there all morning. Can someone else help you? The Chief is in," Jenny volunteered.

"Sure, Max could help me."

Max Dennigraw, the Chief Deputy, was a beefy man with a deeply lined, weathered face and a low voice, so rough it sounded like a Geiger counter. He was square-jawed with a salt and pepper flat top, these days more salt than pepper. An unlit stogie jutted from his mouth. When Max wasn't law enforcing he could be found pursuing his true passion, bass fishing.

"D' you know why I'd rather catch a fish instead of a criminal?" Max would ask. "When I catch a fish, I can either fry him or stuff him."

Max's office was sparse, save for bass trophies and paraphernalia. Bass magazines were on his desk, bass plaques were on the wall. One or two law enforcement certificates competed for the wall space.

"What can I do for you, young Hank?" greeted Max, motioning me to sit.

"Need some background information," I said, slumping in a chair. "You know Rooney Pate?"

"Oh, yeah. Everybody knows Rooney," he said, tossing a magazine aside. "He does a lot of farming 'round here, owns a lot of land. What he doesn't farm, he rents out. He's what I call a player. He's fast and loose. Rich one minute, poor the next. I remember a while back he didn't have two nickels to rub together. Then his crops did real well and he was back with the fast cars and pretty women."

"Is he married?"

"Used to be. Dumped his wife, oh, about five years ago. Likes to play golf and gamble. In fact his friends call him Gambler. He probably goes to Vegas about four times a year and always comes back a winner. During the growing season, he's in town. You can probably find him at his house or at Twin Creeks. Don't play him in cards, leastways where there's money involved. He'll take the shirt off your back. Knox and him often play golf together. Terry'll beat him on the links, but'll usually lose the bets."

"Are they friends?"

"Naw. I think Terry finds him amusing. He's a sport and can keep you laughing, but behind that grin and good ol' boy routine is a sharp mind."

"How many hands does he have working for him?"

"Regulars, not migrants?"

I nodded.

He ran his hand through his prickly hair. "I'd say around ten."

"Any of those problems?"

"What do you mean? To us?"

"Yeah. Have you had to arrest any of them or been called to their homes?"

Max scratched his neck, thinking. "Well... for simple pain in the ass, Red Jenkins comes to mind. He's great when he's on a tractor or combine, but as soon as he gets off the tractor, he crawls into a bottle. He's had some DUI charges and once got the shit beat out of him at a country western place by a jealous husband. He'll spend too much money on the booze, then hang bad paper around town so he can eat.

"Now for just plain meanness, no doubt, I'd go with Ham Wiggins."

"Who? Ham? That's his name?" I asked skeptically.

"Well, his momma named him Hamilton Jacob Wiggins. I suspect the Hamilton was for class and Jacob was a touch of the Bible. He ended up with the shortened version 'Ham,' and he grew into it, literally. He's six feet and at least three hundred sixty pounds. Generally, he's an easy-going guy, not too bright, just happy to be riding a tractor, breathing the fresh air, and tilling the soil, unless he's been drinking or about to get arrested. When he drinks, he gets mean and he can't stand being cooped up in a cell—has to have the open spaces. Those are the times we have problems with him. I remember once he started a fight at a bar, with four guys. Wupped their asses, every one. We were called to break it up and it took five of us with mace and nightsticks to bring him down. Had to interlace a pair of cuffs to get his wrists together. Another time we got a domestic disturbance call at his mobile home. He'd gotten drunk and began tossing his girlfriend around like she was a beachball. The first deputy on the scene was Ronny Mahaffey, just out of the Marine Corps and not used to putting up with much bullshit. Ronny was five ten, a hundred and sixty pounds of blue twisted steel. He told Ham to get in the car, he was under arrest. Ham told Ronny where he could put his nightstick. Ronny warned him once more and told Ham he was about to dismantle him like an M-16. Ham rushed Ronny. Before it was over, Ronny broke one of Ham's kneecaps and a shin, then proceeded to play *Wipe Out* on his 'nads. Ham now walks with a slight limp."

"How was Ronny?"

"Oh, he was pissed. Broke his nightstick. But now, when we have a problem with Ham, we call out Ronny. Ham'll bitch a little, but he'll come along."

"Where does Ham live? I need to see him."

"You ain't gonna arrest him?" he asked with alarm.

I shook my head. "No. Just want to talk to him."

He went to a county map on the wall. "Let me show you how to get there." He drew his finger along the route, and when he got to the end point he said, "It's a brown and white mobile home a half mile on the right down County Road 111, a dirt road. His girlfriend is Sheila Crowder. So she might be home if he's in the fields. She'd been working at one of those jiffy marts, but I was in there last week and I heard she quit. I'd suggest you bring him back here if you want to talk to him. If you have a problem talking to him, Terry or I might be able to help you."

. . .

Ham Wiggins' trailer was located in a stand of pines about fifty yards off the dirt road. The home was a single wide, with gapping sections of absent trailer skirting and speckles of water rust. A faded gray high top conversion van was parked under a dilapidated shed, and a large well head wrapped in insulation stood like a tombstone in the front yard. As I drove into the yard a burly red Chow circled the car growling. I honked the horn a couple of times and cautiously opened the door. The dog, grudgingly, gave ground, bearing his fangs. The trailer door opened and a young woman stepped out onto the prefabbed concrete steps.

She was wearing a pair of jeans with holes in the knees and a black AC/DC t-shirt. Her brown hair was tangled and stringy, her face gaunt, with patches of acne.

"Does he bite?" I asked nervously, pointing to the dog.

She eyed me suspiciously. "It's a her."

"Sorry, I wasn't going to get close enough to check," I said, a poor attempt of levity. "Is Ham home?"

"You a cop?"

"Yeah, G.B.I. The Sheriff wants me to talk to him," I lied. "He's not in any kind of trouble."

She snorted. "Yeah, I bet."

"All I want to do is talk to him. If he was in trouble, do you think I'd show up here by myself?"

She wiped her hands on her jeans, saying nothing, just shifting her weight from one foot to the other. She shrugged, flipping a strand of lifeless hair off her shoulder. "You can find him up the road, about a half mile from here. He and Calvin are working on an irrigation pump."

I drove down the road and spotted the giant tendrils of aluminum irrigation pipe looming over the cornfield. I turned left on a farm trail and saw a pickup parked near the pump. A man tending the pump stopped his work as I approached. A storm was brewing in the west, and the tall stalks of corn waved with the breeze.

"Hi," I said, casually. "You must be Calvin. Looking for Ham Wiggins."

The man wiped his hands with a rag and hollowed, "Ham, someone to see you."

Ham had been kneeling behind the pump and came around.

Max's description didn't accurately depict the man. Ham Wiggins was huge, his face like a bearded pumpkin stacked on a pair of overalls, his cheeks protruding from his head like slabs of meat. His overalls barely contained his bulk, and rolls of flesh exuded from under his oily t-shirt and the sides of the bib. He shuffled toward us with a perceptible limp.

"Yeah, what kin I do f'ya?" he said coldly, his dark, unfocussed eyes evaluating me.

"Max, the Chief Deputy, wanted me to bring you to the S.O. so he and I could talk to you," I explained.

"'Bout what?"

"A young girl, Lydia Carson, disappeared a few weeks back and the Chief thought you might know something about it." I was winging it and wasn't sure whether I was succeeding.

"Don't know nuttin' 'bout it."

"Good. Then you won't mind telling that to the Chief."

Ham hesitated and looked at Calvin. "You need me here?"

Calvin removed his ball cap and mopped his brow. "Go on and get it over with. You didn't have anything to do with it, did ya?"

"Hell, no!" said Ham.

"Then go talk to 'em. Otherwise they'll pester the piss out of ya. Besides, we got bad clouds a-comin'. We'd have to shut down anyway."

When Ham got into the front passenger seat, the car dipped, leaning noticeably to the right. As we were leaving I buckled my seatbelt.

"Can't do that. Most of the straps don't reach around. Besides," he said, patting his bulbous gut, "I've brought my own air bag."

I wanted to get to the Sheriff's Office as quick as I could. I didn't feel comfortable with the man next to me, without cuffs. He seemed sensible, but I could sense his raw power. The sooner I had him in Max's office, the better. Unfortunately, the road was rutted, keeping my speed slow.

We drove past Ham's place. Sheila, wearing her hard rock shirt, was getting into the van, her left hand on the front door, her right clutching the doorframe, lifting her small frame up to the seat. I hadn't noticed her diminutive stature when she stood as the top of the trailer steps. Next to the van she looked like a child, barely five feet tall. What an extreme in sizes. I had a fleeting thought that Ham's and her lovemaking had to be a circus act.

I turned to Ham to make conversation, to keep him docile. "How long have you and Sheila—" Then it struck me. And I recalled Linda Killgore's observations at the airport while searching Lydia's Honda: *The front seat was pushed up indicating the driver was approximately five feet tall. Also the radio was on an FM hard rock station here in Atlanta.* Ham noticed the reaction on my face and with his feral cunning, he knew my thoughts.

I noticed a metallic glint to my right and instinctively recoiled as the blade of a hawkbill knife slashed across my face. Pressing myself against my door, I clawed for my pistol. Ham swung the peaked blade at me again as the car left the road, leaping a ditch. It plowed through a soft field, red soil arching like rusty waves over the hood, then slammed into a tree stump. I managed to grab my gun, pointed it toward the behemoth and fired, the shots exploding in the confines of the car.

There was a pause as we got our bearings. Steam hissed from the radiator and the interior of the car was hazy with acrid gun smoke. The wheels were bogged deep in the soft soil and the right front fender was embedded in a splintered stump. Thunder cracked over the tops of the pines and large drops of water splattered on the windshield. I held my pistol with both hands, pressed tightly against my chest, pointing it at Ham. My seatbelt had protected me from the wreck. My left forearm was flayed from the second knife attack, a flap of skin dangled from my arm, and blood dripped from my right cheek onto my coat and shirt. I swabbed my cheek with my tongue praying there wasn't a hole there.

Ham sat sideways in his seat facing me, the side window behind him shattered, little cubes of glass in his lap, his right arm bent at a strange angle, the menacing knife on the floorboard at his feet.

Ham groaned. "Son of a bitch! You shot me." He had two gunshot wounds, one in his belly, and another in his left shoulder. Thin burgundy fluid seeped from the holes, enlarging into dark irregular circles. "Think my right arm's broke. I can't move my fingers."

I backed away from him. He was still a threat. I tried to open the door, but it was jammed. The light on the radio was off; I knew it was dead.

"Where's Lydia?" I demanded to know.

"Ya motherfucker, ya shot me," he whined in disbelief. "I ain't never been shot before."

"Where's Lydia?" I repeated. "If you want to live, you'd better tell me where Lydia is."

"I ain't saying squat. What you gonna do, shoot me again?"

"Yes... I think I might," I heard myself calmly say. "You killed Lydia, you tried to kill me. If you don't tell me where she is, I *will* shoot you."

Ham sat up, his eyes focusing behind me. I glanced over my shoulder and saw a gray van, his van, coming to a stop on the edge of the road. Sheila came from behind the van, leaped the ditch and walked toward us. "Ham! You there?" she squawked.

"Sheila! Sheila!" Ham screamed from his open window. "He shot me and he's gonna kill me."

"Keep your mouth shut!" I ordered.

"Get the shotgun out of the van!" Ham hollered. "You've gotta shoot him or he'll kill us all."

Pain coursed through my arm as I rolled down my window. "Sheila, call the Sheriff, call the G.B.I. We need help," I pleaded.

She went into the van, emerging moments later with a pump shotgun. "Sheila, go get help. Don't do this!"

She ignored my entreaties, coldly watching me as she meticulously inserted shotgun shells into the gun. From a safe distance she cautiously circled the car.

When she was in front of the car at a distance of about ninety feet, Ham called out to her. "Stay there... and kill him if he tries to stop me from leaving." Ham turned to me. "I'm no harm t'ya. All I want t'do is get away. Then we'll leave ya 'lone and call an emergency wagon fer ya."

"Bullshit," I spat, feeling sticky liquid, my blood, oozing down my neck. "As soon as you get out of this car, you'll get that gun from her and kill me. You've got nothing to lose."

"No, I won't. I swear." He opened the door about eighteen inches and then it jammed into the soft soil. "Damn," he swore at his luck. "Sheila! I'm gonna have t' work ma way through the door. It's stuck. Keep him covered."

Slowly he began worming his way through the door. I tested the fingers in my left hand. They felt fine. I raised the arm and could see the exposed pink muscles in my forearm contract. Though painful, it still functioned. Focused on his task, he didn't notice as I shifted my Smith & Wesson to my left hand. I squeezed the gun's butt. So far, so good.

"I'm half way there, honey," Ham yelled.

She was watching Ham when I leaned out the window, the gun in my left hand, steadied by my right. I sighted the pistol, as I was trained in the academy, smoothly pulling the trigger back while lining the three tritium dots on her image. As the dots fell into a horizontal line, I applied the remaining pressure on the trigger. "BOOM! BOOM! BOOM!" The gun bucked in my hand. I tried to keep my wrist locked, keeping my sights on Sheila. From her reaction, I knew my first shot had found its mark, but she was able to turn the shotgun toward me, unleashing a hail of shot. Lead shot splattered around me, but I kept firing, as I was trained in the Rangers—to maintain concentrated fire power until the threat ceased. She awkwardly racked the shotgun to fire again, but suddenly crumpled to the ground.

The windshield was speckled with cobwebbed holes from the pellets. Some had penetrated the glass embedding themselves in the seat, but others were deflected by the angled glass. I didn't know how many rounds I'd fired, so I quickly reached for my spare magazine and reloaded, pointing my pistol at Ham. He was wedged between the door and the frame, unable to move. He'd witnessed the gunfight and knew Sheila was down. He also had another wound in his left shoulder blade.

"You stupid bitch!" he screamed. "You ain't s'posed to shoot me. You s'posed to shoot him."

"He done shot me too," Sheila wheezed, writhing on the ground. "I need help, Ham. I don't want to die. I can hardly breathe."

"Serves y'right, if you can't shoot any bet'ern dat!"

The rain was now a steady drizzle. My pager buzzed. It was the office, but I couldn't call them. With luck they would get worried and look for me.

"Get back in the car," I ordered. He paused. "If you don't get back inside, that means you're going for the shotgun. I won't have a choice but to shoot you." Ham knew I wasn't bluffing and slithered back inside the car. "Okay, Ham. Let's talk. Otherwise, you both are gonna die out here."

"I don't have to tell you a Goddamned thing," Ham arrogantly replied. "First you shoot me and now you gone and kilt my woman. I ain't tellin' ya nothin'. Sure I've gotten a couple a holes in me, but I'm all right. You'll croak a long time before I do. You want t' wait it out? Fine with me. I'll just relax and take a lil' nap. You've got t' watch me the whole time. Jest let down yur guard fer a moment and I'll take that gun from ya, stick it up yer ass, and pull the trigger."

"Sheila's going to die if we don't get her any help."

"Hell, I saw what y' did t' her. She's dead already. She jest don't know it yet."

Ham was confident. If I tried to crawl out of the car window, he'd jump me. Maybe I could handle him with his bummed arms but it was a risk I didn't want to take. It was a standoff. We stared at each other while Sheila lay dying in the rain.

Five minutes passed when Ham broke the silence. "Jesus!" he screamed, lamely brushing at his legs with terror in his eyes.

I thought a snake had crawled into the car, until I saw them. When Ham had opened the car door, he disturbed a mound of fire ants. Fanning out, the soldiers had found the perpetrator who had invaded their territory and they were attacking, hundreds of the cinnamon-colored creatures crawling up his legs, climbing the car seat, each one stinging and injecting its venom into him.

"Help me, please help me," he pleaded. "I'm 'lergic to 'em. They'll kill me."

"Where's Lydia?" I asked coldly.

"Get 'em off me and I'll tell you. I'll talk. Tell you everything, testify, I promise. Get 'em off me!"

"Tell me first. The longer you try to bargain the worse it's going to get."

"All right, all right! I did it. I kilt her, but it was an accident. Didn't mean to," he rattled. "Now get them off me!"

"Tell me from the beginning. Why you?"

"It was Pate's idea. That's all I know. He... called me to his house one night. God! Get 'em off of me. I'm itching!"

"Talk, Ham!"

"He said he'd pay me five thousand dollars if I grabbed Lydia and convince 'er to have an abortion. If she refused, she couldn't come back. Pate already had somethin' arranged with the doctor. He gave me the information." Ham blew a couple of short panicked breaths. "Told me where she'd be on this trip to Atlanta. The day of the grab, Pate gave me a sports bag and told me to keep this in the van and if anythin' should go wrong I should call him. Everything I needed was in the bag." He paused, slapping weakly at the ants. They had discovered his blood and the message of a new food source had gone out. A phalanx of ants was marching on him.

"Go on," I urged.

"We followed her in the van, 'til she stopped at a fillin' station near Newnan. She parked on the side of the building, used the restroom, then went inside. We parked beside her car. When she came out and was unlocking her car, Sheila approached her to ask for directions. While Lydia's back was turned, I opened the van door and grabbed her from behind and drug her inside. Before she could scream I stuffed a sock in her mouth and wrapped duct tape around her head, leaving her to breathe from her nose. Sheila was wrapping her feet in the tape. The bitch put up a fuss and I had to slap her around to get her to settle down. Once that was done, we drove north to Atlanta, with Sheila following in the Honda. We stopped at a mall near Union City and parked the Honda there. Sheila got in the van while I went in the back with Lydia. I 'splained to her what was going on and that we were taking her to get an abortion. Once we were back on the interstate I took the sock out of her mouth. She screamed and struggled to get loose. The bitch had a lot of spunk, but no one on the interstate could see her or hear her screams. I told her she had two choices: she could get one from a doctor or from me."

He squirmed in his seat, his eyes wide in pain, his hands trembling in fear. "Please, I told you. Now help me."

"You're not finished," I said coldly.

He spoke quickly. "We rode around on the friggin' perimeter for an hour while I tried to talk her into it. I showed her my knife hoping that would change her mind. Then I showed her.... myself, and told her I'd take her if she didn't agree to the abortion. She laughed at me and spat in my face, saying I'd have to kill her before she'd let a piece of white trash take her. What would you do if someone spit in your face?" He moaned, sweeping hordes of ants from his overalls. As soon as he killed some, others would take their place with their incessant stinging. His arms were twitching sporadically. "So I hit her. Once, maybe twice. But I swear, past times I hit Sheila much harder than I did her. When I smacked her, she fell on her side, her head turned kinda funny. She didn't say nuttin', jest breathing like a bird that you sometimes find in your yard after it flew into the side of yer house. Jest moving her jaw up and down for a time. Then it quit. I checked her and figured she was dead. Sheila went nuts. That's all I needed, two fruity bitches in my van. We drove back to the mall and I called Pate. Oh, God. I can't stand it." He weakly flailed at himself, moving closer to me. The ants were swarming on every exposed piece of skin, biting and stinging. He moved toward me.

I fired a shot. The dashboard next to him erupted. "I'll kill you if you stop talking. Now get back."

Shivering like he was frostbit, he continued, his voice quivering. "Pate didn't seem surprised. He told me what to do. Sheila got from the bag an airline ticket to Mexico in Lydia's name. There was a thousand dollars in the bag for her expenses. She drove to the airport and caught the flight, while I drove back to Connally. Pate told me where to dump the body. It's in a well on his property, behind an old sharecropper's shack. The road's growed up, but not so I couldn't get to the well. Sheila stayed in Mexico for a couple of days, got drunk and laid in the sun, then flew back to Atlanta. Pate didn't give us the money at first as he promised. Said once the investigation of her ended, then we'd get paid. Now, please, go get help. I'm having trouble breathing."

The ants' poison was working. Ham was swelling, his skin puffing and his eyes closing. His breathing was labored. Even if he wanted, he couldn't hurt me.

I squirmed through the window, falling onto the ground. The summer shower had passed, and the ground was muddy and slick. I tried to keep my wounds clean. I felt dizzy and walked to the van. Sheila's keys were on the front seat of the van. I drove it back to the mobile home. The Chow ran from the back of the house growling, until I aimed my pistol at her. The dog knew guns and immediately retreated. I found the key to the door of the trailer and went inside.

The place was filthy. Dirty clothes everywhere, dirty dishes and moldy food littering the kitchen counters, peanut shells and beer cans covering the coffee table. A couple of cockroaches slithered under the sofa when I turned on a light. I found a towel that appeared clean and wrapped it around my arm, hoping I wouldn't lose the flesh. Anxiously, I examined my cheek in the bathroom mirror. The cut was deep, about three inches long. I found some gauze in the bathroom cabinet for a makeshift bandage for my face. Then I called the office.

Cole answered the phone. "Jesus, Hank! We've been trying to find you. Where are you?"

I gave him a quick briefing, telling him about the shooting and asking for an ambulance. "Sheila's dead and if Ham doesn't get help quick he's a goner."

Cole surprised me. "Cobb and a deputy are already en route. I'll have Peggy dispatched an ambulance immediately."

"Cobb's en route?"

"Yeah, Max told him. Cobb's been looking for you." Then Cole told me about Norman's wreck. "You were the last person to talk to him and we've been trying to find you, once he was identified at the scene." Normally I would have been shocked at the news, but nothing made sense today.

I heard a car drive into the yard and glanced out the window. "Cole, it's a deputy. Got to go."

"Okay. Peggy's advised Cobb. He's at the scene with your car."

I walked outside, startling the deputy. I had to be a ghoulish site, bandaged in gauze and towels. "Monroe?"

I nodded.

"I'm Ronny Mahaffey. Here, let me help you."

I insisted Mahaffey drive me back to Ham.

Cobb's car was parked on the side of the road, the blue lights spinning. He was standing over Sheila. He saw us pull up and trotted toward us. "Come on, get in my car. You need help. The ambulance will be here in another five."

"Let me see Ham, first," I asked. "Is he alive?"

Cobb shook his head. "I wasn't sure if Ham was still a threat, so I checked the car first."

We trudged through the mud to the LTD and peered through the window. If I didn't know it was Ham, I would have been reluctant to identify him. He had swollen even larger, his skin stretched as tight as a football, only slits for eyes. The ants were still busy with him, crawling over his face, his mouth, through his beard, inside his eyelids, through his hair. Some had found the bullet wounds and were entering and leaving through the holes.

Cobb put his hand on my shoulder. With sirens wailing the ambulance screeched to a stop. "Let's go, son. I've called out the troops to handle this. A shooting team is on the way from Atlanta."

"Not yet," I insisted. "I've got to recover Lydia's body. Ham told me where she is."

"All right. But first let the EMTs look at you. Ronny, can you secure the area until the agents arrive?"

"Yes, sir."

I sat in the rear of the ambulance, briefing Cobb on Ham's confession while a medic treated me. Once I was still, a wave of exhaustion engulfed me. As much I needed to get to Lydia, I wanted to sleep.

More personnel arrived, the Sheriff, the Chief Deputy, the deputies, and agents, followed by the media and the curious.

Cobb contacted Peggy at the office. "Call Luther McCoy at DNR. I want him out here immediately. He knows the Pate area and I need his help in locating something."

Terry and Max joined us at the ambulance. They recognized the van. "Where's Ham?" Knox asked.

Cobb pointed at my car. "In there." Knox walked alone toward my Ford.

"How're you doing, son?" asked Max.

"Tired," was all I could say.

Max turned to Cobb. "Sorry, Cobb. Hank told me he only wanted to talk to him about a matter. Nothing about any arrest."

Max organized the men whose primary function was security and maintaining the integrity of the crime scene. Cobb assigned the agents. Cole was in charge of the crime scene and getting the bodies to the crime lab for autopsies. Echols was charged with processing the crime scene, which included photographs, fingerprints, gathering shell casings and reconstructing the scene. They also took photographs of my wounds. Other agents arriving from Atlanta would assist. Robin and Lanier would go with Cobb and handle the recovery of Lydia's body.

Knox returned. "Damn, Cobb! That's a new one on me. Old Ham looks like the Pillsbury dough boy. Someone needs to get those ants off him before they cart him off. They're in every hole of his body, his eyes, his nose, his mouth——."

"Yeah, Terry, we know," interrupted Cole. "As soon as Stan gets organized, he'll handle it."

"Sir, we need to get Hank to the hospital," announced the medic. "Do any of your men want to follow us?"

The E.R. doctor cleaned and examined my wounds. He was more concerned about my arm than my face. "The skin should reattach itself, but I'm more concerned about infection. We need to keep you in the hospital a couple of days, give you some I.V. antibiotics, and monitor your temperature and white cell count. I'm calling in a plastic surgeon for your face. He should be here in about a half hour. If I did the stitches, you'd end up with one of those Heidelberg scars, looking like a Prussian officer."

The stitches took longer than I expected and I was impatient to leave. The plastic surgeon was methodical. As frustrated as I was at his plodding, I knew it was my face he was mending, and it needed to be done right. As soon as they finished I was out the door, thanking the doctors and nurses, asking them to reserve a room for me. Dennis was in the waiting room.

"Just got off the radio," reported Lanier. "They found the well and they're checking it out. I've got directions. Ready to ride?"

I nodded. My numb cheek made talking difficult and caused me to slur my words.

Running with blue lights, the ride took twenty minutes. Though it was past six, the summer sun was still shining, the evening humid and sticky from the rain shower. We located the trail by the fresh tracks from the search vehicles and followed them behind a weathered shack with a rusted tin roof. An assortment of green DNR trucks, brown Forrest County cars and GBI sedans were scattered around the area.

A group of men were pulling a dark body bag from a hole shielded by bushes and briars. I walked over to Cobb and the Sheriff who were supervising from a distance.

"Terry, you know Lydia. Can you make the identification?" suggested Cobb.

He nervously licked his lips. "Yeah, I'll do it."

I leaned to follow Knox. Cobb placed his large hand on my chest, preventing me from making any forward motion. "You don't need to see her. Remember her from her pictures."

A man unzipped the bag so Knox could view the body, and I caught a whiff of the putrid, rotting corpse. I recoiled, bending at the waist. The finality of it all hit me. Lydia was officially dead. A dear life had been snuffed out, her body tossed away like a piece of garbage. All for greed. By a group of men who thought their position in the community made them immune from the same rules the other citizens followed. Knox viewed the contents in the bag and nodded solemnly, looking at the ground in disgust.

"Let's go see Pate," I said, quivering with rage.

"Robin, it's all yours. We'll be back," instructed Cobb. "Terry, let's go see your golfing partner."

· · ·

Rooney Pate's farmhouse was a neat one-story brick ranch with a slate roof and surrounded by trimmed hedges, expansive oaks and towering pines. His Land Rover was parked out front. Knox knocked on the door, with Cobb to the side and me remaining back, silently hoping he'd come out with a gun. I saw a silhouette pass by the window.

The door opened wide. He was middle-aged man with a ruddy, sun-burnt complexion, and he held a drink in his hand. "Terry! What brings—" Then he saw Cobb and me. "Whoa! This don't look like no social visit. What's going on?"

"We recovered a body on your property." said Knox. "A woman named Lydia Carson. Did you know her?"

Pate shook his head with a puzzled look. "You know, Terry, the way you're asking the question, it sounds like I'm a suspect?"

"A body was found on your property, Pate," emphasized Cobb. "As the owner of the property, it's only natural that you're questioned. If you didn't have any involvement in this, you'll answer the question."

Pate's party demeanor was gone. "I'll tell you what, Terry, and don't take this personal, but it's looking like I might need some legal representation. I'm not saying anything until I meet with my attorney, Davis Adcock. Why don't y'all call him first. If he'll allow it, we'll talk tomorrow."

I stared at the man, trying to contain my hate. This was the man who started it all. This was the man who preyed on the weaknesses of people, their desperation, their greed, their egos, their needs. This was the man whose wickedness led to the deaths of Lydia, Norman, Ham and Sheila. Now he was hiding behind the law, using it to shield him from the exposure of his actions.

Cobb turned and left without saying a word. He walked directly over to me. "We need to get you back to the hospital. I'll talk to the D.A. about Pate. We'll get him." He patted me on the shoulder. "You have to learn when and where to pick your battles. This is not one of those times."

CHAPTER TWENTY-TWO

RETURNING TO the hospital, I was quickly wheeled to my room. I'd hoped to use the next two days to relax and regain my strength, and this was not what I'd been anticipating. In spite of my exhaustion, sleep was not as comforting as I'd hoped. Flashes of the previous day's violence forced themselves into my dreams. Just when I was about to relax I'd jump, seeing the knife flash across my face. I relived Sheila's shooting, hearing her moans and pleas for help.

The next morning at nine, Cobb walked in with the Director. "Young Hank, you don't report to work and I come to find out you've been lounging out here. Gracious, what's happening to you?" He turned to the Director. "You know, he solves a major homicide and now he's of the opinion that he can lay around for a couple of days. The homicide was yesterday, son. What have you done for us today?"

The Director shook my hand. "It's a pleasure to meet you again, Hank." The last time I'd seen him was at the graduation ceremony when he spoke briefly and handed out the badges. "How are you?"

"Pretty good, sir," I said, pushing myself to a sitting position.

"Cobb briefed me on what happened. I admire your perseverance. That's the reputation we need in the Bureau, that agents in the GBI won't quit 'til the job's done. Is there anything we can do for you?"

"Just pay my medical bills and let me finish this case, sir."

He patted me on the shoulder. "That, I can handle."

"Hank, the Sheriff and I gave a joint press conference today on the shooting and we told 'em that it's tied to the recovery of Carson's body," said Cobb. "And they've been clamoring for detailed information. But we've got two situations here: one, to work a shooting and two, to solve Lydia's homicide. Everyone in the office is busy. We don't need any leaks right now. If any reporters show up wanting to talk to you, refer them to me."

"Yes, sir."

I ate a bland lunch, pushing the food around my plate. My upper jaw was sore, so the menu consisted of soup and soft foods. Not very appetizing.

The doctor's concerns proved valid. I was running a low-grade fever and my white count was up. It could have been worse if the doctors had not pumped me full of antibiotics. I took a nap that afternoon. I sensed someone was in the room and opened my heavy eyelids.

There she was in her beauty, her dark hair shimmering in the afternoon light. She was the best sight in the last two days. "Megan, thanks for coming," I mumbled.

Her eyes were shiny and her lip quivered as if she wasn't sure what to say. "You look awful, no, you look beautiful… you… you… look what you did to yourself." She reached for me and stopped. "Is it all right to hug you?"

"Oh, Megan. That would be great," I said, reaching for her. I held her close smelling her hair, feeling her softness, wishing it was possible to enclose her.

She kissed me on the good cheek. "I heard about it on the news. They say you killed two people and found Lydia."

"Uh-huh. Yesterday was kind of busy."

"They did this to you?"

"One of them did. But it's not too bad. I'll be out after tomorrow." I held her hand. I needed her touch.

"Was this what Celeste talked to you about?"

"Yes. I would have never found Lydia without her. At first I thought she was a crackpot, but she was right the whole time."

There was a brief knock and the door opened. I expected a nurse, but I was wrong. She looked familiar, but I couldn't place her until she spoke. "Agent Monroe, I hope I'm not interrupting anything?"

"Ms. AJC," I said, shaking my head in disbelief. "Megan, this is a reporter from Atlanta. You were at the Adams County Courthouse. I'm sorry, I don't remember your name."

"Nita Humphries," she chirped, extending her hand to Megan. "I stopped in to see how he was doing."

"I'm doing fine, Ms. Humphries. I appreciate you coming down from Atlanta to check on my welfare."

"You sound like a hero, Agent Monroe. In spite of the belief of a town, you tracked down the killers of Lydia Carson. The people of Georgia need to know that's the type of agents working for the GBI. I heard a rumor that the death of Reed Norman was linked to Carson. Is that true?"

"I admire your spunk, Ms. Humphries. But all your questions should be directed to either the SAC or Sheriff. If they allow it, I'll talk to you."

Frustrated, she shook her head. "You don't budge much, do you?"

"No ma'am, I guess I don't."

"Well, I am sincere about your recovery. I wish you the best," she said, walking toward the door. "Maybe we can meet and talk off the record someday."

After she left, Megan shot me a stern glance. "You know she was hitting on you."

"Oh, come on. She's just teasing so she can get a story from me, that's all. Unless she has a fetish for the bandaged. And speaking of hitting. Who was that guy you kissed the other night at your apartment?"

"Were you spying on me, Agent Monroe?" she asked, leaning toward me aggressively.

"Megan, you have a definite flair for turning a question."

She paused, considering if she should answer my prying question. "He was a friend, a fellow teacher, who's also getting his master's at Columbus College. He was having some personal problems and stopped by to talk. That's all... but a little jealousy is kind of nice. You wear it well."

Megan checked her watch. "Listen, I need to go."

"Why don't you come back tonight and bring a backgammon game."

She gave me a wink. "You're on."

Shortly after Megan left, Celeste called. I recognized her soothing voice instantly. "Hank, I'm so sorry. I didn't want you to get hurt." There was an irregular cadence to her voice as if she'd been crying.

"I'm all right.... And we found Lydia." I paused, trying to maintain my aplomb.

"Yes, we did!" It was said in a half laugh, a half cry. "And Lydia... well, she's happy now. She wants to thank you."

"Celeste, you knew about Norman and Amanda. How? That isn't something a new angel in town would know. Judy Moon might have known something about that, but not you."

"Well, Hank, I do talk to other angels."

"And you expect me to believe that?"

"I've asked you to believe a lot, haven't I?

There was an awkward silence. We both searched for something to say, neither of us wanting to end our contact with the other. "You know, we aren't finished yet. We found Lydia, but we've got to bring her killers in."

"I'll see what I can do. I'll pray for you."

. . .

That night Megan brought me some casual clothes to wear upon my discharge. We played backgammon into the night, carefully refraining from any talk of the shooting. Astutely, she realized I wanted that behind me.

There was still a lot to do. I had to prove that Pate, Budreau and McTimmons were involved in Lydia's murder. Cobb scheduled a meeting with Emory Vance, the District Attorney, Thursday morning.

I was waiting in the hospital lobby when Cobb arrived. "A two-day vacation's enough for any agent. Now let's get back to work." He carried my overnight bag to his car and as he drove to the courthouse, he briefed me on the discoveries of the investigation while I'd been hospitalized.

The autopsy determined Lydia had died, in layman's terms, from a broken neck as a result of blunt trauma and, yes, she had been pregnant. The fetus was a girl... which brought up an interesting legal question.

Were we working one or two homicides? A review of the airport video confirmed Sheila boarding the Miami flight. Sheila's fingerprints were positively identified among the latents recovered on Lydia's Honda. Hair fibers were found in Ham's van that were consistent with Lydia's hair, and fibers found in Lydia's Honda matched the upholstery in Ham's van. Cobb was optimistic that they would be able to trace the purchaser of the airline ticket and identify Pate, but the ticket had been purchased from a travel agency in Miami, believed to be a front company for drug smugglers. "No se nada," was the pat answer the FDLE agents received when they contacted the business. A security video from the convenience store, Lil' Miser in Newnan, was recovered with a brief segment of Lydia entering the store and paying for a soft drink. Neither Ham nor Sheila were on the film. An obstetrician, upon seeing the news in the paper, called the office, saying Lydia was his patient. With Amanda's permission, he released what information he had. Lydia had been nearing the end of her first trimester and the father, according to Lydia, was Reed Norman. A sonogram had determined that the child was developing normally. Ham's trailer was searched but nothing significant was found.

The District Attorney's office was located on the third floor of the courthouse. Vance's staff consisted of two assistant DAs, three secretaries, a receptionist-clerk, and an investigator. Knox, Robin and Cole were waiting in the reception area for us, and as soon as we entered the receptionist called Vance, who came up from his office to greet us.

Cobb introduced me to Vance.

"We've already met," Vance quickly informed him. "It was at church, right?"

"Yes, sir. Good memory," I said.

"Nonsense. You're not the kind so easily forgotten." I smiled inwardly. Vance was the politician. "I know that Wiggins fellow. Had him in court a couple of times. Not someone I'd want to go toe to toe with. Follow me. We're going to meet in the conference room. Nancy, have Helen join us."

"Yes, sir," said the receptionist.

The conference room also served as a law library, the walls lined with dusty volumes of thick State and Federal law books dating back decades.

Vance sat at the end of the conference table and Helen sat beside him with a yellow legal pad. I sat on one side with Cobb and Knox; Robin and Cole sat across from us.

"I want to thank everyone for meeting with me today," Vance began as if he was addressing a jury. "I know you have a lot to do, but I thought it was best to review what we have in the Carson investigation and decide on where we need to go. Cobb, I don't have much in the way of paperwork yet and I've had to rely mostly on conversations I've had with you and Terry. But from what I understand, some very prominent people have been developed as suspects. If we have to take legal action against these people I naturally will, but I don't want to do it in a haphazard or ill-advised manner. Understand?"

We all nodded.

Vance continued. "Each suspect in this investigation has retained counsel. I've contacted their attorneys, who've advised me that their clients wish to exercise their Fifth Amendment rights and not make any statements or answer any questions. In other words, gentlemen, the suspects cannot be contacted directly, or indirectly such as through informants. If you wish to talk to them, you must go through their attorneys.

"Having given you that little piece of cheery advice, I think the best way to proceed is to review the investigative steps your office took, up until the interview of Wiggins."

"Okay," said Cobb, straightening in his chair. "Normally I would have the case agent present this phase, but because of his face wound, I don't think he should do any lengthy speaking. I'll try to explain what he's done. Hank, if I make any major errors, correct me."

Referring to my investigative summaries, Cobb briefed Vance on my investigation, including my background interviews and the evidence found at the airport. "The break came in the case when Hank learned that Lydia had a confidant, Libby Rudeley, in the nursing home and that Lydia confided in her that she was pregnant and named Reed Norman as the father. The next day Hank interviewed Norman. Norman confessed that Carson had discovered that he, Pate, Ross McTimmons, and J.T. Budreau were running drug money through their businesses. He confessed that he had entered into an affair with her to keep her quiet and she had gotten pregnant as a result of their affair. She refused to abort the child so Pate hired Wiggins to kill her."

"Pate told Norman that?" asked Vance.

"No, sir," I replied. "Norman told me that he didn't know the name of her killer, or in this case, killers. There was a meeting at Pate's attended by Norman, McTimmons, and Budreau, to discuss the dilemma. Pate told Norman he would have it handled."

"I see," nodded Vance, scribbling on his pad.

Cobb continued. "Hank, on an off chance, goes to interview Ham Wiggins."

"Why Wiggins?"

"Because he's a sorry son of a bitch," quipped Knox. "'Scuse me, ladies."

"Wiggins panicked," explained Cobb, "thinking Hank had the evidence on him. And he tried to kill my agent. After shots were fired, Ham confessed, telling Hank that Pate hired him, how they kidnapped her, how they killed her, where they dumped the body, and how Sheila posing as Carson flew to Mexico to cover it up."

Vance leaned back in his chair and said softly. "Meanwhile Reed arranges a meeting in Atlanta and drives head on into a bridge. Such a waste... such a damn waste." He exhaled a determined breath. "Do we have anything at Ham's place or the well that can connect our suspects to either Wiggins' or Reed's statement?"

Robin and Cole reported, explaining what had been found and what had been confirmed.

Vance listened patiently, occasionally asking questions. "Any evidence on Norman's computer?"

"No," Robin replied. "A forensic search was conducted with negative results."

Vance nodded and allowed the room to remain silent for effect. He pulled himself close to the table and placed his pencil on his pad. "It sounds like y'all have done a very thorough investigation. You've got enough to convict Norman and Wiggins, but in answer to the question, 'What do we have on our living suspects?' gentlemen, I don't see it."

"What!" I blurted, thinking I'd heard wrong. "Are you saying we don't have anything on Pate, McTimmons, or Budreau?"

"Yes, son," Vance said regretfully. "Let me explain what we *legally* have. We have statements from two individuals, both of them dead. Their statements can't be admitted because it would be hearsay."

"Dying declaration," I interjected, remembering my Georgia law course. "Norman knew he was going to kill himself when he gave me that statement, and Wiggins knew he was dying from both gunshot wounds and ant bites."

Vance shook his head. "Son, that's stretching it. Did you lay out the foundation to Norman of a dying declaration? Second of all, we'd have to prove that he intentionally killed himself, otherwise how can a man give a dying declaration if he dies accidentally? His death has been ruled accidental. The insurance companies would love for us to prove that he committed suicide; they would only have to pay out about half of the current settlement.

"And as for Mr. Wiggins, a foundation wasn't laid out for him either. In fact, the admissibility of his statement, alive or dead, is questionable. Was his statement given freely and voluntarily, without coercion or threats? Here he is, shot twice by you, and under assault by fire ants, and you tell him that you'll get help if he tells you about Lydia. Mr. Monroe, I understand your motives, and if I was in your shoes I would have done the same thing, but his statement would never be admitted in any court of this land.

"Now, if we eliminate those statements, what do we have?"

The room went stone cold silent. Each agent looking at the other for credible evidence.

"Gentlemen, and lady," concluded Vance, "the work y'all have done on this investigation is exemplary. And I will notify the Director of your works, but I think it's time to piss on the fire and call in the dogs. Thank you for coming."

I was stunned. Pate and the others had beaten me. They had killed Lydia and walked away. Cobb and the others sitting at the table knew our position and as distasteful as it was, Vance was right.

We were in a somber mood as we left the courthouse. "Robin, Dennis, go ahead and write your summaries. We'll see what we can do on this," instructed Cobb.

I got in the car with Cobb. We rode for a while in silence. "Vance is in a tough position," he said contemplatively. "It's kind of like the story of hunting for gorillas. If you're going to shoot the animal, you damn well better kill it. Because if you don't, you're going to be dealing with one pissed off animal. If Vance is going to arrest Pate, McTimmons, and Budreau, he better have evidence, solid evidence, enough to convince twelve men and women that each is guilty beyond a reasonable doubt. If he doesn't have it, then he'll never be DA again. The people who think the three are innocent will consider it a witch hunt and they should have never been arrested. The ones who think they're guilty will believe that Vance screwed up the case and allowed them to get off. Then there're the ones who think if he doesn't do anything, that he's been paid to leave them alone. What I need to do is find Vance a solution."

What was Cobb up to? This didn't sound like the person that Celeste said not to trust. "Any ideas?" I asked.

"I'm not sure. Let me make a few calls. What I'm about to do isn't taught at the academy."

. . .

Only Cobb could have pulled the meeting together. When he requested someone's presence it wasn't due to his position of authority, it was due to his position of knowledge in the community. "You should attend this meeting. It will be to your benefit," was all that Cobb needed to say.

Friday morning was a brilliant day, more suitable for fishing, skiing or having a picnic with friends or family, not sitting in an enclosed office breathing recycled air and listening to frustrating legal limitations and barriers.

The meeting was at nine. Other than Cobb, I was the only local GBI agent present. Waiting outside the courthouse for Cobb were two gentlemen, one white, one black, with the fresh scrubbed look of agents from Atlanta. "I'll introduce you to them later. I don't want to be late for the meeting," Cobb whispered to me. He quickly greeted them and escorted them inside.

As we entered the DA's office, Vance was pacing the floor while Knox read a newspaper. "What the hell's going on?" Vance demanded to know. "You know I've got Pate, McTimmons, and Budeau and their attorneys in the conference room?"

"Calm down, Emory. I've got the case solved. You're going to come out of this a hero," assured Cobb, patting him on the back. "This will get you out of your political box. Give me ten minutes and if you don't agree, say so. You know I can't agree to a thing without your concurrence."

Vance pointed both index fingers at Cobb. "Don't embarrass me."

Cobb dismissed the threat with a wave of his hand. "Let's go talk turkey."

The three attorneys and their clients were seated on the left side of the conference table. We circled to the right and sat across from them. This time Cobb positioned himself at the head of the table with Vance next to him. I sat directly across from Graham who glanced at me with bored indifference and doodled on a legal tablet. Once we were settled, Cobb began.

"I want to personally thank everyone for appearing at this meeting this morning. I trust it will be beneficial to everyone in attendance. You are here as a favor to me and it's duly noted.

"First, gentlemen, I'm not sure how familiar you are with the pending charges against your clients. As you know, they were implicated to varying degrees by Reed and Wiggins for their involvement in the kidnapping and murder of Lydia Carson and her child. And also to varying degrees both their statements to Agent Monroe, here, have been confirmed. Based on what we have learned to date, if Norman and Wiggins were alive to testify, your clients would be charged with violations ranging from a minimum of second degree murder to kidnapping to first degree murder. Would you agree, Emory?"

"Yeah, uh… yes, that sounds reasonable," Vance mumbled impatiently.

"I also believe, and I think you would concur, Emory, that if there was a plea, the State would accept second degree murder pleas from Budreau and McTimmons and a first degree murder plea from Pate. McTimmons and Budreau were indirectly involved in Carson's murder. Pate directed and caused the murder. Correct?"

Emory pursed his lips and nodded.

"Hold on here," interrupted Davis Adcock. He was an imposing figure, with a deep barrister's voice and a full head of wavy brown hair. He wore the traditional blue seersucker suit, popular during the Southern summers. "Cobb, when you asked us to attend, you led us to believe there would be some substance to this meeting. Everyone in the room is familiar with the evidence you have, or rather, the lack of evidence. Vance can't and wouldn't dare bring charges against any one of these men. Now, I can't speak for my associates, but Mr. Pate can tell you that I'm not performing any pro bono work for him. I'd like to know where this is leading, because you're not only wasting my time, but also my client's money."

"Well, Davis, I'm glad you brought up the issue of money. I am trying to save everyone money and time... and position. Since Emory has indicated he would accept second degree murder pleas from McTimmons and Budreau, I believe it would be to their advantage to sign such an agreement today. The same thing for Pate for first degree murder. The murder of Lydia's child would be included in the plea, time to run concurrent."

There was a chorus of polite chuckling from the attorneys and clients. Wylie Blanchard, Graham's attorney, stood up. "Cobb, with all due respect, I'm afraid a little senility has sunk in. As an attorney, why would it be to my client's best interest to plea to murder?"

"Have a seat for one moment and I'll explain. If your client pleads to second degree murder he'll serve how many years? With parole, four or five at the most? And if Pate pleas to first degree murder how much time will he serve? Likely he'll be paroled in seven years.

"Now, what led to Lydia's death? That she was pregnant? No. Pate knows that. The reason she was killed was because she knew about the money that Norman was running through his bank. Norman's affair with her was a short-term remedy. Sooner or later she had to be silenced. Lydia's pregnancy was a good reason to justify her kidnapping to the others, right, Pate? But Pate never intended for her to get an abortion. He knew Norman wouldn't allow them to kill his daughter. Ham just used that as a reason to excuse his actions. She was to be killed all along. That's the reason Pate had the gym bag with the airline tickets, the money, and the scheme to make it appear she'd left the country.

"Hank, the problem in your investigation was that you were trying to catch her killers. You were trying to prove a murder charge against these men. Murder isn't what you really fear, is it Pate?"

"What each of you fear are federal money laundering charges, which bring a twenty-year sentence with no parole. And believe me, with the aggravating circumstances surrounding her death, you'll get the whole helping of pudding. Then we add the federal seizure laws associated with the crime. Budreau, federal agents will be driving those cars off your lot faster than a NASCAR race. Graham, you can tell your daddy that the insurance business is kaput. And Pate, when you get out of prison, the land that your family had for generations will be owned by others."

Cobb reached into his coat pocket and removed a computer disk. "When Lydia discovered your accounts on Norman's computer she made a copy. And I've got it. Very interesting reading. I hope you don't think I'm bluffing 'cause I know your code names, eh, Hot Rod," winked Cobb at Budreau. "I've got the account numbers, both foreign and domestic." Six men sitting across from me went pale. Adcock recovered first, whispering desperately to Pate and Hoyt Watkins, Budreau's attorney.

"Next, I'd like to introduce you to two agents who agreed to attend this meeting: Special Agent Sloan with the Federal Bureau of Investigation and Special Agent Savanowski with the Internal Revenue Service. The United States Attorney's Office and their respective agencies have expressed a keen interest in this case. They were very interested in pursuing this matter, especially when I agreed to turn this disk over to them. I did manage to convince them to refrain until it was decided what we should do with Lydia's murder investigation. Those friendly folks at Justice agreed to decline criminal prosecution if you three agree to the murder pleas."

Now the group was stirring, with emotions ranging from rage to panic.

"This is judicial extortion," complained Adcock.

"Prosecutorial misconduct," added Watkins.

"Then you don't want the deal, I assume. You can take those issues up in Federal court. Mr. Sloan, here's the disk."

"NO!" screamed Adcock, leaping from his chair. "This—this is preposterous." He held out his hands, palms out, trying to calm the climate. "Emory, this is getting out of hand."

"No, it's not," retorted Cobb. "As I said, we've got a situation that allows everyone to go away with something. On the prosecution's side, the GBI and the Sheriff's Department get their arrests, Vance gets convictions, and the community knows no one was railroaded and no one, based on his position in this county, was allowed to evade the law. On the defense's side, your clients avoid a twenty-year sentence and the seizure of their assets. They'll serve between four and seven years. A damn sight better than the federal charges. As their attorneys, you get them the best deal possible knowing that when they're released, they'll have something to come home to, which is your duty as their lawyer. And as for Lydia Carson: justice, in some perverted way, is finally achieved for her killers. Do you have any problem with all of this, Emory?"

"Not at all," he said, grinning, patting the table. "It sounds great to me."

"Gentlemen, Agents Sloan and Savanowski are busy men. They've allowed everyone until noon to come to an agreement. After that, I hand over the disk and the Department of Justice missile is launched and can't be recalled. Understood? We'll leave you to confer with your clients. We'll be in Emory's office should you have any questions."

After we filed out of the conference room I asked Cobb, "Will they take the deal?"

He reached into his side coat pocket and removed a toothpick. He flicked it in his mouth and said, "Yeah, they'll take it. They don't have a choice."

"How did you find the disk?"

"I paid a visit to Amanda. She allowed me to search Lydia's room."

"I searched it and didn't find anything," I said defensively.

"You weren't looking for a disk or computer record. Once Lydia made the disk, the logical place to hide it was in her room. I found it taped under one of her drawers. Thoroughness, young man, is the key to criminal investigation."

I was embarrassed at my carelessness. I'd missed the disk, leaving it up to my SAC to solve the case. "I thought you might be bluffing. But you weren't, were you?"

"I never let people know when I'm bluffing. Otherwise, I've got to prove it every time," Cobb advised with a wink.

"How's Amanda doing?"

Cobb shook his head. "What do you think? After we left Pate's, while you were in the hospital, Knox visited Amanda. She's destroyed. The most precious thing in her life, gone. Once these men plea, she'll have a solid wrongful death suit against some of the wealthiest men in the county. She'll never have to work again, but," he shrugged, "so what?"

An hour later Blanchard and Adcock came to the office. "Emory, we've got a problem. Can we discuss it in private?" asked Wylie.

Emory turned to us. "No, Wylie. If you have anything to say, you can say it in front of these gentlemen. They are honorable."

Hesitantly Blanchard said, "Budreau and McTimmons have agreed to the offer, but Pate won't go for it. We're at a stalemate."

Vance glanced at Cobb for advice. "Stalemate, my ass," said Cobb, his imposing bulk, rising from the seat. "The agreements with McTimmons and Budreau will require that they testify truthfully against Pate, should he choose not to take the deal. Graham's and J.T.'s testimony won't be pleasant, but if Pate wants his day in court, he'll get it."

"And if he won't go with this," added Vance, "he'll be indicted on one count of kidnapping and two counts of murder. Then I'll hand my case over to the Feds and they'll charge him with money laundering, stripping the meat off his bones. With your clients' testimony, confirmed by the GBI's investigation, I'll get a murder conviction. The people in this county don't take kindly to baby killers. Then the Feds take over, and he'll get twenty years and lose everything. He'll be in jail for the rest of his life. It's his choice. Davis, I trust you'll give him your best advice."

Davis' jaws clenched. "I'll talk to him."

An hour later the three attorneys emerged from the conference room. "We've got a deal if the U.S. Attorney's Office will agree not to prosecute on the federal charges," said Blanchard.

"I've got an agreement with me," said Savanowski, reaching into his briefcase and producing a letter.

"Then you've got a deal," Boyd said to Vance. "Second degree for Budreau and McTimmons, and first degree for Pate. Set up a plea date."

I was waiting in the reception area when the attorneys and their clients solemnly filed out from the conference room. Pate and Budreau looked away from us.

Graham walked directly to me. "You're an idiot. You don't know what you wasted, what you tossed away. Hayley wanted you. You could have been a part of us. You could have had everything you desired."

Blanchard grabbed his shoulders. "Graham. Keep quiet!"

Graham shook off Blanchard's grasp. "What's he going to do?" He moved closer to me, violating my body space, until he was inches from me, his breath puffing against my face. I refused to retreat, hoping he'd take a swing at me. "In five years, I'll be out of prison and the people of Connally will have forgotten their regrettable past. I'll be back working in my daddy's business. Where will you be in five years, Agent Monroe? You could have been with Hayley and us, all your dreams fulfilled, but instead, you'll be a midlevel bureaucrat, possibly married, eking out a living, week to week, while I return to my skiing, Twin Creeks and Hayley. Who's the loser here?"

After they left, Cobb came from behind me and placed his timber arms around my shoulder. "Congratulations, Hank. You've solved your first homicide. How does it feel?"

"Not like I thought," I replied demurely.

"Not like T.V., is it? The real world is different. There are no winners in crimes of violence. The dead stay dead, the raped stay raped, the brutalized will forever remain scarred. If you want to stay an agent, get used to it."

• • •

I spent the afternoon digging through an avalanche of paper. Cobb placed me on the workers compensation forms first. I realized the deviousness of the designers of these forms: make the reporting so complicated, so cumbersome and so tedious, that most will simply quit in disgust and file with their own insurer. While I was on my second hour of workman's comp, Peggy called me. "You have a visitor."

"If it's the media, send them away," I told her.

"No, Hank. Don't think it's the media."

I walked to the reception area. A young black man was in the lobby.

I remembered him from Judy Moon's. "May I help you?" I asked.

He motioned with his head. "She wants to see you," he mumbled. "She don't get 'round so good. She's outside."

I followed him to the parking area where a purple conversion van was parked. He slid the side door back. Sucking on her pipe, Judy Moon was sitting in a tattered burgundy lounge chair that had been placed in the back.

She spied the bandage on my face. "Well, Lawd," she bellowed as loud as her frail voice would allow. "What done got hold o' you?" She poked at me with her cane.

"Hello, Ms. Moon."

"Don' go calling me no missus," she ordered. "I'm Judy t' you now."

"Well, Judy, I had a little accident."

"Ha! Weren't no lil' accident, I hear'd. Hear'd you went toe to toe wif dat Ham fella. Shot the fool out of 'em too, ya did."

"Yes ma'am."

"Look like he got a bit of yo ass, too."

"No ma'am, he didn't touch my ass. But he sliced me on the other end."

"Hey, hey, hey," she cackled. "Ah'm jest glad ah didnin haf to do da cuffin for ya. Ah might have had a mite mo trouble wif dat Ham dan you did. Wuz it like I told ya? Y' went an' looked fer da knowledge."

"You were right, Judy. She had learned something that they didn't want her to know."

"See, ya young pup. Y'all think ya haf all da answers, but y'all ain't got da sense. Ya did good to lissen to ya elders, ya hear'd?"

"Yes ma'am."

"Ya 'mind me of one of dem Brittany Spaniel pups. Ya hunt jes like 'um. Ya hit da field all bright-eyed, ya tail a waggin'. Lookin' fer da bird. Ya don know what yer doin' but ya gwan to find da bird. What ya lack in 'sperience ya make up in heart. But no matta what, ya don quit. Ya got da heart, bwa. Ya canna teach da heart."

"Judy, you've been nice to me. Why are people afraid of you? Like you're some witch doctor?"

"Dey 'fraid o' me 'cause I kin see 'em. Right down to da bowns, I kin, like one of dem X-ray machins. Dey don lak dat I see 'em. See what dey really are. But wif you I see inside o' ya too. Down to yer bowns. But inside a you, I seed da good things. Dats why I help ya."

Then her mood became serious. "You done good, bwa. Real good. Da spirits are at peace now. It's been a while, but I feel good things from dem. Moz peoples wouldin did what you did. You got da callin'."

"Thank you, Judy... for your help and all."

"Pshaw!" she spat, with a wave of her thin hand. "I'z just be glad for Lyja sake."

I reached out and took her frail hand in mine, covering it with my other. "Can I come see you again sometime?"

"Lawd, yes. Don get too many gentlemen callers. I'll even take a scrawny one lak you. And I'll answers all ya questions—no charge," she winked. "Well, I'z gots to go. Jes thought I'd stop by and tell ya how I feel."

"Thank you, Miss Moon," I said, as the door was shut.

"Don go callin me Miz!" came the muffled yell from the van.

CHAPTER TWENTY-THREE

I AWOKE to a bright Sunday morning, birds chirping and squirrels scampering. A blue jay was incensed that a band of cardinals had entered his territory, foraging for food. I fed my own bird, who thanked me with his fawning, then dressed for church. I wanted to thank Pheim personally and, maybe, meet with Hayley.

I sat in the same pew as last week, this time, though, allowing enough room for Mr. and Mrs. Sheffield to sit in their reserved section. In a few minutes the elderly couple lumbered to the pew. Mr. Sheffield recognized me and realized I had respected his area. He gave me an appreciative nod. As the organist played, I glanced over my shoulder hoping to find Hayley. I spotted her with her parents in their usual section. Graham was absent. Briefly our eyes met, but she quickly looked down at her bulletin.

The choir filed in, followed by Wright and Pheim. There was a difference in the group this morning. They appeared listless. The organist finished her prelude and Wright rose stiffly from his chair.

"Top of the morning," he greeted, without the usual fervor. He began to speak, but caught himself as if he was trying to organize his thoughts. He leaned over the lectern, looking directly into the faces before him, inhaling deeply like a child, gathering the courage before leaping into the water. "This week has been a trying time for us all. As you probably know, Lydia Carson, a member of this choir, and an active member of this church, was found dead this week. She'd been murdered. On the same day, three other people from this county were also tragically killed and their deaths apparently were related to Lydia's. For those of you who knew Lydia," he turned, acknowledging the members of the choir, "you knew of her goodness, her caring and her devotion to the Lord and this church." He shook his head in disgust. "It's a shame. It's a d-" He bit his tongue. "It's a durn shame. Tomorrow morning, a memorial service will be held here at ten o'clock followed by a graveside service. I hope you all will attend.

"I wish to depart from the usual for a moment and have us sing a hymn for Lydia. If you will, please turn in your hymnal to number seven hundred seven, 'Hymn of Promise'."

We sang:

In the bulb there is a flower; in the seed, an apple tree;
In cocoons, a hidden promise; butterflies will soon be free!
In the cold and snow of winter there's a spring that waits to be,
Unrevealed until its season, something God alone can see.

There's a song in every silence, seeking word and melody;
There's a dawn in every darkness, bringing hope to you and me.
From the past will come the future; what it holds, a mystery,
Unrevealed until its season, something God alone can see.

In our end is our beginning; in our time, infinity;
In our doubt there is believing; in our life, eternity.
In our death, a resurrection; at the last, a victory,
Unrevealed until its season, something God alone can see.

When finished, we all stood in silence, waiting for instructions. Some members of the choir dabbed at their eyes, as did others in the congregation. Wright bit his lip, then blurted, "Go Dawgs."For the first times in years, without prompting, I bowed my head and earnestly prayed.

Later, Pheim approached the lectern and placed his hands on both sides of the podium. "I would like to deviate from the printed sermon today, if you please, based on a personal event that happened this week." He paused as if waiting for an objection. Of course, there were none.

"Angels. How many of you believe in angels?" A few smattering of hands hesitantly lifted in the air.

Pheim smiled. "To those of you who were honest enough to raise your hands...." Pheim raised his arm. "I, too, believe.... More so today, than last week."

"The topic of angels has recently captured the hearts of the public. They're on television, in books, magazines, and even calendars. I think that there is an earnest need for people to have a personal spiritual friend, a guardian angel, if you will, to walk, talk and commune with. However, there is a hesitancy to admit one's belief in angels. It's kind of like believing in fairies. People are afraid they'll be scorned if they admit such foolishness. Christians don't mind admitting their belief in God and their belief in Jesus, but when it comes to admitting belief in the agents of God, well, to us, that's going a little too far. But, I submit, if you are to believe the Bible, you have to believe in angels. And, I promise you, that when you leave the church today, more than likely you will meet an angel.

"Angels generally appear to have three general purposes throughout the Bible and during reports of modern times, they are comforters, protectors, and messengers. In Psalm 91:11 it is written, 'For he will command his angels concerning you to guard you in all your ways,' and the comforting of Jesus after the temptations by Satan is an example of such a purpose. Angels protect us. In 2 Kings, one angel protected Jerusalem from the Assyrians killings 185,000 soldiers one night. Then, of course, there was the angel of death in the story of Moses in Exodus, whose actions finally convinced the Pharaoh to release the Jews from slavery. And angels are the messengers of God. An angel appeared to Joseph when he learned of Mary's pregnancy, directing him to marry her. And, in the Christmas story, angels appeared to the shepherds heralding the coming of Christ....

"Many of the angels are named. There is the archangel, Michael, who is mentioned in the Book of Daniel and Revelation. There is Gabriel, probably the best known of the angels, who also appears in the Book of Daniel and in Luke. Then there are the Seraphim and Cherubim. The Cherubs are symbolic angels and are the inspiration to numerous paintings of the middle ages.

"What makes us different from angels in our duties to the Lord? No doubt angels have supernatural powers, but, think about this: their mission is the same as ours. We are to be devoted servants of the Lord, protecting the weak, comforting the sick and infirm, and spreading the news of Jesus Christ."

Pheim paused, scanning the congregation. "I submit, based on those qualifications, we have angels here in this church. People who protect the helpless from the evils in this world, people who visit the sick, provide food and shelter to the less fortunate, and people who through their witness and personal actions speak of the joy of Christ. I see a lot of potential angels in this congregation. This week I have witnessed the power of such an angel. I invite you to become a part of his angelic host. Let us pray."

I wanted to talk to Hayley after the service. Following the benediction, I briskly headed for the side aisle, weaving past the slower parishioners, hoping to head her off. She was walking up a middle aisle, recognized me and looked away. Then she realized that I was vectoring toward her. She moved ahead of her family, pushing against the throng, moving toward the narthex. When I was parallel to her, I rushed between pews toward her.

"Please, Hayley. Let me speak to you and explain." I touched her gently on the arm, pulling her out of the flow of the crowd and into the pew.

She would not look at me. "You don't know what you've done to my family," she said, tears clouding her green eyes. "You don't have any idea what you've done to me, and the pain you've caused my mother and father."

"Hayley, I did nothing to your family. I had no idea about Graham. Believe me, I wish it wasn't true."

"It's not true. That's what you don't understand. He's only going to plea to avoid the twenty years. Y'all blackmailed him. I can't believe you're so cruel." Her voice was trembling. "I really liked you, Hank. I...I felt that we might go somewhere."

"Hayley," I pleaded.

"Hayley!" said a sterner voice. It was Ross. He caught up to us. "Come on." He turned to me. "Hank, I understand you've got duties and obligations. I just wish you'd come to us first, so we could have dealt with it internally. What Graham did, may or may not be right, but he's family and we've got to protect our own."

"I understand."

"Good," he said firmly. "I don't know about yours and Hayley's relationship, but Graham will always be my son. If you show up at the house it would only cause conflict and uncomfortable feelings. Please don't call on Hayley again."

Startled at the commandment, I looked at Hayley. She gave me one last longing look, walking backwards out of the sanctuary, then turned and left my life.

I sat down in the pew, waited until the crowd dwindled to a trickle, and walked forward. The Reverend was at the front door speaking to a young couple holding a baby.

When they departed I walked up. "Nice sermon, Reverend. Much better than last week, if I may critique."

"Thank you, Mr. Monroe. And I agree. Thank you for providing the subject matter," he said gratefully.

"Reverend Pheim, I want to thank you for your help." I shook my head. "But it didn't turn out the way I expected."

"For neither of us. But one must do the right thing. Sometimes the consequences aren't pleasant. I believe that's what is meant by the term 'duty'."

. . .

Monday morning, while proofing my third investigative summary, my phone rang. It was Cobb.

"Hank, need to see you. Can you come back to my office?" he asked.

I walked in and he directed me to a chair. "The Director just called," he said heavily. He looked ill. He removed his reading glasses. "Hank... uh," he licked his lips, "uh... you're being transferred to Atlanta."

"Sir?" I wasn't sure I heard right.

"You are being transferred to the Atlanta Metro drug squad. Effective next week," he said quickly, spitting out the painful words.

Initially, I was too stunned to comment. Last week the Director was ready to help me in any way. Now he was jerking me away from my cases, away from Megan.

"Is this an example of 'No good deed goes unpunished'?" I asked.

"Hank, the Director realizes what a good agent you are, and feels the G.B.I. can use your talents better in Atlanta," Cobb duly recited.

"Did you have anything to do with this?" I asked bitterly.

"No!" he snapped back.

I leaned back in my chair, rubbing my chin. "Hmmmf, then Graham was right. They might be going down, but they managed to get in the last shot."

"You shouldn't look at it that way. You'll be involved in some major investigations in Atlanta."

"Don't look at it that way?" I repeated cynically. "Can I have your permission to call the Director? I'm calling in my favor."

"Hank, save it. It's a done deal."

"It's politics," I argued angrily. "Some legislator from around here has put the squeeze on him."

"You know what, son? You might be right. But that is the job of the Director. If he ignores the politics of the job, the funds dry up and we'll wind up as overpaid security guards. No doubt, you're important to him, but his first priority is the organization, not your feelings or preferences. Now you've got two choices: you can pout, or you can finish your cases and prepare to move on."

"Or I can quit," I shot back.

"Yeah, you can do that... and Graham will have won."

CHAPTER TWENTY-FOUR

THE WEEK was a bittersweet one. Cobb gave me two days of administrative leave to find a place in Atlanta. I called Lopes, who found me an apartment in a complex where the owners liked cops, providing them discounts. The drive between my new place and Megan's doorsteps was an hour and five minutes—I timed it.

On Thursday the office invited me to lunch at Wingate's. Knox surprised me with his presence, as did Chief Deputy Max Dennigraw, Deputy Ronny Mahaffey, the Sergeant and other troopers from the Post, Dan Maddox of the Connally Police Department and Luther McCoy with DNR.

Saturday, Megan and I visited Callaway Gardens. We lay on the beach, swam and splashed each other in the lake. We rode a two-seater bicycle through the park, under the towering pines and among the azaleas. We stopped at the stone bridges, resting beside cooling waters while smelling the honeysuckle. We visited the butterfly atrium and I marveled as Megan, childlike, played with the fluttery creatures. There was a wedding at the chapel tucked in the foothills of the gardens next to a quaint pond. We waited outside until the ceremony was finished. One of the matrons noticed us. "You two look you might be next," and she handed us small bags of rice. We tossed the grain at the emerging newlyweds.

We pedaled to a hill overlooking the lake and golf course, hid our bike in the bushes and climbed the mount, spreading a cotton sheet over the rushes. We opened a bottle of wine, inhaling the earthy scent of clover, dandelions, and wild onions, ate grapes, apple slices, avocado quarters, and cheese while watching golfers below, appreciating the few well-played shots, laughing uproariously at most of the duffers. The wine, food, and events of the day mellowed us. All that mattered was our closeness.

We had avoided the subject all afternoon. Megan finally spoke up. "I'm going to miss you."

"I hope you believe in the saying, 'Absence makes the heart grow fonder'," I said, tucked close to her with my arms around her.

"I fear the phrase, 'Out of sight, out of mind'," she replied, pressing closer to me.

"I may be forced to leave town, but I will never leave you."

She smiled and gave me a hug.

. . .

That evening while I was packing, the telephone rang.

"Hank?"

I closed my eyes, grateful to hear her voice again. "Celeste. I was hoping you'd call."

"I heard you were leaving," the voice said regretfully.

"I'm being transferred to Atlanta. Leaving tomorrow. I guess it's Pate's way of getting even."

"I'm sorry, Hank. You did a good job. I've been blessed to know you. I... I just wish it had been under better circumstances."

"Celeste, please tell me who you really are. I have to meet you and thank you personally. If you're afraid of being seen around here, we can meet out of town. In Atlanta, perhaps."

"Hank." She paused to consider my offer. "No. No, it's best we don't."

"Please, Celeste," I pleaded. "Your memory shouldn't be merely a voice. I have to put a face, a smile, and a touch to that memory."

"And I'll always remember you, Hank. The living need more of your kind. I have to go."

"No!" I insisted. I was losing her. Once the line disconnected I knew

I'd never hear her voice again. "Please, not yet. I want to know one more thing."

"What's that?"

"I...." I didn't have a question. She knew I was stalling.

"I will miss you, Hank. Always," said the kind, soothing voice. And the line went silent.

I sat on edge of my bed staring at the phone, wishing I could will it to come alive again and reach out for her.

That night, in my dreams, it came to me, like the various colors of a kaleidoscope suddenly rearranging themselves to form a clear picture. I had one final chance to meet Celeste.

. . .

Monday morning. Once again I lugged the Major's cage out of my apartment, and tossed it roughly, against his fluttering objections, into the rear of my Jeep. The trailer was hooked and Megan was waiting for me with a cup of coffee. The cup read: "Remember me always."

We paused from each other at a respectful distance. Then I pulled her close, burying my face in her hair. "I'll return the cup next weekend."

"That would be nice," she said, kissing me softly. Then her voice cracked, "Call me, please."

I grabbed a quick breakfast at Hardee's, then maneuvered my Jeep and trailer into the G.B.I. parking lot. I paid my final farewells to Peggy and Robin, giving each a hug, and a final handshake for Dennis and Stan.

"Johnny, thanks for your help," I said when I came to Cole. "I learned a lot from you."

"Glad to have you with me. Especially in that hospital," he replied. "Come see us anytime."

Cobb was leaning against the squad area wall, watching me make my rounds. He extended his hand for his final greeting.

"Can I speak with you for a moment, sir?" I said, accepting his strong fleshy grip. "In your office."

The request surprised him. "Sure." Once we were seated he asked, "What's on your mind?"

"Before I leave, I want you to do me a favor. Who is Celeste?"

Cobb's bushy eyebrows furrowed. He recovered quickly from the abrupt question, but for an instant I spied a flicker in his eyes that told me the truth. "Who is Celeste?" he answered, the low gravely voice sounding sincere.

I smiled confidently. Now, I was certain of my belief. "She's a friend of yours, but Celeste isn't her real name. Supposedly she's an angel, but, of course, we know better." I paused hoping the uncomfortable silence would encourage him to talk, but he wasn't falling for it.

So I continued. "It came to me last night, finally when I had time to think about Celeste, instead of worrying about my cases. Little snippets of conversations of various people came to me. During a previous Sunday, Reverend Pheim mentioned to me that he couldn't see the forest for the trees. I was the same way. Then during a sermon he preached about angels and their missions. Angels act as comforters, protectors, and messengers. Celeste obviously wasn't a comforter or a protector for Lydia– she was dead. Celeste was a messenger. But during the investigation she acted as a guide, a counselor, if you will. But a messenger can only deliver the message, that's all. She can't guide, nor can she counsel. She can only convey what's been sent. So who sent the messenger? It wasn't Lydia. It had to be someone who wanted to see that justice was done, someone who knew the community, but someone who couldn't risk the potential damage that the investigation might lead to. You, Cobb, were that someone."

Cobb glared over his reading glasses with a bemused look. "Please, go on."

"When Lydia disappeared I assumed I was assigned the case to gain experience. But I was wrong. You knew you had a potential bomb on your hands. Judy Moon told me that Lydia had the knowledge. You knew that... and you knew the knowledge was associated with the bank. With less than two years before retirement and decades living in this town, you couldn't afford the risk of what this case might prove. You'll probably need a part-time job when you retire. But where in this town, be it in private business, with the Police Department, or with the Sheriff's Department, if you've convicted some of its prominent citizens? At the same time, you couldn't assign the matter to your established agents. They've got conflicts of interest and the same concerns, if this proved to be true. But you had a duty and a moral purpose to solve her murder. You needed an agent who, as Judy Moon described me, 'was like a Spaniel pup running through the field looking for the bird'. One that was enthusiastic and relentless. You also needed an agent who was expendable. One, that if needed, could be transferred, without damaging the integrity of the office. I was perfect. Furthermore, by assigning me to the case, it made you appear as if you had no interest in Lydia's disappearance. So if the matter exploded, as it nearly did, you could disassociate yourself from the case. But, Cobb, you still had that moral duty, so you couldn't let me wander aimlessly through the case. You had to guide me, but you couldn't do it directly. So you had to have an alternate, someone who could direct this pup to the bird.

"The way you did it was quite imaginative. You needed a way to contact me and lead me through the maze, but you couldn't use just a voice over the telephone like a concerned citizen or an informant—or it would have to be documented in a summary and you'd have to read it. You couldn't let me provide reports. Why? One, reports would have to go through you and you would not be able to separate yourself from my investigation, and two, if someone filed under the public access laws they would know who was talking to you. So you had to invent an entity that I would talk to, but feel too foolish to report. If someone said they were a leprechaun or a fairy, I would have disconnected the phone immediately. You needed to contrive something that would hold me to the phone, something that would evoke trust. The angel was perfect. My compliments. And you trained her well, for she guided me with caring and concern, but most of all her guidance was useful.

"At the time I didn't notice it, but last night I remembered that when I told her that Reed Norman was the father of Lydia's child, she told me she'd call back in thirty minutes. Why? Because she had to consult with you. She didn't know what to tell me. But when she called back, she was confident and knew how to direct me. You remained in the background. In fact, you kept me busy with other cases. Because you knew, through Celeste, that I was devoted to solving Lydia's disappearance and, in spite of my caseload, I'd keep plugging. But by keeping me assigned to other cases, once again, you're covering your butt.

"Then the call from Atlanta came, pulling me off the case. You knew how long you could give me to solve the case. So you gave me five days. Enough time to solve the case, but, also, a conciliatory gesture to Atlanta. Once again, in case the poop hit the fan, you're covered.

"Then I confronted Norman and he was poised until I mention going to Amanda. He assumed I knew of his and Amanda's history and when he realized I didn't know, he demanded I tell him who had told me. Only someone who was intimately involved in the history of this town knew of their relationship.

"After the meeting with Vance, you knew you had to act quickly in order to prove Lydia's murder. There was no way I could have pulled off what you did with those attorneys. Now it was up to you and you were forced to do your job, but again you positioned yourself as the mediator, so that everyone comes out a winner. Cobb, you maneuvered us all like pieces on a chessboard." I glared at him, at once both admiring his brilliance and ingenuity, and contemptuous of his deviousness and cowardice.

Cobb's expression didn't change. He reached into his shirt pocket and extracted a toothpick. "Nice yarn, Hank." Then he lifted his imposing bulk from his chair and came from around the desk. As I rose, he patted me on the back and shook my hand. "Hank, you've grown in the short season you've been here. You've got the makings of a great investigator."

I backed away. "Please, I need to know Celeste's real name. Give me that, Cobb, please," I implored.

"I'll walk you to your car," he said, ignoring my plea.

"Please, Cobb. I have to see her... just once."

"Mind you, son, I don't know what you're talking about, but maybe this Celeste doesn't want you to meet her. If you care about her as you say you do, perhaps, you'll allow her the privacy she may need."

I reluctantly nodded, inhaling a deep breath. "Yes, sir."

"You didn't go to Lydia's funeral, did you?" he asked.

"No, sir. I'm not good at funerals. I've seen too many of my buddies at those proceedings."

"Of course," he said with an understanding nod. "May I suggest you pay her your personal respects before you leave Connally."

EPILOGUE

I TOOK Cobb's advice and headed to town. Cobb was right. I had grown, but not merely professionally. During this summer I'd grown to love four women, each in an entirely different and varied way, each on a different, but no less emotional level. Love with each individual is unique and special, as singular as a strand of DNA. Love, in the English language, is vague, and these days, even a flippant term.

I turned onto a narrow asphalt drive, bordered by magnolias, and slowly made my way through the maze of gray weathered monuments until I saw the flowers and wreaths at the gravesite of Lydia Carson. A woman wearing a shapeless printed sundress and a wide-brim straw hat was squatting beside the grave, laying a bouquet of sunflowers with the rest. She watched me get out of the car, lowered her head in grief, dabbing a tissue at her nose. Then she walked to her car on the opposite side of the circular road.

I reverently approached the grave, and said a prayer for Lydia's soul. The graveside was crammed with clusters of roses, lilies, carnations and brilliant colored flowers I didn't recognize. I spotted the bouquet of sunflowers and remembered sunflowers were Lydia's favorite, representing cheer, happiness, and optimism. My face tightened, suppressing the urge to cry, and I reached down to lightly stroke the flowers.

A card was attached by a single strand of wire to the sunflowers and squinting through my tears, I read the note. I rose abruptly, searching for the woman. She was standing in the distance, next to her car, watching me with a tender smile. I wiped my eyes in frustration as she disappeared behind a monument, then drove away. I chose not to pursue, for I knew her and now understood, but instead removed the card from the bouquet and gently kissed it. It read:

Lydia and Hank,

May God bless you and keep you in his care during your journeys, giving you the rewards and richness you both so dearly deserve. One day, there will be a season when we all will meet again.

Celeste,
The Angel,
Seraphim